MW00790022

SASHA AND THE BUTCHER

STEPHANIE KAZOWZ

KAZOWZ PUBLISHING

To my partner, Jordan

Playlist

One Night Stand - Janis Joplin
Feeling Good - Nina Simone
I Touch Myself - Divinyls
3AM - Matchbox Twenty
Closer - Tegan and Sara
Untitled (How Does it Feel) - D'Angelo
Can't Help Falling in Love - Elvis Presley
Dreamlover - Mariah Carey
Home - Edward Sharpe & The Magnetic Zeroes
Our House - Madness
Lovefool - The Cardigans
Your Best American Girl - Mitski
Burn - Usher
Stay - Rihanna
Goodbye to You - Michelle Branch
One Way or Another - Blondie
Private Eyes - Daryl Hall & John Oates
Psycho Killer - Talking Heads
Happiness is a Warm Gun - The Beatles
I Will Always Love You - Whitney Houston
I Want the One I Can't Have - The Smiths
I Will Survive - Gloria Gaynor
Do I Wanna Know? - Arctic Monkeys
If I Ain't Got You - Alicia Keys

Content Warning
This book includes:
Coarse language
Vomiting
Heavy alcohol use
Drug use
Fatphobia from a parent
Slut shaming
Biphobia
Explicit sex
Graphic violence
Blood
Graphic deaths/murder

ONE

"Fucking champagne."

With my eyes squeezed shut, I fumbled with my phone, trying to silence the generic marimba melody blasting through the speakers. My fingers tapped the screen until the room finally fell silent. Well, except for the sound of running water.

I internally sighed. Someone was in the shower. It wouldn't be like me to wake up alone after a wedding.

The smell of stale booze and sex clawed at my nose, tempting the bile sitting on the back of my tongue to join the party. I was starting to think that a great night out wasn't worth feeling like a human dumpster fire the next morning.

Taking a deep breath, I sat up, and stars exploded behind my eyelids. I swallowed hard, trying my best not to vomit. Fatigue weighed down my limbs, but I stayed upright. Just barely.

My brain swam in the remnants of too many champagne toasts as I pressed a palm to my forehead, trying to stop the sloshing. An all-too-familiar pain thumped in my temples, and no amount of pressure helped. It felt like the entire wedding party was electric sliding all over my frontal lobe.

Peeling my eyelids open, I tried to ease myself into consciousness. Unfortunately, sunlight blinded me because some asshole had thrown open the curtains.

Thoroughly disgusted with myself, I rubbed my forehead. I'd slept with a morning person, which was, of course, gross and completely unacceptable.

A glance around the room and a whole new wave of nausea turned my stomach.

Crisp white linens covered my legs, navy decorative pillows laid all over the floor, and the furniture was made of dark, sturdy wood. Tasteful art lined the walls, and outside the door, there was a lounge area.

It wasn't my room. It didn't even look like I was in the same hotel. My room at the Budget Lodge had some precious country motif.

While it's never a good thing to wake up in a strange place, I'd made enough questionable turns in life to know how to handle even the most awkward morning afters.

A yawn fought its way out, but my lips stuck to my teeth. My tongue was so dry I had to peel it from the roof of my mouth. I needed a gallon of water pronto.

Adding to my overall discomfort, the AC kicked on, chilling my exposed, clammy skin. After a quick scan of the room, I found my bridesmaid's dress shredded by the door.

Perfect.

Throwing off the covers, I took a tentative step, my foot crushing the beautiful lace bra that did wonders for my cleavage. Adjusting the underwire and sliding it on, I snagged the giant white dress shirt off the floor. A few buttons were missing, but it covered all the necessary parts—sort of.

In a serious stroke of luck, I shook out the duvet, and my panties fluttered to the floor. I whispered thanks to the expensive undergarment goddess in the sky that I wouldn't have to replace another pair.

Walking across the room searching for my shoes, I stopped dead in my tracks in front of the mirror.

Yikes.

Instead of being cute in a "look at how dainty this man's shirt makes me look" way, I looked like an Amazon trying to escape a Men's Warehouse. The shirt struggled to cover my bust, the front gaping so that lace and pale skin peeked out if I moved my arms. Tugging at the hem did nothing as it was just as taut on my hips and ass, barely covering my panties. I was sure to flash a few folks the goods during my escape.

If only my ample ass on display was the worst of it. A paper bag on my head would've been a vast improvement. The once shiny, bouncy curls laid twisted into something more akin to a flaming rat's nest. Black sludge had settled under my bloodshot eyes, and the skin around my lips was stained pink like a kid's Kool-Aid mouth.

"A hot damn mess."

I tried to rub away the leftover makeup with a few tissues and spit, but it only helped move the mess around and irritate my usually pale, white skin into a splotchy red nightmare. Sighing, I turned from the mirror.

Best not to dwell on what can't be changed.

Raking my fingers through my stiff, knotted hair, I searched for my clutch. Moving as quickly as my upset stomach would allow, I checked the sitting area before heading back to the bedroom. With my head under the bed, I kept feeling around despite the room spinning.

The water stopped running in the bathroom.

"Hey Sash, you up?"

Startled, I bumped my head on the bed frame. "Son of a bitch," I gritted out quietly, rubbing the sore spot. I recognized that voice.

Luca Moretti.

Flashes of the previous night rushed back to me—us near the bonfire at the reception with his hands under my skirt, me straddling him in the town car on the way to the hotel, my back pressed against a column in the lobby, me on my knees in the elevator. There wasn't a place from the reception to the hotel room we hadn't dirtied up, at least a little bit.

That, my friends, is a good night.

With a heavy sigh, I started searching for my purse again.

"If you want, we can go grab lunch or something. I know this great Italian place nearby."

I absolutely did not want to grab lunch or something. My hands flew over the plush carpet under the bed until they landed on a shoe and my purse. "Almost there," I muttered.

"Damn."

I froze at the sound of his voice so close behind me. On my hands and knees, I peeked over my shoulder. Damn was right.

Luca leaned against the doorway with a towel wrapped around his narrow waist. His body was lean but broad. Something I hadn't noticed the night before were the scars that marked his tan skin. They added an edge to his appearance that I very much appreciated. But honestly, what was there not to like with him all wet and fresh from the shower?

My gaze lingered on the tiny beads of water dripping from his black, wavy hair to his chest. They disappeared one by one into the bit of dark hair below his navel.

Dragging my tongue across my furry front teeth, I pried my eyes away from his glistening body. I needed to focus on the task at hand.

Too bad everything about Luca was a distraction.

Even his goddamn face left my hungover ass stupefied. The sunlight hit his sharp cheekbones and sizable nose, emphasizing the harsh angles, but warm brown eyes and pouty lips added an unexpected softness to his face.

He was no pretty boy. No, he was a rough, handsome man.

The longer I stared, the bigger his smile grew. He let out a chuckle, and it occurred to me that I hadn't said anything back to him and was instead staring at him like he was the last piece of cheesecake in the fridge.

Shaking off whatever spell Luca's mere presence put me

under, I gave him a toothy smile. "Hey, I was just looking for my other shoe." I kneeled, steadied myself, and stood up as gracefully as a hungover bridesmaid could.

"I see." Pushing away from the door frame, he strolled toward the closet. As he rummaged through his suitcase, I ogled his firm backside and thick thighs. I let out a little sigh of appreciation, and he glanced back at me around his legs, wiggling his ass at the same time. "I figure fair is fair." His smile made my heart stutter, almost making me forget operation get the hell out of dodge.

Tearing my attention away from his bouncing backside, I lifted his pants off the floor, huffing when I came up empty-handed yet again. I stalked around the room, becoming more frustrated by the second. This was not the easy exit I wanted.

"Looking for this?" In Luca's big hand was my heel.

"Yes, thank you!" I reached for my shoe, but he raised it above his head. Quirking an eyebrow, I put my hands on my hips. "Keep away? Really?"

He leaned into my space, the smell of his soap filling my nose. I wanted to nuzzle into his chest, kiss, stroke and—

"Get lunch with me."

For fuck's sake.

Rolling my eyes, I jumped up and snatched my shoe from his hand. I tugged down the tails of the shirt, and yet another button popped off at the top of my bust. So much for tasteful cleavage. I sucked my teeth and tried to smooth the front of the shirt. Let's be honest—nothing about this busted ensemble was tasteful.

Balancing on one foot, I slipped on my right shoe and then teetered on that slim heel to slide on the left. "I'm sorry. I have to go."

Luca's eyebrows pulled together. "So that's it?"

Standing to my full height in the four-inch heels, I was over six feet tall but still an inch or two shy of his hairline. "Does there need to be more?"

His eyes narrowed, and his mouth set in a straight line. "No, I guess not."

I had my out but couldn't take those first steps away from him. So we stood there, staring at each other. I couldn't look away from his dark stubble or stop thinking about it rubbing against the inside of my thighs. His pink tongue darted out to wet his lower lip, and my lips parted in response. God, I wanted to taste him.

Luca watched me with hooded eyes, his body leaning toward me, but he didn't take a step closer. He didn't need to. Doing nothing more than standing there, I struggled to keep myself from reaching out to touch him. A blush crept up my neck.

"How about your phone number? Can I get your phone number?"

The softness in his voice gave me pause. It coaxed me to give in, to give Luca whatever he wanted. "I don't think that's a good idea. I'm not in the market for whatever you have in mind."

His hand brushed through his wet locks, muscles flexing with the movement. "You're not in the market for a repeat performance of last night?" He picked up a flattened ringlet, twirling it with a gentle tug. I can honestly say it had never occurred to me to be jealous of my own hair until that moment. "I know you had a good time. What I don't know is why you're running out this morning."

Annoyance cleared out some of the lust haze Luca's closeness created. "Who says I'm running? You're not asking for more sex. You're asking for meals, for dates. I'm not interested."

His hand moved to my earlobe, rolling the small piece of flesh between his thumb and finger. I leaned in, hating and loving the feel of his touch, hating that I loved it so much. "What if we kept it purely physical? Can I have your number then?"

I couldn't help but smile at his perseverance. Shaking my head, I tried to find the right words to make him understand. "Luca, you aren't the type. Your first instinct after a one-night stand was to take me for Italian. Lunches lead to dinners, dinners lead to meeting the friends, meeting the friends leads to meeting the family. See where I'm going with this?"

Luca gently wrapped a hand around my neck, his fingers sliding under my hair. Goosebumps covered my arms the second his calloused fingertips grazed the sensitive skin there. It became harder to remember why I needed to leave.

I shuffled closer to him, and the corners of his lush lips pulled into a small smile. Our chests grazed with each breath, rising and falling at the same time. Tiny drops of water soaked into the front of the white shirt. "A bit conceited, don't you think? Who says I'd fall for you?"

I barked out a laugh as I pushed on his chest to create a little distance. His warm, wet skin under my palms made my fingers curl in, scratching him in the process. He was enticing. Too enticing.

"No one, but I'd rather not risk it." Taking a step back—the hardest thing I'd done that morning—I took a deep breath. "Last night was great, the best, but I need to get going." Pinching the shirt's fabric between my fingers, I pulled it from my body. "Thanks for lending me the shirt. I'll get it back to you."

Luca's smile fell, and his hands dropped to his sides. Dark brown eyes bore into my face, resigned to see me leave. "No problem. It's the least I can do after destroying your dress."

Moving toward the door, I was hyperaware of his large body following closely behind. I tossed my nasty, tangled mane back and looked over my shoulder. "Don't apologize for that. It might've been my favorite part."

Giving him a dazzling smile, I winked and sauntered out of the room. The adorable family decked out in swim gear—staring at me like the disaster I was—made the ride down to the main floor kind of awkward. But what can you do?

The elevator doors opened, and I entered the lobby. With my head held high and shoulders back, I strutted from the hotel.

There's no such thing as a walk of shame if you're not ashamed.

After a brief stint as the half-naked woman on the sidewalk, my phone beeped, letting me know the rideshare had arrived.

As I slid into the Prius, the girl driving turned and stared. I buckled the seatbelt and pulled the shirttails down to cover my lacy underwear the best I could. Looking up from my poorly concealed crotch, I found pretty blue eyes locked on my body.

I leaned forward, resting my elbows on the back of the front seats, offering a generous amount of cleavage thanks to the missing buttons. "It's not that I'm not flattered to be ogled by such a beautiful woman, but I'm tired and just want to get home."

The driver blushed and sprang into action. "Sorry. I just —Sorry."

Leaning back in the seat, I smiled at her in the rearview mirror. "Like I said, it's not a problem. Just bad timing."

I slept the rest of the day away, waking up to my birth control alarm at eight p.m. My phone was full of missed calls and texts from clients, my assistant, Ashley, and an unknown number.

Ignoring the work calls, I texted Ashley back and went to the kitchen. My phone rang as I made it back to bed.

"Thank God! I was about to file a missing person's report," Ashley shouted.

Balancing a glass of cab filled to the brim, I settled back into bed. "You can't even file one until I've been missing for 48 hours. Don't be so dramatic."

Ashley scoffed. "I'm not being dramatic. You didn't answer my texts, and you missed Metal Brunch. You never miss Metal Brunch."

The dry red washed over my taste buds, and my sore body relaxed. It felt like Luca had sexed every muscle to death. "I'm sorry I worried you guys. It was a long night, and I needed sleep more than I needed waffles." I pointed my toes, then flexed my heel, testing my calf muscles. The ache was ridiculous. "I feel like I was run over by a sex truck."

There was a scuffle as she whispered to someone, and then there was a masculine groan.

"Okay, spill."

I sat up in bed—my friend senses tingling. "Only if you tell me who that was."

"Just Malcolm. He was dropping off some leftovers from his date." A door slammed shut, and she laughed. "He's gone."

Complication, thy name is Ashley. "That's weird, Ash."

"No, it's not. He was in the neighborhood and knew I wouldn't bother cooking while Ben's out of town."

I shook my head. Ben was her latest live-in boyfriend. He was perfectly fine, perfectly dull.

"Whatever you say."

"Don't. It's not like that with Malcolm. You know that."

"Mm-hmm."

"We're friends."

"Sure."

"Oh, fuck you, and tell me who put that pussy in a coma."

I snorted. "Wow. Please never say that again."

"Okay, okay. But seriously, Sash, what happened to you? One minute, you're at the reception. The next, poof, you're gone."

I downed the rest of my wine, wiping my lips with my fingertips. "I left with Luca Moretti." Tapping my fingers against my lip, I finally said in a breathy whisper, "He may very well be a sex god. I don't know that I've ever been this sore."

Ashley was quiet for a minute. "Wow. You must be in love."

She laughed, and I fell back into my pillows with a groan. "It would've been perfect, but he wanted to take me to lunch. Who wakes up from a one-night stand and is like, 'You know what? I could really go for a bolognese. You in?' It was weird."

"You know, some people are just polite. Who knows, maybe he wanted to carbo-load for round two."

"No, not this guy. If you want energy for another go, you order room service. He wanted a post-bang date."

"Why is that so bad?"

"It's not. I'm just not that girl. After Beth, I realized I don't have the time or attention span for a real relationship. It's not fair to the other person."

Ashley sucked her teeth. "Beth was a high-maintenance princess. No amount of time was ever going to be enough for her. Don't let that train wreck color your opinion on dating. Also, dates don't equate to marriage, Sash."

Squeezing my hand into a fist, I tried to keep my temper in check. "I fucking know that, but I also know that I would rather not have another Beth on my hands. That started as a casual thing and ended up being a fucking mess. I still feel guilty."

Ashley cleared her throat. "I'm sorry. I shouldn't be pushing you into things you aren't ready for. Consider my lips zipped."

We sat in silence for a couple of minutes, and I picked at a loose thread on my duvet cover. Opening my mouth to speak, Ashley beat me to it.

"So, you're really not going to see Luca again? Even with his freight train sexual prowess?"

So much for zipped lips.

"I don't plan on it." I shook my head. "It's a shame Luca couldn't be down with lots and lots of sex with no commitment."

"We all can't be like you."

"You're just jealous."

Ashley sighed dramatically. "You're right." There was some rustling on Ashley's end, like wrappers being opened. "It might be time to end things with Ben. We haven't had sex in two months. Two fucking months! I'm going crazy."

"Two months? That's . . . I . . ."

"You sound like I told you I have cancer."

"Sorry. I just can't imagine going that long while living with my partner."

Another sigh. I knew Ashley was miserable, but what I didn't know was why she kept trying to make it work. "I know. I can't believe this is my life now. Malcolm asked me if I had stock in Energizer. Dick."

"And you're just friends?"

"Shut it."

"Okay, okay."

"Look, I gotta go. I've got an early meeting with those people from Amerent."

"I forgot that's tomorrow. Good luck."

"Thanks. I have a few things to review with you once I get back to the office, so block me off some time."

"Sure thing. Sleep tight, Ash."

"You too."

I settled further down between the sheets. Exhaustion from the night before made me ready for bed, even though it was only 9:30. Turning off the lamp, I snuggled deeper into the covers. Ryan purred on the pillow next to my head, his fluffy tail tickling my neck.

As I drifted off to sleep, my phone rang.

Yawning, I answered, "Hello?"

"Sasha?"

Oh shit, I knew that voice. The memories of him moaning over, under, and behind me quickened my pulse. Why the hell was he calling me? You don't just call people. No one wants an unexpected phone call.

"Luca?"

"The one and only."

I patted down my hair and straightened his shirt that I was still wearing.

He can't see me. Why the hell am I tidying up?

Grimacing, I tossed the cover off my legs. "So, you got my number."

"That I did. My cousin's a very helpful guy."

I rolled my eyes and muttered, "Michael."

"Don't blame him. I told him I found something of yours."

"So, you're a liar. Good to know."

"Hey! I didn't lie. I found lots of things last night. That patch of freckles under your knee. What happens when I bite the inside of your thigh. How you like my fingers—"

"I got it. Thank you. What do you want?"

My fingers twisted the ends of my hair while Luca said nothing. I pulled the phone from my face to check and see if he'd hung up when he finally said, "I just want an hour of your time."

"No."

"You don't even know what I want to do."

I tugged my hair at the root. "What do you want to do?"

"One drink. I want one drink with you." I could hear the smile in his voice.

"No. I already told you."

"Okay. I won't ask again."

"Really?" My shoulders curled with disappointment. I knew that wasn't fair. I'd said no countless times in the past twelve hours, but I kind of hoped he would push through. I generally hated the "wear you down" tactic, but having him chase me for just a little of my time had been nice.

"Yes, really. I'm not a stalker, Sasha. I'd hoped you'd change your mind after having some time to think about it, but it's okay. It's not like you're the only woman in St. Louis."

I shot out of bed, itching to put my foot up his ass.

"Well, I'm glad you have so many options."

"Shit. That's not what—" Panic laced Luca's voice, but it wasn't enough to soften my hurt ego.

"No, no, no. You're absolutely right." I paced my bedroom, gesturing and carrying on as if he was there with me. "I'm sure you have no problem getting women." Letting out a bitter chuckle, I gripped the phone even tighter. "A tip though? Maybe don't mention your harem of lovers, even if you're being rejected. It's kind of a dick move." Luca stammered out nonsense, but I cut him off. "Please don't call me again. Although, with so many options waiting, why would you?"

I ended the call.

Huffing out a frustrated breath, I tossed my phone into the pillows. Poor Ryan darted under the bed to avoid my tantrum.

I'd actually felt bad for turning Luca down. Part of me was even ready to say yes to spending a little time with him. But that last bit of bullshit undid all the goodwill he'd built. The reverence I had for his abilities in bed, next to beds, in hallways, in cars, etc., etc., dimmed by the second.

My reasons for turning him down, admittedly, sounded arrogant, but fuck if he didn't take the cake. Well, you know what? That guilt for bailing on him was dead.

Luca Moretti could go fuck himself and that long list of willing women. Good thing I had long lists of my own.

TWO

Backstage at The Monocle, I gripped the wooden pole, watching in the mirror as Jazz laced my corset. She tightened the middle one more time before she created a perfect bow. Admiring how the green rhinestones matched my eyes and set off the flame of my red hair, I tried to ignore the pressure on my chest. Too bad the boning dug into my sides, making it hard to take a breath.

"Fuck, Jazz. I still need to breathe."

A hard slap to my ass pushed me into the beam. "Oh, hush, you can take it." Her elegant fingers traced the column of ribbon that laced me in, her black eyes never leaving mine in the reflection as her hands crept around my now-cinched waist. She pressed her soft curves into my back, leaving no space between us.

"Have a good show, Sasha." Her lips grazed the shell of my ear as I arched against her.

Backing away, she went to the other side of the dressing room, her hips swaying.

Jazz was the newest addition to our burlesque troupe. From the minute I met her, I knew she'd be trouble. I never crossed that line with the Shimmy Sisters, but Jazz tested my resolve. Everything about her oozed sex. The way she spoke, walked, danced, hell, even the way she looked at me, put me on edge. It didn't help that she was leaps and bounds smarter than me and an accomplished lawyer. She was the total package.

Jazz pulled her stockings on slowly, a smirk playing on her lips. Flipping her black, curly hair over her shoulder, she winked at me. It'd been like this for months, a constant build-up to nothing.

Leaning against the wooden beam, I motioned for her to continue. Watching Jazz dress was almost as good as watching her take it all off.

Polished nails raked up her impossibly long legs, stopping to toy with the bands that cut into her toned thighs.

Fuck me. She's hot.

Frilly panties barely concealed her perky ass, and a gold bustier pushed up her small chest. I wanted nothing more than to explore her lithe, tight body, and she knew it.

She slipped the garter belt on, adjusting the top against her flat stomach. Gold flecks covered her body, making her dark brown skin glow. Tilting her head, she met my gaze with a look of pure desire.

Sashaying over to her dressing station, I murmured, "Here, let me." Kneeling before her, I attached the clasps to the top of her thigh highs. I traced the straps, gently grazing her legs with my fingertips, and was rewarded with a shiver that ran through Jazz's whole body. I gazed up at her through thick false lashes, enjoying how discombobulated she was. "There you go." My breath caressed the exposed skin between her legs.

"Uh, thanks." Her lips stayed parted, and her eyelids lowered.

"No problem." Before I got off my knees, I placed a kiss above each thigh-high. Goosebumps spread over her skin, and her hips tilted toward me. The heat from her body drew me in, making me forget where we were.

"Places, ladies! Three minutes to lights!" Evie rushed through the backstage, ushering all the performers to line up and dragging me back to reality.

I moved away from a stunned Jazz, her chest rising and falling a little faster than before. "Good luck, Jazzy." As I walked toward the stage door, her eyes stayed on me.

Jazz's attention added an extra bounce to my step. Thinking about all the things I could do to her—all the things she could do to me, all the things we could do together—made me giddy.

Trying to lose some of that goofball energy, I shook out my limbs. Stage time was sexy time.

Evie announced me, and I parted the heavy, velvet curtains, my leg leading the way. As the first notes of "Feeling Good" filled the room, I strutted toward the audience. The bright lights kept the crowd faceless as I slowly removed the long gloves with my teeth. As the song swelled, my clothing dropped, and my body jiggled without restriction. Going to the edge of the stage for the finale, a face I hadn't seen in weeks caught my eye.

Luca Moretti sat on the edge of his seat, his eyes wide, mouth hanging open. It took everything in me to keep going and ignore the way my heart thumped violently against my chest.

One more turn and I winked at him as the tassels spun. Blowing a kiss to the audience, I swished off stage.

My heart raced, and a blush crept up my neck. Surprise audience members always threw me for a loop, but knowing Luca watched me dance turned me on in a way I didn't like. That the prick still got under my skin pissed me off. I only hoped my little show had gotten him so hard he needed to dump ice down his slacks.

The music for the second group number started up as I slipped into my silk robe. When the green room door opened, I sat down to make a slight makeup change for the last number.

"I'm hurrying, Evie. Be ready in five!" I kept my head down, searching for my mascara.

"I think I can get you there faster."

Startled, I dropped the eye shadow pallet in my hand and spun around.

"What are you doing? You shouldn't be back here, Luca."

He inched toward me, his eyes drinking in every inch of my body. "It's okay. I know the guy who owns this place."

Standing to meet his attempt at dominance, I snorted. "Of course you do. What I should've said is, I don't want you back here. I need to get ready for the last number."

Luca's body pressed me into the makeup table, his southern hemisphere giving my performance a standing ovation. "I'll be brief."

The smell of his cologne drew me closer to him as his hands skirted up the bottom of my robe, firmly palming the curve of my body. Under the silk, my thighs trembled. How had I forgotten what his hands felt like?

"Nothing about you is brief, Luca."

Grinning, he lightly kissed me. "I'm glad you remember."

Luca pulled the sash to my robe, and the fabric fell open. His forehead furrowed as he caressed the skin around the pasties. "I like these."

My head fell back, and my eyes shut as he gently tugged the tassels, not enough to remove them but enough to pull the skin. "If you like these, you should see what I wear off stage."

Hot breath on my neck was the only warning I got before his mouth latched onto my pulse. He groped and squeezed his way down my soft body before he grabbed my ass, lifting me onto the table.

I leaned back to get his attention and asked, "What are you doing?"

His face was flushed, his eyebrows pulled together as he shook his head. "Honestly? I don't know. You make me a little crazy."

He leaned in to claim my mouth in another sweet kiss. When he pulled back, his face was more relaxed. "I think it's time for you to feel a little crazy, Sasha."

The way he whispered my name like it was something to savor sparked a fire inside me. I wrapped my legs around him, bringing him into my body. His trouser-covered erection rubbed against the thin fabric of my panties, and it took everything in me not to moan. Swallowing hard, I whispered back. "You can try."

He gave me a lazy smile, unwrapping my legs from his torso, and knelt before me. "Deal." His large hands grasped my knees, pushing them wide as his fingers traveled up my thighs. Luca kissed and nipped the soft skin, paying particular attention to a spot so close to where I wanted him most. I cursed, curling my fingers around the edge of the table. The more he sucked, the wider my legs fell open.

"Luca," I panted. He had to do something more. I was about to crawl out of my skin.

His dark brown eyes looked up at me as he pushed the damp silk between my legs aside. Never breaking eye contact, his tongue barely brushed against me. Arching my back, I put one hand on the back of his head, but he wouldn't move closer.

The next pass of his tongue was harder, pressing against my slit without going in.

"Fuck, Luca!"

He continued his slow torture, each lick having more pressure than the last. My abdomen clenched. I ached to be filled.

"I need your fingers."

Without pulling away from my body, he sighed, his breath a chilled wind on my heated skin. "No."

His mouth went back to work, his tongue dipping in only to pull out. Sweat beaded on my forehead while my core tightened, begging for more. With my eyes shut tight, head lolled back, and teeth digging into my full red lip, I prayed for relief.

Luca's tongue pressed against my clit, rolling against it while his hands squeezed my ass. I writhed under his ministrations, equal parts frustration and pleasure.

The door creaked open, and my head snapped up to find a shocked Jazz standing in the doorway. "Uh. I'll keep them out for a minute while you wrap up." She strolled out of the room with a smirk on her face.

My attention returned to Luca as he stood and brushed off his knees.

Laying splayed across the makeup table, all I could think about was finishing what he started. "What are you doing?"

His red, wet lips distracted me as he wiped his mouth. "Creating incentive."

Tilting my head, I waited for him to continue.

"Have dinner with me."

It was like he dropped me in an ice bath. Gathering up my robe, I covered my body. "God. Really, Luca?" I flipped my hair out from under the collar. "I thought you'd finally seen the light."

Turning my back on him, I straightened up the mess my ass had made on the table. As I reached for a knocked-over can of hairspray, he grabbed my wrists. Pinning them to the table, his body wrapped around me. "It's been a month, and I can't stop thinking about you. You can't tell me that this doesn't feel good." He kissed my neck, nuzzling my ear. "I want to see if we're compatible in other ways."

I looked up at him in the mirror. His face was so genuine.

Maybe this could work.

He must have seen the moment of weakness because a smile spread across his face. "Just give me a chance, Sasha. If you hate it, we can fuck and say goodbye."

I shook my head and laughed. "Fine. One dinner."

Luca wrapped his arms around my waist, pulling me into his hard body. "Thank you. I'll text you."

In the mirror, I watched him walk out. Not one second later, the girls poured into the green room, and Jazz sat at the station next to me. "I didn't know you were dating someone. I wouldn't have been so—" She batted her eyelashes at me and dramatically pouted her lips. "If I knew."

"I'm not dating anyone."

Her eyes didn't leave the side of my face as I tried to cover the marks on my neck. "Then who is he?"

I tried to temper my annoyance. Annoyance with myself? Annoyance with Luca? I wasn't sure. "A guy I fucked. That's all."

Lifting an eyebrow, she turned toward her mirror. "If you say so."

Thankfully, she left it. I didn't even know what to say about Luca. I was in lust with him, willing to go on a date to get in his pants. Resting my cheek in my palm, I sighed.

What's happening to me?

"What do you think about this fabric? Is it too Western? The Regents wanted kitsch, but if I give them this, I might be going against my moral obligations as an interior designer and a person with functioning eyeballs."

Ashley tapped her toe, waiting for me to answer, but I only stared at the text Luca had sent me.

"Uh, yeah, sure."

Swiping the phone from my hand, Ashley darted out of reach. "What is so important you can't help me with this curtain emergency?" Her eyes widened, and a grin lit up her face. "Oh. Luca. He's taking you to his family's restaurant?" She glanced up at me, then back at my phone. "Oh, girl."

"Shut up. It's no big deal." When Ashley didn't immediately agree, I narrowed my eyes at her. "Right?" She lifted an eyebrow but didn't answer.

I swiveled in my chair, turning away from the windows that faced out to the rest of the small office. I didn't need Miranda in reception to see me panic. "What's he thinking? I barely agreed to this date, and now I might meet a cousin, aunt, or, heaven forbid, an immediate family member." Tossing my head back, I let out a groan.

Ashley plopped down in the cozy chair on the other side of my desk. "He probably didn't even think about it. Maybe it's his favorite restaurant, and that's why he picked it. Moretti's is the best Italian in St. Louis. He's probably just trying to make a good first impression."

Flopping my head in her direction, I huffed out a breath. "Whatever. I guess I'm heading out then. I need to get ready."

"It's 4:30. How long do you plan to primp for?" Ashley frowned as she unwrapped a piece of chocolate from my candy dish.

Gathering up my things, I tidied my desk. "I need to stop by Kristina's so she can do something with my hair, fit in a quick mani/pedi, and get home with enough time to change and put on fresh makeup." When I looked up, Ashley was holding back laughter. "What?"

"For someone who doesn't want this date, you're certainly going to a lot of trouble."

"Listen, just because this is a terrible idea doesn't mean I'm not going to show Luca the same courtesy I do any other highly anticipated lay." I swung my purse over my shoulder and walked around the desk. "Hopefully, I can trick him out of his pants before the date even starts."

Ashley patted my back as she flicked the light switch. "Whatever you say, Sash."

Giving Miranda a tight smile, I threw up my middle finger and left the office to the sound of Ashley cackling.

Moretti's was empty. Not a single person was standing outside the restaurant, which was bizarre for a Friday night. The stylish host station stood vacant, and no one was at the glossy bar. The lights were dimmed for dinner service, but no one was being served.

"Uh, Luca?"

A loud crash came from the back of the building. "Back here."

"Back where?"

"The kitchen."

Looking down at my pristine little black dress, I sighed. All that prep for nada.

Walking through the dimly lit dining room, I shook my head in disbelief. All the tables were bare except one two-top. Candles adorned the small table, and rose petals were sprinkled on the floor. He'd gone full-on romance, and I was ashamed to say I didn't hate it.

I pushed past the employees' only door and found Luca bent over in front of the oven. That man's backside was a thing of beauty.

"Am I early?"

With his back to me, he answered. "Nope, just taking care of a few finishing touches. Have a seat."

One stool from the bar sat at the metal prep table. Luca finally turned toward me as I made my way across the cramped space. While his eyes raked over the simple sheath dress and the curves it hugged, he wiped his hands on the front of his apron. "You look beautiful, Sasha."

It was absurd for such a handsome man even to exist, let alone be there cooking for me and calling me beautiful. In his black trousers, white button-down with the sleeves rolled up, and stained apron, he was an intoxicating picture of high-powered domesticity.

"Thank you." Taking a deep breath, I hummed. "It smells great in here."

"Why, thank you."

Luca came to my side, his hand resting on the small of my back as he ushered me to the stool. The smell of his expensive cologne enveloped me, and I had a hard time not burying my nose in his neck. Clearing my throat, I turned my attention to the kitchen to keep myself from doing something silly, like biting him.

Every burner held a pot or pan simmering with some kind of magical deliciousness. Sliding up on the stool, I made a show of counting the cookery. "Are we feeding the entire neighborhood?"

Luca's cheeks crimsoned, and his hand rubbed the back of his neck. "I know, I know. It's been a while since I got to man the kitchen here. I might've gotten a tad carried away." He looked around the kitchen, shaking his head. "I'll have to take the leftovers to my mom's tomorrow." Returning to his spot behind the stovetop, he stirred and tasted whatever was in the biggest pots. Clearly pleased with the taste, he smiled at me. "She's my biggest fan."

Leaning forward, I dipped a spoon into a pot that had a marinara simmering. As soon as the sauce hit my tongue, my eyes slid shut, and a not-so-quiet moan fell from my mouth. The balance of spices was perfect, and he'd added a kick of crushed red pepper flakes for a bit of heat. It was heavenly.

When my eyes fluttered open from sauce-induced bliss, Luca's serious gaze pulled me in. Smiling broadly, I leaned toward him. "I think she might have some competition. That is the most delicious sauce I've ever tasted. You should be a chef!"

He cleared his throat and focused on stirring the pot in front of him a couple of times before looking back at me. "I actually went to culinary school. This was supposed to be my kitchen." He tasted the sauce and nodded. "But things change."

Luca fussed with the hand towel over his shoulder, no longer making eye contact.

Great, I'd opened a can of worms.

"I'm sorry. I can't imagine having to make a change like that."

He nodded, staring at the bubbling sauce intently. "I started working here when I was 13. I've always loved cooking, and my cousins had no interest in taking over for my uncle, so I was the obvious choice." A timer dinged, and he removed a pan from the oven. His movements were graceful and practiced. A true professional. "My older brother trained to take over for my dad, but there was an accident, and he passed away." He looked up at me with sad eyes. "Family obligations pulled me from the kitchen, and now I'm running Moretti Properties and all its holdings. A job I never wanted and am barely qualified for."

With a humorless laugh, he wiped his hands down the front of the apron. "Okay, enough of that. I'm supposed to be wooing you into submission, not dragging you down with my regrets." He grinned, but it didn't reach his eyes, which was just wrong. Regret, or sadness, or whatever he was feeling, should never cast a shadow over one of Luca's smiles. A lump settled in my throat, and I fidgeted in my seat. I wasn't sure why I cared so much. An uncomfortable silence settled over us as he finished prepping our dinner.

Bouncing my leg, I joked, "The last time I cooked was six months ago. It was supposed to be mac n cheese, but it ended up burnt n black. Ryan wouldn't even eat it."

Luca looked away from his work with a small smile. Tilting his head, he started plating the food. "Who's Ryan?"

Fluttering my eyelashes, I dramatically sighed. "Just the love of my life. Too bad he loves another." Luca's smile faltered, so I quickly added, "Catnip. He won't give it up, and I refuse to share. You know?"

"Your cat." He put down his utensils and laughed.

I scrunched my eyebrows in false confusion. "Yes?"

"You're a weird one, Sasha." Shaking his head, Luca pulled a pan from the oven and took off his apron.

Hopping down from the stool, I circled the prep table and wrapped my arms around his waist, pressing my body into his. "That I am, but isn't it more fun that way?"

Luca hugged me close. "It is." He pressed a sweet kiss to my forehead before pulling away. "Now, you go have a seat, and I'll be in with our plates."

Swaying my hips as I walked out of the kitchen, I could feel his eyes on me. I tapped my chin and looked everywhere but at the decked-out table. "But which table?"

He scoffed loudly from the stove as I settled into the chair facing the kitchen door. When Luca pushed through with the plates, the kitchen's bright light created a halo around his tall, broad body. He smiled at me as he put down a beautifully plated dish. "I might've overdone it, huh?"

"No, not at all. But be warned, I now expect flower petals to surround me at all future meals."

Uncorking a bottle of expensive wine, Luca laughed. "So, there will be future meals?"

"Let's see how this one goes." I accepted the glass of red from him.

"Deal."

We fell into a comfortable silence. Well, maybe not comfortable, but I was inhaling my pasta with a gusto I'd never experienced, so I was doing just fine. When my plate was empty, I finally looked up at Luca.

He was leaning on his elbows over his half-full plate, the glass of wine in his hand nearly empty. One eyebrow lifted, and the corners of his mouth pulled up. "I take it you liked it?"

I carefully dabbed the corners of my mouth. "Obviously. That was the best meal I've had in a while. You're a cooking god."

Inclining his head, he thanked me.

"Can I ask you something?"

He nodded, taking a sip of wine.

"Did you know I was in the show the other night? Is that why you were there?"

Choking on his wine, he shook his head wildly as he coughed. After taking a small sip of water, he cleared his throat. "No, of course not. I wasn't lying when I said I would leave you alone. My friend really did invite me. He has a thing for Evie. You can imagine my surprise when you walked out and started to take your clothes off."

I chuckled. "I guess that'd be a pretty big surprise, huh?" Swirling my wine, I studied Luca. "I was shocked when I saw you in the front row."

"I would've never known it, the way you just kept on dancing."

I shrugged. "I'd already written you off."

"That's fair. I was a prick."

Leaning back in my seat, I sipped the delicious wine. "No, you were honest. I just didn't like the implication that any woman could take my place. I get we don't know each other, but to go from pursuing me so aggressively to a 'who needs ya' attitude just because I rejected you pissed me off. I may be open to casual sex and one-night stands, but I won't be disrespected."

Luca leaned more forward. Everything about his posture was humble. "And that's why I'm apologizing for being a dick. I was hurt and tried to hide it by pretending to be a player. That's not me. Honestly, I hadn't had a one-night stand in probably ten years. I'm a little out of my depth here."

His honesty continued to knock me off balance. I scooted closer to the table, and my foot hit his. "You seem to be doing just fine. I'm here, aren't I?"

The air of guilt remained, but a small smile crept upon his face. "You are, but I had to resort to sexual extortion." He downed the rest of his wine and poured another glass. "When you left the stage, I don't know what came over me. I was in that dressing room before I knew what I was doing." He blew out a breath and looked up at the ceiling, wiping a hand down his face. "Then your friend walked in on me—Oh, God."

That did it. I fell into a fit of laughter.

"What?" Luca's eyebrows pulled together, and he set down his wine glass.

Covering my mouth with my hand, I tried to calm down. "You're not what I expected. You're so terribly sweet. Innocent."

"I'm sorry if I don't go around fucking women in public. I'll try to do better."

I only laughed harder.

Standing to his impressive height, he came around the table and pulled me from my chair. My body shook with laughter, even as his hands smoothed down my back. Gripping my ass, he pressed me to him, trapping my hands on his chest.

"I love your laugh, Sasha, even if it's at my expense." My laughter died down, but my smile remained just as big as his.

I wrestled my arms free and threw them around his neck. "You say that now."

"I know a few things that won't make you laugh." He leaned down, putting his face an inch from mine.

Going to my tippy toes, I tried to close the distance, but he pulled back, smiling. "Let me get your dessert."

His hands left my body, and I sagged with disappointment. "I thought that's what you were doing."

Walking back to the kitchen, he tsked. "Ms. Mitchell, you're going to have to work a little harder than that to get in these pants again."

Plopping down into my chair, I huffed. "Challenge accepted."

THREE

Luca and I lay on the couch, pretending to watch whatever movie he put on, our hands skimming each other's bodies. Tracing his jaw with my fingertips, I kissed his chin. "It's our third date."

Placing another soft kiss on his scratchy cheek, I felt a smile spread across his face. "It is."

"If you count the burlesque show, we've seen each other every Friday for four weeks."

His hands skated down my back, coming to rest on my ass with a light squeeze. "Correct."

"So that begs the question, are you putting out tonight?"

A laugh burst from Luca's mouth, vibrating through my chest and startling Ryan off his cat tree. Growling and flipping his tail with annoyance, he strutted from the room.

I had to agree with Ryan. This was no laughing matter.

Leaning up on my elbow, I glared down at his grinning face. "What's so funny?"

His silk sock brushed against my foot as he hooked his leg around mine. Rolling me, he pinned me against the back of the couch. With his body pressed against mine, the beginnings of what I was after nudged my hip.

Luca caressed my cheek, and I leaned into his warm hand. The smile on his face slowly faded as he gazed at me. "Sasha, I want nothing more than to give you whatever you want."

I turned my face, smiling as I kissed his palm. "Great. Take off your pants."

He chuckled, shaking his head. "No."

"What do you mean, no?" I complained, my smile falling.

Luca placed a sweet kiss on my nose and pulled back so our chests were no longer pressed together. Like the desperate bitch he made me, I dug fingers into his shoulders, trying to close the distance he created.

"I mean, no. Not tonight."

Disappointed, I let go of his shoulders. One hard shove and his top half flew off the couch. "Why the hell not?"

"It's not the right time." Detangling our legs, he sat up on the floor.

The erection he was sporting made it hard to believe what he was saying. His tousled hair and swollen lips made him positively fuckable, crossing all my wires. I didn't understand why this was happening. "Is it because I ordered in and didn't cook? Trust me. I did you a favor."

He shook his head, those dark waves falling into his brown eyes. "No, tonight was perfect. I just don't think now is the right time. We should wait until we're ready."

Lifting an eyebrow, I stared at the tightening in his slacks. "If your dick is anything to go by, I'd say we're ready."

Luca stood, putting his crotch at eye level, taunting me. The streetlights had come on, and Luca was taking his balls and going home just when the game was getting good.

"Sash. I don't want how we met to dictate what kind of relationship we have. I'm enjoying getting to know you, and I hope you feel the same way." He picked up his shoes and sat down to put them on.

"I do, but I don't understand why we couldn't have been naked when you told me about being Peter Pan in the school play." I straddled his lap, halting his attempt to tie his shoes.

"Hell, we could've even acted it out." My hands brushed his shoulders, sliding to his firm chest. "Let me be your Wendy, Luca."

The desperation in my voice disgusted me, but I was beyond pride at this point.

I pressed myself into him, but he only smiled. "Remember, dome of secrecy. Very few people know about my stint in tights. I expect you to take that information to the grave."

I nuzzled his neck, placing small kisses on the sensitive skin until shivers racked Luca's body. Grinding on his lap, I whispered in his ear, "My silence can be bought." I nipped his earlobe, and he gripped my hips more firmly, holding me down against his hardness. A quiet moan left my lips as I rocked against him. "I'll blackmail you. Or is it extortion? I'm not really clear on the difference." I gave his neck a quick bite.

Luca's body stiffened. When I pulled away, he no longer looked playful. I framed his face with my hands, trying to bring his gaze back to me. "Hey, what's wrong?"

Blowing out a breath, a sorry excuse for a smile settled onto his handsome face. "Nothing, I'm just being weird, aren't I?"

I shook my head. Guilt settled into my chest for pressuring him into something he was clearly not into. "No, I'm being pushy." I moved to get off his lap. "I'm sorry. You're free to leave without further molestation."

Before I stood completely up, Luca pulled me back to his lap. My lips parted to ask what he was doing, but he kissed the bejesus out of me, smothering any possibility of speech.

His lips were soft but demanding. As he tugged my bottom lip between his teeth, a moan fell from my mouth. My hips rolled against him, trying to regain our previous passion. His tongue stroked mine in time with the movement of our bodies. He dug his fingers into my fleshy ass, the bite of pain welcome and only adding to my pleasure. The course material of his slacks rubbed against the flimsy material between my legs, and heat started building, every move bringing me closer to a big finale.

Before I could topple over the edge, Luca's kisses slowed. His hips stopped moving with mine, and no matter how hard I strained to stay flush against him, he pushed me back on his lap.

When he pulled away, we were gasping for air. Resting my forehead against his, I stared into his eyes, panting, trying to regain control of my body. No one had ever made me so desperate.

He placed my hand over his racing heart. "You feel that? That's why I want to wait. We could be something special. I don't want to rush it."

I nodded as he set me on the next cushion. Adjusting himself, he stood. The tent in his pants was enough to poke an eye out. How did he expect to leave with that thing standing at attention?

Looking down, hunger clear in his eyes, he bent over and kissed me. My fingertips just grazed his hairline before he pulled back, keeping me from grabbing his thick, black hair and holding him hostage.

"I need to get out of here before I fuck this up." Luca sighed as he took a step toward the door.

I nodded, not really understanding why he was holding out on me. I picked the cat hair off my dress, unwilling to watch him leave when I was so wound up.

"Sasha."

"Yeah."

"Please look at me."

Reluctantly I did, and damn, I wished I hadn't. Luca's messy hair and swollen lips made me want to leap off the couch to maul his sexy ass. "I'm looking."

"I'll call you?"

I wanted to scream, "Why bother?" So, we could make another date where he would be perfect and charming. Get me to the edge of happy-good times, then bolt? No thanks. The thought of another blue ovary night left me cringing.

Despite the horny bitch in me trying to avoid another orgasm-less night, I wanted to spend more time with Luca. We'd only scratched the surface, but he was already more open than my last partner, albeit more complicated. I didn't know how to navigate our budding relationship.

"Sure. Get home safe."

He kissed my forehead and left without saying anything else.

Ryan hopped up on my lap, clearly pleased it was just the two of us again. "What a letdown. Huh, bud?"

He purred, his head ramming into my hand as I petted him.

"I guess I'm taking care of myself yet again."

For the fourth Friday in a row, I took a battery-operated trip to bliss.

"Not acceptable. They were supposed to be here yesterday, and now you're telling me it'll be another week?"

A set of retro wingback chairs I'd sent out to be reupholstered was MIA, and I had a pissy client breathing down my neck. The vendor was an artist who hand-painted fabrics and didn't seem too concerned with deadlines or signed contracts.

As he droned on about the delays, I paced my small office.

Movement from across the hall caught my eye. Ashley pushed Malcolm out of her office and slammed the door. Shaking his head, he stepped away before turning back and leaning against the wall. He looked like a moody spread in a fashion magazine. The white of his shirt contrasted beautifully with his dark brown skin, and his charcoal slacks were tailored to fit his impressive height—pure perfection, except for the scowl on his face. Rubbing a hand down his waves, I caught his eye, and he glared at me, jaw tensing, then stormed out of the office.

"Just friends, my ass."

"I'm sorry, what was that, Ms. Mitchell?"

"Nothing. I want those chairs here by Friday, or I'll be letting everyone know exactly what they can expect when they work with you. You got me, Adams?"

There was a pause, and then, in a mouse-like voice, Scott replied, "Yes, Ms. Mitchell."

"Great. See you in two days." I hung up, done with the entire conversation, and man.

An hour later, Ashley peeked out of her office. When she looked at me, I raised an eyebrow. Since when was she hesitant to barge into my office?

Shaking her head, she stomped inside. "Today is a total fucking nightmare, Sash." She flung her body onto my cozy chair, her dark cloud-like hair bouncing as she landed.

I closed my laptop. The bathroom remodel I was working on would have to wait. "What happened? Malcolm looked pissed."

At the mention of Malcolm's name, she shot straight up in the chair. "Oh, that fucker. He was mad? I should shove my heel up his ass."

Leaning back, I held my hands up. "Hey man, I'm not the enemy. What did he do this time?"

"He had Ben followed." Ashley shrunk back in her chair, staring at the opposite wall.

"Wait. What?"

She cracked her knuckles, a habit she struggled to break. "Yeah. Apparently, I have shit taste in men, and Malcolm thought it was his job to have my boyfriend followed."

"That's so weird. I don't even know what to say."

"Right? But guess what he found out?"

All I knew was if Ben was cheating on her, I'd murder that fool.

"Ben doesn't go to the office."

My rage dissipated. Frowning, I said, "I don't think I understand."

Ashley rolled her head on the back of the chair and looked at me, tears filling her dark brown eyes. "Ben got let go three weeks ago and didn't tell me. He's been pretending to go to work. How did I not notice?" She pressed her palms into her eyes, dropping her chin to her chest. "I'm fucking terrible."

She choked on the last word and started sobbing, gasping for air. I rushed to her side with a box of tissues. "Oh, come on, Ash, you're not terrible. He is. Keeping something this big from you is not okay."

She cried into my neck. "But . . . but what does it say about me that he didn't think he could tell me? And where did he go when he was on that 'business trip' last week? Oh God. What if he's cheating on me and lying about his job?"

I rubbed circles on her back. "Then I fucking castrate him, set the rest of his bits on fire, and we dance on his dick ashes."

"You're demented." Hiccupping laughter sprayed snot and tears all over my shirt, both grossing me out and filling me with relief.

"That I am, but I'm your best friend, so what's that say about you?" Tears streamed down her brown, dimpled cheeks, and I wanted to tear Ben apart with my bare hands. "I have an idea. Why don't you come with me to Sammie's gallery opening tonight?"

Ash dabbed her eyes with a tissue, shaking her head. "No. No, I need to go face the bastard." She blew out a harsh breath. "Anyway, I thought Luca was your plus one these days."

My stomach dropped. He'd turned down my invitation without even giving a reason. Not even an "I already have plans." Usually, I would've already moved on to the next warm body, but Luca had me all fucked up.

"He can't make it."

Ashley frowned. "Oh. And you're upset?"

I shrugged. "I guess? I think I'm more annoyed that this is throwing me so much. Pre Luca, I would've already had another date, but instead, I've been trying to decide if that's wrong."

Ash's sniffles died down. "Have you had the relationship talk?"

Snorting out a laugh, I shook my head. "It's been three dates. We haven't even slept together since the wedding. So no, we haven't defined the relationship or whatever."

Tipping her head to the side, she studied my face. "Have you been with anyone else since your first date?"

"If I'm honest, I haven't been with anyone else since the wedding."

Ashley blinked rapid fire. "What? But it's been . . . and you . . . no sex?"

"Correct. It has *not* been fun."

She blew out a breath. "You must have it bad for Luca."

I frowned. She wasn't wrong. All signs pointed to me being thoroughly whipped by a man who was withholding his amazing dick game. This was not the Sasha I knew.

Luca had dictated the pace of our relationship. Hell, that we even had any kind of relationship was because he decided it. I'd gone without sex for nearly two months, and I was fucking done. Pulling my phone off the desk, I sent a text.

"You texting Luca?"

"Nope. Dimitri."

Her face twisted into a wicked smile. "Ah." She stood up and walked toward the office door. "Well, have fun with that. I hope he's everything you need."

"He always is."

I stood at the back of the gallery, watching Dimitri weave through the crowd holding two champagne flutes. Men and women stared at his striking figure in a mixture of lust and awe, and I didn't blame them. The man wore the shit out of a suit. One wink from Dimitri and everyone in a five-foot radius was a little hot and bothered.

He had the whole tall, dark, and handsome thing down, but something was off.

Dimitri was too perfect, too pretty. Flawless. All night, we'd flirted and touched, but I didn't find the excitement I usually did with him.

"Your champagne."

I smiled, thanked him, then took a large swig. The bubbles tickled my throat, and I had to fight back a cough.

His chilly hand rubbed my exposed back, trying to soothe me. "You okay, Sash?"

I nodded, gently wiping below my eye. "Went down the wrong pipe."

Dimitri smiled at me with his perfect, straight, white teeth.

Nothing. No quickening pulse, no fluttering in my stomach. Just nothing.

I pressed myself into his body, and he reacted immediately, wrapping me in his arms as he had done a hundred times before. Lowering his head, he placed a light kiss on the corner of my mouth. I pressed my hands to his shoulders to get more leverage, determined to enjoy the night.

"Sasha."

At the sound of *his* voice, panic seized my chest. Waiting a beat, I slowly pulled back from the kiss, trying to gain some composure. Looping one arm with Dimitri's, I forced a smile onto my face. "Luca, nice to see you." Gesturing to Dimitri, I made introductions. The two men shook hands, neither particularly pleased.

"We actually know each other, don't we, Moretti?"

"Oh, I know you, Chronis." Luca's glare barely softened when he looked at me. "Can I have a word?"

Dimitri laughed. "You know what, man? I need to make my rounds. I'll be back in a few minutes." He kissed my cheek and strolled away, leaving me with a fuming Luca.

"So—" he abruptly cut me off and pulled me by the elbow into a backroom of the gallery. Slamming the door, Luca spun on me. He looked positively deranged.

"What do you want to talk about, Luca?" I sat on a tall crate, trying to keep my expression neutral. Inside, I was a mess. Seeing Luca had me all twisted up, and I worried that my dud of a date hurt what little we had built.

Luca paced the small space before stopping right in front of me. When his hands found mine, I released the breath I was holding. Touching was good. Touching meant he didn't hate me.

"Why are you here, and what are you doing with Dimitri Chronis?"

"Sammie's a college friend, and I had a plus one. I asked you first, but you were busy. Remember?"

His hands tightened around mine. "I do, but if I'd known this is where you needed a plus one, I would've said yes. I needed to be here tonight, but we could have come together."

As if on cue, a bite-sized brunette came crashing through the door. "There you are. I need you out there, Luca." Her eyes widened when she saw us so close, holding hands. "Oh. Sorry. I'll be out front."

And then she was gone.

"I have a million things I want to say, but I really do need to be out there." Luca's jaw ticked as he eyed the door.

I tried to drop his hands, but his grip tightened. "It's fine. Just go. I need to get back to Dimitri."

Without warning, he pulled me into his body, his lips crushing mine. Every ounce of our frustration and anger poured into that kiss. I bit his lip so hard I tasted iron. Luca answered by digging his fingers into my fleshy hips.

The moment demanded more. I wanted more.

Dragging my hand down his body, I gripped his hardening member. A low groan sounded from the back of his throat as I worked him over his pants until they became too tight. I swallowed the sound with my kisses, thrilled that he was losing control.

I pulled away from him, and he started to complain until my hands hit his belt, tugging his hips to me. Making quick work of the buckle, I unbuttoned his slacks. Pushing his pants and boxers down, I caught sight of my primary target.

It's been too long, old friend.

I licked my palm before wrapping my hand around his hot,

hard length. As I stroked him, I couldn't pull my eyes away. The way Luca thrust his hips created an ache in me. I needed more than was wise in the back room of a crowded gallery.

Twisting my hand, I kissed the long column of his neck as his head fell back. He twitched under my fingers, his chest rapidly rising and falling. Kneeling, I took him into my mouth. The moan that fell from his mouth sent a shot of heat between my thighs, making me squeeze them together to get some relief. I could have come just from the noises he made. They were so raw and guttural, unlike the polished businessman Luca presented himself as. Humming around him, I couldn't get enough of the salty taste of his skin and the weight of his cock on my tongue.

Luca was big, so I took his shaft in as deep as possible, using my hand on the rest so every inch was touched. My tongue swirled, and I hallowed my cheeks, giving him no time to adjust.

It wasn't long until he was pulling my hair back. "Fuck. I'm going to come." His husky words sent a shiver of delight down my spine. I winked at him and continued to suck the life out of him. A moment later, he came deep in my throat. Not leaving a drop, I cleaned him up with my tongue. Luca's glassy eyes watched me intently as I tucked him back in his pants and gingerly wiped the corners of my mouth.

"You're needed out front." I smiled sweetly at his stunned expression. Standing, I brushed off my knees.

"You're here on a date with someone else, and you sucked my cock in the backroom."

"That does appear to be what happened."

He gathered me up in his arms, one hand holding my chin tightly. "I know we don't owe each other anything, but I want you to know I haven't been with anyone else since the wedding."

"Ditto."

Luca exhaled, and I laughed. He was obviously relieved by my lack of extra circular activities. "I'd like to keep it that way. Is that okay with you?"

I paused. "Under one condition."

"Yes?"

"I get 100% access to your sex genius."

Luca licked his lower lip, his eyes promising he'd give me exactly what I wanted. "Deal. Get rid of the Greek asshole and find me. I'm taking you home."

I saluted him, and he slapped my ass. Sticking my tongue out at him, he chuckled as I slipped out of the room.

When I found Dimitri, he was chatting up a slender ginger. His hand lingered just above her ass.

"Hey Dimitri, I think I'm going to head home with Luca." I smiled at the blushing girl on his arm. "You good?"

Dimitri's grin should've scared the little thing. He was going to devour her. "Yes, ma'am. Claire's offered to show me to her favorite watering hole."

He leaned in and pecked me on the cheek. His lips grazed my ear as he whispered, "Call me if Moretti fails to deliver."

I looked him in his cold gray eyes. "Oh, he won't."

Dimitri pursed his lips, but he was in no position to say anything. With one more wave, he and his arm candy left the gallery.

I was finally free to claim my prize.

Searching the room for my own tall, dark, and handsome, I found him in the back of the gallery. Luca argued with a slightly older man as a beautiful woman stood between the raging bulls, shrinking into herself.

I joined the tense group, my hand lightly grazing Luca's shoulder. He turned, his face softening as he kissed my cheek. "Sasha, this is my cousin Marco." Marco's grip was unnecessarily tight when he shook my hand. "And this is my sister-in-law, Adriana." Her hand was as limp as a dead fish.

I put on my "new business" smile. "It's nice to meet you."

Adriana smiled, but a tightness in her face kept it from being natural. Marco placed his hand on the small of her back and whispered in her ear.

"Luca, it's late, and I think we've put in enough face time at this thing. I've got Maggie closing once the show is over, so I'm going to take Adriana home now. We'll see you at your parents' on Sunday."

With a polite nod, the doom and gloom twins left.

I turned to Luca, who looked defeated.

"You own this place?"

He tore his eyes from their retreating backs. "My family does." He blew out a sharp breath. "Damn. I just wanted Adriana to have fun. You know?"

One hand ran through his hair as he stared at the ground. "Why couldn't Marco just try? For once?"

Luca looked lost, so I wrapped my arms around him. His body tensed but then relaxed. He wound his arms around me, his chin resting on top of my head. We swayed side to side with my nose burrowed into his shirt. After a few minutes, his breathing slowed, and I peered up at him. "All better?"

He smiled, pressing himself more into me. "I will be once I get you alone."

I liked the sound of that.

FOUR

When Luca said he was taking me home, what he meant was that the event was going to end, and he was going to triple-check all the employees' work, going as far as processing credit card payments and stacking serving trays. Once he was satisfied with everything, we headed back to his place.

At 2 a.m., he deposited a tipsy me into a town car. Sliding on the leather seats, I marveled at the chilliness against my thighs. "Luca, these are the softest seats in the world and the coldest. Feel my thighs." Tilting my ass at him, he grabbed my hips and pushed me back into a seated position. After securing my seat belt, he nodded at the driver.

"How much champagne did you drink, Sasha?"

"Enough." I frowned at him. Was he really drink-grubbing after I sat in the gallery for seven fucking hours?

I twisted my body to stare out the window. All the excitement of choosing Luca—at least for the night—flew out the window. He was already policing my behavior, just like Beth. I would not be a part of another relationship where someone treated me like a delinquent. So many people tried to mold me into what they wanted. I just wanted someone to appreciate me for me.

Not sure if it was the booze or my fragile feelings, but tears stung my eyes. Mortified, I leaned toward the driver. "You know what? Can you please take me home? I'm suddenly not feeling well."

Luca stared at the side of my face as I settled back into my seat. "Sasha?"

Blinking, I fought to keep the tears at bay because I couldn't stomach him seeing me cry.

"Sash. Look at me."

His warm fingers lifted my chin as he gently turned my face. Frowning, he tilted his head as he studied me. "What's wrong?"

Shaking my head, I twisted my hands. I tried to steel myself against his concern. I'd already been more open with him than was smart. The fact that I expected him to find my shenanigans charming proved how comfortable I'd gotten. Trying to swallow down my disappointment, I smiled at Luca. "Nothing. I'm just drunk and tired. I think I should just go home."

His eyebrows pulled closer together as he cupped my cheek. "I said something, didn't I? Was it asking about the champagne?"

My eyes darted away from his face. I couldn't stand how hard he was trying. He was being so sweet, but I had experience with this. It starts out all light-hearted and fun, but then they want me to stop going out so much, stop performing, stop being me. Beth almost succeeded in making me into her "perfect partner." I wasn't about to lose myself again.

Luca sighed. "I didn't mean it like that. I was asking because I don't make a habit of taking inebriated women to bed. I was trying to." He moved his hands around like he was trying to find the words. "Have realistic expectations."

I grinned at him. His cheeks were bright red, but this time, he didn't look away. "So, you were checking to see if I was still going to fuck you?"

That did it. He rolled his eyes and laughed. "Jesus, I wished you didn't say it like that, but yes."

Amused and pleasantly surprised, I studied his face. "So, you weren't disgusted with my lushness tonight?"

Quickly, he shook his head. "No, you were stuck watching me count trays. It would've been weird if you didn't take advantage of the free-flowing champagne."

"Hm. I don't know what to do with that." I shifted back in my seat.

"Why don't we go back to my place? I'll make us a late-night snack, and we can take it from there." His long fingers laced through mine.

He was smiling so sweetly that I couldn't help but smile back. "Why do I feel like mind-blowing sex is off the table now?"

Luca chuckled and told the driver to continue to his place.

The streetlights sporadically lit Luca's face as we traveled through the city. My eyes traced the bend in his nose that hinted at previous breaks.

Was he bullied as a kid? I needed to get my hands on some childhood photos. My alcohol-soaked mind tried to wrap around the idea of this gentle giant being beaten up. His nose wasn't the only imperfection on his otherwise beautiful visage. He had nick-like scars on his face and body and one large, faded scar that ran down his side.

I wanted to trace that line with my fingers, better yet, my tongue. Without realizing it, I inched closer to Luca and slid my hand up his thigh. Much to my dismay, he stopped it before I grabbed the goods. Tearing my gaze from where our hands were joined, I frowned at him.

Why'd he stop me?

With hooded eyes, he licked his bottom lip. "Not in the car, Sasha. At least, not this time."

I grinned at him. "It's going to be when the time's right? Right?"

Hearing his words recited back to him, he looked away. Even in the dim light, I could tell Luca's ears were red.

"Don't tell anyone, but I think that's sweet." I squeezed his hand, wishing I was squeezing something else.

He gifted me a shy smile and gave my nose a quick kiss before ushering me out of the car.

Carefully stepping around a chunk of missing asphalt and through the grass next to the sidewalk, I waved as the car pulled away.

"Wow." Luca's house was a classic three-story brick row house with a mirrored unit attached.

"You like it?"

"Uh. Yeah. This is real estate goals." I turned and faced the park across the street. "I don't think you could do much better."

"It's all right." He chuckled as he unlocked the door to the duplex.

I stared at the trees and flowers, enjoying a rare cool summer breeze, and tried to check myself. Seeing his domestic-as-hell neighborhood made me comfortable. Pair that with how good Luca made me feel, and I was worried.

How mushy was I going to get? Sloshed Sasha was very mushy. In my drunken state, I could finally be honest with myself. I loved how sweet he was. The fact he wanted our second first time to be special was beyond precious, even if it annoyed the hell out of me.

I loved how he seemed to like me despite my pile of flaws. My family couldn't even make that claim. Ashley was the only person to take on all this mess.

Scariest of all, I loved how easily I pictured myself with Luca. On paper, we didn't make sense—hell, in conversations, we barely made sense—but there was something about him that was right. He felt like home.

Luca pulled me from my spiraling thoughts, shouting my name from inside. "Sasha! You coming in or . . ."

Blushing like the foolish chump I was, I scurried inside. If I was going to successfully seduce one, Luca Moretti, I needed to get my head on straight.

Kicking off my stilettos, I dropped to my generous five-ten

height. Luca slipped off his beautiful Italian leather dress shoes and continued to tower over me as few people did.

I followed him through the main floor as he pointed out rooms and things he thought I would find interesting. If asked, I couldn't have told you a damn thing about those rooms. All my focus was on the way his back flexed with each arm movement and how his long strides made his ass perfectly pinchable. My attention otherwise engaged, I ran into him when he stopped in a homey kitchen.

I spun around, taking in every detail. It was as if the design came from one of my notebooks. Butcher block countertops, white cabinetry, clean light fixtures, and top-of-the-line appliances all combined to form my idea of the perfect kitchen.

"Does it meet with your approval?" Luca's hands skimmed my waist.

I leaned back into his embrace, his cologne enveloping me. "It does. It's cozy, warm, and inviting. I expected granite and sleek lines, but this honestly feels more like you."

He brushed my hair to one side and placed a kiss beneath my ear. "I'm glad you like it."

Before I could turn and wrap myself around him, Luca let go and headed toward the stainless-steel fridge. "Now, do you want grilled cheese or pasta?"

The eternal battle raged in my body. Food or sex. Rarely did I have to choose. The champagne dancing through my body whispered sweet nothings of bubbly carnal pleasure, but my stomach complained of too few hors d'oeuvres at the art gallery.

Luca started laughing. "You look like I asked you to decide which arm to cut off. Let's go with grilled cheese. I want you to see just how varied my skills are."

I sat down at the kitchen island and watched Luca slice green apples.

"If you're making me a grilled cheese, why are you cutting apples? Are you trying to make sure I get in a fruit serving?"

Luca smiled down at the apple he was cutting. "You really

don't cook, do you?" He finally looked up at me, his hair falling in his eyes. I shook my head and leaned over to brush it away. Like a good girl, I sat back in my seat and let him continue prepping our bougie, late-night snack. "It's for the sandwich. I'm doing a green apple, bacon, gouda, and Havarti grilled cheese."

My mouth hung open. "You can do that?"

He nodded.

"You are a god."

Luca laughed so loud that I was sure the neighbors heard him. Covering his mouth to muffle the sound, his eyes crinkled in amusement. "You're a goof, but I'm glad I'm so impressive."

"In more ways than one," I whispered back to him.

He leaned across the cutting board. "Why are you whispering?"

"You were whispering, so I figured it was appropriate."

His eyebrows shot up. "Oh yeah, my neighbors." He gestured to the wall with the knife. "My sister-in-law and nephew live next door, and the kitchens share a wall. I try to be quiet late at night in this part of the house."

"Ah. So, no loud activities on this beautiful butcher block. Noted." I brushed my fingertips over the top of my cleavage, and Luca's eyes zeroed in on the movement. "What about your bedroom? Any shared walls?"

His head shook. "Not one."

I smiled. "Excellent." Resting my elbow on the counter, I tapped my fingers against my collarbone. "Do I need to burn those sandwiches, or are you going to deliver the goods, Gordon Ramsay?"

Luca focused back on his cutting board and shook his head. As he chopped and assembled the sandwiches for the skillet, I stared at him shamelessly. He was so handsome. Even his imperfections turned me on. I was close to saying fuck the sandwich, but he had already done so much work.

"Hey, Luca?"

He kept his eyes down. "Yes."

"Can I steal a shirt? This dress may be sexy, but I am a little uncomfortable."

That got his attention. He checked me out from top to bottom, his teeth snagging his lip before he cleared his throat and dropped some butter on the hot skillet. "Sure. Upstairs, first room on the left."

I hopped off the stool and left the kitchen.

Photos of what I assumed were his family lined the stairwell. One picture showed a younger Luca, his arm thrown around a devastatingly handsome man, who had to be his brother, in tuxes, laughing. The next was of the same hottie and Luca's sister-in-law. She looked like a completely different woman—no limp noodle present, only a drop-dead gorgeous woman marrying a man she clearly loved.

At the top of the stairs was a photo of Luca and a little boy. It had to be his nephew. The way they smiled at each other made me all teary-eyed. Luca looked right with a child in his arms, and I worried about what that thought meant for me. I wasn't even sure I wanted children, but now I was picturing Luca holding babies that may or may not have my green eyes and his black hair.

Oh God, we'd have goth children.

Shaking off drunk, weirdo thoughts, I hurried up the rest of the stairs.

Luca's bedroom was precisely how I imagined it would be— Light gray on the walls except for a single navy accent wall behind the bed, white linens, and dark wood. It was masculine, stylish, and far too neat.

Going into his closet, I pulled out a worn Wash U t-shirt. Slipping out of my dress, I pulled it on. My ass was hanging out the bottom, but what did I care? Maybe it would get the ball rolling.

My hands caressed the duvet cover, and I moaned at how soft it was. The mattress had the perfect amount of give when I pressed down. There was no way around it. Standing was no longer for me. I needed to be lying down.

Tossing my dress aside, I slid into bed, sighing with pleasure as

I ran my bare legs across the thousand-thread-count miracle sheets. This was the life.

Heavy footsteps on the stairs drew my attention, and I popped up. Luca walked in, wearing a big smile and carrying a tray with two sandwiches and two tall glasses of water.

"I knew I'd lose you to the bed."

Smiling sheepishly, I scooted to rest my back against the headboard. "Sorry, but when I felt the covers, I had to give this baby a test drive."

Luca set the tray of food down on the side table. "I get it."

Walking away from the bed, he unbuckled his belt, pulling it off and hanging it in the closet. Next, he unbuttoned his pants, let them pool at his feet, stepped out of them, and then folded them nicely. He gingerly set the pants in a basket full of dry-clean-only items.

Then Luca loosened his tie and carefully rolled it, placing it in a drawer in his built-in closet. In an impressively short amount of time, he unbuttoned his dress shirt, folded it, and added it to the basket. Finally, he pulled his undershirt over his head, tossing it in a different basket.

When he turned back to me, I was too distracted by his well-rehearsed routine to be rightfully impressed by his near-nudity.

Grabbing the tray, he sat down on the bed. "What?"

I shook my head with a laugh. "Nothing."

His dark hair fell in his eyes as he handed me a plate and glass. "No. Clearly, something's funny. What is it?"

"That was the most intense undressing I've ever seen."

Luca studied his closet with a frown. "I don't know what you're talking about."

"Okay, Luca." I took a bite of the promised sandwich, and, holy shit, was it delicious.

Before he'd started the second half of his sandwich, mine was gone.

"Do you want it?" He tried to hand me his plate.

"I really shouldn't."

He shook it in my face. "Oh, come on."

Snatching it before he could change his mind, I all but yelled, "Fine! I was trying to be polite."

Laughing, he stood up and went into the ensuite. The sink started running, and he came out with a toothbrush in his mouth. Pulling it out, he eyed the white foam as if he was willing it to stay on the bristles. "I have an extra toothbrush on the counter for you."

Nibbling on the sandwich half, trying to make it last longer, I nodded.

He went back to the bathroom, and I listened to him gargle.

When he came back all minty fresh, he hopped onto the bed. "I was thinking. Maybe we could do the Farmer's Market tomorrow morning? I usually get my produce for the week there."

Setting the plate on the serving tray, I stood up from the bed. "I guess? I'm not really a 'farmer's market' kind of gal, but if the end result is delicious treats made by you, I'm in."

While I brushed my teeth and made use of my small toiletry go bag, I heard Luca leave and come back to the room.

I patted myself on the back for getting my whole routine done in ten minutes. Wiping down the counters of the small mess I had made, I laughed. Luca was a total neat freak, but it made him so much more human.

Flipping off the light, I went back into the bedroom.

The first thing I noticed was my dress was no longer on the floor but instead hung up in the closet. The food tray was gone, and the pillows straightened.

The most significant change was the huge Italian man passed out on top of the covers.

Straddling his hips, I kissed him deeply.

Nothing.

I pinched his nipple.

Nada.

I'd been emotionally vulnerable, yet I was still going to bed unsatisfied. Disappointed, I sighed and reluctantly pulled myself from his body.

And what an impressive body it was. Five stars. Would ogle again.

Rolling to the other side of the bed, I got under the duvet. That's when Luca moved finally moved. He lifted his body to get under the covers, pulling them out from their neat tucks around the edges. Once under the sheets, his hard body wrapped around me as his arms pulled me closer.

Waiting for the usual cuddle awkwardness to set in, I held my breath.

Luca pulled me even closer and kissed my ear. In a sweet, sleepy voice, he whispered. "Goodnight, Sasha."

I instantly relaxed. His warmth made me feel content, something I hadn't experienced in a while, if ever. How could a person I'd only known for a couple of months make me feel so safe?

As if he heard my thoughts, his arms squeezed me tight, and he mumbled nonsense in my hair. I bit back a laugh at just how cute he was. Then, I internally gagged at how sappy I was getting.

Catching myself in a happy moment, I vowed to enjoy my time with Luca. In the end, people like me weren't meant for people like him, but I would live it up while he was mine.

Smiling to myself, I pulled his hand to my mouth and gave it a small kiss.

FIVE

I peeled my tired eyes open and looked around the room as I reached across the bed, only to find cold sheets.

"Who the fuck has an alarm set for Saturday morning. And who the fuck wakes up before it?" I mumbled into my pillow as I swatted the noisy box. I didn't even know people still had dedicated alarm clocks. Why not just use your phone?

I rolled over to check the time.

Six a.m. On a Saturday. After copious amounts of champagne.

Nope. Luca had lost his damn mind.

As I snuggled back down, Luca burst through the door, whispering. "Oh shit! I'm so sorry."

I grumbled into the pillow.

"Are you awake? If you are, we could get cleaned up and head to the farmer's market now. The earlier you go, the better."

Flipping to my back, I glared at a fully dressed and ready-to-go Luca with the fire of a thousand suns. "Are you fucking kidding me? It's six a.m. Wake me up in six hours, and we'll brunch."

I pulled his pillow over my face and inhaled deeply. He smelled so good, and his pillow held a perfect impression of his scent. My body relaxed, and I started to drift off.

The bed dipped, and I figured Luca had seen the error of his ways and was going to join me in the beauty that was sleeping in on a Saturday morning.

Slowly, the soft sheets glided over my legs, and the cold air of the room hit my skin. I tossed the pillow and shouted, "Hey!"

Luca kneeled between my legs, his hands hovering over my thighs. Raising one of my perfectly shaped eyebrows, I waited.

With a sexy smile on his face, he gently caressed the insides of my thighs, making my legs spread even wider. "Sasha, if you get up right now, I can get everything I need from the farmer's market to make you a beautiful dinner."

His calloused fingers tickled as he moved past my pussy. A frown took over my face. His teasing bullshit only made my mood fouler.

"After dinner, we can have dessert. Doesn't that sound nice?"

His large hand spanned my stomach, moving under the shirt I was wearing while his other landed next to my head to support his weight. Minty breath fanned across my face, his lips a little too far away to kiss.

"Depends. You know, I'm trying to keep realistic expectations." I winked and arched up into him. "Are you my dessert?"

A lazy grin spread across his face as he pressed himself in between my legs. His growing excitement was hard against my thigh, and I threw one leg around him, pinning him against me.

"That's the plan." With those words, he closed the distance between us. I eagerly met his lips, parting mine to sneak my tongue out. He let me set the pace of our kiss just a moment before his tongue invaded my mouth, caressing and teasing mine as his hips matched the motion. He rolled against me, turning me into a clawing, desperate mess.

His hand moved up to cup my breast. Unable to cover the whole thing, he tried his damnedest to leave no inch untouched. The rough texture of his jeans rubbed against the wet satin between my legs, and I cursed into his mouth. My body was vibrating as I edged toward an orgasm, and the bastard was still fully clothed.

Luca's mouth trailed kisses down my neck, occasionally stopping to suck. As long as his tongue kept stroking my skin after, he was welcome to mark me up with a million hickies. I didn't care. That mouth was addictive, and I was hooked.

His fingers pinched my nipple as his mouth enveloped the other through the shirt. Sensitive from all the stimulation, the soft fabric felt rough against my tight tip, and his tongue's movements caused delicious friction. Needing more, I arched my back, pressing myself into Luca's skilled hand and mouth. Gripping his thick, coarse locks, I held him close to my body. His heat made my skin clammy, but I wouldn't give an inch.

Anticipation kept my eyes locked on his movements. When his brow furrowed in concentration, my lips curved into a small smile. I was his sole focus, and he was mine. Despite the heavy weight of his body, my chest filled with lightness. Warmth spread through me that was more than just the friction between our bodies. Luca was burrowing into my heart, whether I liked it or not.

No longer allowing any space between our lower halves, Luca pressed me into the mattress. My legs were like a vise grip around his hips, my heels digging into his firm ass. One of my hands let go of his hair, trying to reach down to get a squeeze, but Luca's teeth tugged my nipple, making me bunch his shirt instead.

"Jesus, Luca."

His hum against my chest sent shivers through my body. My breath was all over the place as I tried to match his hips' rhythm, but the beginnings of my climax made me jerky and erratic.

One pinch, bite, and thrust, and I fell over the edge. Luca kept moving against me, helping me ride out the waves of pleasure.

Panting, I grabbed his face and kissed him hard, all teeth, tongue, and desperation. When he pulled away, all I could do was smile.

Luca's lips were bright red and swollen, thanks to his devotion to pleasing me. I flattened out the tufts of hair my fingers had pulled, reveling at the thickness.

With twinkling eyes, Luca kissed my nose. "So, you ready to get up?"

My hand grabbed his hard cock. Letting out a sexy moan, Luca tipped his head back, eyes shutting tight.

"I think you're up enough for the both of us. Let me help you with that."

When he peered down at me, my heart stopped. Gone was the sweet, playful, dry-humping Luca. In his place was the man that had tongue fucked me in a hotel lobby. The look in his eye let me know I was minutes away from not walking right for a couple of days.

And oh God, did I want that.

He gripped my wrist, pinning it to the bed. My other hand stayed put, too excited to stop him from going on.

"You're really trying to fuck up my plans." He leaned his face inches from mine, his minty breath caressing my cheeks. "Listen closely. You're going to get your ass up, put on a pair of my shorts and a T-shirt, then we're going to go to the farmer's market. I will make you dinner tonight, and we will have a civilized, good time. After that, I will fuck you just how you want. Not before, okay? I'm doing this the right way."

Luca confused the fuck out of me. His rock-hard cock strained against his jeans, but he was determined to wait. Well, it was his dick's funeral.

Letting go of my body, Luca pulled away, his expression softening. As his eyes devoured my body, I returned the favor. A simple T-shirt stretched across his broad frame, but I knew it was pricey by the feel of the fabric. His dark denim did little to conceal my number one fascination.

Looking at Luca made my body overheat. No person should ever be that sexy. It isn't fair to the rest of us.

Reaching his hand out, he pulled me from the bed. A quick

but firm swat to my ass sent me toward his closet. "Be quick. There should be a pair of Adriana's flip-flops in there."

I frowned, but he was already out of the room. Rubbing my ass cheek, I considered my choices. My generous figure and his slim hips meant his clothes were tighter than my own.

Pulling out the black flip-flops, I rolled my eyes. I couldn't believe I was going to go in public wearing basketball shorts and flip-flops. High maintenance was not a bad thing in my book. I enjoyed looking a certain way, and there was nothing wrong with that. He owed me big time for schlubbing it in public.

Downstairs, Luca was pouring coffee into two to-go mugs. Much to my disappointment, he'd tamed his trouser monster.

"Ready to go, even if I look like I'm about to do yard work."

Smiling, Luca shook his head. "You're beautiful no matter what you're wearing. Now, let's head out before you find another way to sabotage the day."

An hour into my first farmer's market experience, I was actually enjoying myself. Stalls were situated under tents and the shade of the trees that lined Tower Grove Park's pathways and the surrounding streets. People busied themselves, searching for the perfect tomato while the faint noise of city traffic fought against the band playing twenty stalls away. All in all, the farm-in-the-city vibe was something I had never thought I'd like but was proving to be an excellent way to spend a Saturday morning.

It didn't hurt that Luca only let go of my hand to pick up produce or pay for one of our many snacks. My cheeks hurt from laughing at the faces Luca made while inspecting the goods. He was very particular even when it came to which plum we would get for our sixth or seventh goodie of the morning.

"See how deep and even the color is on this one?"

I nodded, and he shoved it under my nose.

"And smell how fruity it is?"

Inhaling deeply, I said, "Yes."

He took my hand and placed the plum in my palm. "Feel that weight? How there is only a little give?"

My fingers tightened around the small fruit. "Yes."

Luca grinned down at me. "That's how you know you've got a good plum."

He paid the vendor, and we moved on. I took a bite, and juices dribbled out of my mouth. "Oh my God, so good. Here, have a bite."

Grabbing my wrist, he brought the plum to his mouth and took a huge chunk out of it.

"Hey! You ate half the damn thing."

Luca chuckled, pulling me to his side. His warmth was welcomed despite the late August heat. After he swallowed, he sighed, "Second best thing I've tasted today."

He pushed aside my hand full of fruit, covered in sticky juices, and kissed me deeply. His tongue moved slowly against mine, caressing it gently, savoring me. Breaking the kiss, he didn't move too far away. The corner of his eyes crinkled as he gazed down at me.

"Yeah, that's the best thing I've tasted in a while."

I gave him a wry smile, but before I could make a joke about where I wanted him to taste, a voice I could go the rest of my life without hearing again shouted my name.

"Sasha?"

Turning away from Luca, I tensed as Beth Cooper cut through the crowd, dragging a woman behind her.

"Shit."

Luca followed my eyeline. "Friend of yours?"

"Something like that." I threaded my fingers through his, bracing myself for impact.

When Beth reached us, she was positively beaming. Even though she was smiling, the tightness around her eyes let me know she wasn't about to be nice.

"What are you doing here, Sasha?" Her brown eyes looked me up and down, lingering on the flip-flops. "Dressed like that?"

Luca squeezed my hand. Squeezing back, I gave him a big smile. The last thing I needed was for Luca to stick up for me. That would only prolong this nightmare.

I turned toward Beth and a woman I recognized as an old college hook-up. "Luca shops here weekly and asked me to join him. We're picking up stuff for dinner." Glancing down at my body, I laughed. "As for the fit, I plead the fifth. It's too early for me to make sound decisions."

Positioning myself closer to Luca, I began the painful introductions. "Luca Moretti, this is Beth Cooper, my—"

Beth's hand shot out as she interrupted me. "Ex-girlfriend."

Luca froze next to me, but he shook it off and took her hand in a firm handshake. When their hands dropped, I looked at Beth expectedly, but she was apparently not going to introduce her companion.

Taking it upon myself, I addressed the fourth member of our group. "It's good to see you again, Courtney."

Beth's eyes widened, and she stared at the woman holding her hand. Courtney's cheeks crimsoned as her pretty blue eyes looked anywhere but me. I'm not going to lie. I loved the fact she remembered me and, maybe more importantly, she was uncomfortable with the possibility of re-hashing our tryst with her girlfriend. If that made me an asshole, so be it.

Beth dropped Courtney's hand. "You know each other?" Her head whipped back and forth like she could glare the truth away.

"You could say that. We shared a suite in college." Beth relaxed a smidge, and we couldn't have that, so I added, "And I taught her how to go down on a girl." I winked at Beth. "You're welcome."

It was petty, but Beth had always made snide comments about my partner count, so I figured why not use her slut-shaming against her? I felt a twinge of guilt for Courtney, but honestly, she had to know that Beth was the fucking worst.

A sneer washed over Beth's beautiful face. "Of course you did.

Is there a woman in the state that you haven't fucked?" Her eyes turned to Luca with disgust. "Or man?"

"You know me. I like to fuck."

Beth scoffed, and Courtney looked mortified by the whole interaction. I gave her an apologetic smile but offered no words to go with it.

An uncomfortable silence settled over us, so I finished my plum. Taking my time to suck the juices from my fingers, I went one by one. All eyes were on me.

Tossing the pit in the trash, I turned to a fuming Beth. Her eyes darted to Luca, and I was apprehensive for the first time since this little ambush started. Suddenly, my goading seemed like a bad idea. Beth could be cruel when she wanted to be, and I didn't want Luca caught in our crossfire like poor Courtney.

"Luca, was it?" He nodded, his jaw tight. "You know what? Good luck with her." Her glare sunk into me as she continued to talk to Luca. "The only person Sasha loves is Sasha, so be careful with how much of yourself you give."

Balling my hands into fists, I kept myself from grabbing her by those beautiful black locks and smashing her face into the trashcan. How dare she pretend like I didn't love her? Like I didn't give her all my time. Like I didn't change for her. This bitch wanted to get fucked up.

Before I could act on my homicidal thoughts, she grabbed Courtney's hand and stormed away.

I took a deep breath and turned to Luca, but his eyes stayed glued to the spot where Beth had just been.

Without looking at me, he asked, "That's your ex?"

"Yeah." Unease settled between us.

"She's pretty awful."

"Yeah."

When he finally looked at me, the joy from earlier was gone. "Must have been a pretty nasty breakup."

"Look. I'm not perfect by any means, but what she said was bullshit." I waved my hand in the direction she'd gone. "I did my best, but she was always pushing me to do things that weren't me. To be someone I wasn't. We weren't right for each other."

Luca grimaced. "Things like going to the farmer's markets and waking up before noon on a Saturday?"

"No, more like fundamental changes to my personality and life." I huffed out a breath. "I don't want to get into the hellscape that was my relationship with Beth. Just know, if I didn't want to be here, I wouldn't be."

"I guess. It's just, we're so different, and I'm—"

Grabbing his hands in mine, I tugged him closer to me. "Luca, I can honestly say no one has ever caught my attention quite like you. I don't think you have anything to worry about."

He stared at me for a moment before eventually smiling. Placing a short, sweet kiss on my lips, he pulled his hands from mine and cradled my face. "Good, because I wasn't lying when I said I can't stop thinking about you."

A blush crept up my neck. He was too sweet, and it made me nervous. "You're exaggerating."

Luca's thumb brushed my bottom lip, and my skin prickled with goosebumps. "I'm not, Sasha. Can you promise me one thing?" I didn't move an inch as his eyes clouded over. "Will you tell me if you start to lose interest? I would rather know before you move on with someone else, maybe have a chance to turn it around."

My heart thumped in my chest. This was real. He was asking for all the trappings of a relationship—exclusivity, honesty, early mornings at the farmer's market, sex that meant more than coming.

I crossed my trembling hands behind his neck. Luca scared me, but what was even scarier was that I wanted all those things with him.

"I promise."

SIX

After salvaging our morning at the farmer's market, Luca dropped me off at my apartment.

"My place, 7 p.m. Don't be late."

Pressing a quick kiss to my lips, Luca didn't give me a chance to take it any further. He pulled away, laughing at my whine of disappointment. "Oh, come on. We aren't having sex in my car at 11 a.m. on a busy street."

I shuffled out of the car, grumbling. I honestly didn't care if my whole neighborhood brought out lawn chairs and enjoyed the show.

My phone buzzed against my hand as I searched for my keys at the bottom of my purse. Mom's smiling face flashed across the screen.

"Hey, mom."

"Honey! How are you?"

The keys slipped from my fingers as I tried to jab them into the lock. "Shit."

"Language."

"Sorry." I blew the hair out of my face and pushed through the door. "I dropped my keys, and it's been a rough morning."

She sighed. "What happened, Sasha?"

Dropping my bag on the couch, I went to the kitchen to grab some water. "Just a run-in with Beth. It was nothing, just super awkward."

"That girl. I told you she was trouble. You never—"

Slamming the bottle of water down, I tried to rein in my annoyance. "Stop. Okay? I already had to deal with her, and I'm not going to discuss this with you. Anyway, why'd you call?"

"I'm sorry. I just don't like hearing you upset." When it became apparent I wasn't going to say anything else on the Beth subject, she continued. "I wanted to see if you could come to dinner on Sunday."

I swallowed down a sigh. A night with the parents was a necessary evil, one I did not take lightly. "I guess. What's the occasion?"

"Well, I ran into Janet Donovan, and she said her son Casey split up with his wife and is staying with her. I thought it might be nice for you to catch up. When's the last time you two saw each other?"

Glaring at the granite countertop, I opened and closed my mouth several times, unable to come up with the right thing to say. This would be the third man my mother had tried to set me up with since I'd turned thirty. All three met Mom's standards—they were Catholic, employed, and terrified of their mothers.

"High school graduation. I believe he was permanently attached to Marie Lank. You know, his soon-to-be ex-wife."

"So, you have a lot to talk about!" My mom was unbelievable. The woman was dancing on the grave of their marriage.

"Mom. I'm not doing that. I don't need a recently separated man crying on my shoulder, trying to cop a feel."

"Sasha! Casey is a nice boy. He wouldn't do that."

"Just like Max was a nice boy? You need to stop trying to fix me up."

"I had no idea Max was still married! And what do you expect me to do? I want grandbabies, and at the rate you're going, it's never going to happen!"

Laughter bubbled from my mouth. "Would it make you feel better to know I'm seeing someone?"

"A man?"

"Yes. A fucking man." I spat out.

"Sasha, I—"

"Forget it. I won't be at dinner. Tell Casey what's up from me. I'll talk to you later." I hung up to Mom's sputtering. She called me three more times before giving up.

For a few hours, all I did was eat potato chips and French onion dip while watching season three of The Office. A knock on the door pulled me from the mindless time suck.

Ashley stood on my doorstep sobbing.

"Oh, Ash. Come here, babe."

I pulled her into my apartment and sat her on the couch, waiting for her sobs to stop.

Hiccupping, she stared at me with watery eyes. "B-B-Ben."

"Calm down, sweetie. Take a breath." I brushed the tears from her cheeks, trying to calm her.

Ashley wrung her hands, her eyes dropping to her lap. "I confronted him. Instead of being sorry, he just threw a bunch of shit at me about Malcolm and me being too demanding. Then he left."

Her sobs started up again, and I wrapped her in my arms. "Oh, Ash, I'm so sorry. Fuck, Ben."

She shook her head against me. "No, he's not wrong. Malcolm and I are too close. I never realized how much it bothered him."

I pushed her shoulders back, making her look at me. "No, fuck that. Ben could've told you he felt weird about Malcolm, but he didn't. Instead, he brings it up when he's caught in a real fucking mess. As for being demanding, it's not unreasonable to expect your live-in boyfriend to tell you when he gets fired."

Wiping her nose on her sleeve, she nodded. "I don't know what to do. I don't want to go back to our apartment."

"Then, you stay here. I have an extra bedroom. It'll be like college."

Ashley laughed. "We almost killed each other in college."

"This time, I promise not to fuck someone four feet away from your bed." I held up three fingers. "Girl Scout's honor."

She nodded. "Okay. Thanks, Sash."

I grabbed my phone. Ashley clearly needed me.

"Who are you texting?" Ashley had finally grabbed a tissue and blew her nose.

"Luca. We have dinner plans, but you're more important."

She snatched my phone before I could send off the message. "Don't cancel. I'll be fine."

"Are you sure?"

She gave me a sad smile. "I am. I just need a little alone time."

"Fine, but I still have a couple of hours before I need to head over."

Grabbing a throw pillow, Ashley cuddled into my side and grabbed the remote. "Great, we can make it to the season finale."

———

"Oh damn, Sasha. If Luca doesn't put out tonight, I will."

"I'll keep that in mind." Winking at Ashley, I slipped on my heels.

Her laughter followed me as I walked out the front door.

Even though it was only a fifteen-minute drive to Luca's, it felt like an eternity. I was fucking nervous, which was ridiculous.

Finding a parking spot right in front of his duplex, I pulled in and shut the car off. I checked my lipstick, hair, the backs of my earrings, pretty much anything to delay the inevitable.

"Come on. It's just dinner. Get out of the fucking car."

Dragging my feet to his front door, I shook out my hands.

With my fist raised to knock, I jumped back when the door flew open. Adriana rushed out, a scowl twisting her pretty face.

Luckily, I took a step back and avoided a collision.

"Oh, shoot! Sorry about that." She frowned at my emerald bandage dress. "Sasha, isn't it?"

As I was about to answer, Luca rushed out the door.

"Adriana, don't be that wa—" His eyes landed on me, and he swallowed. "Sasha! You're here!"

"I am." I awkwardly smiled at Luca while glancing back at the sad, angry woman standing a foot away.

Luca pulled me to his chest for a tight hug. The smell of his cologne and Italian spices wrapped around me. His solid body against me felt right. We fit together.

When he pulled away, Adriana surprised me by still standing there staring at us, her eyes shining with unshed tears. Muttering a curse, she spun around and ran into her apartment.

The door slammed, and Luca rested his hand on it. "Damn it."

Awkwardness settled around us. I didn't know what the deal was with his sister-in-law, but obviously, there was something about me she didn't like.

"Should I go? I don't want to upset anyone."

Luca's shoulders sagged as he turned toward me. "No, you're not going anywhere. Adriana's a worrier." Lacing his fingers with mine, he led me inside. "She'll get over it."

"Did I do something? She's only met me once." I didn't like the idea of being perceived as a problem.

Stopping abruptly, he twisted toward me. "You didn't do anything. Adriana has her own baggage she's putting on us." He pecked my lips. "Let's try not to let her ruin our night."

His fingers squeezed mine, and I nodded. I didn't want to dwell on Adriana, so I would try to enjoy the evening.

Luca's crooked grin made my heart race. I loved everything about his face. Going to my tiptoes, I kissed the tiny scar near his eyebrow.

"What's a girl got to do for a glass of wine?"

Doing a little bow, Luca waved his hand toward the kitchen. "This way, madam."

I chuckled as I sashayed past him, but I didn't make it far before his hands pulled my hips into him.

"This dress is amazing, Sasha." Luca's full lips brushed against my ear, his hard body pressing against my backside.

"Thanks, Luca, but if you don't let me go, we won't make it to dinner."

His hands tightened before letting me go. "You're right. Whose brilliant idea was this?"

Moving away from him, I tossed my hair over my shoulder. "Your's, and I'm holding you to it."

I hopped up on a stool, flashing a good amount of thigh, and Luca groaned, "Worst plan ever." He set a full glass of red down in front of me. "It should only be another few minutes before dinner is ready."

Luca bent over and checked the oven.

What a sight.

His slacks showcased his ass in a way that made me want to send a thank-you note to the designer. The man could dress, but the body underneath could wear anything. I couldn't wait until after dinner when I could tear his clothes off and get reacquainted with every inch of his delicious body. My cheeks heated, so I took a sip of wine, enjoying the glorious view in front of me.

"Are you staring at my ass?"

"Yes."

Without looking back at me, he said, "Good. I'd hate to be the only one without eye control."

We both laughed as he plated the food. It was amazing to watch him work with such precision.

"Why don't you go have a seat at the table? I'll be right in."

Walking into the adjoined dining room, I shook my head. Flower petals circled the table, and candles covered every surface.

This motherfucker was going to get it once we ate his probably perfect meal.

I stood there, trying to figure out what I'd done to deserve this, and Luca nearly bumped into me as he carried out our plates.

He set them down, his face scrunching up. "Is it too much?" I didn't answer. He scanned the room, never looking at me. If he had, he would've seen how big my smile was. "I wanted tonight to be special. You're amazing, and I want this to be amazing."

I grabbed his face and crushed my lips onto his. It took a beat, but then his hands cupped my ass, his tongue exploring my mouth. Pressing my body against his, I trailed my fingers up his neck and pulled his earlobe. He groaned but broke our kiss.

We were both panting. The difference was that while I was smiling, Luca was straight-faced.

"Sasha, sit."

Pulling out a chair, he waited for me to sit. I watched with rapt attention as he shook out a napkin and laid it on my lap, his fingers grazing my exposed thigh. He was hell-bent on dinner proceeding as planned.

Taking a seat, he took a sip of wine.

We ate in silence. The egg raviolo first course and steak main were delicious, but Luca's throat moving as he swallowed was even more delectable. Every bite was slow, deliberate, and maddening. The pink of his tongue peeked out, slowly dragging across his full bottom lip, collecting a small drop of wine. His fingers traced his wine glass, and I could almost feel them skating down my sides. Those brown eyes consumed me from across the table, making me shift in my seat.

"Are you ready for dessert?"

I nodded as I stood to join him, but he pushed me back into the chair. Leaning down behind me, he nibbled my ear. "Let me grab the tiramisu and coffee."

When he left the room, I finally took a breath. I was so fucking worked up that his mouth on my ear would've been enough to make me come.

Luca returned to the dining room, carrying a tray with one piece of tiramisu and one coffee.

"Why's there only one?"

He smiled.

Clearing the plate from in front of me, Luca lifted me onto the table. He sat in my chair and grabbed the tiramisu. Stunned, I couldn't find the words to ask what he was doing.

Handing me the small plate, he slid his hands up my calves to my knees, slowly parting them. He brushed a kiss on one knee, then looked up at me. "Take a bite."

The fork glided through the layers, the sponge springing up. I put it in my mouth and, without breaking eye contact, slowly slid it out between my red-painted lips.

I'd never had such perfect tiramisu. Humming in delight, I went to put the plate down, but Luca stopped me. "No, you eat your dessert, and I'll eat mine."

His words had my core throbbing. Cutting off another piece, I smiled at him. "Sounds good to me."

As I ate another bite, Luca kissed up my thighs, his hands pushing up the hem of my dress.

I stilled as his head inched closer to my pussy. His eyes shot up to me and then at the small plate in my hand. Raising one of his thick black eyebrows, he lifted his chin. I took another bite, and he continued his trip up my thigh.

Another bite, and he pulled me to the edge of the table. I set my feet on the arms of the chair and let my knees fall open even wider. Luca's hot breath hitting my wet panties sent a shiver up my body. He ran his tongue over the scrape of fabric, his nose pressing against me.

My hips shot up. "Fuck, Luca."

"Eat, Sasha." His fingers dug into my thighs, stilling me.

Even though his eyes stayed on my pussy, I nodded and took another bite.

Luca's hand slid up my hips and gently pulled down my panties. I lifted to help, leaving most of my ass hanging off the table. My body ached, waiting for him to touch me. My toes curled into the armrests, anchoring me and giving me a sense of stability.

As the fork sliced the remaining tiramisu, Luca flicked my clit. I gasped, nearly dropping the plate on his head. Slowly, his tongue slid up my slit, each time a little harder. My thighs shook, the tension building in my body.

His flat tongue pressed against my clit, rolling against the pulsing bundle of nerves. My hips jerked away from him. It was too much and not enough all at once, but his hands squeezed my ass, keeping me in place.

Rocking against his tongue, my hands flexed, and the fork and plate clattered to the floor. I grabbed his hair, pulling him closer as if it was possible. Two thick fingers slid into me, curling to hit my g spot as he sucked. My body trembled against him, seconds from coming undone.

Luca's free hand grabbed my ass with bruising force as his teeth nipped my clit. That was it. Heat rushed through me as I spasmed around his fingers. I pulled at his hair, but his mouth continued to work against me, prolonging my orgasm.

"Luca, stop." I panted. "I need a minute."

He grunted and pulled away with my fingers still locked in his hair. Reaching up, he pried my hands from his strands and stood. Licking his swollen, wet lips, he moved his glazed-over eyes up my body.

Reaching around me, he unzipped my dress and pulled it over my head. His hands grazed my soft stomach, the pooch I'd made my peace with years ago, and I jerked away from him, laughing.

"That tickles."

His lips pulled into a lazy grin. "I know. I like watching you squirm."

Lowering his face, he claimed my lips in a wet, messy kiss. I tasted myself on his tongue, and I grew excited again. My fingers fumbled with the buttons on his shirt as I worked to get him as naked as I was. Becoming impatient, he pulled back a moment to yank the shirt over his head.

In the candlelight, I could make out the definition of his torso. Perfection, he was perfection. I promised myself that I would memorize every dip, line, and scar. I wanted to remember everything about Luca.

He trailed kisses down my neck, biting my collarbone. The way he sucked the thin skin, I knew I would be a bruised-up mess in the morning. His hands reached around to unclasp my bra, leaving me naked and vulnerable on his dining room table.

Only when I was totally bare did he pull away. His eyes swept over every inch of my body like it was the first time.

"You are the most beautiful woman I've ever seen, Sasha." The lust in his gaze left me with no doubt of his sincerity.

Heat crept up my neck. This whole situation was out of my depth. Everything with Luca was so easy but so heavy. There was no way around it. I was falling for him.

Shit.

Pushing down the panic threatening to take over, I inhaled. The smell of us on him calmed me enough to keep me on the table and not running out the front door bare-ass naked—but just barely.

I reached out with shaky hands for his belt, fumbling until he stopped me. Grabbing my chin, he forced me to look him in the eye. "Hey, it's okay. We don't have to do anything else. I'm happy just to hold you."

Those words set a fire under my ass. I wanted this man. Launching at him through his hold, I wrapped my arms around his neck, my mouth attacking him with little to no finesse.

Luca didn't seem to mind as he eased me back on the table, his hips pressing into mine. He rose and unbuckled his pants. Leaning up on my elbows, I watched him drop his trousers. There were no boxers underneath.

Jesus Christ.

Without thinking about it, I sat up and took him in my hand.

Luca's groan spurred me on, and I kissed wherever my mouth could reach. His hips thrust into my hand, his fingers twisting in my hair. Part of me wanted to make him come like this, push him past the point of control until he was fucking my hand and coming all over me, but he had other ideas.

Jerking out of my hold, he reached down to his pants. When he pulled out the foil square, I laughed. "Didn't think we'd make it through dinner?"

Shaking his head, he rolled on the condom. "I know us, Sasha."

Luca stepped back between my legs, one hand gripping my hip, the other on the back of my neck. "And I know I always want to fuck you, and you're always begging for it."

My laugh became a strangled moan as he thrust into me. The stretch to accommodate him stung, but I was so wet it didn't matter. Wrapping my legs around his waist, I tilted my hips up, forcing him deeper.

"Sasha." It was a plea that my hips answered with another slow movement.

"Luca, fucking move."

He thrust into me. Hard, sure movements that hit me deeper than I thought possible. His hand tilted my neck up, trying to accommodate our height difference. The hand on my hip gripped me tightly, possessively, as his hips slapped into mine—every thrust building the tension in my belly.

Resting his forehead on mine, Luca stared deeply into my eyes. His hips drove into me harder, leaving me breathless.

"You feel so fucking good. I need you to come."

I nodded, shutting my eyes to focus on how amazing he felt inside of me, but Luca's hand squeezed the back of my neck, forcing me to look back at him.

"Eyes open, I need to see that beautiful green. I need to see you."

My lips pulled into a smile. He was so fucking intense, but surprisingly, I loved it.

Carefully, he laid me back, and his hand left my hip to squeeze my breast. I curled my fingers around the edge of the table to keep myself from sliding across the glossy top as he drove into me.

His mouth closed around my nipple, and he swirled his tongue and sucked hard. Arching my back into him, I cried out when he gently tugged with his teeth. He did the same to the other side until I was nearly yanking his hair out and squirming under him. All the while, he continued to move between my thighs like a man possessed.

Luca moved up my body until his tongue was fucking my mouth, owning me. I didn't know how much more I could take. I was in sensory overload and desperate for a final push to release everything he'd built up.

Pulling away, he locked eyes with me as he sped up his thrusts. Luca moved one of my legs over his shoulder, and the position let him in even deeper.

One more deep, life-changing thrust, and I fell over the edge. My vision got fuzzy, and I threw my head back onto the hard table with a loud thud. It didn't matter. My whole body shook as I struggled to take a deep enough breath. Luca had officially ruined me in the best way.

Above me, Luca murmured my name like a prayer, his eyes unfocused but locked on my face. Each meeting of our hips was punctuated with a rumble until his body tensed, and he came deep inside of me, letting out a deep groan.

His eyes momentarily shut like he was savoring the moment. I brushed his sweaty hair from his forehead, wanting to see his whole face. His lips tilted up, and he opened his eyes, taking my hand and kissing each finger. The gesture made my breath catch, and a more subtle warmth took hold of my chest.

I was fucked.

Panting, Luca gently pulled out. He walked into the kitchen, presumably to toss the condom.

Left alone, I clutched the table, fingers aching, legs spread wide. Failing to muster up the energy to sit up, I was still splayed across the table when Luca strolled back into the room.

"Damn, now that's the best buffet I've ever seen."

My head flopped in his direction. "I think I'm broken."

He laughed and helped me sit up. "Well, perk up, Mitchell. I'm not done with you yet."

Sitting buck naked on his dining room table, watching his bare ass tidy up the room, I knew for a fact I wasn't even close to done with him.

SEVEN

LUCA MORETTI

I can't tomorrow night. What does your
Saturday look like?

Uh. I'm free after 8.

Not ideal, but I'll make it work.

"Damn."

"What's up?"

I pulled my eyes from the disappointing text and looked at Ashley inhaling pork fried rice. We'd been working on a contractor issue for most of the morning, so we treated ourselves to a sodium fest.

"Just trying to find time to actually see Luca. Outside of that quick lunch last Wednesday, I haven't seen him in two weeks. I thought after finally sleeping together in the parameters of a relationship like he wanted, I'd be swimming in orgasms." I stabbed the takeout box with a fork and dropped my head. "I'm dying."

Ash swallowed, washing it down with a swig of Coke. "That sucks."

Chewing the delicious takeout, I waved my fork in the air. "It is what it is. We're both busy people. I mean, I'm the one who canceled dinner on Monday to close the deal with The Armbruster Hotel. I can't be mad at him for doing the same thing."

Nodding, Ashley tossed her empty carton in the trash. "Sure, but it doesn't mean it doesn't suck."

"Mm."

"I think Malcolm and I are coming to your show tonight."

Taking another bite, I lifted an eyebrow and smiled. Malcolm had been a fixture at our apartment for the past two weeks. Was it like that when she lived with Ben?

"Shut it. He has a thing for Jazz and wants me to introduce them."

Ashley's eyebrows drew together, and the corners of her mouth dipped. Someone wasn't happy about their *friend* boning someone else.

"I'll let you in on a little secret. You have a better chance with Jazz than Malcolm."

Her frown dropped, and a smirk took its place. "Tonight's going to be fun."

"And that's why you're my best friend." I laughed as she skipped out of my office.

The rest of the afternoon was a flurry of paperwork and phone calls that nearly made me late for call time.

Evie rushed into the dressing room and gave me the stink eye before continuing her pre-show speech. "I want to see smooth transitions between acts. And I'm moving Sasha to before the last group number." There were a few sighs, but Evie kept chugging along. "Now finish getting ready. We go on in thirty!"

The glue kept getting tacky too fast, so the falsies wouldn't go on straight. "Damn it!" I tossed them down and took a deep breath.

"Relax, Red. You've got plenty of time to get gussied up." Jazz leaned in over my shoulder as she reached for the ruined eyelashes. Her sweet perfume filled my nose, reminding me of the last time we were so close. The smile on her face drew my eyes from her modest cleavage, and I blinked.

"Thanks."

The sequins on Jazz's bodice rubbed against my bare shoulder. My stomach twisted, and not with the excitement that usually followed our brief flirtations. I immediately thought of Luca and knew I needed to shut down whatever this was.

Jazz stared at me in the mirror expectantly.

"Do you need something?"

Her grin faltered as she stood to her impressive height. "No. Not right now."

She left the green room, and I let out a breath of relief.

One tally in the good girlfriend column.

The show was a blast, but I couldn't help but scan the audience for a certain Italian Stallion. It surprised me how disappointed I was not to find him in the crowd. It wasn't like I invited him, but I'd hoped he'd surprise me.

The dressing room slowly cleared out as I changed into street clothes.

"You want to grab a drink at the bar?"

"I was planning on heading straight home, but I could hang with the girls for a bit."

Jazz smiled and held the door for me. We squeezed past some of the other performers and pushed our way to the bar.

Leaning down, she yelled in my ear, "I'm going to try the other side of the bar. Be right back."

Not one second later, two large hands pulled my hips back. Craning my neck up, I was shocked to find Luca grinning down at me. "Hey, lady. Great show."

Twisting in his grasp, I threw my arms around his neck. My lips crashed into his, claiming him in front of a packed bar. As Luca's hands made their way to my ass, hoots and hollers met my ears. I'd missed Luca and couldn't have cared less that we were giving everyone a show.

A tiny voice inside freaked out at how much I had missed

him, but his tongue silenced it with vigorous strokes. All the stress of the past two weeks melted away.

"Got your drink, Sash."

I spoke too soon.

Luca pulled away at Jazz's voice, leaving me in a breathless daze. When I finally pulled myself together enough to face her, I was relieved she looked amused.

"Uh, thanks."

As I reached for the drink, Luca pressed into my back. With my free hand, I gestured between the two. "Jazz, this is Luca. Luca, this is Jazz."

They shook hands with me pinned in the middle. Her sweet perfume mingled with his clean cologne, and it was just plain uncomfortable. For me, at least.

Jazz's eyes cut to me, her face twisting into a smirk. Rolling my eyes, I took a sip of my gin and tonic, focusing on it and not the two beautiful people I was sandwiched between.

Loud enough for just me to hear, she whispered, "Just some guy you fucked?"

Surprised, I inhaled with the straw in my mouth and started coughing. Luca moved to my side, his hand rubbing my back. "You okay?"

"Yeah? You okay?" Jazz sipped her drink with her hip popped out.

Glaring at her, I nodded. "Fine." Through watery eyes, I looked up at Luca. "You need a drink?"

He smiled and shook his head. "I shouldn't. I have an early morning. I just wanted to grab a little time with you." He leaned in and whispered, "I missed you."

Biting my lip, I pulled away from a smiling Luca. "Jazz, I think we're going to head out. I'll see you at practice?"

Jazz let out a laugh as she looked back and forth between us. "Sure, I'll let Evie know you had to leave. Have a good night." She turned and went back to the bar with a smile.

Happy to see Jazz was fine and even a little amused by my situation, I pulled Luca through the bar, barely keeping myself from sprinting to my car.

"Did you drive here?"

"Nope, Pete dropped me off. I figured I would bum a ride from this hot little redhead I know."

Snorting, I unlocked the car and threw in my bag. "Little is not the word to describe any part of this body, but I'll take the hot. Thank you."

Luca laughed as he folded his long frame into my compact car. "You have to be pretty little to drive one of these. Jesus, is this actually a clown car?"

"It's all about the gas mileage, baby. Well, that and being able to carpool to the big top."

The ride to my apartment was quiet. I usually had time to prepare before I saw Luca. For some reason, I couldn't remember if my apartment was clean.

Walking through the front door, I said a silent thank you to the universe that Ashley had picked up. She was a saint and, hopefully, wouldn't be home for a while.

"Do you want a drink? A glass of water?"

Luca shook his head, his body already pressing against me. When his lips touched mine, my sense of control snapped. I wrapped myself around him, one foot remaining on the floor for balance.

My fingers made quick work of his tie and button-down. I knew he would hate seeing all his clothes tossed about the apartment, but he would just have to get over it.

He pulled my baggy clothes off, leaving me in lacy hip-huggers and nothing else. Taking a minute to give me a once over, he traced my sides with his fingertips. "Damn."

I trembled under his touch, but it was the intensity in his eyes that threatened to bring me to my knees. The space between us crackled with energy, every breath adding to the haze settling around us.

"Let's go to my room before Ashley has the unfortunate experience of walking in on me having sex. Again."

"Ashley's staying with you?"

I didn't want to get into the whole Ben thing. "Yep. She broke up with her boyfriend."

"Ah. Then bedroom, it is, although I was looking forward to another dining experience."

"You know what?" Laughter spilled from my mouth. "Doesn't matter. Bedroom. Pants off. Now."

"Yes, ma'am!" With a little salute, Luca sauntered to my bedroom and stripped off his remaining clothes.

I stood in the hallway and watched the show until he shimmied out of his boxers, and his tight, firm ass beckoned me to join. Turning the corner into my room, I found Luca on the bed, spread out and ready to go.

"Now, now, Ms. Mitchell. You appear to be overdressed. I insist you get more comfortable."

Stage Sasha came to life. I looped my thumbs in the sides of my underwear. Prowling toward the bed, I teased the fabric down, only to pull it back up. Luca's eyes were locked on my body, his hand stroking himself. Biting my lip, I slowed my steps, mesmerized by the show he put on. His thumb brushed the tip, and he licked his bottom lip, lifting his chin at me to continue.

I turned to give a side silhouette, then pulled my panties all the way down. Bending at the waist, I popped my ass out. Flipping my hair, I rolled back up. Luca's eyes roamed over every exposed inch of skin, his full bottom lip catching between his teeth.

I glided toward the bed, my fingers trailing down my chest, his eyes following their path, adding a phantom weight to my hand. I was used to being watched, but the adoration and greed in Luca's gaze were unlike anything I'd ever experienced. It made me feel powerful and, on some baser level, like I owned him.

When I reached the edge, he reached out and grabbed me by

the hips, pulling me over him. My red curls flew everywhere, eventually settling on his face. He blew them away, laughing. "Your hair is everywhere."

Reaching over to the bedside table, I pulled out a scrunchie and tied up my knotted mane. "There. Better?"

"Much. I can see your face." His thumb brushed my cheekbone, and I leaned into his hand.

The way he looked at me made me feel vulnerable. He saw me, not just the bullshit I put out into the universe. It was equal parts freeing and scary.

Tension settled between us as we stared at each other, his hands running down my sides.

Finally, Luca leaned up and kissed me. His tongue caressed mine as his hands moved my hips. Every movement stroked him against me, the proof of my arousal creating slickness between us.

Without looking, I reached for a condom. As quickly as I could, I rolled it on his length and then eased myself down on him, both of us groaning in relief.

I began to move up and down, rolling my hips at the bottom to add extra pressure on my clit. Luca's thumb stroked me, his other hand gripping my hip. Speeding up to chase the orgasm just out of my reach, Luca surprised me when his hand came down hard on my ass. "Open your eyes."

I hadn't realized they were closed. Looking down, Luca had a slight smile on his face, but his forehead furrowed as he thrust up to meet my hips. A blush crept onto my cheeks as he gazed at me with pure adoration. I was in foreign territory. The urge to close my eyes, to hide from the intimacy, was there, but with each passing minute, the connection with Luca kept them open, kept me present.

It wasn't long before our movements became sloppy, and my body gripped around him in a devastating climax.

I rolled my hips to ride out the waves of pleasure. Luca thrust up a few more times, finally finding his own ending.

Gently, I lifted myself from him, careful to keep the condom in place. He rolled it off and tossed it.

I stretched out, watching Luca's muscles flex as he walked to the bathroom. My body was sore from dancing. Add that to the Luca effect—I'd need a day to recover. As he walked back toward me, his smile grew bigger and bigger. What was he thinking?

He slid in between the sheets, resting his head on my chest, his hand tickling my thigh. "What am I going to do until Saturday?"

My fingers ran through his thick locks. "You mean for the next two days? Uh, work?" I laughed at his disgruntled sigh. When I didn't stop laughing, he blew a raspberry on my stomach.

Grabbing a pillow, I walloped him in the back of the head, and we started to wrestle playfully, although I don't think it was a very fair match.

After a particularly good pinch to his nipple, Luca snatched my wrists, pinning me down. Settled between my legs, the beginnings of another erection nudged my pussy.

As I smiled up at his goofy grin, my heart swelled.

"Sasha, I don't think I can go a week, let alone weeks, without seeing you."

"Ditto, but we can't exactly help how busy we are." A lock of hair fell into his eyes. I wanted nothing more than to brush it back, but he had my hands restrained.

His sigh fanned across my face as he lowered his body down. Leaning on his elbows, he released my wrists. This position created a delicious weight against my lower half, and I couldn't help but wrap my legs around him, shifting my hips to accommodate and tempt him into another round my body didn't need but demanded.

"How about we have a designated night? Doesn't matter what we have going on. We end the night together."

It sounded like a great idea. "Like tonight? We both had plans, but you still came to my show?"

"Exactly. No matter what, I'll be in your bed, or you'll be in mine every Thursday night."

"Why not a weekend night?"

"Because I want to see you more than once a week. I don't want to waste this deal on a night I'll probably see you anyway."

We both laughed, the vibrations making my thighs tighten around him.

"Okay, deal. Thursday nights are ours."

That first Thursday night together, we didn't get any sleep.

"Happy three-month anniversary! Oh, jeez, can we stop doing these monthly anniversaries? I sound like an asshole."

I set my shoes in the rack Luca demanded I use when I came over. He told me it was to make them easier to find, but he didn't exactly have any other stilettos in the joint.

Checking the living room, I found it empty. He told me to be over by eight for a late dinner, yet he was nowhere to be found. "Hello?"

"We're in here!" Luca's voice carried from the kitchen.

I did not expect to find Luca elbow-deep in a pumpkin with what could pass as his mini-me by his side.

I awkwardly waved at the pair. "Uh, hey there."

Little Luca peered up at me through thick black lashes. His little cheeks were rosy as he leaned up and whispered something in Luca's ear.

"She is pretty, bud."

The little boy's mouth fell open at his uncle's betrayal. With a serious pout, he wiped his small hands covered in pumpkin guts down the front of Luca's shirt.

I couldn't help but laugh at the pride shining on his angelic face. Luca tried to look angry, but his smile gave him away.

"Sasha, this little troublemaker is my nephew, Dante. Dante, this is my girlfriend, Sasha." Luca stood up, shaking pumpkin guts off his hand onto the newspaper. "I'm going to grab a fresh shirt."

On his way out of the room, he dropped a kiss on my cheek. "Sorry, Adriana had to go out last minute. She should be back soon."

Shaking my head, I looked at the adorable little surprise. "No problem. Kids aren't the worst." I gave Luca a peck on the lips and a swat on the ass. He chuckled on his way upstairs.

Cautiously approaching the table, I took the seat farthest away from the pumpkin massacre.

"Dante, it's a pleasure to meet you." I stuck my hand out, and he wrapped his tiny fingers around it. Two respectable pumps, then he flipped our hands over, placing a little kiss on my knuckles.

"Well, now. Aren't you a charmer? How old are you? Eighteen?"

Dante's face lit up, his smile showcasing a couple of missing teeth. "No, I'm six, almost seven."

"Where did you learn to be so suave?"

He frowned. "What's suave?"

Leaning in, I smiled. "It means charming. Did your uncle teach you the hand kiss thing?"

"Oh, no! It's what princes do when they meet princesses."

"That's very gallant, Dante."

He shook his head.

"Chivalrous?"

Another head shake.

"Polite towards women?"

He nodded. "My mom says manners are important."

"Your mom's a smart woman." Turning toward the pumpkin, I gestured to the mess. "What are you guys going to carve? A goofy face?"

Dante shook his head, his hands shuffling through some notebook paper. When he got to the last page, he held it up. "I want it to be a vampire's face. Uncle Luca said we could use paint for blood."

"That sounds pretty cool."

"Yep. Then we're gonna bake the seeds and eat them. My uncle is the best cook."

As if on cue, Luca walked into the kitchen. "Did I hear my name?"

"Dante here was just telling me about your sweet pumpkin plans. How can I help?"

Luca's eyebrows lifted toward his hairline. "You want to carve pumpkins?"

"Duh. I can make a template and help with the blood. I am an artist, after all."

"You are?" Dante's sweet voice was right next to me. He'd scooched over a chair.

"I am! I can paint, draw, and even do a little photography."

His brown eyes went wide. "That's so cool! My mom can sew. She made my Halloween costume!"

"That's awesome. What are you going to be?"

"A vampire. Mom made me a really cool cape. Do you want to see it?" He jumped up from his chair and ran to Luca. "Can we go get it?"

"After we finish up here, bud."

Stomping his foot, Dante crossed his arms and glared at Luca. "But I want Sasha to see it!"

Standing up, I flanked Luca. "No worries, kiddo. I'll be here all night. I'll check it out after we finish the pumpkin."

Looking between the two of us, Dante huffed out a breath. "Fine. But you're sitting next to me." He grabbed my hand and led me back to the table.

Pulling out the cleanest chair, Dante waited for me to sit, then tried to push it in.

"Let me help." Luca effortlessly moved me closer to the table. He leaned down and placed another kiss on my cheek. "Thank you."

I patted his hand on my shoulder. "No worries."

A Thanksgiving Day flu kept me from dinner with my parents and them from meeting Luca for the first time. After four months of dating, I finally felt ready, but the bug of death decided the meeting was not meant to be.

Perhaps more disappointing than missing a delicious meal, it would be the first Thursday night we had missed since we started the tradition. I told him to stay away. He didn't need to get sick.

Shuffling through my apartment to get another glass of water, I noticed Ashley had left her phone charger on the counter. She'd gone to dinner at Malcolm's sister's and stayed the night with him since I was ground zero for gross, snotty illness. The front door opened, and I snatched up the charger cord. "You forget something, Ash?"

In the kitchen doorway, I ran into a hard chest.

"Luca! What are you doing here?"

He took several steps toward the counter and put down several bags. As he removed his jacket and scarf, he gave me a once-over. "When Sasha Mitchell tells me she's too sick for a sleepover, alarm bells go off. At first, I thought you might be trying to get out of me meeting your folks, but I knew it was the real deal after Ashley texted me to check on you."

Placing my hands on my hips, I tried my best to be indignant but failed. Luca wasn't entirely off base. There had been some second thoughts about him meeting the entire family on Thanksgiving. I mean, who does that? It would've been better for him to meet my parents first, then the rest of the bizarro Mitchell clan at a later date. Like, maybe never.

Before I could say anything, there was a tickle in my throat, and a coughing fit took over. In a flash, Luca was by my side, guiding me to the couch.

"Okay, Sash, here's what's going to happen. You're going to sit here and watch one of your trash shows about tiaras, house-wives, or murder, and I'm going to heat up some homemade chicken noodle soup for you. Then I'll make you tea or whatever else you need."

"That's some queen shit." I blew my nose, then tucked the tissue in my robe's pocket.

Luca grinned and gave me a peck on the lips. He didn't even cringe at being so close to my chapped nose and stale, sick breath. "I'll be right back."

I settled into the couch as Luca made a racket in my kitchen. In between the curses, I heard him questioning why I didn't have *normal* kitchen gear. After twenty minutes, he came in with a big, steaming bowl of soup.

"Well, I'm glad I made the soup at home. You only have one dull knife."

Shrugging, I sat up to accommodate the delicious-looking soup. "I don't cook, remember?"

He shook his head, gesturing back toward the kitchen. "But that kitchen's just ridiculous. You don't even have any soup spoons."

I held up the large spoon. "What do you call this?"

"A serving spoon." He deadpanned.

"It's what I use for soup, so it's a soup spoon."

Ignoring Luca's grumbling, I scooped up a big spoonful and slurped it down. Even with my sense of taste severely diminished, I could still tell it was top-shelf soup. I finished the chicken noodle magic in less time than was probably attractive and set the bowl on the coffee table. Luca settled down next to me with a cup of tea.

"That was amazing, Luca. Thank you."

He smiled and put his cup down. "No problem." Pulling my blanket-covered feet toward him, he settled them in his lap and started to rub. Luca frowned at the TV as he massaged up my legs. "If I have any daughters, no beauty pageants. This is barbaric." I wheezed out a laugh, catching his attention, and he gave me a timid smile. "What?"

I shook my head. "Nothing. I just don't know how I got so lucky. Why are you doing all this?"

Squeezing my foot one more time, he looked back at the TV and said, "Because I love you."

I promptly fell into a coughing fit.

EIGHT

"Did you say it back?" Ashley sat on the edge of my bed, sipping her coffee.

"No. I just froze and coughed up a lung."

She cringed. "Poor guy." Taking another sip, she winced and stuck her tongue out. "Damn, that's too hot."

Setting the mug down on the floor, she said, "You know, he didn't seem upset when I got home this morning."

I sat up a little taller. "That's the thing! He said it and acted like everything was normal. Like it was no big that he said the L-word."

Ash laughed and shook her head. "You're thirty and can't even say love. Poor Luca."

"Hey! I'm great! A little emotionally broken, but great!" I tossed my snotty tissues at her, but they didn't make it far.

Dramatically sighing, Ashley gathered them up. "You are great, but that won't make up for being emotionally unavailable."

I nodded. I knew she was right. "It's just . . . Everything always turns to shit when I say those three words."

"But that's not Luca's fault. Forget all the losers in your past. How do you feel about him?"

I picked at the fuzzies on my sweater. Talking about my feelings was not something I wanted to do while feeling like the living dead. I glanced up at Ashley through my lashes. "I know how I feel." My voice was barely above a whisper.

"And?" Ashley's eyebrows nearly disappeared into her hairline.

"And I'm not going to tell you before I tell Luca."

Ashley smiled and nodded. "Good girl."

Monday morning came, and I felt a million times better, thanks to Luca's excellent nursing skills. Every day, I woke up to a healthy breakfast waiting for me, and then every night, he showed up with a new homemade soup. He never mentioned his Thanksgiving declarations or seemed upset with me. It took me until Sunday night to realize he wasn't playing any games. He was just a mature adult.

How fucking novel.

Sitting in my office, I tried to plan a fitting way to tell him how I felt. Ignoring the forty-five unanswered emails in my inbox, I devised a wine-and-dine plan for Thursday night, our night. Reservations and grooming appointments made, I strutted into Ashley's office to tell her just how brilliant I was. What I didn't expect to find was Malcolm on his knees in front of Ashley.

"Pro-tip: that works better if her pants are off."

I plopped down on the small couch as Malcolm scrambled to pick up the flowers that were all over the floor.

"Ha, ha. Very funny, Sasha." Ashley rounded her desk and sat down with a grunt. "That asshole Ben sent me flowers. It's been months, and he's still trying to weasel his way back into my life."

The two of us watched Malcolm silently pick up every petal. He scowled at the mess as his large hands moved with delicate precision.

A small sigh from across the room caught my attention, and when I looked at Ashley, her eyes were fixed on Malcolm's ass.

Like a creepy voyeur, I watched my best friend perv on her "platonic" friend.

"I think I got it all."

Ashley jumped at the sound of Malcolm's voice. "Thanks." She made a show of picking up a piece of paper off her desk and studying it.

Malcolm wiped his hands on his pants, and the two knuckleheads stared at each other, not saying anything for a full minute. It was like I'd walked into an awkward scene in a rom-com, the kind of on-screen magic that would make me turn off the movie and try to find something with a little more humor and a lot less pining.

As I tried to find a tactful way to escape the room, my phone rang, offering me an out.

"Oh, I need to grab this." Neither spared me a glance as I slipped past Malcolm and out of the room.

"Sasha Mitchell."

"Hi, honey! You sound better!"

"Mom . . . hey." I'd dodged her all weekend. "I'm almost back to 100%."

"That's great." I heard the car door chime.

"You going somewhere?"

"I'm actually heading back into the house. If you didn't answer, I was going to drive over to your apartment."

You decline three calls, and Maggie Mitchell was ready to drive across the city.

"Sorry, I slept through most of the weekend."

"Did Ashley take good care of you?"

Closing my office door, I slid down into my comfy chair. "She was actually with Malcolm most of the weekend."

"You should have called. I would've been there in a flash."

I noticed Miranda had refilled my candy bowl. Snatching a piece of dark chocolate, I tore it open and popped it in my mouth. "Don't worry about it. Luca stopped by."

"What a sweetheart! When can I expect to meet him?"

After missing Thanksgiving dinner, I hadn't considered rescheduling. If I was honest with myself, which I was trying to be, my brain was stuck on Luca.

"Oh well, Luca and I—"

"How about Thursday? It's your dad's last day off before he's scheduled to be at the station for the weekend."

My gaze fell on the reservation confirmation, still on my computer screen. I knew we were both free that night, but we were free for naughty, sexy times, not awkward family time.

Weighing the options of him meeting them this week or over the upcoming, more pressure-filled holidays, I kissed my beautiful night goodbye.

"Sure. That sounds great."

"Wonderful! Be at the house by 6:30."

"You got it. Love you, Mom."

"Love you, Sweetie."

Setting my phone on the desk, I picked up a pillow and proceeded to smother my face with it. I screamed every obscenity I could think of, including some I'm pretty sure I made up. Out of breath and thoroughly annoyed, I texted Luca our plans for Thursday. He sent back a heart emoji. Fucker.

The drive to my parents' was silent. I'd tried to cancel plans three times before we even left my apartment, but every time, Luca talked me off the ledge. "If you don't want me to meet your parents, just say so."

Luca's attention was on me, but I didn't have the guts to look him in the eye. "I don't want you to meet my parents."

The robotic voice told us we had arrived, and he pulled into the driveway. The ranch-style house was just as it ever was—light brick with large front windows, a two-car garage that only my mom parked in because Dad's workbench and tools took up half the damn thing, and perfectly manicured flowerbeds that laid empty: a perfect middle-class suburban home and the site of my teenage angst.

Leaving the car running, neither of us moved to get out. Luca waited for me to make a move, but I had no idea if I would get out of the car. I'd much prefer staying in the safe confines of Luca's expensive ride and listening to whatever the hell NPR was droning on about. I threaded my fingers together and squeezed them in my lap, focusing on steadying my breath.

Unbuckling his seatbelt, Luca shifted in his seat. His gaze burned into the side of my face, but my eyes stayed locked on my now red fingers. "Sasha, I don't want to push you into something you're not ready for, but I can't help but feel like we aren't on the same page when it comes to us. I want you to meet my parents, my friends, hell, everyone. I'm very proud to be with you."

His words struck a chord, and I twisted toward him. "It's not that I'm not proud of you, Luca. It's actually the opposite. I don't know what I did to deserve a guy like you." My voice cracked, and I rapidly blinked.

Luca cupped my cheek, his thumb brushing my quivering bottom lip. "Then why don't you want me to meet your parents?"

Dropping my gaze, I tried to find the right words. "My parents have the uncanny ability to bring out the worst in me, and they love to talk about how messed up I am. I guess I'm just worried that once you see the real me, you won't be so in . . . in."

"In love with you?" His fingers spread into my hair, holding me in place. "I'm in love with you, Sasha. No parent bullshit will change that. Please try to trust me."

The first tear fell down my cheek. Nodding, I fisted his shirt in my hands. "I'll try."

He brushed his lips against mine in a kiss completely at odds with the harsh hold we had on one another. His soft, feather-light caresses left me breathless, yearning for more.

Luca pulled back, breaking the sweet kiss. "Now, let's get our asses in there before I show you just how much I love every single part of you." The heat in his gaze sent a spike of arousal through my body. A quick scan of the car confirmed that my fat ass wouldn't fit over the console between our seats.

Damn sports cars.

"Stop plotting our fucking and get out of the car."

Shutting off the motor, he got out, and I slowly followed. Before I made it three steps, Luca was at my side, wrapping his arm around my waist. He kissed behind my ear and whispered, "Seat laid down, your back against the dashboard, legs on either side of my hips as I fuck you from below. Or seat pushed back, your hands on the dash as you bounce up and down on my cock. Those were the first two that came to mind."

I laughed. He knew me too well. Despite the panic weighing down my chest, Luca could still make me laugh and take my mind off the nightmare at hand. Warmth beat back the bad feelings trying to overwhelm me, and for the first time that day, I thought everything would be okay.

Stopping just shy of the front steps, I wrapped my arms around his neck. "I love you." The words spilled out. I hadn't meant to say it there, in front of my childhood home. I'd wanted to say it in a much more meaningful and potentially sexy way, but thems the breaks.

A breathtaking smile spread across his face as he scooped me up, his lips attacking every inch of skin he could reach. I squealed with laughter, dragging my fingers through his hair and egging him on.

Pressed so tightly to Luca, his arousal brushed against me.

"New plan. We get back in the car and tell your parents we had an emergency."

Shaking my head, I patted him on the shoulder. "No. No, I need to show off my amazing boyfriend."

He threw his head back in a sigh. "If you must." His smile didn't dim even a little as he pecked my lips. A slap to his ass, and we shuffled up the stairs.

I raised my hand to knock, but Mom was already opening the door.

"Sasha!" Grabbing my shoulders, she wrapped me in a tight hug. I struggled to reciprocate because she had my arms pinned down. One second later, she shoved me into the house and set her sights on Luca.

"You must be Luca! Get over here. Let me get a look at you!"

Ushering an unsure Luca into the well-lit living room, she patted his hand. "It's so good to finally meet you. Sasha is so secretive about her life that I feel like you're a complete stranger."

"Mom."

Her gaze cut to me in a warning to shut up, and then she looked back at Luca with adoration shining in her eyes. He rubbed the back of his neck, a small smile on his face.

Taking both mom's hands in his, he turned on the Moretti charm. "It's so nice to meet you. I can see where Sasha gets her good looks."

I winced.

A girlish laugh left Mom's mouth as her eyes sized me up. "You're too sweet. You should've seen her in High School. We could've been twins." She glanced at an old Christmas photo on the wall and smiled softly. "It's been a few years since we could swap clothes though. Isn't that right, honey?"

I nodded and focused on the old pictures lined the walls. Photos of me with the volleyball team, with my high school boyfriend at prom, and me at graduation in a tight white dress hung like a memorial to the girl I used to be. If you didn't know any better, you'd think I died my senior year of high school.

"She's always had a sweet tooth." Mom's hand gestured to all of me.

Luca slowly dropped Mom's hands and joined me at the time warp wall. He chuckled, and I turned to look at him.

"What's funny?"

His eyes crinkled in amusement. "You were all knees and

elbows." His hands slid around my middle, and he palmed my lower stomach. "A cute kid that grew into a beautiful woman."

I leaned into him. His presence was a shield from the passive aggressiveness that permeated the house.

"Why don't we head into the dining room? Your father's already in there." Her tone was light but decidedly less chipper than a minute ago.

Mom left the room, and Luca pulled me closer to him. "Wow."

"Yeah. If you think she's something, wait till you meet my dad."

We walked into the dining room, and Dad stood up, puffing out his chest. Sticking his hand out, he waited for Luca to grasp it before he spoke. "You must be Luca."

"I am. It's a pleasure to meet you, sir."

Dad grunted, dropping his hand. "We'll see about that."

Mom carried in the pot roast and rolled her eyes. "Come on, Greg. Leave the poor boy alone." Setting her classic blue Le Creuset down, she motioned to the table. "Sit down, kids."

Luca pulled my chair out and scooted me in before taking the seat next to me. Mom dished out the pot roast, mashed potatoes, and veggies, adding more carrots to my plate than any other.

"This looks wonderful, Mrs. Mitchell."

"Thank you, sweetie."

After a few tense moments of chewing, I glanced around the table.

Luca focused on his meal, his eyebrows scrunching up. It was a telltale sign he was breaking down the ingredients. I knew he would quiz me on the way home about which herbs my mom used and whether I tasted the hint of this or that. It was his favorite post-dinner game.

Shifting my focus, I looked across the table at Mom. She cut off a small piece of meat and nibbled it while eying my gorgeous man. I could almost hear her thoughts.

How did she get such a handsome man?

She must be doing something sexually to keep him interested.

Oh, Jesus, help her.

At least he's a man. Maybe we'll get those grandkids.

Her eyes swung toward me, and the age-old urge to shrink and make myself smaller hit. Over a decade out of the house, and I still felt those adolescent digs. When her gaze dropped, her mouth pinched to the side, and I wondered which diet I would find in my inbox when I got home. The irony? She was always dieting, always miserable, and always hangry as hell. I couldn't remember a time when she wasn't on some diet or new "life plan."

Dad cleared his throat, jarring us all from our inner thoughts.

"So, Luca, what exactly do you do?"

Wiping his mouth with a napkin, Luca swallowed. "Property development in the city. We're currently buying up old factories and renovating them into condos and office space."

Dad nodded thoughtfully. "You're going to revitalize the city?"

"That's the idea."

"Do you think more high-priced condos are what the city needs?"

"I—"

"Don't you think gentrifying neighborhoods is the wrong answer?"

"Actually—"

"You're essentially pricing people out of their own neighborhoods."

"Moretti Properties—"

"How do you deal with the guilt of kicking people out of their homes?"

"Dad! Let Luca talk!" I sat up in my seat, ready to jump up if need be. Luca's hand squeezed my thigh under the table.

"It's okay, Sasha. Your dad's just concerned about the city, as he should be." Luca looked across the table at my dad and smiled. "It's true. My father wasn't always conscious of the needs of the people who live in the city, but I'm actively trying to undo the damage our developments cause. I make a point of offsetting any new development with affordable housing options. Part of what makes the city so great is the diversity in the neighborhoods. It would be terrible if we lost that in the name of revenue."

"Dad, where is this coming from? The last time I was here for dinner, we argued about whether gentrification was really an issue."

"Sasha, I may not believe that left-wing bullshit, but I know you do. I'd hate for you to compromise your ideals for a man."

What a mind fuck. I didn't even know what to say. Dad and I had never seen eye to eye politically, but now he was vetting my boyfriend? Part of me was a little impressed, considering how much research he had to do to put on this little farce.

"Why don't you leave the leftist political vetting to me?"

Dad's lips twitched. "Deal."

After a beat of silence, mom swooped in. "Luca, how old are you?"

"Thirty-five."

"I bet your mom is anxious for you to settle down. Give her a few grandbabies?"

"Mom!"

Luca laughed. "My mom adores my nephew Dante and can't wait to have more grandkids." He leaned forward like he was telling a secret. "Don't tell your daughter, but I'm excited to have a brood of my own. I was one of two, but I'd love to have three or four."

This dinner was taking a turn. Luca's feelings on kids weren't surprising, but I'd never put myself in the equation. My mind reeled with how easily I pictured us with kids.

With sparkling eyes, Mom sighed with delight. "That's wonderful. Greg, isn't that wonderful?"

Dad grunted and lifted his chin my way. "Maggie, some people are still growing their careers and need to focus on that. There's always time for a family later."

My education and career were two points of pride for my dad.

Both my parents were very Catholic, so my love life had always been a point of contention, but now I understood what my dad hated most was the idea of me wasting my MBA or career on being someone's wife and mother.

Frowning, Mom said, "If you wait too long, you lose the chance to have the family you want." She looked at Luca and, in a strained voice, said, "I always wished we could've had more kids."

"I can understand that, Mrs. Mitchell. And I can assure you both that I would never want to leave my partner with any regrets, whether it be because of careers or children." Luca looked at me, eyes soft with apology. With his shoulders tense and his smile slowly dropping, I grabbed his hand and squeezed.

Smiling broadly at my mom, I said, "I hope you made your apple pie for dessert."

And with that, we moved on to the less touchy subject of religion.

"You were a big hit." I shimmied out of my skirt and tossed it in the corner of Luca's room.

He eyed my pile of clothes with a little frown. "Please, your dad couldn't have hated me more."

Sitting on the edge of the bed, I yanked my tights off, purposefully whipping them into Luca. "Not true! Imagine if we told him I was knocked up. You'd be dead."

"You're not wrong." Luca came over and sat next to me. "I'm sorry if I played along with your mom too much. What I said was true, but I'm sure I freaked you out."

I reached back and unclasped my bra. "If I'm honest, I was more freaked out by how easily I could picture us with kids."

Luca framed my face with his hands, turning me toward him. A timid smile pulled at his lips. "Really?"

"Really." I covered his hand with my own, leaning my cheek into his palm. "I told you I love you, but more than that, I like you. The days I see you are better than the days I don't. I see a future here, Luca, and that scares me. I've never felt this way."

Luca kissed me like it was the first time. His lips devoured mine, burning me with his claim. Laying me back, the soft cotton of his shirt grazed my nipples, sending shivers through my body. I tugged at the buttons, my lips unwilling to break from Luca's.

The wool from his slacks was harsh against my inner thighs, and the zipper pressed against the damp lace between my legs, making me hum with pleasure. Luca pulled away to remove his clothes. In a surprising move, he left them scattered on the floor.

Leaning up on my elbows, I took in the Adonis in front of me as his eyes traced every exposed curve of my body. The hard ridges of muscle flexing, begging to be touched.

Slowly, he lowered himself between my legs. "Is it a terrible cliché if I rip your panties off?"

I laughed. "Go for it."

With a toothy grin, he tore the scrap of fabric from my body. The pinch of the elastic snapping pulled a surprised yelp from me.

Luca's hand gripped my stinging hip while his tongue teased my nipple. Goosebumps prickled up all over, and I pressed myself fully into him. I grabbed his hair, my hips grinding against him, searching for the right angle to slide him into me. "Luca, I need you inside me now."

His teeth bit down, and my back arched, pushing my chest into his face. "Luca!"

He leaned back and looked me in the eye. "Sasha, I want to feel you. All of you."

I froze. I'd never had sex without a condom.

"I . . . Uh. Okay."

"If you're not ready, I completely understand. It's a big step."

In one night, I'd told him I loved him, that I could picture us having children together, and now I was going to have unprotected sex with him. I waited for anxiety to set in, but it didn't.

"No, I want to." Pushing my hips up, I gave him the go-ahead.

He slowly pressed into me. Physically, there was no real difference without a condom, but emotionally, I was a raw fucking nerve.

When Luca was fully inside, he paused and kissed me deeply. With my hand on his chest, I felt his heart race against my palm. I made his heart race. The thought made me light-headed and so fucking happy.

He pulled back, resting his forehead on mine. "I love you, Sasha."

"I love you, too. Now get moving, or I'm taking over."

NINE

The sound of the shower starting nudged me awake. I glanced at the clock, happily noting Luca slept until seven. That was a first. He was always up at five, no matter how late we stayed up.

Appreciative of the extra shuteye, I decided to give him a little surprise. Tiptoeing into the bathroom, I glimpsed Luca's muscular ass through the foggy glass of the shower door. I could've watched that man rub his body down all day, but doing it myself would be much more fun.

Sneaking in behind him, I skimmed his back with my fingertips. "Need a hand?"

He jumped a little in surprise but turned around with a big smile. I took the loofa from his hand and soaped him up. My hands lingered on his abs as I dragged my nails down his taut skin, the muscles flexing under my touch.

Kneeling before him, I looked up through my wet lashes. God, he was glorious. Slowly, I washed each leg. I took my time, getting every inch. Dropping the loofa, I grabbed his ass with a rough squeeze before moving down to rinse his legs thoroughly. Every time my mouth came near his cock, I exhaled. Luca's legs tensed, and his breathing became labored.

Nothing like a little tease first thing in the morning.

Once I was sure I wouldn't be washing my mouth out with soap, I kissed up Luca's thighs. His hands pressed on the tile wall behind me, his back protecting me from the spray of the showerhead.

I gently kissed his tip, flicking my tongue out to taste the moisture gathered there. Parting my lips, I inched down his sizable length. Luca rewarded me with a throaty groan, sending a wave of pleasure through me.

Moaning around his head, I took in his entire length, relaxing my throat to accommodate all he had to offer. A few months before, I couldn't imagine taking all of him, but over the months, I'd become an expert in Luca's pleasure. One of my hands cupped and fondled his balls while the other gripped his ass. I loved his ass. I loved digging my fingers into the thick muscles and feeling them tense and relax.

Luca thrust forward with a grunt, hitting resistance. "Oh shit. Sorry, I . . . I—"

Gagging, I pulled back, only to take him to the back of my throat again. I bobbed up and down, sucking and swirling my tongue around the tip. One of Luca's hands twisted in my hair, tugging when he filled my mouth.

"Like that, Sash. Fuck."

Humming, I continued to move on his shaft. The vibrations made his legs shake, and his hand in my hair tightened, making my scalp sting. I slid a hand between my wet thighs, and I stroked myself, trying to relieve the ache building there. My muscles tightened as I pushed two slick fingers inside. If I did it right, we'd both come at the same time.

Just when I thought he was one second from blowing, Luca pulled me up by my hair, his lips crashing into mine as he lifted one of my legs and slammed into me. His mouth swallowed my yelp as he fucked me into the cold tile wall. Every thrust pushed my shoulder blades harder into the slate, his body allowing no room to move. I held on to his shoulders, afraid of slipping, as my legs turned to jelly. In a matter of seconds, I'd completely lost control of the situation.

Luca was a man possessed. He pumped into me, taking my breath away with every thrust. His thumb found my clit, and he mercilessly stroked me into a panting mess.

I dug nails into his back and bit his neck to stay grounded, paying the feeling forward.

"Luca! Fuck!"

Luca's brown eyes bore into me, and this time, I didn't have to be told to keep my eyes open. I wanted to. I wanted to be there totally in the moment with Luca.

"I fucking love you, Sasha."

His words, his eyes, his fucking fantastic body pushed me over the edge. I screamed out my release, coming so undone I leaned all my weight onto Luca.

Before the shake of my orgasm waned, Luca thrust hard one more time, coming as he buried his face in my neck.

We stayed locked together, panting and murmuring sweet words until we both recovered. Cuddling in the shower was a novel experience for me. It was intimate, weird, and a bit chilly. Luca gently pulled out, leaving me feeling a little sore but a whole lot satisfied.

He readjusted the water's temperature and then rinsed off. Propping me up, he moved me under the warm stream of water and shampooed my hair. "Good morning." He kissed my nose before grabbing the conditioner.

Yawning, I gave him a sleepy smile. "Morning."

He carefully rinsed my hair and soaped up my body. It wasn't until we were drying off that either of us spoke.

"I want you to come to my family's holiday dinner."

Combing through my wet, red waves, I watched him in the mirror. "When's that?"

"Saturday before Christmas."

"Okay."

He shook his head, his face scrunched in confusion. "Really?"

I laughed. "Yes, really. You met my family. It's only fair."

He blew out a breath, wrapping his arms around me. "Thank you, baby. I'm so excited for them to meet you. Dante's been singing your praises since Halloween, and my mom's eager to meet the mysterious red-haired beauty."

Turning in his arms, I wrapped mine around his neck. "Oh, I like that. Mysterious red-haired beauty."

Nodding, Luca smiled down at me. "I think Dante's going to try to steal you away."

Our lips an inch apart, I smiled. "Don't worry. I don't like younger men." Luca chuckled, and I kissed his cheek. "Although Dante does call me a princess. I do like the idea of being royalty."

"Who wants to be a princess when you can be a fucking queen?" He nipped my bottom lip and trailed his lips down my body.

Luca proceeded to make us both late for work by showing me just how he would bow down to his queen.

Nerves hit like a motherfucker as we pulled up to the Moretti's house. Strike that. Mansion. It was a fucking mansion.

I gawked at the expensive foreign cars that lined the drive as the valet took Luca's keys and pointed us up a beautiful walkway.

I brushed my fingers against the velvet of my dress, silently cursing. I regretted the length as soon as I stepped out of my apartment and saw Luca dressed to the nines. The simple emerald skater dress would have been overkill for the Mitchell family Christmas dinner, but here I was, committing a fashion faux pas at some rich people's extravaganza. Maggie Mitchell always said you could never be overdressed, but I thought I was being reasonable. I should've known better than to trust Luca. Never trust a straight man to tell you what to wear to a damn event.

"Will you stop worrying? You look amazing."

I grunted.

"Do I need to take you upstairs and show you how much I love this dress?" His hand snuck under the hem, his icy fingers digging into my fleshy ass.

I swatted him away. "I'm already dressed inappropriately. Please don't grope me where your family can see." Proprietary wasn't something I usually worried myself about, but meeting the parents always put me on edge. Meeting parents that lived in a mansion put me on a ledge. Beth's mom was a nightmare. I only prayed Luca's was nothing like the Senator.

Luca sighed. "I'm sorry, Sash. I didn't really think about what this thing's like." Bending his neck down, he stared me in the eye and murmured, "I'm a terrible man. Please forgive me."

He stuck out his bottom lip, his brown eyes begging for forgiveness. It was clear where Dante learned his lethal pout.

"Fine, you're forgiven, but you owe me."

"It's my pleasure to be indebted to you, Ms. Mitchell." He leaned close to my ear. "But I promise you will be the sexiest, most beautiful woman at this party."

I laughed. "I hope you'd feel that way. This is your family. It'd be kind of gross if you thought cousin Stephanie was hot."

Luca looked away, and my nerves started to get the best of me. "Uh, it's not just my family."

I stopped walking and stepped into the grass to stay out of the way of the dawdling old folks. "What do you mean? You said your family's Christmas dinner. Who else is going to be here?"

"My parents, Adriana, Dante, Marco, some other cousins, and a few family friends. It's really no big deal."

I pulled him by the jacket. "It absolutely is a big deal! It's one thing to show up underdressed for the immediate family. It's another to show up to some mini-gala looking like I'm ready to go to the fucking Ice Capades."

Luca's shoulders slumped. "Do you want to go home?"

Staring at the perfect colonial decorated in tasteful holiday splendor, I bit the inside of my cheek. I was being a big fucking baby, but I wanted Luca's family to like me. Adriana already had some unknown issues with me, and I needed someone on my side other than a seven-year-old.

"No. Let's go."

I started to walk away, but Luca pulled me back.

"What?"

He reached into his coat and pulled a long velvet box. "I was going to give this to you tonight, but maybe now is a better time."

My hands shook a little as I opened the box. Diamonds and emeralds sparkled back at me.

"Oh, Luca, this is too much."

"Nonsense." He took the necklace and went behind me to put it on. "It was my grandma's."

I touched the cold stones and shivered at the sheer weight of them. "I don't . . . I can't—"

Luca's hot breath on my neck shut me right up. "Yes, you can. I want you to have it. The emeralds are the exact color of your eyes." He kissed the nape of my neck. "It was made for you."

I nodded, trying to catch a glimpse of the shine around my neck. Removing my earrings, I put them in my clutch.

Luca turned me and smiled. His hand pushed back my bouncy red curls, grazing my neck. "Perfection. You ready to go in?"

"Let's do it."

We entered a beautiful foyer. A classic chandelier sparkled and set the tone for the entire room. Black-and-white marble buffed until you could see yourself fed into a grand staircase and a few hallways. Traditional grandeur wasn't my aesthetic, but it fit like a glove in a space like that. Tasteful Christmas decor of holly, poinsettias, and garland touched every corner, and I wondered who they hired for their holiday decorations.

"Oh, Luca, honey! You're here."

A middle-aged, dark-haired woman with striking European features glided toward us. She looked like a young Sophia Loren —a woman who only gets better with age. Sophia Loren could get it, and the same was true for Mrs. Moretti.

"Mom, everything looks amazing." The two beauties hugged and then turned their identical gazes toward me. Luca's mom gave me a once-over, a smile playing at her lips as her eyes landed on my neck.

"This must be Sasha," Mrs. Moretti said, pulling me into a tight hug. "I'm so glad to meet you. I've heard so many wonderful things about you."

When she let go, I gave her my best smile. "Thank you for inviting me. You have a beautiful home."

She gave a slow perusal of the room before bringing her focus back to me. "Thank you. I've been thinking it's time for a facelift. I understand you're an interior designer."

I glanced at Luca, and he shrugged. "I am. My best friend Ashley and I started our own business two years ago."

"Then we need to have a chat sometime. I'd love to hear what you think." A woman waved at her from the end of the hallway, and Mrs. Moretti frowned. "Please, excuse me." She patted Luca's arm before gliding away.

"One down."

"Come on. It's not that bad."

I glared at Luca and walked into a festive sitting room. Cream furniture was arranged to allow for foot traffic from the fireplace to the bar set up in the corner of the room. Offering me the very thing I'd need to survive the night, I made a beeline to the bar. The bartender's bright blue eyes locked on me, and he shoved his wild blond curls behind his ears as he watched me walk across the room.

With a broad smile, he asked, "What can I get you?"

"Gin and tonic, please."

Luca's big hand spanned my back. "A Manhattan."

While our drinks were being made, I surveyed the guests. The older gentlemen in the room sent appreciative glances my way while their spouses openly gawked at my short dress. The looks were curious, but there wasn't an unkind face in the crowd until Adriana rounded the corner.

It was like she had Sasha-dar, and her eyes immediately landed on me, her neutral face falling into a slight frown. Before I could smile or wave, a little body hit my legs.

"Sasha! You're here!"

"Hey, Dante!" I ruffled his dark hair.

"Dante! Don't jump on people." Adriana grabbed one of his little hands as she tried to smooth back the chaos I caused. This woman needed to take a chill pill.

I picked up my gin and tonic and took a sip. "It's okay, Adriana. I have a soft spot for the little guy."

Her lips pulled into that signature stick-up-the-ass smile. "Well, he needs to learn to behave accordingly."

Dante was fucking seven, but he wasn't my kid, so the frigid queen's rule was law. I planned on sneaking him some extra candy canes later.

Luca pivoted, kissing Adriana on the cheek. "You look beautiful tonight."

Her cheeks crimsoned as her eyes dropped to her floor-length red gown. She would've been an absolute vision if her face hadn't given off an air of constipation.

"Thank you, Luca." She laid a limp hand on his arm. "Can I steal you for a minute? Marco's in the library and wanted a word."

Luca looked at me, concern lining his face. "Will you be okay alone for a minute? I'll be right back."

Internally, I was screaming no, but this wouldn't be the first time I had to work a strange room alone. "I'm fine. I've got Sean here to chat with."

Luca sent a stern look to the bartender and nodded. Adriana followed Luca out of the room, Dante in tow.

Standing in front of the bar only gave everyone a better vantage to stare at me. Finely dressed guests walked by the room, some stopping to take a peek before moving on to what must have been other rooms set up for entertaining. The funny thing was, every time I tried to catch their eye, suddenly, the floor was fascinating, or the ceiling held the secrets to the universe.

Cowards.

Downing my drink, I asked my All-American Sweetie for another and then went in search of apps. After far too many pastry puffs, I turned down a hallway, searching for a bathroom to touch up my lipstick. An angry, feminine voice caught my attention. Leaning against the wall next to a set of cracked double doors, I let my nosey nature take over.

"Why is she here? What do you think you're doing?"

"Just stop."

"It's like you don't care about anyone but yourself."

"Adriana, I don't have to explain myself to you."

A loud smack sounded, and heels clicked closer to the door. I hurried down the hall, out of sight.

"You're heartless, just like your brother."

Adriana stormed down the hallway back toward the crowd. A couple of minutes later, a defeated Luca followed.

Every fiber of my being wanted to walk out the front door and never look back. There was some weird shit happening, and I wasn't sure if I wanted to know why Adriana felt like Luca owed her something.

I walked casually back to the party, woodenly smiling at people as I passed. I just needed to make it to my coat, and I could escape.

I reached the foyer when Luca found me.

"There you are." His face was solemn as he wrapped me in his arms, placing a possessive kiss on my lips. The more his tongue caressed mine, the easier it was to forget we were making out in his parents' house surrounded by his family or that I was trying to ditch him not one minute ago.

My lungs screamed for air as he pulled away. I smiled as I wiped the lipstick off his swollen bottom lip with my thumb. "Can I talk to you before we sit down for dinner?"

Luca frowned but nodded. After a quick look around, he led me upstairs to a bedroom. When he flipped the lights on, I found myself standing in a teenage boy's dream room. Band posters covered every inch of the walls, and the entertainment center was packed with every gaming system known to man.

A shelf filled with cookbooks was the only thing amiss—a little reminder of how odd Luca must've been as a teen boy. Was he picked on for being a culinary prodigy? Was that how he got all those scars?

"Your bedroom?"

Luca smiled and nodded. He sat on the bed, smoothing out the comforter as he waited for me to talk.

Standing in front of him, I forced him to look me in the eye. "Why doesn't Adriana want me here?"

He flinched as if I had slapped him. His hand rubbed down his face. "Damn it."

I took a step back. "Are you fucking Adriana? Did I come in between some secret affair?"

Luca jumped up in a panic. "Fuck! No, no! Jesus, she's my sister-in-law!"

His outburst made me feel less disgusted but more confused.

"How do I explain this?"

I took his spot on the bed as he paced the room. When he turned toward me, apprehension was written all over his face. "My family's rich."

That's what he agonized to come up with?

"Yes, and?" I waved my hand at the ridiculous size of his childhood bedroom.

"And there are dangers being this wealthy."

He was being deliberately slow with his explanations. "Can you jump to the part that's the deep, dark secret? I feel like I'm the weakest link on a CW teen drama."

"She's worried that I'll die just like my brother."

"I thought you said it was an accident."

Luca shook his head, his gaze on the floor. "According to the police report, it was an accident, but Dante had been receiving threats for months but ignored them. We didn't find out about them until it was too late."

Tears filled his eyes, and his hands fisted in his pockets. The slump of his shoulders tore at my heart.

Moving quickly, I wrapped my arms around him. I needed him to know I was there. His muscles relaxed as he returned my embrace, but his breathing was still labored. Muffled by his chest, I asked, "What does that have to do with me?"

"After Dante died, Adriana completely shut down. She isn't the same woman my brother married. Paranoid doesn't even begin to explain it. She's convinced the same thing will happen to me. She doesn't want anyone else to go through what she has."

My heart ached for Adriana, and I felt terrible for all the mean jokes I had made in my head at her expense.

"Have you received any threats?"

His body tensed under my arms. Pulling away to look him in the eyes, I couldn't catch his gaze. "You have! Fuck, Luca!"

Dropping my arms, I tried to walk away, only to be trapped in Luca's grip.

"There've been threats, but I'm not my brother. I'm not ignoring them. My father and I will find these assholes, and they'll be dealt with." His voice was rough and forceful, sending a shiver through my body. This was the powerful millionaire Luca Moretti I rarely saw, the man who owned a good chunk of the city and had no business being with the likes of me.

"Should you get a bodyguard or something?"

Luca smiled down at me. "There are always eyes on us. I'm not taking any chances."

"Us?"

"You've had a tail since the night at The Monocle. There's always someone there, just in case."

"You've got to be kidding me." Heat coiled in my belly, but I wasn't sure if it was anger or something else altogether.

"Sasha, nothing's more important to me than your safety. I will not let my circumstances hurt you."

"I can't decide whether I should punch you in the gut for having some goons following me or push you down on that bed and fuck you into a coma for being all protective." Pushing the loose hair from his eyes, I tried to make peace with this new reality. "Promise me you won't keep me in the dark anymore. Honesty, remember?"

He sighed, a small smile on his face. "I promise. I'm sorry I didn't tell you before. I didn't want to scare you away."

My fingers walked up his chest. "You could never scare me away, Luca. I'm the crazy bitch that loves you."

His lips parted. After a moment of him staring at me and not saying anything, he shook his head and kissed me. It was a warm, gentle caress that made me sigh.

With his forehead resting on mine, we smiled like fools. I felt closer to him than ever before. He'd shared something scary and huge with me—something that, for some, would be a deal-breaker.

My heart raced at the thought of him being in harm's way. Any bastards that wanted to snuff out this beautiful man would have to go through me.

"Let's head down before mom comes looking for us and finds me fulfilling an adolescent fantasy on that desk over there."

We tried to hurry down the stairs without being noticed, but that wasn't in the cards.

A man who looked like Luca in thirty years stood at the base of the stairs, glaring at us. Sneaking away from a bedroom is not how I wanted to meet Luca's dad.

As we reached the bottom step, Mr. Moretti scoffed. "Luca, your mom's been looking for you. It's time to sit down for dinner."

Luca tensed, letting my hand go, only to wrap his arm around my waist. "Dad, let me introduce you to Sasha Mitchell."

I plastered on a professional smile and held my hand out. Mr. Moretti had a firm shake as his eyes gave me a once-over. His forehead creased when he noticed the gems sparkling around my neck.

"Pleasure to meet you. Thank you for including me in your holiday celebration."

"Luca's mother wouldn't have had it any other way. Please excuse me. I need to find my wife."

The salt and pepper fox walked away, leaving me to wonder what a girl had to do to be accepted into this family. "That went well."

Luca hugged me from behind. "Don't mind him. He doesn't like anyone."

"That's reassuring," I grumbled.

The moment we entered the dining room, all eyes were on us. Luca was entirely in his element as he led me down the longest table I'd ever seen in a home to the head of the table. The other guests sized me up, many scowling as they openly judged me. Holding my shoulders straight, I was determined not to wilt under the scrutiny.

Fuck them!

As soon as Mr. and Mrs. Moretti made their grand entrance, the room lost interest in me. Well, except for one willowy brunette standing close to the door. Her eyes stayed glued to my face, not even wavering when Mrs. Moretti approached her. It wasn't until she was directly addressed that she stopped her stare down.

"Nicki dear, come sit with the family."

The gorgeous woman strutted behind Luca's parents. *Could she walk like a normal person?* She looked like she was built for the runway and could only fiercely move from point A to point B.

Mrs. Moretti motioned to the spot next to me.

Without a word to the room, Mr. Moretti pulled out his wife's chair and sat down in the head seat. Luca followed suit, pulling my chair out before sitting.

Ole, long and elegant next to me, sighed as she pulled out her own chair.

What a fucking hardship.

They brought the first course out, and Mr. Moretti stood, silencing the room. "Thank you all for joining us this evening. Rosa has certainly outdone herself this year." The room erupted in applause, and Mrs. Moretti's cheeks flushed. "The holidays are a tough time for our family, but being here together with all of you makes our losses easier to bear." Mr. Moretti gazed at Dante with misty eyes. The little boy was oblivious to his grandpa's heartfelt speech because he was busy puffing his cheeks out at Luca.

"Tonight, we have three generations of Moretti men sitting at the head of this table, and I couldn't be prouder." With a sly grin, his eyes zeroed in on Luca. "Unless my son finally finds a wife and gives me a dozen or so more grandchildren."

Laughter filled the room, but I shrunk down in my chair. Was that a dig at me? Mr. Moretti's eyes bounced over me, landing on Nicki, and he winked! In disbelief, I watched her cheeks deepen into an outrageous blush.

Luca's dad made some kind of toast, and glasses around me clinked. Then the parish priest, Father Anthony—a cousin or something of Luca—said the blessing, and everyone started to eat. But I sat frozen, staring at the gorgeous woman to my right.

Who the fuck is she?

"You okay?" Luca's hand squeezed my knee as he leaned into my personal space.

Slowly, I turned to look at him. "Are you fucking kidding me?"

I must have been louder than was "appropriate" because Luca glanced at the people sitting near us. Adriana was scowling at Mr. Moretti, but everyone else was digging into their food, unaware of the tension at the head of the table.

"What's wrong?"

In a lower voice, I whispered, "Who is this fucking woman sitting next to me?"

He frowned, clearly confused. "Nicki? She's a family friend and acts as legal counsel for my family and our businesses along with her father."

A foul taste sat on my tongue. "And why would your dad mention grandkids and wink at her?"

Understanding dawned on his oblivious face. A deep frown pulled his thick eyebrows together as he looked past me at Nicki. Quickly, his gaze fell back on me, a hint of panic evident in his eyes. "Shit. I wasn't paying attention. Dante and I were making faces."

My heart softened because, of course, the big oaf wasn't paying attention.

"Nicki and I dated in high school, but then she fucked Dante, and that was that. I can't believe Dad is even entertaining that bullshit. We're just colleagues, nothing more." He pressed his lips to my temple. "You have to believe me, Sasha."

The tension in my shoulders eased up a bit. "I do, but I don't think I can stay at this dinner. Your father clearly has a problem with me, and I can't guarantee he won't get slapped upside the head if he has any more cute comments to make."

"Luca, what has you and your friend so engaged? Maybe the rest of us would be interested." Mr. Moretti smirked at me, and my hand itched to backhand the jerk.

Instead of letting Luca answer, I grinned back at Mr. Moretti and said, "Just how money can't buy manners."

Mr. Moretti's lips remained upturned, but his jaw twitched. "What a fascinating observation. Luca, where did you find this interesting woman?"

"Honey." Mrs. Moretti's hand landed on his arm.

"No, Rosa, I'm just trying to get to know our son's *friend*."

"Dad." I restrained Luca from standing up.

"It's fine." Leaning forward, I stage-whispered at the pompous ass. "Mr. Moretti, I met Luca at your nephew Michael's wedding. Then I got to know him *very* well—if you know what I mean." I exaggeratedly winked at the arrogant asshole.

Across the table, Adriana choked on her wine. Dante's little hand pounded on her back as she caught her breath. A huge smile spread across her face, and she almost looked like the woman in the wedding photos.

In a louder voice, I added, "You, on the other hand, I think I know well enough." Standing up, I tossed my napkin down on the table. "I'm just going to show myself out."

Taking a few steps, I noticed all the mouths hanging wide open and laughed. When I reached the door, I turned dramatically. "Just so you all know, Luca said this was a family dinner, not a formal event. So, I apologize for my inappropriate attire. Although it gave you all something to talk about, so maybe I should say you're welcome."

With a swish of my hips, I turned and sashayed from the room. All eyes followed me as I left. For the people staring at my ass, I gave them a little more bounce to gawk at.

Loud shouting erupted in the dining room, and then heavy footsteps sounded in the hallway. Two massive arms circled my torso, and the comfort and calm that came from a Luca hug warmed me. "I'm so sorry, baby." His lips grazed the top of my hair.

I shook my head. "Just take me home. I need one of your grilled cheeses and maybe some time on the dining room table."

Luca turned me in his arms. "Whatever you want." His smile was soft as he kissed me.

Walking out the front door, Mrs. Moretti called out to us. "I'm so sorry." She hurried, obviously distressed. Wrapping her arms around herself to ward off the cold, she stopped next to Luca. "My husband can be a prick. Please don't hold that against the rest of us."

Her watery eyes softened my anger. "It's okay, Mrs. Moretti—"

"Rosa."

"Okay, Rosa, but we're just going to go home. We can try this another time."

One eyebrow quirked up, her whole face lightening with humor. "Home? Are you two living together?"

What?

"Not yet, Mom."

Not yet?

"Oh." Her smile faded. Why did she look so disappointed? "Well, get her home safe, Luca."

The valet brought the car around, and we drove home in silence.

Not yet.

Luca unlocked the door, and I put my shoes in the little holder he loved so much.

Not yet.

Peeling off my outer layers, I moved on autopilot as Luca watched me with worried eyes.

Not yet.

When I was seated at the kitchen counter, he finally approached me. "Sasha, what's wrong?"

Luca leaned down to get a better look at me, his big brown eyes doing little to snap me out of my stupor.

"Not yet."

His thick eyebrows pulled together. "Not yet, what?"

"We don't live together."

A small smile tugged at his lips. "Right. And?"

"You said 'not yet.' Meaning there will be a yet."

His fingers caressed my cheek. "Hopefully. I can't think of anything better than having you here always."

I nodded. The idea of waking up every morning to Luca's face, of coming home to his delicious cooking, of bumming around on Sundays, of maybe getting a dog, was intoxicating.

"But we don't have to do anything you aren't ready for. I'll wait. I'll always wait."

Luca's words warmed me, and my body trembled with excitement as I considered the next steps with Luca. At the end of February, my lease was up.

My hands slid up his chest, moving with the steady rise and fall of his breath. "Two months."

"Until?"

I smiled, fisting his shirt. "Yet."

TEN

Ashley set a box on the counter and gave me a funny look.

"What?" I tried to shove my dull rainbow-sheathed knives into the cutlery drawer.

"Are you really going to keep those? Luca has professional-grade knives. I don't think you need your cheap knives anymore." She started pulling out novelty wine glass after novelty wine glass from the box.

"If the kitchen master didn't want to house my more eccentric kitchen gear, he shouldn't have left me to the unpacking. This is his punishment for going into the office on move-in day."

Ash laughed as she held up a wineglass that said: I'm not slurring. I'm speaking in cursive. "I can't believe you've kept all of these. You're a hoarder."

Finally wedging the green butcher knife between two expensive thingamabobs, I slammed the drawer closed. "I'm not a hoarder. I'm an appreciator. I'm sentimental."

"You sure are mental . . ."

"Shut it." I grabbed the glass from her hand and contemplated the open cabinets. Luca already had a complete set of any kind of glass you would need. My heart broke. There wasn't any room for my precious keepsakes of drinking. "Just leave them there for now."

Sighing, I went back to the living room and plopped down on the couch. Ashley followed close behind with two seltzers.

"How you doin' champ?" Her sweet face held an unnatural frown.

I took a sip of the wild cherry bubbly and tried to collect my thoughts. "I'm okay. A little disappointed Luca's not here, but I get it. It's just weird to think I live here now."

Looking around the already-decorated room, I wasn't sure where my art was supposed to go.

"It'll get easier once you make it more your own. Give it time."

I nodded, not comfortable with how out of sorts I was feeling. The day's excitement fell flat as soon as Luca walked out the door. He left me to figure out how to shoehorn my life into his. Without him there, it was easy for doubt to creep in.

Ashley touched my knee, drawing attention away from my morose musings. "Are you having second thoughts?"

"No, not at all. I want to live with Luca. I just don't know how all this works. I don't know. I feel weird about being here without him on day one. It'll be fine when he gets home."

With a cautious smile, Ashley finished her can and checked her phone. "If I'm going to be ready for my date, I need to head home. Are you sure you're going to be okay alone?"

A Cheshire grin spread across my face. "I'll be fine. What is this, date number three with the wonderful Theo?"

Standing up, Ashley blushed as she gathered up her coat and purse. "It is, and I need to make sure the apartment is ready for company."

I followed her to the door. "Well, have fun, and don't do anything I wouldn't do."

Ash snorted and hugged me. "So, then, nothing's off the table. Noted." Pulling away, she wrapped a scarf around her neck. "Call me if you need anything."

"Will do. Now get out of here!"

Waving, I shut the door and locked it. Ryan rubbed against my ankles, purring. "Hey, buddy. Let's find a place for your cat tree."

Three hours and five drinks later, I was drunk and no closer to figuring out the cat tree situation. Luca texted every hour, apologizing for his lateness, but I couldn't bring myself to tell him it was okay. It wasn't okay. I was fucking pissed.

Sighing, I left the cat tree in the hallway and headed upstairs. I pulled on a silk chemise and roughly tugged out the tucked corners before slipping into bed. Ryan's soft purring relaxed me, but sleep never came. Around three a.m., a loud crash sounded downstairs.

My heart racing, I stumbled out of bed and grabbed a heavy vase from the hallway. Tiptoeing down the stairs, I readied my weapon to attack the humongous figure hunched over the fallen cat tree. I quietly moved behind the intruder, raising the vase in the air. Before I swung down, Luca turned and grabbed my wrist, pulling me into his body.

"Jesus, Sash! It's me."

I lost my grip on the vase, and it crashed to the floor, breaking into several large pieces.

"Shit!" I scrambled out of his hold and knelt, trying to gather the pieces. I hoped the vase wasn't a one-of-a-kind, but my gut told me Luca wouldn't have a Target original in his house.

Two cold hands gripped my shoulders and pulled me back up. "Leave it." Luca's voice was tight, but in the darkness, I couldn't make out why.

Wait. Is he annoyed?

"I can't just leave sharp ceramic all over the floor. Ryan could hurt himself, or one of us could step on it."

Luca reached across the hall and flipped on the light.

In an act of self-preservation, my eyes shut. "A little warning might've been nice. Some of us just got out of bed."

Opening my eyes, they adjusted slowly to the bright light as I watched Luca pick up the cat tree and straighten some boxes that had fallen over. "Sorry. I didn't mean to wake you. I also didn't expect there to be an obstacle course in the doorway when I got home."

His snark straightened my spine. Resting a hand on my hip, I tilted my head. "Oh, I'm sorry. Was I supposed to get everything unpacked by myself? How lazy of me not to unpack my whole life in one day."

Luca pinched the bridge of his nose. "I didn't mean it like that. I—"

"No, no, no. You're absolutely right. Why don't I just throw my stuff out? Huh? It'll make this whole process easier for *you*."

Throwing his hands to his side, Luca huffed, his eyes widening in disbelief. "What's going on? Why are you upset?"

Taking a step toward him, my hands balled into fists at my sides. "First, you left me on move-in day. Today was supposed to be fun and exciting, but instead, I was alone in your house while you were off figuring out contracts with Nicki and Gabe. Second—"

Luca's face turned red, and he scowled as he shouted at me. "Because I *so* wanted to go to work today! Dammit, Sasha! Do you think I wanted to leave you and what is now *our* house to go in and deal with someone else's mess? No!"

I took a step back. Luca had never raised his voice to me like that, and I wasn't sure how to feel. Noticing my slight movement, he took a breath, and his whole body slumped. After a few cycles of inhaling and exhaling, he closed the distance between us.

"Oh, baby, I'm so sorry. It's late, and I'm exhausted and disappointed, but I shouldn't take it out on you." His lips pressed gently against my forehead. "Please forgive me. I wanted to be here with you. You have to believe me."

Sighing, I pushed my face into his chest and nodded. The soft wool of his coat was still cold from the crisp February air, and the smell of cigarette smoke clung to the fibers along with the distinct stench of sweat. Gabe, Nicki's dad, smoked like a chimney. It was one of the things Luca hated about his father's chosen advisor.

"You have no idea how hard it was to focus, knowing you were here alone. All I wanted to do was get home and properly celebrate us finally living together."

I looked up into Luca's ridiculously gorgeous face. "Okay. I believe you, but why didn't you clear out space for me like you promised? It feels like there's no room for me here."

A small smile crept onto Luca's face. "Honestly? I didn't think about clearing space anywhere but in the bedroom. Obviously, that was a mistake."

My lips twitched, but I kept from smiling. "You gave me three-fourths of the closet space."

"I know how much you love your clothes." His smile grew as his hands skimmed down my back, stopping at the hem of my chemise.

A firm squeeze from his hands and I pressed myself into him. "I do, but don't think that gets you off the hook for the rest of it."

Luca's smile dropped, but his eyes still shined with amusement. "Of course not. Tomorrow, I'm at your beck and call."

My fingers danced up Luca's chest to his neck. "What about right now?" I blinked, and Luca swept me into his arms. Laughing as he took the stairs two at a time, I gasped out, "I meant the vase. You have to clean up the vase!"

An hour later, Luca cleaned up the broken pieces and found a place for Ryan's cat tree. We fell asleep in each other's arms as the sun peeked through the curtains.

I was home.

———

"And you seared the meat before putting it in the oven?"

"Yes, mom. I followed your recipe to the T."

"Okay." Mom sighed over the phone. "I'm just so happy for you, honey. You couldn't've found a better man."

I scoffed as I cut the potatoes. "You over your little crush on Casey Donovan?"

"Luca and Casey aren't even in the same category of man, honey."

Laughing, I tried to remember it was good that my mom had taken a shining to Luca, even if it bordered on fangirling. "Yeah, well, thanks for the recipe and help. I can't wait to surprise him with dinner. It's the perfect way to say happy one month living together."

"I like hearing you this way, Sasha."

Dropping the potatoes into the boiling water, I asked, "What way, mom?"

"Happy." A timer went off in the background. "Listen, sweetie. I gotta go if I'm going to have dinner ready by the time your father gets home. Give Luca our love."

"Will do. Love you, Mom."

"Love you, honey."

Checking the oven, I set a timer for my potatoes and then laid out on the couch. Ryan curled up on my stomach as I flipped through Netflix, searching for something to watch. I started the next episode of the Great British Bake Off, ready to be wowed by feats of culinary magic when my phone buzzed on the table.

LUCA MORETTI
Earliest I'll be home is 9. Sorry baby.

But it's Thursday.

I'll be home before it's not. What's up?

I huffed out a breath. He'd been late home every day this week, but to be honest, so had I, but we'd promised to be home for dinner tonight.

You can still order Indian without me. I'll heat mine up when I get home.

I didn't want to ruin the surprise, but it seemed like it didn't matter anyway.

> It's fine. Be safe getting home.

I put my phone down and stared at Ryan. His green eyes stared back at me as if he was trying to console me. His tail curled around him, and he rubbed his face against my hand.

Living with Luca was great when he was there. We both had demanding schedules, but his hours were so erratic that I could never plan for them. The only guaranteed alone time I had with him was Thursday nights and Saturdays, but now I was losing that. Our sex life had been regulated to the middle of the night when he got home and early in the morning before work. I saw more of him when I didn't live with him, which was complete bullshit.

As I took the potatoes off the stove, there was a knock at the door. Excited to have someone distract me from my annoyance, I rushed to open the door.

A disheveled but smiling Adriana stood there. "Good, you're home!"

"How can I help?"

We shuffled into the hallway. "Dante can't find his copy of *The Giving Tree*. Maybe he left it over here last weekend when he spent the night?"

"Let's check his room." Going upstairs to the guest room designated for Dante, Adriana slowed as she passed her wedding pictures. Her fingers brushed her lips, and she wrapped her other arm around her stomach. We'd never discussed Dante. Anytime the conversation veered that way, she'd change the subject, suddenly need a glass of wine, or use the bathroom.

Giving her some privacy, I left her on the stairs and searched the room. Under the bed, I found a stack of books, and on top was the little man's favorite bedtime story.

"Found it!" Standing up, I joined Adriana in the doorway.

Her eyes were glassy, but a small smile pulled at her red lips. "Thanks, Sasha."

As we made our way back downstairs, Adriana inhaled dramatically. "What smells so good?"

Instantly, my mood soured. "Pot roast." I gestured toward the kitchen. "I made Luca dinner. Too bad he isn't going to be home to eat."

Adriana arched a dark eyebrow at me and smirked. "You cooked?"

I reluctantly smiled. Since the Christmas dinner fiasco, Adriana had defrosted toward me. She was actually kind of funny when she wanted to be.

"I did. Would you and Dante want to come over and join me?"

She looked at the door. "Sure, I haven't put the lasagna in yet. Let me grab Dante. I'm sure he'll be ecstatic."

I finished mashing the potatoes right as Adriana and Dante made it back over.

"Sasha!"

"I'm in here, bud!"

A small body collided with my hip. "You're cooking?"

"Yes. Why is everyone so surprised?" I blew a strand of hair out of my face as I pulled down some plates.

"Because you never do. Remember the pancakes?" Dante's sweet face smiled up at me.

The image of Luca and Dante trying to choke down a breakfast that looked like hockey pucks made me laugh. "You're right, but this will be different, I promise. Now go take a seat at the table."

He nodded and sprinted away. Adriana grabbed juice for Dante and a bottle of wine for us. I carried the food to the table and dished out the plates, careful not to make a mess on the ridiculously expensive tablecloth.

Dante hesitantly sniffed as he inspected the fork full of potatoes. As he chewed, his face screwed up in concentration, just like his uncle. For a kid, he was quite the foodie.

"Mm. This is so good."

Adriana hummed in agreement.

"Thank you! Make sure you rub it in Luca's face later."

Dante finished chewing and speared a piece of roast with his fork. "Why isn't Uncle Luca here?"

He chewed, giving me a closed-mouth smile.

"He's working. I was going to surprise him with dinner."

Dante rolled his eyes. "What a dummy."

"Dante!" Adriana scolded, fighting back a smile.

"What? When Sasha's my wife, I will always be home for dinner."

I tried not to laugh. "I appreciate that, Dante."

He nodded. "It's the truth. When I'm big enough, you'll be my wife, and Uncle Luca will have to deal."

Adriana snorted, drawing Dante's attention. "You okay, mom?"

Nodding, she took a sip of wine. "I'm fine, just shocked by how grown up my little man is." Dante sat a little straighter and dug into his plate of food.

Dinner ended up being fantastic. Dante told us about an upcoming field trip to the Arch, and Adriana tactfully filled me in on a date she'd had the weekend before. While I'd planned for a much different evening, catching up with my favorite Morettis was nice.

After stuffing ourselves, Adriana and I cleaned up and chatted while Dante finished his dessert.

"You know, it was always like this with . . ." she gave me a meaningful look, then went back to drying a wine glass. "He worked insane hours, and if that wasn't enough, Nicki was always there. One time, Dante even joked that she was his work wife."

My fingers gripped the dirty plates under the water. "How did you deal with it?"

She laughed. "I didn't. We'd fight, make up, and then do it all over again the next day."

"It's just hard. Nights like this make me wonder what the hell I'm doing."

"Believe me, I understand. It sucks."

"It really does." I scrubbed a plate even though it was already clean. "I've never felt this way before. I don't think I realized just how much time he spends with Nicki. I get he has no interest in her, but I'm jealous that she gets to be with him all day, you know? At this point, I'm even jealous of Marco for getting to spend so much time with him on this new project."

Adriana stiffened but then relaxed. "I get it. Just remember, Luca is madly in love with you and has no interest in any other woman, especially a backstabbing bitch like Nicki."

I turned to check on Dante, and he was beautifully oblivious to our conversation. Setting down the plate, I glanced over at a pink-faced Adriana.

"Are you okay?" I placed a soapy hand on hers.

"I'm fine."

We finished the dishes in comfortable silence—both of us too tied up in our own thoughts to make small talk. Being with a Moretti man was no walk in the park, but did it have to push me out of character? I had to admit that for the first time in my life, I was jealous.

Son of a bitch.

As I made that ugly discovery, the front door opened and closed. I looked at the clock and was surprised to see it was only 8:30. Dante abandoned his cleared dessert plate and ran from the kitchen. "Uncle Luca!"

Adriana and I shared a look before following the sound of laughter to the front door. "What are you doing here, buddy?"

"Sasha made dinner, and it was so good!" In what could only be called a stage whisper, Dante added, "I think you're in trouble."

Luca's eyes jumped to my face, his smile dimming. "I think you might be right."

Putting Dante down, the little boy ran to my side and tugged on my hand. "Remember what I said."

I laughed, hugging him. "I will."

Dante kissed my cheek and then ran to his mom, pulling her out the front door. Adriana waved, laughing at her miniature tornado of a son.

The door shut, leaving Luca and me alone in the hallway.

"Why do I feel like my nephew just proposed to you?"

I turned from him and went back to the kitchen. Over my shoulder, I said, "Because he did. When he's big enough, I'm going to be his wife."

Grabbing a kitchen towel, I wiped up the little water that had sloshed from the dishes. Luca silently looked in the fridge and pulled out the plate I'd made for him.

I turned, and his sad eyes met mine. "Wow, this looks amazing. I'm sorry I wasn't here."

Shrugging, I pulled the towel through my fingers. "It's whatever. My future husband was here and enjoyed it."

Luca shook his head, placing the plate on the island. "I'm going to have to have a talk with my dear nephew." He cornered me against the countertop. "I can't believe you cooked for me."

"Happy one month living together."

Without warning, Luca's lips crashed into mine with a punishing force. His fingers wove through my hair, tilting my head up for better access. I couldn't move, and my lungs ached from lack of air, but Luca wasn't slowing down. His tongue tangled with mine, completely dominating me.

Abruptly, he pulled away. Gripping my thighs, he lifted me to the countertop. "Fuck. I love you so much. This week has been the fucking worst. I've missed talking to you, laughing with you, taking my time with you." He stepped between my legs, his already hardening length pressing against me. "Have you missed me too?"

His teeth nipped my ear and pulled. I moaned out a yes.

"I promise to try harder, baby." His hips thrust into me, causing my spine to curve into him.

"You better." It was shameful how quickly I forgave him, how my body demanded compliance. Quickly, I unbuttoned his shirt, tearing it from his body. I brushed my hands down his toned torso. My man had his shit together. His abs flexed under my fingertips, making my hands tremble with anticipation. When my eyes made it back to his face, he was staring at me with pure hunger. "Pants off."

Luca didn't have to be told twice and dropped his pants and boxer briefs.

Shimmying, I wiggled out of my underwear. I hiked up my dress, spreading my legs, showing him exactly how much I had missed him. Running my fingers through my folds, I wasn't surprised at how wet I was.

Luca's pupils dilated as he stepped into my space. This time, I grabbed him by the back of the head and brought him down to me. I bit his bottom lip hard enough to earn a grunt.

Luca's hands gripped my hips as he entered me in one powerful thrust. I yelped, the stretch causing minor discomfort, but I wouldn't want it any other way. Wrapping my legs around him, I urged him on. His thrusts came wild and fast, just like his heartbeat under my palm.

I dug my nails into his shoulders, pushing him back so I could look at him. His messy black waves, red and swollen lips, and hooded brown eyes locked on our joined bodies created a vision that pushed me closer to my climax.

"Fuck Sasha, you're so fucking perfect." He thrust faster and harder as I held on for dear life.

My walls began to pulse, my whole body shaking. "I love you, Luca."

Smiling, Luca pulled my face to his, kissing me while his hips slapped against mine, pushing me over the edge.

White flashes behind my tightly closed eyelids accompanied

my shaking limbs as my climax peaked. Moaning into my mouth, Luca thrust a few more times, his body slumping against me as he came.

I brushed the sweaty hair from his forehead as he kissed my neck and collarbone. His attention became more persistent, and just as my body readied for round two, Luca's stomach growled. Laughing, I shoved his shoulder toward the saran-wrapped plate.

As he slid out of me, I flinched—the hazards of a good time.

Easing down from the counter, I grabbed his boxers and cleaned myself up a bit. When I looked at Luca, he was already digging into his plate of food. "Hey! Warm that up!"

Luca glanced up. "Baby, this is delicious."

"It's better warm," I grumbled.

He smirked. "No offense, but I don't want to spend the time heating this up when I could be between your legs. After the next round, I promise I'll warm up that helping."

"Well, as long as you promise." I smiled, and I stole a bite of cold mashed potatoes.

ELEVEN

When Luca asked me to put in a bid for the new Moretti condominium contract, I immediately said no. Working together sounded like a surefire way to kill our already limited personal time. I knew Luca, and there was no way work wouldn't come home with us.

After several weeks of back-and-forth bartering and a trip to the property, I gave in.

What a fucking mistake.

I searched high and low for the perfect fabric to upholster the chairs that would sit in the lobby. It was apparent that I had to go custom, and because the universe had a sick sense of humor, Luca loved Scott Adams' designs.

Months before, I swore never to use the irresponsible asshole again. After consuming all the dark chocolate in my candy dish, I made a note to tell Miranda to refill it and dialed Adams.

"Adams Custom Design, Scott speaking."

"Scott? It's Sasha." My voice came out flat.

"Really?"

Huffing out a sigh, I said, "Yes, really."

"What happened to you never working with an unprofessional taint like me again?"

"I have a new contract, and you're the only one I know who can create the upscale look I need."

"I see. Well, I want an apology." I could hear a smile in the fucker's voice.

Scraping up what little dignity I could, I took a deep breath and said, sorry.

Scott broke out into a fit of laughter. "Shit. I never expected you to do it." I waited while he calmed down. "What's the gig?"

"A Moretti condominium. It's being completely gutted and redone."

"How'd you swing that job? They always work with Jones Design."

I tapped my pen on the desk. Since winning the contract a month ago, I'd run into this question a lot. The fact I got a job because of my partner embarrassed me. Luca swore our proposal was the best, and we would've won the work whether or not I was his girlfriend, but I knew I would've never gotten the opportunity to make a pitch without our connection.

"Luca Moretti asked me to put in a bid, and we won." Scott made a noise like he was going to say something, so I cut him off. "That's beside the point. Are you available?"

Scott laughed. "I can make the time. Come to the studio tomorrow, and we'll get to work. I promise to make my deadlines."

"You better. This is big for both of us."

"10-4, Red."

"Bye, Scott."

Ending the call, I let out a groan.

Pulling together the updates I had to deliver to Luca's office at three, I didn't notice Ashley slip into the room.

"You heading to Moretti's today?"

Nearly jumping out of my skin, my hand flew to my chest as I scowled at the bubbly nightmare. "Jesus, Ash. Please announce your presence, or I'm getting you a fucking bell."

She laughed as she plopped down in the chair in front of my desk. "Sorry, I can't help how stealthy I am."

"Mm-hmm. How was your 10 a.m. with that boutique hotel?" I went back to sorting all the documents.

"It's a done deal. We're going to renovate the entire thing over the next few months, so they don't have to close."

Ashley smiled from ear to ear. The only thing better than her eye for design was her sales pitch. The girl had the gift of gab.

"That's great! A year from now, SA Designs will be the go-to for hospitality in St. Louis."

Checking the candy bowl, Ashley pursed her lips as she dug through the remaining Werther's Originals. "Maybe then we can take a vacation. These hours are making having a personal life impossible."

"Sure, but it's worth it, right?" I frowned and glanced up from my tidy pile of papers.

Her eyes widened, and she sat up straight, her hands flying out in a defensive move. "Of course! This is our dream." She lifted one shoulder as she looked back down at the desk. "I just wish I could have this and a steady relationship. After Theo, I realized I don't have time for a man right now, and that really sucks." She ran her hand over the slicked-back hair that gathered into a big poof at the back of her head, patting on top with a frown. "I'm twenty-seven, and I thought I'd be a little further along in the romantic department."

Guilt hit me hard. While Luca and I had been struggling to make time for each other, we had the benefit of living together. Even if I only saw him two evenings a week, I at least caught a glimpse of him here and there.

"Ash, I'm sorry. I wish I could take more off your plate. How about we take a girls' trip somewhere fabulous after we wrap up the Moretti project and the hotel?"

Ashley relaxed back in the chair. "That sounds heavenly. Let's do it."

"Great." Shoving the folders into my bag, I walked around my desk toward the door. "Now I have to go sweet talk Luca into letting go of those hideous, fucking expensive-ass light fixtures he's dead set on for the hallways. Wish me luck."

Ashley followed me out, flipping the light switch. "Godspeed, Sasha Mitchell."

I booked it and made it to Luca's office just in time for our meeting. I set the cupcake I picked up for Lauren on her desk with a wink. Luca's executive assistant was a fucking saint. She kept me looped in on his schedule and even reminded him when he had been at the office late too many nights in a row.

I loved Lauren.

Nicki's monotone voice greeted me before I even stepped into Luca's office. The woman was a bore. The few times I had to interact with her, I found myself imagining new ways to incapacitate her and flee. It was a good thing she was beautiful and intelligent because moss had more personality than her.

"I need you to get these contracts signed by 4 p.m. today." Nicki was leaning over Luca, her dark, wavy hair brushing his shoulder.

Had the woman never heard of personal space?

I took a deep breath to try and shake off my annoyance. "Mr. Moretti, I'm here for our meeting."

Luca looked up and grinned. Pushing his office chair back to stand, the wheels ran into Nicki's toes.

"Ouch! Luca!"

With a word of apology, he grabbed Nicki's shoulders to steady her, then hurried around the desk to meet me at the door.

"Sasha, what a pleasant surprise. I forgot we were meeting today."

Wrapping me in a tight hug, he kissed my lips with a passion entirely inappropriate for the office. He tasted like coffee and peppermints. When he pulled away, his smile made me laugh.

Using my thumb, I tried to wipe away the lipstick smeared on his lips. "I hope you're not greeting every contractor this way."

Luca's hands skimmed down to my ass and squeezed. "Only the sexy redheads I live with."

Patting his chest, I took a step back. "Good."

Behind Luca, Nicki rubbed her foot while watching us with a bit of a frown. "Hey Nicki, how are you?"

"I'm doing well. Thank you, Sasha." She stared at Luca's back. "Luca, I'm going to head back to my office unless you need me for this meeting."

Luca turned and smiled at Nicki while lacing his fingers with mine. "You can go. Thanks for your help on past projects, but I think Sasha and I got it going forward."

Nicki dropped her foot to the floor and nodded. Without another word, she left the office.

Once we were alone, Luca shut his office door and turned the lock.

"Nicki used to help with the designs?" I walked over to the desk and sat in one of the visitor's chairs.

Luca settled down in his chair. "Yeah, she has a good eye and kept the designers on track."

"Gotcha." Reaching into my bag, I pulled out my plans. Luca worked to clear space by pushing other folders and what looked like proposals to the side. As I handed him my papers, a logo in a pile Luca made jumped out at me.

Jones Design.

I dropped my folders before Luca had a hold of them, the papers falling out onto his desk. "Damn it, Sash."

"What the hell is this?" Grabbing the nicely bounded proposal, I noticed the address listed on the cover was that of the condominium.

Luca swallowed hard. "A proposal."

My fingers tightened around the pages, creating a crease. "And why do you still have it? Once you awarded SA the contract, why would you hold on to another company's plans? Are you comparing my work?"

Luca shook his head in a full-on panic. "No, not at all. Dad had Nicki drop it off on Monday. He wanted me to look it over one more time before all the ordering was finalized. I swear I wasn't—"

"Then why the fuck is it still on your desk four days later?" Red seeped into my vision.

He looked down at his desk.

"Holy shit, you were going to compare the plans!" I dropped the packet like it burned me. It was one thing for people to judge me personally, but to judge my professionalism was something I couldn't stomach. I needed to get out of Luca's office and lick my wounds. Spinning toward the exit, I moved as fast as my stilettos would allow.

Quickly, Luca jumped up and got in between me and the door, his shaking hands gripping my shoulders to hold me still. "Sasha! I was just going to review it as a favor for Dad. I had no intention of making comparisons."

"Question. Once you award a contract to your other vendors, do you continue to review proposals?" I jammed my fingertip into his pec.

Wincing, he shook his head no. I stepped back out of his hold and into a full warrior-princess stance.

"And so why are you reviewing another company's proposal a month after giving SA Designs the job?"

"My Dad—"

I held my hand up. "No, Luca. Why are you reviewing another proposal? Are you not satisfied with our progress?"

"You know I'm satisfied. Your plans are amazing, and you're right on schedule."

"So again, I ask, why are you reviewing another proposal? Why not tell your dad to fuck off and trash it? Or if that's too extreme, just trash it and tell him you reviewed and compared? Why did you keep the proposal?"

With panic written all over his face, Luca's mouth hung open, waiting for the right words to come out.

I moved around him. "Perfect." Shaking my head, I scoffed. "I don't know if I can be here right now." Turning, I opened the door.

Without looking back at Luca, I said, "I have a show tonight. Don't expect me home. I'll crash with Evie or Ash."

As I passed Lauren's desk, she gave me a pained smile. Stepping into the elevator, I turned to find Luca watching me from the middle of the office. "Sasha." His voice was a whisper. Tears threatened to fall from his eyes, but he clearly didn't care because he continued to stand there as his employees gawked at their distraught boss.

Before concern and guilt made me fold, the elevator doors closed, and I slumped against the wall.

What a terrible fucking day.

Sitting at the bar, three sheets to the wind, I complained to anyone who would listen. That ended up being mostly Jazz.

"Why would he ask me to do the job but then change his mind?"

Jazz's hand gently patted my thigh. "I don't know, Sash. I'm sure he didn't change his mind. It's probably just family shit."

She shrugged and took another sip of her cocktail. The long falsies hit her high cheekbones as she closed her eyes in enjoyment. When the tip of her tongue brushed against her bottom lip, I realized I was leaning in far too close. But I didn't pull back.

A lazy smile pulled at her lips as she moved her hand to my hip. It was all wrong, but instead of stopping her, I inched closer in my seat.

"I just feel like he doesn't value me as a business equal, like I'm some kind of joke, you know?"

I stared at her like she had the answer to stopping the aching in my chest. I felt worthless, but Jazz had only ever showered me with compliments and adoration. The whole situation wasn't smart, but I wasn't interested in being smart. I wanted to feel better.

Her dark eyes softened as she moved even closer. Our noses were almost touching, and I smelled the whiskey from her drink on her lips. Her cold fingers caressed my jaw before her palm cupped my cheek.

"You're far from a joke. He's the joke for making you feel anything less than amazing."

Jazz's eyes dropped to my lips, and finally, I found the intelligence to move away. "Sorry, Jazz." I covered my face and shook my head. "Shit, I'm a fucking asshole."

I laid my forehead on the bar as she laughed. "You're fine, Sasha. I knew I was pushing my luck."

Turning my head to watch her slam back the rest of her drink, I rested my cheek in whatever booze someone had spilled there.

Placing her glass on the bar, she asked for her check. After signing the slip, she moved to stand up. "Let's get you home, yeah?"

Shaking my head, I refused to stand. "I can't go home. Luca lives there."

Jazz laughed. "That's the point. Give me your phone. I'll get you an Uber."

"Don't bother," I grumbled.

I struggled to put my coat on and shuffled out of The Monocle. Sitting out front was a black town car. Jazz eyed the sedan and gave me a questioning look. "Luca's. He sends it when he can't come to shows. Asshole thinks I can't get home."

Wobbling, I grabbed onto Jazz and gave her a big hug. "Sorry for being the worst. You're so fucking hot and nice, Jazz. If I weren't all in love or whatever, I would fuck you so hard. Believe that."

Her shoulders shook under my hold. "Thanks, Sasha." Pulling away, she gave me a peck on the lips. "Now get the fuck home before my drunk ass makes a mistake."

I slipped into the sedan while Jazz went back inside to wait for her ride.

"Fun night, Ms. Mitchell?"

"A fucking blast, Pete." I deadpanned. "What'd I tell you about that Ms. Mitchell shit?"

"Sorry, Ms. Sasha, a force of habit."

"Mm-hmm. Is Luca home?"

Pete glanced at me in the rearview mirror. "No. I believe he's still at the office."

Rage erupted from inside me. That fucker wasn't at home wallowing in my absence? "Then take me there."

"I don't think that's a good idea."

I leaned between the front seats. "Well, I don't really give a fuck."

A short car ride and I was out front of Luca's office building. Taking the elevator, I used the silver doors to straighten myself out. Post-show Sasha was hot, but add in being shit-faced, and it was a mixed bag.

The doors slid open to a dark floor, with only two offices still lit—Luca's and Nicki's.

Strutting toward Luca's office, hushed voices met my ears. Much like that afternoon, Nicki sat far too close to Luca, but this time, his hands covered his face.

"Well, this is cozy."

My voice shattered the serene scene on the couch. Luca jumped up and away from Nicki, red-eyed and disheveled. Nicki was as perfect as ever, not a hair out of place.

"Sasha, you're here." He looked at me in disbelief, his eyes never straying from my face.

Motion from the couch pulled my focus back to Nicki. Anger bubbled up in my stomach because she was witnessing this weak moment. She had no right to be in our fucking business. If looks could kill, that bitch would've been drawn, quartered, and served to a cannibal.

Noticing my glare, Nicki cleared her throat and slipped on her heels. "Excuse me."

She tried to leave the room, but I wouldn't move. Instead, I made her squeeze through a tiny crack of space. I wanted her to feel every ounce of discomfort I felt when she was around.

Petty? Probably. Did I care? Fuck no.

When we were finally alone, I spoke. "So, this is why you stay late so much? Couch time with Nicki?"

Luca's eyes darted between me and the couch until realization dawned on him. His hands gestured between himself and the spot Nicki had just sat. "What? No! Never. I didn't want to go home if you wouldn't be there, and Nicki saw the light on when she was leaving. She was checking to see if I was okay, nothing more. I will always come home to you, baby. I don't want anyone else."

Nodding, I waltzed over to the couch and sat down. Guilt stabbed at my stomach. "I guess people in glass houses shouldn't throw things or whatever."

Luca frowned as he joined me on the couch. "What are you talking about?" Leaning forward, he took my hands. His nose scrunched up at the smell of alcohol on me. "Are you drunk?"

I giggled. "Yep."

He sighed as he squeezed my hands, his thumbs rubbing small circles on my skin. "Tell me what happened, baby."

Tears filled my eyes. I'd never felt this way before, so fucking weak for someone else. "I got drunk and almost let Jazz kiss me. Well, she did kiss me, but not the way I was going to let her. You know?"

Luca's body tensed, a scowl taking over his features, but he didn't drop my hands. If anything, his grip tightened. "No, I don't know. Explain it to me." His voice was sharp and cold.

"I felt like shit, Luca." I noticed his jaw relax as his eyes softened. "Jazz listened to me complain, and then I almost let her kiss me, but I didn't." I rushed out the last bit, not wanting to leave Luca with any doubt. "When I was leaving, she gave me a peck goodbye. Like this." I gave Luca a quick peck and a small smile tugged at the side of his mouth.

"So, it wasn't a kiss like this?"

Leaning over, he pressed his lips gently to mine, but it wasn't long before his hands were in my hair, and our tongues were tangling. I pushed up the hem of my skirt and straddled his lap.

One of his hands squeezed my ass while the other gripped the back of my neck possessively. I rolled my hips, enjoying the rough texture of his trousers against my lace-covered pussy.

With one slap to my ass, Luca pulled back. "So, not like that?"

Gasping for air, I never stopped moving my hips. "Nope."

He smiled as he stilled my hips. "Good." He kissed the tip of my nose. "I'm so sorry, baby. I wasn't thinking, and I hurt you. Never again."

I nodded. "I felt so worthless, Luca. It confirmed every bad feeling I had about working together. Like I wasn't good enough for the job."

Luca's fingers dug into my hips. "You are more than good enough. You're fucking brilliant, Sasha. I'm sorry if for one minute I had you doubting that."

Everything wasn't okay, but I understood enough about Luca to know he meant what he said. "I'm still mad. Probably will be for a little while."

He nodded, his hands releasing my hips to come and cup my cheeks. His thumbs brushed under my eyes before he took my lips in another sweet kiss. Pressing down on him, I rocked against his hardness. I wanted to forget the ugliness of the day, to let Luca use his power over me to take the pain away.

Eager to have him inside me, my fingers shook as they unbuckled his belt. Unbuttoning his pants and pulling out the bottom of his shirt, I rose up on my knees. Tearing my lips from his, I put all my focus on pulling his erection from his boxers.

Pushing my panties to the side, I slid down on his length, my body lighting up at the connection. Luca let out a strangled groan, his head falling back against the couch. His throat bobbed, begging to be kissed.

As much as I loved watching him come undone under me, I needed to see his face. I needed reassurance that he was mine.

"Look at me, Luca," I demanded.

His head rolled forward, and his perfect brown eyes bore into me. I gasped, fingers curling into his chest. There it was—the love, the devotion, the desire Luca had for me. His apology was in the way his red eyes traced my features in awe and wonder, and some of the hurt melted away.

Slowly, I moved up and down on his cock, feeling every inch, every ridge. His hips jerked up to meet mine, and I stopped.

"Don't move."

Luca panted, lowering himself back down, leaving only his tip inside.

Sliding back down, I rolled my hips at the bottom. My movements sped up as I came down harder and faster. My breath came out in huffs and moans. Luca's eyes never left mine.

"Baby, I'm going to come." His words were breathy as he gripped my body hard.

Clenching my walls, Luca tensed and released. Riding out his climax, he used his thumb to press on my clit as he thrust up from below. My orgasm came fast and hard, my whole body convulsing. Sweaty and panting, I fell into Luca's body. Wrapped in the warm light of his desk lamp, a sense of peace settled over me. We kissed and murmured, "I love you." Neither of us was in a hurry to separate.

When we finally stood up from the couch, we heard the elevator doors close.

TWELVE

Tzatziki spilled out of the gyro just as I thought I had a handle on the damn thing.

"Isn't that the best gyro you've ever had?"

I tried to block out Scott's continuous commentary and focus on the delicious bit of food I was wolfing down.

"Admit it, Red. You're glad we had to stay late. If we didn't have to make all these alterations, you'd never have gotten to try Athena's."

My eyes darted toward the blond doofus. Washing down the lamb and pita with a sip of water, I rolled my eyes. "Oh yeah, Scott. This is so much better than being home in my bed." Shaking my head, I wiped my hands. "You're just lucky Luca's out of town. Otherwise, you'd be making these adjustments by yourself." Scott laughed as I gathered up the takeout containers and trash.

"Only a few more details to peg down, and we're done with this phase."

I looked down at my watch and sighed. "I don't know about you, but I'm ready to get the hell out of here."

"Ouch." Scott threw a hand over his heart. "This is my home, my kingdom. Are you saying you don't enjoy the fumes of my artisanal shop?"

I couldn't help but laugh. The dude was a dork, but he wasn't as bad as I'd initially thought. When my carpenter fell through on some one-of-a-kind pieces, Scott talked local furniture hotshot Axel Lapusan into taking the project. With access to Axel's genius hands, Scott and I made a few tweaks and changes to the pieces we had in mind. Those tweaks and changes are what led me to be sitting on the floor of Scott's workspace, surrounded by swatches and notepads at 1 a.m.

Shaking the cramp out of my leg, I tried to smooth my hopelessly wrinkled pencil skirt. "I think I'm starting to understand why you're such a space cadet. I feel high off the paint and ink fumes."

Scott popped up from the floor, his hands full of notebooks. "What'd we say about name-calling, Red?"

"What'd I say about calling me Red, airhead?" I nudged Scott's shoulder, causing him to drop a couple of notebooks.

Blowing a loose lock of hair from his forehead, he bent over to pick up his notes. Scott was tall and lean, bordering on lanky, but he had one phenomenal ass. I figured it was from his bike-only lifestyle.

"I've never met someone who both loves their red hair but also wants no mention made of it." He peeked up at me while wiggling his ass in the air. "And stop staring at my ass before I get the wrong idea."

He brushed past me with a wink and headed over to his desk.

Shaking my head, I gathered up my folders and notes. When I looked up, Scott's eyes rested on my chest. "Ahem. Weren't you just saying something about staring?"

Scott's tan cheeks blushed as he boldly looked me in the eye. Moments like that reminded me he was only twenty-four. "Sorry, Red."

I righted my body and gave him a soft smile. "Remember, Nicki's calling tomorrow."

Flopping down onto one of the chairs he was working on, Scott let out the groan of the century. He was not Nicki's biggest fan.

"Sorry, man. Luca's in Chicago again, which means she's in charge of wrangling the final signatures from Axel. I'm sure by now she knows you aren't my intern."

A deep frown etched into his youthful face. "How can someone so beautiful be so . . . so—I don't even have the words." His eyes met mine, the plea for compassion there before he uttered a single word. "Can't you talk to her? I mean, it's your fault we have to deal with her."

I arched an eyebrow in his direction.

"Fine! I'll talk to the plankton, but if she makes one snide comment about my age or professionalism, I'll find out where she lives and graffiti all over her car."

Grabbing my purse, I nodded. "Very professional of you, Scott. I'm out of here. See you next week when you get those proofs done."

"Drive safe, Red."

A black sedan sat outside our duplex when I got home. Pete rolled down the driver's window and gave me a small wave.

"Hey, Pete."

"Ms. Sasha." It was a compromise, I guess. At least I was no longer "Ms. Mitchell."

"You know you don't have to wait for me to get home, right?"

Pete shook his head. "And you know when Mr. Moretti is out of town, I have strict orders to make sure you make it in every night."

Leaning my hand against the body of the car, I lowered my face down to Pete's. "With Luca's new project in Chicago, this sentinel act is getting a little ridiculous. He's already been gone twice this month. I know Maria can't appreciate you being out this late at night."

The twinkle in Pete's eye at the mention of his wife made me smile. "Maria understands my loyalty, Ms. Sasha." A slight smile pulled at his lips. "If you want to help me out, come home earlier."

Backing away from the car, I gave Pete a salute. "10-4, buddy. No more late nights at the office."

Once I opened the door, I waved to Pete and hurried inside. It might've been April, but the nights were still a bit chilly.

Ryan sat perched on his cat tree right inside the living room, fast asleep. "Thanks for waiting up for me, Bub." Coming home to an empty house was hard, and I found myself talking to Ryan more and more. I wasn't sure if Ryan appreciated it.

Getting ready for bed, I checked my phone for Luca's usual 'goodnight' text.

Nothing. He hadn't texted me all day. I scrubbed my front teeth with renewed vigor as I stared at the crease between my eyebrows.

The day before, Luca hadn't reached out to me until I texted him. The more I thought about it, the more agitated I got. Since he went on that first trip to Chicago a few weeks ago with his dad and Marco, I'd been doing a lot of the work in our relationship. Hell, I'd even been relegated to initiating sex.

Anger and dissatisfaction twisted my gut. I was frustrated sexually and emotionally. It didn't help that my stomach hurt from eating too much gyro.

I spit out the toothpaste without running any water. It would leave a gross, crusty mess for Luca when he got back in three days. Gargling, I fought the urge to rinse the toothpaste grime away.

The white paste would drive him bonkers, but he could deal with it. Birthday or not, his little Houdini act was bullshit. Was my bathroom sabotage passive-aggressive? Yes. Was that going to stop me? No.

Finishing up in the bathroom, I shut off the light and slid into bed.

In the dark, lonely bedroom, I couldn't stop wondering what Luca was up to or why he hadn't made time to call me. My mind concocted all kinds of scenarios, from torrid affairs with jazz lounge singers to being kidnapped by stalkers hell-bent on his riches.

Huffing out a breath, I realized I was being ridiculous and needed to relax. I tried counting backward from one hundred, then from one thousand.

Annoyed by the lack of drowsiness, I couldn't stay still. I pulled out my vibrator and tried to tire myself out with an orgasm. I came, but sleep still evaded me.

Flipping on the lamp, I looked around the room for something to do. My eyes landed on the dirty clothes basket that was pretty empty. Slipping out of bed, I grabbed the basket and turned it over. I kicked and tossed the clothes all over the floor.

Satisfied by the mess, I went back into the bathroom, pulled all my hair products out from under the sink, and set them on the counter.

I smiled at the minimal chaos. Luca would flip when he got home. As I reached for the light switch, my deranged smile in the mirror caused my hand to drop to the counter, knocking over a styling wand.

"What the fuck is wrong with you? Are you really this big a fucking loser?"

Without a second thought, I turned on the faucet and rinsed the toothpaste down the drain. I returned all my products to their designated cabinet and tossed all my dirty clothes back into the basket.

Getting back into bed, I grabbed my phone.

I miss you.

Only a minute passed before my phone lit up with a text.

> I miss you so much, baby. Love you. The next 3 days can't go by fast enough. I'll call you tomorrow.

Smiling to myself, I fell into a peaceful sleep.

When Luca wasn't home, Saturdays meant brunch with Ashley, Sarah, and Adriana.

"Pass the champagne. This is a weak-ass mimosa."

Ashley frowned at me but handed me the bottle. "I'm sorry, princess. I didn't know we were getting sloshed."

"It's brunch." I shrugged as I poured myself a generous glass of champagne. Dropping in a few berries, I sipped the more potent cocktail.

Sarah laughed and toasted me. "I could use a little drunken breakfast fun."

"Trouble in perfect husband paradise?" Ash said with a lifted brow. She always got weird when it came to Sarah and Michael's unnaturally perfect partnership.

Sarah frowned. "No, not exactly."

Adriana gestured with her mimosa in hand, nearly spilling it on the table.

Blowing the bright red bangs from her forehead, Sarah tilted her face toward the ceiling. "Michael is ready to be a papa, and I want to have a little more time with just us." When she looked back at us, apprehension was written all over her face.

"Makes sense. You just got promoted and are getting situated in the new position. Is Michael being pushy?" I couldn't imagine the sweet, baby-faced man being a jerk, but you have to ask.

Sarah waved a hand as she set down her drink. "No! No, nothing like that. I just feel like I'm letting him down. And after he's done so much for me." Her gaze dropped to the tabletop, where she drew patterns in the condensation from her glass.

Ashley cleared her throat. "Him changing for you doesn't give him the right to dictate the pace of the rest of your lives. It's not like you didn't make sacrifices for him, too."

Nodding, Adriana patted Sarah's hand. "Ash is right. You should probably talk to him about how you're feeling. From what you've said, I'm sure he would be mortified if he knew you felt pressured."

Sarah took a drink of her mimosa. "I know you're right." Taking another sip, she shook her head and looked at me. "Enough about me. Tell us what you have planned for Luca's birthday!"

A devious smile spread across my face. "When Luca gets home Monday night, I'm going to greet him in this little lacy number I picked up online. From there, I'm sure you can guess where the night goes. I had Lauren clear his Tuesday for me, so it will just be him and me for twenty-four hours. No work, no interruptions. My vagina can barely contain its excitement."

Adriana laughed. "I think Dante and I will spend the night at Grandma's."

"Might be for the best." I winked at her.

Ashley had a pained smile on her face. I could've kicked myself for being so braggadocious about Luca and my planned sexcation. Work had only gotten more time-consuming, and she was still single and hating it.

"Ash, you need me to top you off?"

"Sure. I'm going to grab another waffle. Does anyone need anything from the kitchen?"

"More bacon, please!" Adriana raised her hand, the champagne making her more peppy than usual.

Ashley shuffled out of the dining room, and Sarah shot me a questioning look as I poured Ash a full glass of champagne with a splash of O.J.

We needed to get Luca's condominium and the hotel done. Ashley needed a break, a man, and a—hell, I didn't know what. I just wanted my bubbly best friend back.

She shuffled back into the dining room and dropped a plate of bacon off in front of Adriana.

"Ashley?"

Her gaze stayed on her plate as she cut into her waffle and took a big bite.

I pressed on. "I was thinking about our vacation."

She took another bite but nodded, letting me know she heard me.

"Let's do Mexico. Like in college!"

A small smile pulled at her lips as she chewed. A particular night involving a hot coed and a remote part of the beach probably flashed through her mind.

"Just me, you, and whatever trouble we can find."

Her big brown eyes finally looked at me, and I knew I had her.

"I was looking at our schedules, and we could go as early as the first week of June. What'd ya say?"

Ash swallowed and dabbed her mouth. "I think I can make it another month."

Relief washed over me. "Great."

"Oh. I want to go to Mexico!" Adriana popped another piece of bacon into her mouth.

Wiggling her eyebrows at me, Ashley said, "You're both more than welcome to join. Imagine the four of us and unlimited margs."

"That sounds fun. I'm not gonna lie. Every time I talk to Celeste, I get a little jealous. She's been traveling and having all these grand adventures while I'm sitting in meetings trying to figure out how to spin my client's bullshit ideas."

"Then it's settled. We're going to Mexico! Now I have a serious question: Is there more champagne in the kitchen?" Adriana asked as she shook the empty bottle in my face.

Laying in the living room, completely trashed and full of breakfast foods, I binged a TV documentary series about swingers on Netflix. Pete had already come by to check on me, and I assured him I'd be staying in for the night.

My phone lit up with a text from Scott.

> **SCOTT ADAMS**
> You owe me for taking a work call from Nicki on a Saturday.

Laughter shook my body, causing Ryan to jump off my stomach where he'd been peacefully napping.

> Poor baby. What'd she do this time?

> She said it was cute that Luca was giving so much "new talent" a chance. She hoped we wouldn't blow it.

My body flushed with anger. Both Scott and I worked damn hard to be where we were. In fact, we were both on the cusp of being on the same tier as Axel Lapusan. The buzz surrounding SA Designs BEFORE we got the Moretti contract had been growing.

> Bitch is just jealous. She's her dad and Luca's lap dog. She's a law degree playing paralegal.

Scott sent a gif of an explosion.

> You're right, but you still owe me.

> Fine, next late-night meal's on me.

> Perfect.

Dropping my phone on the coffee table, I snuggled into the

couch and watched an ancient, terrifying man try to get with a pretty young thing.

In classic day-drinking fashion, I passed out on the couch. Rolling off, I woke up to Netflix asking if I was still watching, and four missed calls and one voicemail from a local number.

Switching off the TV, I started the long trek upstairs to bed. As the voicemail played, my heart raced.

"Ms. Mitchell. This is Officer Russo with the St. Louis Police Department. Please give me a callback—"

I immediately pulled the phone from my face and hit call back on the number. I stood on the stairs, waiting for the officer to answer. After three rings, they finally picked up.

"Officer Russo."

"Uh, hi. I'm returning your call. This is Sasha Mitchell."

"Ms. Mitchell, I was calling regarding Luca Moretti. You're listed as his emergency contact?"

My heart fell. The lump in my throat made speaking difficult, but I squeaked out a yes.

"I'm sorry to inform you that Mr. Moretti sustained multiple gunshot wounds tonight during an alleged mugging outside the Emerald Nightclub. He's currently receiving care at Barnes-Jewish Hospital. I would advise you to make your way down as soon as possible."

"Is he . . ." I couldn't say the words. Luca had been shot, and I couldn't even ask how bad the damage was. I stared at the picture of him and Dante, promising myself I would give him all the little Lucas and Sashas he wanted if he was okay. At that moment, it was clear that Luca was my future, my life.

"He's stable, Ms. Mitchell."

Tears spilled from my eyes, my whole body shaking with relief and fear for Luca. I couldn't control the sobs that racked my chest. Swallowing down the bile rising in my throat, I calmed my breathing.

"I'll be there soon. Thank you, Officer Russo."

Quickly, I grabbed my purse and rushed to Adriana's door.

After knocking for what felt like an eternity, I gave up and ran to my car. I would call her when I got to the hospital. My first concern was seeing Luca.

Driving like a bat out of hell, I made it to Barnes in fifteen minutes. I parked in the garage, and then it hit me.

Why is Luca in St. Louis?

THIRTEEN

I don't remember making it into the hospital or asking for Luca's room information. I don't remember the elevator I must've taken to the floor or navigating through the maze of hallways.

Why is Luca in St. Louis?

Slow, plodding feet dragged me through the sitting area like my body knew only bad things were waiting for me. Like my feet were trying to save me from my future.

He wasn't supposed to be back for two more days.

Tears blurred my vision, but not one fell. I repeatedly swallowed, trying to consume my heartache before it made a sound.

He lied to me.

My stomach was in knots, and pain radiated through my chest. I scanned the hall for a trashcan. Pressing my hands against my stomach, I folded in on myself, dry heaving over the can.

He lied to me.

Wiping my mouth with the back of my hand, I staggered down the hall. Before I was completely prepared, I was standing outside his room. Leaning against the wall, I took a deep breath. Fear of what was about to happen froze me in place.

He was the love of my life. Period. End of story.

And now, I was going to lose him.

A small voice in the back of my mind tried to soothe the pain in my chest, telling me it wasn't what I thought, that Luca loved me.

A voice coming from Luca's room drowned out that internal cheerleader. "I couldn't let them take you in the ambulance alone." Nicki's calm tone grated on my ears.

"I told you to go home. They've called Sasha. She'll be here any minute, and I don't want her to see you here." Luca's voice was raspy and low. There was steel there I'd never heard. A harshness that made me wince.

"So? You're not going to tell her the truth?" For the first time, composed and emotionless Nicki sounded out of sorts.

"No. If I do, I'll lose her. I can't lose her." A tremor at the end was the only evidence of humanity in his voice. Who was this man?

"You'll lose her anyway. Your lies, your, your—"

"Enough! You knew the deal from minute one. Don't think I'll allow you to dictate anything to me, Nicki. Now get the fuck out of this hospital before Sasha sees you." A shiver ran up my spine. Luca was merciless. Cruel was never a word I would've used to describe him, but damn if he wasn't living up to it.

When Nicki spoke again, her voice was thick with disgust. "What are you going to tell her, Luca? Huh? Sasha's smart. How do you expect to get out of this one? You were shot outside one of your nightclubs on a Saturday night. A Saturday night that you were supposed to be in another city! It's not like you got hurt making your way home to her."

Silence.

"Face it. Honesty or not, you've already lost her. At least if you're honest, she'll be able to move on."

I pressed a fist against my mouth. Sobs threatened to spill from my lips, but I wanted, needed, to hear more.

"Nicki." Luca's voice was low and lethal. "Your concern for my girlfriend is moving, but I will not tell you again. Get the fuck out of my room. I'll handle Sasha."

Rage and heartbreak fought in my chest for dominance.

He was going to handle me? Fuck him!

As Nicki's heels clicked toward the door, an officer approached me.

"Ms. Mitchell?"

With a shuddered breath, I took a step toward the cop and into the quarreling couple's line of sight, wiping my eyes to clear the blurriness. Glancing into Luca's room, I watched his face pale and Nicki's mouth fall open.

When her eyes left mine and landed on the officer next to me, she came back to life. Without looking at Luca, she shuffled from the room, keeping ample space between us, and hurried down the hall.

Nodding to the officer, I couldn't make any words come out of my mouth as he shook my hand.

"Great. I spoke to you on the phone. I'm Officer Russo. As you can see—" his hand gestured toward Luca, "Mr. Moretti is doing fine. I was just heading in to take his statement, and then I'll be out of your hair. So if you'll have a seat in the waiting room, I'll—"

"Oh no, it's okay. Luca would want me there with him when he gives you his statement." I surprised myself with how composed I sounded.

"Well, okay. Let's do it to it then." Officer Russo smiled, but it fell as he looked at Luca.

I lead Russo into the room, taking the chair at the end of the bed and leaving the one closest to Luca free.

"Mr. Moretti, I'm glad to see you awake. I hope you're feeling all right."

Luca's eyes jumped between the officer and me. "As well as you can feel with two holes in your body."

The urge to scan him for injury consumed me, but I fought back my impulses with the image of Nicki standing in that very room.

"Good, good. Let's make this quick, then. Can you give me a rundown of what happened tonight?"

Luca's eyes no longer strayed to me. Pulling his lips into a charming smile, he proceeded to give his statement.

"Around 8 p.m., two work associates and I were outside the Emerald nightclub, about to go in."

"Ms. Nicole Ricci and Mr. Marco Moretti?"

Luca's smile flattened into a line, tension apparent in his face. "Yes."

"And then what happened."

"A man approached and attempted to steal Nicki's purse. I was able to snatch it back, but in the course of the struggle, the guy got off two shots."

"What did this man look like?"

"Over six feet, brown hair, nothing too memorable about him. It was dark on that section of the sidewalk."

Officer Russo jotted down every word Luca said, his eyebrows pulling into a frown. "You got into an altercation over a bag?" Luca nodded, and the officer shook his head. "In the future, please let the bag go. No life is worth the latest Chanel."

"I'll keep that in mind, officer. Is there anything else? I'm feeling pretty tired and would like to have a minute with my fiancé before I pass out from the meds."

"That should be it for now. I'll be in touch."

I bit my tongue to hold back the line of curses I had for that bastard calling me his fiancé and smiled at the exiting officer.

Without looking at Luca, I asked, "So now I'm your fiancé? Is that how you decided to handle me? By deciding we're engaged? What the hell's wrong with you?"

Swinging my head toward him, I watched all the color leave his face.

"How much did you hear?" His voice was soft, nothing like the aggressive tone he used with Nicki.

"Enough." I stood up and started to walk around the room

slowly. "You're not in Chicago." My eyes refused to look at him. Just hearing him breathe in the room irked me.

"No."

Counting the titles on the floor as I paced, I waited for him to say more, but he didn't. "So you lied."

Silence. Deafening silence.

Nothing about us had ever been silent, but now, when I needed his words the most, he offered nothing.

"Were you ever even in Chicago?"

A whispered no fell from his lips.

I stopped in front of the window. Staring at the highway, I gnawed on the inside of my cheek.

"It's not what you think, Sash."

It was my turn for silence.

"You have to believe me. It's not what you think."

A rage I'd never felt tore through me. "You want to know what I think?" I spun around to glare at him, causing some hair to land in my mouth. "I think you're a fucking liar and a cheat. I think you've been fucking Nicki, and it wasn't enough to do it after hours. You needed to have real couple time, huh?"

"No! I would never—"

"And I'm the fucking fool over here wondering why my boyfriend isn't trying to fuck me, isn't making time to call me when he's away. It's because you were too busy with her." My finger pointed in his direction, but I kept a safe distance from the bed, avoiding his hands that kept reaching out to me.

"Sasha—"

"No, Luca! I love you, and you fucking betrayed me! Is it because she looks like a fucking model? Because it sure as hell can't be because of her wit and personality. Or is it because she's daddy-approved? Tell me! Why the fuck did you do this to me?"

The bed squeaked as Luca shifted toward his suit jacket on the chair. His hands strained as they pulled out a felt box.

Pressing my back against the window, I blinked rapidly as my eyes filled with tears. "What the fuck is that?"

His chapped lips pulled into a small smile as he flipped open the lid. A diamond the size of a Chicklet sparkled at me. "An engagement ring. I've been carrying it around for months, waiting for the right time."

My fingernails dug into my palm. "And this is it? Do you honestly think that proposing will get you out of this . . . this—whatever this is?" I yelled.

Luca kept his hand extended, waiting for me to take the fucking ring.

Crossing my arms over my stomach, I gathered all my strength. "Tell me, Luca. If this isn't what it looks like, what is it?"

Finally, his hand fell along with his eyes. "I can't tell you that, Sasha."

I let out a sharp laugh, my head lolling to the side. "So I'm just supposed to ignore the fact that you've been God knows where for the past few days? That if you hadn't been shot being such a 'gentleman,' I would've never known? Tell me, would you've ever told me?"

Staring at the ring, he shook his head.

"And will you tell me the whole truth now?"

Another slow head shake.

"One more chance, Luca, or I'm out the fucking door. Tell me what's going on." I pleaded with him, no more strength left in my voice.

Beautiful brown eyes filled with tears looked back at me. "I love you, Sasha. I . . . I." A sob racked through him as he tried to get to me, but the wires and cords kept him tethered to the bed. "Please . . . I just can't . . . you have to believe me."

Slowly, I moved toward the door. With each step, Luca became more frantic. The machines beeped. His words became punctuated with hiccups and sobs as he tried to pull himself free of the wires. Two nurses rushed past me and tried to restrain him, but his pain-filled eyes never left me. He thrashed against their gentle hold, and the two women shouted for help. Two burly nurses ran in and held him down. They added a syringe of something to his fluids bag, and his movements slowed. Sluggishly, he whimpered and quietly begged me to stay.

"Sorry." Tearing my eyes from Luca, I ran from the room. I didn't stop running until I reached my car. Somehow, I made it home without crashing.

"Taking or leaving?" Ashley held up my treasured wine glasses.

"Box'em, and I'll have the movers get them. I really just need to have my clothes and beauty shit right now. The rest I'll stack to be picked up this weekend."

"You got it."

Adriana stood in the kitchen doorway with a garbage bag full of clothes. "Sasha, I'm going to put your winter clothes in my guest room. I'll make sure the movers get them."

I absentmindedly nodded as I jammed shot glasses in paper.

"I still can't believe Adriana is helping you move out."

When I looked up, Ash was staring down at the pile of paintings I had already taken off the walls. "Yeah, well, she still thinks I should wait and talk to him. But what is there to talk about? Worst-case scenario, he is fucking Nicki, and I leave. Best-case scenario, something else is happening, and he doesn't trust me enough to tell me, and I leave."

Her eyebrows furrowed, and she moved towards me. "I just don't see Luca as a cheater. It's gotta be something else."

Shrugging, I kept filling the box in front of me. "Doesn't matter. Being a liar's not much better." Looking at the clock on the wall, I sighed. "Listen, can we just get this done? He's being discharged tonight, and I'd rather be anywhere but here when he is."

Frowning, Ashley didn't say anything else.

An hour later, I had all my essentials in our cars, the rest stacked at Luca's and Adriana's. Locking up, I handed Adriana my key. "The movers will be here on Saturday at 10 am. It shouldn't be a problem for Luca. He's usually at the office or wherever."

Pulling me into an impossibly tight hug, Adriana whispered. "I'm so sorry. I wish I knew what to say."

I patted her back. "You don't have to say anything. It's Luca's secret, and he isn't sharing."

My heel caught on the top step as I watched Pete pull up to the curb. The back door swung open, and before I could run, Luca was charging toward me.

"What the hell is this? Where are you going?"

Sneering at his demanding tone, I pushed past him. "Where were you this past week?"

Luca grabbed my elbow. "St. Louis."

"Doing what?"

His finger dug into my skin. "I can't—"

"Tell you. Got it. Have a nice life, Luca."

Using all my strength, I ripped my arm from his hold.

"Sasha—"

Reaching the driver's side door, I looked him dead in the eye. All I saw was fear and panic. "No! This is it. You always acted like I would be the one to lose interest and break your heart, but here I am, completely broken. Stay away, Luca. Just stay away."

As I drove away, I couldn't tear my eyes away from the crumpling figure in my rearview mirror.

"Scott, just follow the floor plan we created, and I'll be there in half an hour to finish up."

"Fine, but now that the wallpaper is up, I am second-guessing this pillow for the lobby and—"

"If it's heinous, we'll make adjustments. I'll be there soon. Bye."

Before the neurotic mess pulled me into another round of "which cushion, which vase," I hung up.

We were one week away from the grand opening of the condo and two weeks out from Mexico.

Leaving Luca made our working relationship more than awkward. It was clear he was dragging out the project, but it wasn't getting him anywhere with me. I sent Ashley and Scott in my place for any face-to-face meetings.

I'd successfully dodged him for six weeks, but soon I'd have to suck it up and see him at the grand opening event. He wasn't going to keep me from such an excellent networking opportunity.

Shutting down my computer and gathering up my stuff, Malcolm startled me when he slipped into my office and shut the door.

Arching an eyebrow at the door, I looked back at him. "I think you have the wrong office. Your lady love is across the hall. You know, 5 foot nothing, curly brown hair, dimples?"

He laughed and glanced towards Ashley's empty office. "I'm pretty sure she'd be pissed if she knew I was here."

Confused, I sat back down. "Okay?"

Malcolm dropped a folder on my desk. "I was sorry to hear about you and Luca. I really liked that dude."

Flipping open the file, I nodded. "I did too, until he fucked another woman and lied to me." I pulled out picture after picture of Luca and Nicki. None of them looked like they were intimate in any way. "What are these?"

Malcolm rubbed the back of his neck, keeping his eyes on the pictures in my hand. "My brother-in-law, James, is a PI. I asked him to follow Luca."

It was official. My life was a fucking joke. "Why?"

Settling into my comfy visitor chair, the way Ash did daily, Malcolm unwrapped a piece of candy. "Believe it or not, I care about you, Sasha. It just didn't make sense to me that he was cheating on you. I've seen you guys together, and after everything Ash told me—"

"Ah. There it is. Ash." The exhaustion of the past month and a half settled in my bones. "Listen, even if he wasn't cheating, he was still lying. I can't be a part of that."

Malcolm nodded as he sucked on a hard cinnamon candy. "I get that, but aren't you curious about what he's been up to?"

I scanned the photos, and they were just a bunch of Luca meeting with other rich assholes at bars, offices, restaurants. "Not really." I closed the folder and handed it back to Malcolm. "He's not my concern anymore."

"But—"

I stood up and flipped off the desk lamp. "No. Even after he came clean about the dangers associated with being with a rich motherfucker like him, I told him months ago I was all in. He was the one who decided he couldn't trust me, and I won't stay with someone who isn't 100% sure about me. I deserve my very own ride-or-die. Why would I expect more from my friends than I do the love of my life?"

Malcolm stood up and followed me out into the hall.

Unlocking the door, I let out a breath before turning around. The sadness in Malcolm's eyes gave me pause. He was honestly worried about me. With a shaky smile, I said, "If I'm honest with you, it doesn't matter what Luca's up to. If he were the one to tell me, it wouldn't've mattered. He could've killed a man, and I would've asked if he needed help burying the body. That's how much I loved him, and that's how much I've lost."

Malcolm's lips parted, but I covered his mouth before he could say another word. "I mean it. Let it go."

A hot puff of breath against my palm was his only response.

Pulling my hand away, I smiled. "Great, now get the hell out of here."

The promise of a Mexican vacation is all that kept me moving forward.

FOURTEEN

The closer we got to the gala, the more my hands trembled.

"Sasha, are you going to be okay?" Scott's baby blues kept glancing at me from the driver's seat. "I can turn this car around, and we can forget this whole thing. Although I think it might be a crime for this much sexy not to show up." He suggestively winked at me as he gestured between us. I let out a shaky laugh, and he grabbed my hand.

"No. Luca isn't going to ruin our victory lap."

Scott valeted the car, and we walked into the lobby arm in arm.

"Wow. We're fucking good." Scott's eyes took in every detail we'd agonized over. I'd never worked so closely with a vendor. Without Scott, this contract would have been impossible. I owed a lot to the goofball on my arm.

"Shhh. Rule 101 of rich people is to keep the 'fucking' under wraps."

Scott nodded his head. "Noted." A tray of mini something or other breezed right past us. "Let's get our hands on some of those apps. I'm still hungry."

"Even after that steak?" I took a step away and looked him up and down. "Where do you put it all?"

Wrapping his arm around my shoulder, Scott grinned down at me. "Play your cards right, and I'll show you later."

I shook my head and pushed him away. "Let's keep this professional, Adams."

Shooting me a sly smile, Scott laced his fingers through mine and led me toward the bar. His hand pulled away, only to rest on my lower back. I knew I should put an end to the familiarity, but Scott was so comforting, like my own little knight in hipster armor.

Pushing the "should's" from my mind, I leaned into his side.

"The lady will have a—"

"Gin and tonic."

Goosebumps exploded across my skin at the sound of Luca's voice. His presence begged me to look to the left, and with one glance, I regretted ever getting out of the car.

He was a fucking wet dream. All James Bond and shit in his tux. When my eyes finally met his, I saw it all—anger, hurt, exhaustion.

I struggled to come up with something to say as Scott maneuvered us so he stood directly in front of Luca and I was to the side. Extending his free hand, he tried to get Luca's attention. "Mr. Moretti, it's good to see you again."

When it became apparent that Luca had no intention of shaking his hand, let alone looking at him, Scott's hand dropped, and he turned toward me. "You good with a gin and tonic."

I nodded, my eyes held captive by Luca's glare.

Scott ordered his drink, his hand sliding from my back to around my waist. I appreciated the support because I was one second from melting into the beautiful marble floors.

"You came." Luca's words were breathy.

"I did."

Only then did Luca's gaze move from me to Scott. "With him."

I narrowed my eyes at his profile. "I don't see how that is any of your business, but yes, I came with Scott."

SASHA AND THE BUTCHER

My voice dripped with disdain, begging for a fight, but when Luca finally looked back at me, his eyes were filled with resignation.

As his plump lips parted, Nicki joined our happy little group.

"There you are! Your father wants you to make the welcome speech." Her slim fingers patted his chest as she wrapped her other hand around his arm.

Gripping my handbag with a force sure to leave finger marks in the beautiful fabric, I gave her a small smile. "Hello, Nicki."

"Sasha. Hello." She had the decency to pull her hands off Luca as she muttered something about him having five minutes. One last look of confusion at Scott, and she scampered off.

"You better get going. Wouldn't want to disappoint your father."

Finally, Scott handed me a drink, and I took a sip to fortify the bitch act I needed to get me through the night without becoming the girl crying in the bathroom. Luca watched me take another large sip through the tiny straw, his eyes never leaving my red lips. I could see the desire there, the longing.

Too fucking bad.

"I think Scott and I are going to go and find those little bacon-wrapped asparagus things we saw the waiters carrying around." I took two steps away, only to have a large, calloused hand grip my elbow. Scott continued walking, not noticing the big, worked-up goon holding me back.

"Sasha, please. Can we just talk?"

The threat of tears kept my eyes forward on Scott's disappearing back. "Are you going to tell me everything?"

His fingers flexed on my elbow as he inched near me. "You'll hate me if I do."

Taking a deep breath, I turned into his body. My chest was grazing his with every intake of air. Allowing my fingers to grip his lapels, I begged. "I hate you right now. What's there to lose? Please, just tell—"

"Luca!"

Based on Luca's tensing body, I didn't have to turn around to know it was his father. The change in his posture caused me to let go of his jacket. He was turning into that other Luca, that heartless man I didn't recognize.

"I'm sorry. I can't." Luca let go of me and took a slow step back. His face remained stoic, but his eyes were full of regret. In a hushed voice, he said, "I love you. Know that."

Then he was gone.

Body sagging, my hand landed on the bar for support. I was shaken and unsure if I could make it another minute in the richly decorated room. I downed the rest of my drink in a gulp, and the bartender asked if I wanted another. Waving him off, I shook my head. There was nothing behind that bar that could lighten the pressure on my chest. What I needed was fresh air and to get the hell out of there.

Walking through the crowd, I fought the urge to glance at the small platform set up by reception.

As the door was opened for me, my name came over the speaker: "Sasha Mitchell and her team did a wonderful job creating a posh, livable space that we at Moretti Properties believe will set a new standard for upscale residential living here in St. Louis City."

Luca's eyes never left mine as he spoke. After a few more thank yous, he lifted his glass, and the group all toasted to the future of Moretti Properties.

Using the noisy room as cover, I slipped out the front door. It wasn't long before Scott found me and drove us home. Without a word, Scott followed me into the apartment. I dropped my purse on the couch and set off for the kitchen.

"Sasha, I—"

"Stop. If you're going to stay, you can't talk about what just happened." I kept looking through the drink options available.

"But—"

Over my shoulder, I fixed him with my withering stare.

"Got it. My lips are sealed. What do you got to drink?"

Pursing my lips, I took inventory of my scant liquor cabinet. The breakup with Luca decimated my usually well-stocked reserves. "Uh, I have a little vodka and a little bourbon."

"You can have the vodka."

I slammed the bottle on the counter. For a second, I thought about grabbing shot glasses, but what would be the point?

Taking a long pull from the bottle, I eyed Scott. We'd gotten close, but why was he here? His eyes watered a little as he swallowed the brown liquor, and a pink blush covered his cheeks. Scott set the whiskey down and lifted his eyebrows. "Now what?"

I shrugged and took another pull. The vodka burned less as my body grew accustomed to the poison.

"Do you want to watch something?"

I shook my head.

Scott moved toward me, his body pressing me into the countertop without even touching me. The shine of leftover alcohol on his lips had me inching closer. His tongue darted out to lick away the moisture, and my hand gently settled on his arm. One more deep pull from the bottle as the clear liquid settled in my body, creating a false sense of warmth. For a minute, I pretended Scott was the reason for the heat in my belly. I'd never been one to lie to myself, but desperate times and all that jazz.

His worn hands were steady as he took the bottle from me and set it on the counter. "What do you want, Sasha?" He rested his palms on the edge of the granite on either side of me.

Smoothing my hands over his chest, I knew what I wanted, and he wasn't it. How I wished he was. I chewed on my lip, trying to focus on Scott and Scott alone, knowing there wasn't a chance in hell that would happen.

His gaze dropped to my mouth. A moment more of hesitation and Scott would make the choice for me. All I had to do was close my eyes and let the vodka trick me into feeling more than was there.

Closing my eyes, I held my breath and waited.

How many times had I done that before, Luca? Why couldn't I go back to that Sasha? The Sasha who conquered and got hers?

Scott's warm breath tickled my nose as he kissed the tip. The tenderness jolted me, and my eyes flew open. Extending my arms, I pushed Scott back.

"What are you doing?" The sharpness of my voice startled both of us.

Scott's warm hands slid down my arms, and he pressed my hands to his chest. His forehead wrinkled as he took in my struggle to get away from him. "I was just kissing you. What's wrong?"

Tearing my hands from his, I rounded the island to put some much-needed space between us. "That wasn't . . . That wasn't a—"

"Was I supposed to just fuck your mouth with my tongue, Sasha? Is that what you wanted?" He snorted out a breath as he tugged at his hair. "I'm sorry I wasn't—"

My hands gripped the countertop as a blush bloomed across my entire body. "No. I'm just fucked up, Scott." The swirl in the granite gave me somewhere to stare as I tried to climb out of the clusterfuck I'd caused. "Look, you're too good of a guy to use. You . . . you deserve more."

I messed with a bottle cap as Scott moved around the kitchen. He pulled me back against his chest and wrapped me in his lean arms. "Stop. You don't have to explain yourself." We both exhaled. I laid my arms over his, hugging them to my waist. Standing in my low-lit kitchen, we swayed back and forth until Scott started to laugh.

Leaning back, I peeked at him over my shoulder. "What's so funny?"

Kissing my cheek, he shook his head. "I'm not getting laid because I was too sweet. I need to rethink my approach."

A peel of laughter tore from my mouth as I bumped him away with my ass. "Rule 101 of heartbroken women. Just fuck the girl, no cutesy kissing shit."

He grabbed the whiskey, taking a big gulp before grabbing the bottle of vodka and heading toward the living room. "Noted."

And like that, Scott and I went back to our ridiculously unprofessional relationship.

A couple of hours later, Scott was passed out on my couch, and I was slipping into a silky negligee when a banging at the front door startled me from my nighttime routine. Trying to keep the late-night visitor from waking the entire building, I rushed to answer, passing an unconscious Scott snoring on the couch.

"Who is it?" My eyes darted back to my unconscious companion as nerves twisted my stomach.

"It's me."

The gravel in Luca's voice grated against my heart.

My hands smoothed down the door, stopping to hover over the deadbolt. "What do you want?"

"Let me in, Sasha."

A shiver shook my core at the command. My fingers rested on the lock. "Why?"

"Just let me in."

The vodka churned in my system, whispering encouragement. All I could think about was Scott asking me what I wanted.

Luca.

It would always be Luca.

Letting out the breath I'd been holding, I turned the lock and cracked the door. That was all the invitation Luca needed. He was in my apartment before I knew what was happening, and the door shut with a soft click.

For every step Luca took toward me, I took two back until I was trapped against the end of the couch. Wild eyes devoured every inch of my exposed skin as Luca's hands balled into fists at his sides.

While I was in a scrap of silk, Luca was still in his dress shirt and slacks, his neck the only skin exposed to my greedy eyes. We stood staring at each other, the alcohol causing me to sway into him while he leaned toward me. My heart begged to be next to his. The traitor didn't care about my pride.

Ryan took this opportunity to jump from the cat tree down onto the slumbering Scott. When my blond friend popped up from the couch, cursing my furry son, Luca finally looked away from my body.

"What the fuck is this?" Luca advanced on Scott, and I jumped in between the two.

"Sasha, what's going on? What's he doing here?" Scott leapt off the couch. The drunk fool tripped over the ottoman, trying to get his bearings.

The sound of Scott's voice set a fire under Luca's ass, and he sprung toward the confused goofball. Leaping onto Luca's back, I wrapped my arms around his neck. "Scott, I think it's time for you to head home!"

Luca tried to shake me off gently, but I hung on like a mold spore.

Straightening up, Scott was fighting a losing battle with gravity. I worried about him leaving, but he had a better chance with a ride-share than with a pissed-off Luca. "I'm not going to leave you with this guy. Look at him."

Scott's words stopped Luca's struggling. His hands gripped my thighs, and he sat on the couch, pinning me behind his back. "I would never hurt her. Please, just go."

Feeling Luca's body somewhat relax, I nodded to Scott. "I'm fine. Luca won't hurt me."

Scott frowned but nodded. When the front door closed, I released Luca and pushed him off the couch.

With a grunt, he landed on the floor.

"What the fuck are you doing here, Luca?"

He ran his long fingers through his hair, not even trying to stand up. "I needed to see you. I can't do this."

"Can't do what, Luca?" Pulling my feet under my ass, I leaned against the arm of the couch.

He leaned back on his palms, his eyes guarded as he looked at me. "I can't do this us apart thing. It's killing me."

Scooting to the edge of the cushion, I smelled the scotch on his breath. "You know the solution. Tell me the truth."

I blinked, and he was kneeling in front of me, unfolding my legs and moving between them. "I can't do that. Please, trust me."

The heat from his palms fueled the growing need in my belly. I tried to push him away, but my heart wasn't in it. "I can't trust you when you don't trust me, Luca. Don't you see that? Without trust, this is just make-believe, not a partnership. Fucking while playing at commitment. We could never be more than that."

Luca flinched. "You can't honestly mean that."

Dropping my gaze, I tried to beat back the pain in my chest from the further cheapening of my genuine love. Words begged to tumble from my lips, but I couldn't will them out.

His two large hands framed my face, forcing my eyes back to his watery, bloodshot gaze. "I love you more than anything in this world, more than myself."

Tears rolled down my cheeks. In a choked-out whisper, I begged, "Then tell me. Please."

"I can't," Luca croaked out as he dropped his hands. The finality in the air was suffocating. This was over. We were done.

He moved to stand, and my breathing became shallow as my heart raced. He was leaving. Panic seized my limbs, and I grabbed him, smashing my lips into his. Luca pulled me to the edge of the couch. His fingers dug into my thighs, forcing me to wrap around him. The soft material of his tux met my exposed pussy, sending a thrill through my core. He pressed into me, unyielding until we connected completely. His thickening arousal cradled between my legs made me slick with need. It was everything I'd been missing, everything I'd been starving for.

One hand grabbed his thick hair at the root, pulling it hard. The other tore at his shirt, buttons popping in every direction. I leaned away to shove away the open shirt, a sigh falling from my lips when I saw his chest. He was skinnier and less defined than when I last saw him. His gunshot scars served as an unpleasant reminder of why we were so miserable.

As if he knew where my thoughts were heading, he distracted me by squeezing up my body, his hungry eyes plotting his next move. There was no softness in his expression, just determination. My body thrummed with awareness of the predator between my legs, but I wasn't scared.

With a snarl, he tore the silk of my nightie from my body. I matched his aggression by pulling him to me by the shoulders, nails scoring him, sliding down his back, and leaving bright red trails. My teeth bit into the thick cords of muscle where his shoulder met his neck. I wanted to mark him one last time as mine.

My heart stuttered at the thought that this was it, but the adrenaline kept me moving, marking, and devouring.

Luca groaned, the sound vibrating through me. He pulled me from his neck with a tug of my long hair. The pain only made me more excited. When his lips met mine, he claimed every inch of my mouth with forceful thrusts of his tongue. His moans swallowed mine as he pinched and pulled my pebbled nipples.

I sunk my teeth into his bottom lip until I tasted blood. With a yelp, he pulled back, his tongue licking away the red droplets. The smile he gave me was a challenge. At that moment, we weren't lovers. We were adversaries, each trying to leave a mark that wouldn't fade when this moment was over.

He grabbed my ankle, opening me up to him completely. Bringing my calf to his lips, he gently bit into the fleshy muscle.

"Take off the kid gloves, Luca. I know you have it in you." I would not let him love me. He would fuck me, and then he would leave. That's how it had to be.

The smirk fell from his lips, and a slight frown took its place. Leaning back, I waited for him to make his choice. When his forehead smoothed, and his hand tightened on my leg, relief flooded me, and I knew I had him for one more night.

Luca stood up and unbuttoned his pants, letting them fall to the floor. "Turn around." My skin heated at the command as he quickly stepped out of his boxer briefs.

Standing, I moved around him and motioned for him to follow. "I have condoms in the bedroom."

His breath hitched, and for a split second, I wanted to turn around to apologize, but we were too far gone. There would be no softness tonight. I pulled the box of condoms out of the side table. I bought it when we broke up but hadn't opened it yet.

Luca flipped the light switch, shedding an unflattering glare on what was happening between us.

My body hid the shake of my hands as I opened the packaging, but it was enough that I saw it. I took a deep breath and turned to hand him the foil packet. His jaw twitched as his eyes tried to cut through to me. There was a plea there that I refused to acknowledge.

I had to do this.

Reaching out, I grabbed his hard length, pumping him until he was thrusting into my palm. Turning the full force of my green stare to his dark gaze, I muttered the two words that would put more distance between us. "Fuck me."

Luca thickly swallowed and gave a slight nod. "Turn around." This time, his voice held no fire, no excitement. I was killing him.

I bent over the edge of my bed, my face resting on the crisp, soft cotton. Jittery with anticipation, I listened to Luca's deep breathing. His giant hand came down hard against my ass cheek, and I jolted forward. Without time to brace myself, another swat came down on the other side. I moaned, my hands fisting the duvet.

"Is this what you want, Sasha?" Luca's voice was devoid of emotion.

I nodded. Luca's roughness excited me. I'd always appreciated it when he took a firm hand, and he knew that. The difference this time was the lack of silliness we'd always had in the bedroom. This time, there were no smiles. I didn't expect there would be for a long time.

His foot kicked mine further apart. I heard the foil rip before I felt him at my entrance. Luca drove into me with no preamble, punching the air from my chest. He gave me no time to adjust to him before he began to move furiously. Long, hard thrusts that inched my bed closer to the wall. Panting, I moaned as my pussy fluttered around him. Lifting my leg onto the bed, Luca entered me even deeper.

A hand came down on my ass, and I screamed out his name. Overwhelmed, I wanted him to stop but also to keep going.

Trying to focus on my release, I buried my face into the comforter, but Luca had other ideas. With my hair wrapped around his hand, he pulled my top half up, making me scramble to get my hands under me as he put a soul-scorching kiss on my lips.

Every move of his body served one purpose.

To brand me.

My body shook with the oncoming climax when Luca withdrew from me. I flopped down on the bed, panting, sweating, and confused. Before I could ask what he was doing, he flipped me onto my back in the middle of the bed.

Moving over me, he entered me as fiercely as before, only this time, his thrusts were slow, inching out only to slam back in. I met him stroke for stroke, tipping my hips to take him deeper, trying to close the impossible distance between us.

I dug my fingernails into his ass and held him to me. Luca groaned, gathering my hands in his and pressing them above my head.

The bed squeaked from our movements—the room filled with the sounds of our broken love.

Latching his mouth to my nipple, he sucked and nibbled until I was arching into him.

When his free hand found my clit, I came harder than I ever had. My limbs quaked, and tears streamed down my cheeks from the sheer intensity. Sweat covered every inch of my body as I slid against Luca.

Moments later, Luca came groaning my name as he laid a sweet kiss on my lips. He stayed buried in me as he kissed me, whispering words of love and adoration that only broke me further.

"Get out."

Pressing up on his hands, he gazed down at me, his eyes full of tears. I couldn't take it, so I focused on his neck and the darkening bruise where I'd bit him.

"Sasha."

I shook my head, so he grabbed my chin.

It wasn't until a tear fell on my nose that I looked at him.

"I love you, Sasha."

"I know."

FIFTEEN

"You should've told Axel to pick a different place," Ashley said for the hundredth time.

I couldn't tell if it was the chilly spring air or the glowing lights from Moretti's, but a shiver traveled down my spine.

"I'll be fine, Ash. We'll have dinner, finalize this partnership, and I'll be home with Ryan before anyone realizes the dreaded ex was at Moretti's."

Her small hand grabbed mine, and she squeezed. "Okay. I won't say it again."

Pausing at the door, Ashley spoke with the hostess.

As she showed us to a table at the back of the restaurant, all I could think about were rose petals on the floor and Luca's promises. Swallowing hard, I pushed back the tears that threatened to come. One year later, I still had Luca flashbacks.

My vision tunneled as we passed the kitchen door. I thought about how special I felt that first night. Course after course, Luca shared parts of himself with me. I pressed a hand against my chest, trying to ease the ache that thinking about him caused. It was nowhere close to the life-altering dread that turned my stomach the minute he left my apartment, but it still sucked.

When a waiter came barreling through the door, I snapped

back to reality. Ash gave me a pitiful smile, and I shook my head, letting out a heavy breath. I could do this. I could fight my memories.

Watching the door, I wondered how late the guys would be. Fifteen minutes later, Ashley was ordering wine as Axel and Scott arrived. The tardy assholes certainly knew how to make an entrance. Every head turned as the two men walked gracefully through the restaurant.

Scott was ridiculously handsome in a navy suit, patterned shirt, and pocket square. I loved a man who knew how to accessorize. The cheeky bastard had a wink and smile for every woman he passed, spending an extra beat on a little brunette sitting a table over from us. After getting the blush he was looking for, he happily pulled me from my chair and gave me a smooch on the lips.

I laughed and pushed him away. "What would the cutie over there think?"

Wrapping his arm around my waist, he peered over his shoulder at the blushing beauty. "Oh, she's still in."

Snorting, I glanced across the table at my best friend and her sometimes bed warmer. Axel looked every bit the lumberjack in a red flannel shirt and dark denim. Only Axel could walk into a Michelin-star restaurant ready to finalize a multi-million dollar deal, looking like he just chopped wood for the winter. I didn't miss the hunger in Ashley's eyes as they traveled over Axel's body. His full lips pulled into a smile, and he kissed her cheek, sitting beside her.

Scott's lips lingered by my ear. "Should we be worried that Ashley's going to eat Axel for dinner?"

"Leave them alone. At least someone's getting some." Slapping Scott's arm, he plopped down next to me, pulling Ashley's gaze away from her hulking focus.

"Well, if you two can refrain from ripping each other's clothes off, I have the contracts here." Scott patted his leather messenger bag.

"No promises." Ashley smiled, no embarrassment on her face. Truly, a woman of my own heart.

We all had a good laugh as the waiter returned with a bottle of wine, offering Ash a small amount to taste. After doing the whole swirl, smell, and taste deal, she nodded, and the waiter poured us all a glass.

Axel raised his and gave us all a toothy grin. "To the new SA Designs."

We all cheered and clinked glasses.

"I just can't wait to get into the new space." Ashley bounced in her seat, her hand grabbing mine. While she was excited, I was still in worry mode. Converting a warehouse into both work and office space looked easy on paper, but the build had proven to be one nightmare after another. Luckily, the end was in sight.

"Only one more month!" Scott slapped Axel's back and took another sip of wine.

"And only another million things to do." Axel returned Scott's pat, causing wine to dribble from Scott's lips.

Axel and I were the realists of this not-so-little endeavor, or as Ashley and Scott referred to us, Mom and Dad.

Ashley glared at Axel and grabbed her menu. "No need to be a downer, Ax."

"Sorry, shorty. Didn't mean to rain on your parade." Axel leaned in, resting his hand on the back of her chair.

Pleased with his apology, Ash perused the specials.

I snuck a peek across the table, and Axel's soft expression piqued my interest. With his eyes trained on Ashley's face, he smiled like a man in love. Looking between the two of them, I wondered if my friend felt the same.

"I want one of every app! And every dessert!" Ashley was in "everything is great and okay as long as we act like it" mode, and I was thankful for that.

Scott waved down the waiter and ordered enough appetizers to feed the restaurant. Once we all ordered our mains, Scott pulled out the contracts. With a dramatic flourish, he pulled out an expensive, fancy pen.

"Let's sign this thing!"

We all took turns jotting our John Hancocks.

I tried to come up with some sweet words to mark the occasion, but none seemed right. "So that's done."

A silence fell over the table as we all looked at each other. A slow smile pulled at our lips until we were all full-on smiling like lunatics. No words were needed. Our hands joined as we leaned into the table, moving closer to one another. It felt good to bask in this new chapter of my life—to look at my friends and know we were on the verge of something amazing.

"Excuse me."

A hand on my shoulder pulled me out of our silent love fest. When I looked up, I nearly shit my pants. Marco Moretti stood there, holding a bottle of champagne.

Snapping my mouth closed, I swallowed.

"Marco, how good to see you." A forced smile wavered on my face.

Smirking, he leaned down into my personal space. "Well, that's a big fucking lie." Turning to my friends, he gave them the Moretti smile I'd grown so fond of, one I never wanted to see again. "Champagne, compliments of the house."

Our waiter showed up with four champagne flutes, and Marco filled one at a time. He took forever, and his smug smile let me know he was aware of exactly how uncomfortable I was.

After what felt like a millennium, he nodded and told us to "enjoy" before walking away. I wanted to leave it at that, to forget Marco even existed, but I couldn't keep my eyes from following him to a table on the other side of the room.

If I thought seeing Marco made me sick, I was wrong. That was a simple cold compared to the full-on system shutdown that seized my body when I saw Luca sitting there, real as can be, and he wasn't alone.

Across from him sat Nicki Ricci. Beautiful, graceful, fucking

Nicki. As if that wasn't enough, an iceberg-sized diamond on her left ring finger sparkled in the candlelight. My lungs burned as I tried to take another breath. It was like my body had forgotten how to function. When air finally forced its way into my chest, I panted out the growing panic.

Completely unaware of my stare and subsequent meltdown, Nicki continued to eat.

Crushed, I looked back at Luca. When our eyes met, I saw nothing of the man I loved. His dark eyes were as hard as his five o'clock shadow-covered jaw. I received no softness. Only a head tilt in acknowledgment before he turned back to Nicki.

I couldn't pull my eyes from him and willed him to look at me again, but he stayed focused on the woman in front of him, telling an animated story. I shook with the desire to run, but my limbs couldn't move.

Sweat covered my palms as my hand tightened around the cold glass.

I left him. I. Left. Him. If he was engaged, it shouldn't matter to me. I shouldn't care.

But I fucking did.

"Sasha. Sasha!" Ashley's voice pulled me from my spiral. When I finally turned to her, her glare was burning into the side of Luca's head.

"I need to go to the restroom."

Her eyes snapped to me, the disgust evaporating. "Sure, I'll come with."

Shaking my head, I let her know I was okay.

On shaky feet, I made my way towards the bathrooms. Before I was out of earshot, I heard Ashley tell Axel that we should've gone somewhere else. The sadness in her voice hurt, and the confusion in Axel's made me feel guilty. He wanted to treat us to a nice dinner, not send me into an imploding episode.

Stumbling into the small room, I locked the door behind me. My shoulders curved under the weight of my heartache. The mirror offered me little comfort as my perfectly painted face suddenly looked hollow, my green eyes dull.

I busied my hands, wetting a paper towel and holding it to the back of my neck.

"Get it together, Sasha. You're a bad bitch. You're better than this. Do *not* let Luca ruin your night."

Pacing the tiny pink bathroom, I tried to pull myself together. I adjusted my boobs, making my cleavage even more enviable, and took a deep breath. Checking my appearance one more time, I unlocked the door.

Before I could get a foot across the threshold, I was pushed back into the room. With his back to me, Luca flipped the lock.

"You know this is kidnapping, right?"

His shoulders tensed, but he didn't turn around.

A minute passed without him saying or doing anything. "We just gonna hang out in a bathroom all night?"

Luca rested his hands against the door and shook his head, taking slow breaths like he was trying to calm down.

"If you're just going to stand there, can I leave? I have a table full of people waiting for me."

Nothing.

"Listen, asshole—" reaching my limit, I grabbed his shoulder to spin him around, "I—"

Luca turned, his hands landing on my shoulders, pushing me against the wall as he bellowed, "Just shut up!"

His dark eyes narrowed, his jaw twitching in agitation. In a softer voice, he said, "Just stop for a minute."

I nodded slowly. Luca's grip loosened, and one hand ran through his hair.

He tilted his head, trailing his other hand down my arm, and laced our fingers together. The gentle gesture was in complete opposition to the anger on his face. The warmth of his palm and the way our hands fit together reminded me just how dangerous he was to my resolve.

Shaking my head, I tried to pull my hand from his, but he held on tighter. "What are you doing, Luca?"

Our hands swung between us. "Honestly? I don't know. You make me a little crazy."

I fought the urge to smile at the memory of that night in the dressing room. The night he earned a date.

"I need to go. Ashley, Scott—"

"Yeah, I saw him." His fingers tightened. Disgust pulled at his lips as he pressed his body into mine.

"No! You're not doing this when little Ms. Perfect is out there sporting the rock of the century." I tried to push him away, only to get my hands stuck between us.

Luca shook his head. "What does that have to do with anything?" Disbelief must have shown on my face because Luca quickly added, "Oh, you think her and me? No, no, no! She's engaged to one of my accountants, Aldo. We're just having a working dinner."

As soon as my body relaxed in relief, I tensed. I shouldn't have cared. I shouldn't have been relieved that he wasn't engaged. But I fucking was.

"Oh."

Luca's plump lips twitched into a cautious smile. "You were jealous?"

"No, I just . . ." My eyes dropped to where my hands sat pinned between our chests. One breath and I looked back into his impossibly dark eyes. "I just don't like hypocrisy."

"Oh, that's it." His long fingers caressed the side of my face, and it felt like fire licking at my skin. "It had nothing to do with you still having feelings for me."

Violently shaking him from me, I moved against the countertop. "Fuck you, Luca! The only feelings I have for you now are disappointment and annoyance."

Instead of being the verbal hit I wanted, my words gave Luca confidence. Crowding my space again, he was every bit the business tycoon the world knew him as.

"You can't be disappointed without caring." Bending a little to meet me eye to eye, he cupped my cheeks in his palms. "I still love you, Sasha. Tell me you still love me."

I didn't say a word. Luca's fingers slid into my hair and tightened. "Say you love me." His Adam's apple bobbed. "Please." Raw emotion poured from Luca's eyes. Every day of hurt, every hour of longing, every minute of missing suffocated us. He was breaking me.

For a moment, I allowed myself to revel in his hands on me, in his eyes looking at me, but I knew nothing had changed. "It doesn't matter if I love you."

"But it does!" Luca's face twisted with frustration. "All that matters is that we love each other."

The honesty in his voice made my body weak. Grabbing his forearms, I tried to anchor myself. "You know that's not true. You—"

His lips silenced my words. Leaning back, I tried to break the kiss, but his fingers twisted in my hair kept me in place.

When I didn't kiss him back, he nibbled a trail to my ear and then down my neck.

"Luca, you have to stop."

Pulling back, he looked me dead in the eyes. "No, you have to stop. You've made us miserable for a year. Aren't you tired of this?"

"I'm not miserable." Luca laughed, making me more adamant. "I'm not! I have my friends, my business, my distractions. I'm fine."

Dark, bottomless eyes regarded me. "Yeah, your distractions. Are you honestly trying to say that those random fucks come close to what we had?" Luca hoisted me up on the countertop, sliding the hem of my tight dress up. "How I made you feel."

My body instantly heated as he stepped between my legs, but my brain was sounding the alarms. "Luca, I . . ."

Strong fingers dug into my ass, pulling me flush to his body.

His grip was firm and sure. With no space between us, all I could do was breathe him in.

When his lips touched mine again, I was done fighting. Sure, I knew I would regret everything, but a part of me knew I would regret not kissing him more. I'd been starving for him for a year.

Breaking our kiss, I grabbed his chin. "This is it, Luca. No more after this."

He sighed. "Fine, whatever you say."

I stopped him as he tried to kiss me. "No. I mean it. After this, if you see me out, you don't follow me to get me alone. You don't approach me." I ran my fingers gently over his jaw.

"Do you think this is the first time I've seen you in the past year?" I thought over our time apart, unable to think of a single time we would've been in the same place. "St. Louis isn't that big of a city. I've seen you, and I've avoided you. Tonight, I just couldn't."

"Oh."

Shaking his head, he gripped me harder. "You know what? Fine. I'll pretend you never existed. Happy?" My body shrank under his glare.

"Ecstatic." All I could think was, "be careful what you wish for."

Without further ado, Luca's lips crashed into mine, his hands exploring the curves he knew better than anyone.

My palms flattened down his chest and abdomen until I hit his belt. Luca thrust his hips toward me, tilting to give me easier access.

In no time at all, I had his pants and boxer briefs pushed to his knees and was stroking his hardening cock. I buried my smile in his shoulder as he moaned against my throat. Working him until my thumb brushed over a bead of moisture, I marveled at how right he felt in my hand.

Luca took a step back to pull down my panties, the cold countertop causing me to jump. "Fuck, that's cold."

He smiled, reaching for his wallet. As he rolled the condom

on, he never made eye contact, the smile falling from his lips. With the way he scowled, it was like that condom was every person I'd fucked in the last year.

Guilt I didn't want to accept crept in, making my chest feel heavy. Somewhere in me, I felt like I'd betrayed Luca. There's no reasoning with my heart, no explaining the whys, only that I've kept us from what is ours, gave away what should've been Luca's.

"What'd your erection ever do to you?"

Shaking his head, he looked at me with a strained smile.

Silently, he moved between my legs, easily sliding into me. My green eyes never left his dark stare. Every thrust was silently punctuated with the words I knew he wanted to hear me say, wanted to say again.

I. Thrust. Love. Thrust. You. Thrust.

I wondered when this fucking love would die. When would be enough? The lust driving me a moment ago was gone. My body was finally getting the message. Luca's thumb brushed my cheek, wiping away a tear. My breath caught with the sweet kiss he placed on my lips.

Arousal was the last thing on my mind. I prayed for him to come so I could leave and fall apart alone.

Moving his thumb from my face to where our bodies joined, he rubbed my clit slowly. The determination on his face let me know he refused to come before me. Our chests brushed together with labor breaths while he worked his hips and thumb to set my body on fire.

Closing my eyes, I tried to remove Luca from the equation and enjoy what he was doing to my body, but one whiff of cologne, and I couldn't help but open my eyes and look at him.

"I don't think I'm going to come, Luca. I—Just finish."

His body stopped moving. In a strained voice, he said, "I'm sorry, Sasha." Pulling out, he tossed the condom and turned his back to me, his broad shoulders moving up and down. "I just thought, maybe, I don't know. Maybe enough time had passed. I was wrong." When he turned around, his face was blank. "Let's just get back to our dinners."

He waited for me to slip my panties back up and fix myself in the mirror. The silence was crushing as his eyes observed my every move. I wondered if this would be the last time we would ever be this close again, and I hated the fact that I cared.

Unlocking the door, Luca led the way back to the dining area.

As soon as we both made it past the first tables, loud gunshots sounded. Luca pushed me down, his enormous body crushing me. More shots flew through the window, and his torso jerked erratically.

"Are you okay?" I shouted.

Luca's eyes glazed over as his hand cupped my cheek, a small smile on his lips. "I'm—"

His eyes fluttered closed, and his body went limp on top of me.

"Luca!" I wrapped my arms around him, my fingers landing in hot, sticky liquid.

The squealing of tires and the shouts of the restaurant patrons were barely audible next to the buzzing in my ears as Luca's breathing slowed to a stop.

SIXTEEN

"You're fucking high if you think I'm not getting in the back of that ambulance, Marco!"

His jaw flexed as he stared me down. I kept my bloody hands from wiping away the tears that blurred my vision, as they still shook from anger, from fear, hell, from the desire to wring Marco's neck.

After the medics gently removed Luca from my body, they revived him and got him on a stretcher. All that was left was getting him to the hospital.

"You're not his wife. You're not family, so you're not going, Red!"

Marco turned on his heel and jumped into the back of the ambulance. I took a step, and Ashley grabbed my arm. "Come on, Sasha. I'll drive you there."

The taillights disappeared around the corner before I yanked my elbow from Ash's grasp and ran to her car. The ride to the hospital was silent. For the second time, I was heading to the hospital because Luca was fucking shot.

Marco's words ran through my mind. I wasn't Luca's wife, but when he said it, my whole body rebelled. Luca belonged to me! I should've been the one holding his hand, telling him every-thing would be okay, promising that I'd be there.

Instead, I sat shotgun in a Prius, hoping we didn't hit too many red lights.

Ashley dropped me at the front doors, saying something about parking and being right up. The smell of antiseptic hit my nose, and it transported me back to the last time I rushed to the hospital, wondering what the hell Luca had done.

I didn't listen to the nurse's directions but eventually stum-bled upon the Moretti clan in the emergency waiting room.

"Sasha!" Dante's small body smacked into my legs. I held my hands up to avoid touching him with crusted blood.

"Hey, buddy." His big brown eyes, so much like Luca's, were ringed in red, and he was wearing the *Star Wars* pajamas I bought him for his birthday. He cried as he fisted my dress tightly.

Looking up for some help, or at the very least some hand sani-tizer so I could comfort my little guy, I locked eyes with Luca's mom. Her black hair was haphazardly up in a bun, and instead of her usually tailored outfit, she wore yoga pants and a hoodie. Rosa's eyes were puffy and her skin red and splotchy, but she mustered up a smile for me as she came to claim her sobbing grandson.

"Come on, sweetheart, Sasha needs to get cleaned up, and then you can visit with her." She looked at me for permission, and I nodded.

I found the floor's bathroom and tried to get all the blood off my skin. In a fit of stubbornness, I refused to clean up at the restaurant. I was too concerned about getting in the back of that fucking ambulance. My reflection let me know that was the wrong choice.

Specs of blood covered my entire body and face, staining my arms and hands pink even after vigorous scrubbing. The only saving grace of the whole debacle was that the black dress I wore hid the blood drying against my skin.

Instead of crying or getting sick, the blood made me angry.

Every speck of Luca's blood on my face only reinforced the desire to find these assholes and end them. I'd never been a violent person, never even hit another human, but that night, I could've murdered a man and been cool to brunch the next morning.

Taking emergency makeup wipes from my purse, I cleaned my face and pulled my long hair into a ponytail. A little less bloody, I joined the ever-growing number of Morettis in the waiting room.

As soon as my ass hit the plastic seat, Dante climbed into my lap. Putting a blanket between us, I wrapped my arms around him, nuzzling him under my chin. Rosa came and took the chair next to me.

"How are you?" Her brown eyes shone with tears.

"I'm okay. How's Luca? At the restaurant, he . . ." I glanced down at Dante and found him staring right at me. "He had to be revived."

Nodding, Rosa grabbed my hand. "They rushed him into surgery as soon as they got here. We should know more soon."

Adriana ran into the waiting room and scooped Dante into her arms, grunting with the effort. Dante was a tall eight-year-old, something I'm sure he got from his father, as his mother barely managed his weight.

With a quick hello to me, Adriana focused on her mother-in-law. "Oh, Rosa, I'm so sorry I couldn't come sooner."

"It's okay, dear."

As Rosa filled Adriana in on the little we knew, Mr. Moretti and Marco walked in. Both men immediately spotted me, but while Mr. Moretti scowled, Marco bit back a smile.

"Rosa, come here."

Mrs. Moretti rolled her eyes but gracefully went to her husband. Pulling her to his chest, he closed his eyes and took a deep breath. When his lids opened, there was less fire there than before. Well, that is, until he looked at me.

"What's she doing here?"

Rosa patted his chest. "Dante, come on. She was there at the restaurant."

"And?" His black eyes never left me.

"She practically fought me to get into the ambulance," Marco added with that same irritating smirk from the restaurant.

"Why would she do that?"

Taking a step back, Rosa looked between her husband and me. "Because she loves him, you—" she then proceeded to light his ass up in Italian.

Adriana laughed but covered her mouth, and Marco moved to stand near us, placing his hand on the small of Adriana's back. The tips of her ears turned red, and she refused to make eye contact with me.

Interesting.

"Sasha, can I have a word?" Mr. Moretti's deep baritone pulled my attention away from the cozy pair.

"Uh, Sure."

I followed him down a few halls before he stopped. When he finally fixed me with his stare, I wanted to run away. Luca's hardass face was nothing compared to his father's. This right here was why this man had power. He demanded it.

"Why are you here?"

"Luca was shot."

He sighed. "Yes, I know. But why are *you* here? Last I checked, you ran out on him."

"I did—"

"You did. You broke my son. So again, I ask. Why are you here? Are you planning an encore?"

"No. I just wanted to make sure he was okay. I care about him."

A derisive snort in my direction let me know how the rest of this conversation would go.' Mr. Moretti took two giant steps forward, pinning me to the wall. I tried to sidestep him, only to have him grab my arms violently. "Listen, Ms. Mitchell. You're not welcome here. I want you to say your goodbyes to my wife and Adriana, then leave. Do not come back. Do not call my son. Disappear. You got me?"

When I didn't respond, he shook me, and my teeth clattered from the force. "Understand?"

I nodded—anything to get him to let me go.

"Good."

Without another word, he left me scared in the hallway. Shaking my sore arms, I tried to compose myself. That was the scariest fucking thing I'd ever experienced. Well, besides the drive-by.

I eyed the tender skin Mr. Moretti had left behind. Pressing my fingers into the red flesh, I found it hard to believe what just happened. Regular people don't get violent and intimidate folks. That's not normal.

Slowly, I wandered back to the waiting room, wiping away my tears and taking calming breaths. Turning the corner, I pulled my lips into a small smile.

Fake it till you make it, or whatever.

Mr. Moretti's glare followed me as I walked through the room. The hairs on the back of my neck stood on end, and it took everything in me to keep my shoulders from curving under the pressure. My gut screamed to run, not bother with the goodbyes, but I knew that would only put me under more scrutiny.

When Rosa looked up at me, her eyebrows drew together. "Honey, are you okay?"

I guess my smile didn't fool her. Shit.

"Uh, yeah." Pressing my hands down the drying blood on my dress, I grimaced. "I think I'm going to head home and change. You can't see it, but this dress is pretty much soaked."

Rosa tilted her head, disbelief etched into her features, but she nodded. "Okay. You be safe, and we'll see you in the morning?"

I managed a weak smile. "You bet."

Dante was fast asleep in Adriana's arms, so I gave her a quick wave and asked her to call me with any updates.

Ashley walked into the hospital as I made it to the lobby. "You wouldn't believe how full the parking garage was. I guess it is a full moon."

Of all her quirks, her obsession with the moon cycle was one of the more bizarre. I once asked her if she believed in astrology, and she told me that it was just a bunch of nonsense. Classic Gemini.

"We're going."

I passed right by her and out the door. It took a minute before she caught up and started leading me to her car.

"What happened? I thought we were in for the midnight vigil. Is Luca okay?"

"I don't know." I pulled at the drying fabric, anxious to get it off.

Ash grabbed my arm, tugging me to an abrupt stop. "What happened, Sasha? You couldn't get here fast enough, and now you're running away like your ass is on fire. What happened in the twenty minutes you've been in there?"

Looking anywhere but in her eyes, I stayed silent. Her tiny fingers dug into my already bruising arm, and I winced, jerking out of her hold.

"What the hell?" All five feet, four inches of Ashley were tense and ready for battle. "What. Happened?" Her dark eyes flashed dangerously.

"Can we just get to the car? I need to get out of this dress." I tugged at the fabric, blinking back tears.

Ash frowned, her mouth parting, then snapping shut. With a tight nod, she started walking again.

It wasn't until her tiny Prius had pulled out of the parking garage that Ashley spoke. Her voice came out rough like she was holding back tears. "Did Luca die?"

"No. He hasn't. He's in surgery."

Blowing out a breath, Ashley shook out her hand. "Okay, that's good. So, what had you so shaken?"

"Mr. Moretti."

I watched the city lights go by, wondering what I was supposed to do.

"Okay?"

"He's scary, Ash. Like violent, threatening scary." We stopped at a red light, and Ashley turned toward me, her eyes demanding I continue. "He told me to leave, not to come back, and not to talk to Luca. Then he grabbed me and shook me. All while we were in some empty hallway alone. I was legit scared he was going to hit me." I turned away from Ash and faced the road. "What the hell am I supposed to do with that?"

"You tell Luca!" The light turned green, and I motioned for her to drive. "Sorry." She gestured to the car behind her. "I don't think he would appreciate his dad manhandling you. And you know what? Fuck that guy."

The farther we got from the hospital, the tighter my chest felt. I didn't have a billionaire trying to murder me with his eyes, but I should have been there with Luca.

Ashley's hand squeezed mine. "Are you okay?"

"I don't know what I'll do if he dies. I . . . I . . ." I shook my head as tears started to roll down my cheeks.

"You love him."

Hiccupping a laugh, I shook my head. "If I do, I'm not going to tell you before I tell him."

"Good girl."

Around four in the morning, I got a text from Adriana saying Luca was out of surgery and stable.

I jumped out of bed, got dressed, pulled my hair into a bun, and ran out the door.

The waiting room was as packed as it had been when I left. One pair of fierce, dark eyes bore into me like I was a plague coming to take down the entire family.

Lucky for me, a certain eight-year-old had my back. "Sasha! Uncle Luca is going to be okay!" Dante danced around, holding a glazed donut in his hand.

"That's awesome. Is he awake yet?"

He shook his head and ran off, leaving me with his grand-parents.

"He's all hopped up on sugar. Today's going to be a rough one." Rosa's laugh turned into a yawn. "Come sit. They expect him to wake up any minute now."

"Okay."

I gave Mr. Moretti a wide berth and sat on Rosa's right. Immediately, she grabbed my hand and patted it with the other. "You know, you're good for my Luca. You're strong, smart, and don't let him give you any shit. Why can't you two just make it work?"

I jerked my head back, trying to catch Rosa's gaze. Instead, I locked eyes with Mr. Moretti's glare. "I can't live with secrets, Mrs. Moretti, and Luca can't live without them."

"But you love him?" Her voice was full of emotion.

"I do." I stuttered out, my eyes never wavering from Mr. Moretti.

Patting my leg, she sat up. "Then it'll work itself out. I'm going to check with the doctors."

Marco and Rosa passed each other, and he handed her a cup of coffee before dropping into her now vacant seat.

"So, you're back?" He stretched his long legs out and threw his folded arms behind his head. His eyes shut like he was settling in for a nap.

"Obviously."

Marco grunted. "I guess we're stuck with you then?" A smile graced his lips, but his eyes stayed closed.

"Guess so."

Mr. Moretti opened his mouth to say something, but Rosa flew into the waiting room with a doctor. "He's awake! Come, Dante!"

The worried parents followed the doctor, leaving Marco and me alone. I fidgeted with my baggy shirt, well, Luca's baggy shirt. Maybe I should've put more effort into my appearance if this was going to be the first time I said I love you in a year.

"You look fine. Stop fussing." Marco watched me with one eye open.

A blush covered my face. I was acting like a fucking lovesick fool. "I'm just a bit of a mess right now. You know?"

Adriana walked in carrying a zonked-out Dante, and Marco's gaze immediately fell on the pair. "Yeah, I get that."

The four of us sat in tense silence for about half an hour before Luca's parents returned. Rosa's cheeks were red and tear-stained, but she was smiling. "Sasha, honey, Luca wants to see you."

I turned to Adriana with wide eyes. Never in a million years did I expect to get in that room so soon. Adriana gave me a big smile and a thumbs up. Marco laughed and shooed me away.

Squeezing past Mr. Moretti, he breathed in my ear, "Don't forget what I said."

Chills ran through me, but I eased past him. My desire to see Luca alive and well outweighed any fear of the promises lurking in his icy stare. A doctor motioned toward a door, and I took a deep breath.

There Luca was, hooked up to a million machines and looking pale and all wrong. His dark hair was in every direction, and his beard, which just hours ago rubbed against me, made him look even more haggard.

"Sasha." His voice croaked out in disbelief. Greedy eyes traced my body as if he thought he would never see me again.

"In the flesh." I shuffled to the chair next to his bed. Gently, I picked up his hand and squeezed it between mine, dropping small kisses on his knuckles. Closing my eyes to gather my thoughts, I sighed in relief. "God, Luca. I was so scared." When he didn't say anything, I opened my eyes and looked at him. Tears welled in his eyes as his teeth sunk into his bottom lip. "What's wrong? Do I need to call a doctor?"

I tried to drop his hand to stand up, but his fingers gripped mine, keeping me in place. "No, I just can't believe you're here."

He laughed and hiccupped. "Why are you here?"

Nodding, I understood this must confuse him. I shocked myself by how much had changed for me in the last twelve hours. "When I saw you lying there, bleeding, something clicked for me." I scooted the chair closer to the bed, closing as much distance as possible between us. "I realized I wouldn't be able to live knowing you were gone, that I hadn't been living since you've been gone. I love you, Luca. I never stopped. I don't think I ever will."

Ugly sobs tore through Luca as he covered my hand in kisses. But he didn't say anything. As the minutes went by without him saying a word, panic settled in my stomach. "Uh, this is where you'd usually say something."

Luca wiped his eyes with the back of the hand not hooked up to IVs. "I love you too, Sasha, but you know that."

A cautious smile spread across my face. "I want to be with you, Luca. Secrets, whatever. I know you'll eventually share it all with me. I'm not happy about it, but hopefully, you'll see I'm here, no matter what, and will open up."

Tension filled the small space between us, and Luca set my hand down. "Sasha, I don't think—"

Folding my hands together on the bed, I sat up straighter. "No. You can't be—"

"I am. If tonight taught me anything, it's that you have no business being in my world. What if you were the one that got shot?" Tears continued to fall down Luca's cheeks.

"But I wasn't! You saved me, Luca!"

"And I would do it over and over, but what if I'm not there? I wouldn't survive if you got hurt because of me. I love you too much."

"I love you too!" Jumping up from the chair, I started pacing the room. This wasn't going the way I imagined. I would say I love you, and he would say I love you too, then I'd nurse him back to health, and we would live happily ever after.

"I know, baby, but like you said, it's not enough. Love isn't enough. You're not safe with me, and I won't put you in danger."

"Oh, fuck you! Don't use my words against me. I just told you that I was wrong. How can you do this?" My hands clawed at my chest, pulling on the shirt like I could get to my splitting heart.

Full-on sobs racked Luca's body. "Baby, I don't want to, but you're my number one priority."

I trembled with anger. If he weren't lying in a hospital bed, I would've thrown myself at him and forced him to submit. But as it was, the machines started to beep louder. Stepping to the end of the bed, I grabbed his toes. "Please don't do this. Please."

Luca wiped his eyes and shook his head. "I have to. I love you, Sasha Mitchell. I always will, but you have to be safe. Please go."

Ignoring his words, I moved to his side and gently grabbed his chin. Pressing my lips to his, I tried to convince him using the only language I had left. His free hand coiled in my hair, tugging strands from the messy ponytail. Desperation and love exploded between us, neither willing to stop until our lungs screamed for oxygen.

Well, that and a panicked nurse's shrill demand for us to stop.

Stammering and begging for Luca to change his mind, I fought the tight hold on my arms. The hospital staff ushered me from his bedside, slamming the door shut in my face.

Outside his hospital room, I slid down the wall, and my heart collapsed in on itself. I thought I'd felt pain before, but that was nothing to losing Luca, really losing him. All hope was gone. I didn't even try to hold back the tears and snot.

I'd never doubted Luca's love for me, and if love is why he was not with me, then I knew he would never break his word. I said love wasn't enough to stay together. But for Luca, love was enough to keep us apart.

SEVENTEEN

Three days.

For three days, I sat at home, eating my weight in cookies and ice cream and drinking enough vodka that my blood could get a vampire drunk.

My little pity party was broken up by Scott and Ashley showing up unannounced.

"Hey! Put me down!"

Scott laughed but kept walking toward the bathroom. Nausea rolled my stomach, so I tried to focus on a fixed spot, but I bounced up and down with each step. His shoulder jammed in my stomach, pushing up my little feast with every jostle.

"How the fuck are you carrying me, beanpole?"

"Wow, I don't think I like this, Sasha." Hurt laced his voice, but the smile on his face kept me from taking him too seriously. "For your information, I lift weights. If you'd ever given me a go, I think you would've been surprised by just how much I'm capable of."

"Good for you. Now put me down, asshole."

"Gladly." Entering the bathroom, he sat me in the bathtub.

I scrambled up to my knees, but Ashley was already there. Cold water blasted me in the face, waking me up.

Sputtering water, I glared at my two bitch-ass best friends as they laughed at me.

"Go shower, and we'll fix you an actual meal."

"I've—"

"No, you haven't. The number of empty cookie boxes on the living room floor tells me you're in a full meltdown. I'm making eggs."

At the suggestion of soft, smooshy, maybe even a little runny eggs, I leaned out of the bathtub and grabbed the edge of the toilet. The previous night's regrets spewed from my mouth, leaving my stomach empty and my mouth disgusting. Chocolate was not meant to be vomited. I'd wronged the gods.

Scott rubbed my back and sighed. "Oh, Red. What have you done to yourself?"

Resting my cheek on the toilet, I looked at him through blurry eyes. "Self-medication or self-destruction. Who can really tell the difference?"

Scott helped me strip and set me up in the shower. He sat on the floor and waited for me to finish cleaning myself, mumbling something about how he wasn't going to be responsible for me passing out and drowning.

Such a drama queen.

After plying me with water, pain relievers, and five small bites of a veggie omelet, the three of us sat on the couch. My head rested in Ashley's lap, her manicured nails scratching my scalp, while my feet laid in Scott's lap, and he rubbed my calves.

"Okay, Sash, what happened?"

Tears flooded my eyes, and I curled in a little, only to have Scott pull my legs straight. "None of that, Red. No hiding from us."

I sighed and nodded. "I told him I loved him, and he told me to go."

"That's it?" Ashley screeched.

"Well, no."

Her fingers pulled at a knot in my hair.

"Ow!"

"Tell us what happened, or I'll find every knot."

"Fine! I told him how scared I was when I didn't know if he'd live. I told him I loved him and wanted to be with him no matter what. He said he loved me, but he's too scared of me getting hurt to be with me. He's a fucking coward."

My hands balled into fists near my chest. I was clearly moving on to a new stage of my grief—blinding, unyielding rage.

Scott squeezed my feet. "It sounds like he was shaken up. I mean, he was the only reason you weren't shot, Sasha. Maybe he has a point." I snarled at him, and his hands on my feet went still. "Or maybe I'm an asshole." He slid out from under my feet. "I'm going to grab another glass of water for you."

I'd never seen Scott move so quickly. Once he was gone, I noticed how quiet Ashley was. Pulling myself from her lap, I sat up. "What are you thinking, Ash?"

Her fingers fumbled with the stud in her ear. "I don't know. It's all so strange." I motioned for her to continue. Furrowing her brows, she turned her whole body toward me. "Okay, so when I was with Ben, I had a feeling something wasn't right, but I carried on like nothing was wrong, and look how that panned out."

"And you think Luca has something going on?"

Releasing a deep exhale, she threw her hands up. "I mean, people don't just get shot twice! I know he's rich, but you don't see other millionaires and billionaires out there getting shot up!"

"Okay." She was making sense. I was embarrassed I hadn't seen it before.

"And all the lying. If he wasn't cheating, then what the hell is so bad he couldn't tell you?"

Nodding, I glanced down at my hands. "After we broke up, Malcolm brought me a file on Luca, and I didn't want to see it." Ashley's only response was a deep intake of breath. "I thought it was just white-collar bullshit, you know? As far as I knew, he was shot in a mugging gone wrong. Now I'm wondering how bad things really are."

"As much as I hate to say it, maybe you should talk to Malcolm and get that file."

Ashley and Malcolm had a big falling out after he gave her some information about Axel. I didn't know the details, but apparently, it's a part of Axel he doesn't share with just anyone, and Ash was horrified that her friend tried to use it as ammunition against him.

"You wouldn't mind?"

"No. Not for this. Just promise me you'll be careful. Back off if it's dangerous, okay?"

I couldn't promise that, but I could nod, so I did.

Checking my phone for the hundredth time, I nearly chucked the damn thing against the wall of the dressing room. It had been three weeks since I called, texted, and emailed Malcolm, and he had yet to surface. I let out a growl and slammed my phone down.

Jazz's forehead wrinkled, but she never asked if I was okay. She knew I had enough people policing my emotions and didn't want to be another person I avoided. No, she had become one of the best distractions around.

After our near kiss, Jazz told me I was too dramatic to fuck with. She wasn't wrong. Luckily, her rules kept me from turning her into one of the dozen warm bodies I took up with over the past year. Instead, she became a close friend that I found insanely fuckable. Going out with Jazz guaranteed a good time with zero judgments.

"You going to leave that eyelash half on?"

Looking in the mirror, I sighed. I'd misapplied the right lash. "Well, shit. Thanks."

"Let's try to make it through this last number before you combust, 'kay?"

I pressed the eyelash down, making a fish face to focus. Blinking rapidly, I blew out a breath when the eyelash stayed put.

"Go fuck yourself, Jazzy." I gave her a dazzling smile, and she laughed. Blowing me a kiss, we lined up at the stage door.

The number went off without a hitch, and the crowd whistled and begged for more. One man in the front row caught my eye. Dark hair flopped over dark eyes, and for a moment, I thought my prayers had been answered and Luca was there.

That optimism only lasted until I was able to make out his cruel face sneering at me. My instincts were screaming that I was in danger. Standing in his crosshairs, I was vulnerable, and it wasn't because I was in only pasties and panties. This man was devouring me with his eyes. Never had a smile been so hard. My cheeks ached with the effort. Evie kept talking, promoting upcoming shows and the bar specials that were still going on.

With one final group flourish, I hurried off stage.

I waited until the last possible second to leave the dressing room, praying that the creep master would be long gone.

Of course, he wasn't.

Next to Chloe stood Mr. Menacing. He rubbed his chin and moved toward me.

Standing on my tiptoes, I searched the crowded bar for Jazz, only to find her wrapped around an equally tall and lean goddess.

I was on my own.

Quickly, I darted between people, trying to make my way to the side exit, but someone grabbed my elbow. Panicked, I tightened my grip on my stage bag and swung. It landed with a resounding thud against Malcolm's stomach.

"Shit. Sasha, it's just me." He coughed, looking at the bag in his hands. "What the fuck is in there?"

"About twenty pounds of makeup and thirty pounds of shoes. Why the fuck are you sneaking up and grabbing women in bars?"

He pulled the bag from me and threw it over his shoulder. "I shouted your name, but you were zoned out. Can we head back to your place? I have what you were looking for."

Throwing a quick peek over my shoulder, ole creepy bastard

was watching us with interest. I pulled Malcolm's free arm around my shoulder and moved toward the exit.

"There's a creep watching me. Ham this shit up."

Malcolm kissed the top of my head, glancing behind us. "Got 'em."

We quickly got in my car and drove away. Silence settled between us, making me antsy.

"So, how's it going?"

Malcolm raised his eyebrow at me. "Seven months, and you want to make small talk?"

Pushing my hair back, I rolled my eyes. "Fine, what do you have on Luca?"

"I think it's better if I can show you while I explain."

Stopped at a red light, I turned toward his smirking face. "Whatever."

Seven excruciatingly silent minutes later, and we were home. "Thank fuck! Come on, let's sit at the table."

Malcolm laid out a bunch of folders.

"All right, let me get this all out before you ask any questions. Okay?"

I nodded, plopping down in a chair.

Opening the first folder, Malcolm removed a series of photos and laid them out in front of me. Immediately, my eyes zeroed in on the creepy man from the show. "Hey, that's—"

"What did I say?" Malcolm said impatiently.

"Fine. Sorry. Please proceed." I slumped down in the chair, crossing my arms under my chest.

"Okay. I want to start with Luca's dad and then work our way to the present day. These five men are Dante Moretti's inner circle: Gabe Ricci, Alessandro Russo, Giuseppe Moretti, Antonio Bruno, and Stefano Romano, your shadow for the night. All these men were raised in the lifestyle."

I leaned forward and traced the pictures with my fingertips. "Gabe works with Luca now, and Giuseppe is his uncle." Frowning at Malcolm, I asked, "Lifestyle?"

"Organized crime. The Mafia, Sasha."

I laughed, but Malcolm's expression remained grave.

"But they own Moretti Properties and a million other businesses. Why would they be involved in the mob?"

"Money, power, thrill, take your pick, Sash. It's not uncommon for the rich to have illegal dealings. In this case, Dante Moretti built his legitimate empire on dirty money."

Shaking my head, I couldn't believe it.

"Let me show you."

Opening another folder, he set a stack of financial documents in front of me.

"I did a little digging on the family's financials."

Despite knowing all my interrupting was pissing him off, I couldn't help myself. "What exactly do you do for a living, Malcolm?"

Letting out a little laugh, he shook his head. "You never listen to me, do you?" I shrugged. "I'm a forensic accountant. My brother-in-law's a P.I., and I work with him sometimes." He pointed to the top page. "Now, let me explain what I found. After going through all the legit business and personal accounts, I found this account named DM. It has a steady stream of cryptocurrency deposited in and a few wires from accounts that I was able to trace. Nothing too exciting there. It wasn't until I dug into the wires and deposits from about a decade ago that I found something."

He flipped the pages, fanning them out in front of me. "Deposits from business owners and politicians, most notable to you, Senator Cooper."

"Beth's mom?"

Malcolm nodded. "The frequency of the wires suggests they were most likely payments for blackmail or extortion. And this isn't the only account like this."

"Fuck."

"Indeed."

"And Luca is what? The head honcho?"

"I believe they call it a Boss, maybe Don. The preference seems regional." I wanted to smack the smug smile off his face.

"How? I don't . . . It's hard to believe. I was expecting insider trading or something equally douchey."

Malcolm finally sat down, opened the last folder, and slid it my way. The picture on top was of a bloody crime scene. "What do you know about Dante Moretti, II?"

I scanned the photo, taking in the number of markers surrounding a body riddled with bullet holes. "Just that he was threatened and then killed. Luca made it sound like a stalker or something."

"A rival group killed Dante. I believe you know one of their associates, Dimitri Chronis."

"Sorry, what?"

"I don't know how you did it, but you've somehow involved yourself in an old-fashioned turf war."

"But Dimitri's just a harmless fuck boy."

"You're not too far off. He is just a small-time black market art dealer, but his big brother, Cy, is the one who called the hit on Dante. I suspect he's behind the shooting last month at Moretti's and is working his way up the ranks."

I opened my mouth to speak, but no words came out.

"When Dante died, Dante Sr. tapped Luca to take over. James said his cousin Marco was vying for the spot, but Dante Sr. wanted his boy to take it."

"So what kind of shit is Luca involved in?"

"That's where it gets interesting. From what I can see, he mainly focuses on legitimate businesses. It's only in the last two years that he's had a hand in the illegal side of the family. He relies on Marco to be the heavy, but they run the whole gamut of shit. Blackmail, extortion, gambling, guns, drugs, sex work, pretty much what you'd expect."

"Why didn't you tell me about this shit last year?"

"Because I didn't dig this deep. Everything I saw was white-collar and not that dangerous. I thought you'd want to know that your boyfriend could do time, but I had no idea it was this serious or dangerous. I'm sorry I didn't do a thorough job last time around, but Luca is not who you thought he was."

"He's a bad guy. He's a fucking criminal." The words were ash in my mouth.

"Yep."

"And I should leave this all be. Forget him." A sharp pain stabbed behind my eye.

"Absolutely."

I started shoving all the pictures and documents back into the folders. "Well, thanks for this. Can I keep these?"

"Sure."

Stacking the folders, I laid my hand on top of them and dropped my chin to my chest. Deep breaths couldn't calm me. My sweet Luca was a fucking criminal. He'd probably killed people or, at the very least, hurt someone.

Suddenly, all the scars made sense. He was a part of a violent world.

I tried to wrap my head around this new information but couldn't reconcile the man who so gently loved me with some hardened criminal. I needed to hear the truth from his lips. I would—

"Are you going to be okay?" Malcolm startled me out of my thoughts.

I shook my head.

"Do you want me to call Ashley and get her over here?"

Lifting my eyes, I shook my head. "I'll be okay. Ashley would only complicate things."

He nodded. We both knew how black-and-white things were to Ashley. Her world never operated in the gray.

For the first time that night, I really looked at Malcolm. By his usual standards, he was a mess. His edges were crisp, but his styled waves had grown out to curls, and a thick black beard covered his usually cleanly shaven, dark brown skin. Instead of a tailored suit, a simple t-shirt and dark jeans covered his unbelievable six-seven frame. The man was still unbelievably attractive. His relaxed look was maybe sexier than his typical clean-cut style, but he looked exhausted and rumpled. His separation from Ashley was taking a toll.

"How long are you two going to fight?"

Shrugging, he pulled his phone from his pocket. "Until she answers my calls, I guess. I fucked up, but I really thought I was doing the right thing. I don't know, I just miss her."

We stood in the dining room silently while he scrolled through his phone.

"My Uber's here. Please be careful and don't do anything rash. Don't make me regret giving you this information."

"Yes, father."

He cracked a smile as he waved goodbye.

Against my better judgment, survival instincts, and all the logic in the world, I knew I needed to see how deep Luca was in this organized crime bullshit. I was about to be extremely reckless, and I could only blame it on the drive to know who exactly the man I desperately loved truly was.

EIGHTEEN

I sat in the corner of Sunrise for four consecutive mornings before Beth Cooper finally made an appearance. When we were together, she never started her day without a hipster-approved latte.

The barista called her name, and as she turned, her brown eyes widened when she saw me at what used to be "our table." Lacking her usual grace, she collected her coffee, looked toward the door, and then back at me.

Pulling my lips into my most inviting smile, I motioned for her to join me. Her eyes bounced back and forth, but eventually, she huffed and glided over to me.

"Morning, Beth."

"Sasha. To what do I owe the pleasure?" Beth stared down at her latte.

"Go ahead."

She sat on the edge of the chair across from me. "What?"

I rolled my eyes. "Take the picture. It's a crime to let good latte art go undocumented, right?"

A lovely blush covered Beth's cheeks as she gently set her mug down and snapped a couple of pictures. "You always thought these pictures were corny."

She's not wrong.

I glanced out the window at a Prius trying to parallel park while cars zoomed around them. The Grove didn't have much traffic, but it could get hairy when spots were few and far between. Sighing, I turned back to her. "That never stopped you before. Why would it stop you now?"

Beth smiled and finally took a sip of her drink. She closed her eyes, her long lashes kissing her cheeks, and for a second, I was looking at the girl who stole my heart. After a deep breath, she opened her eyes and stared at me.

When it became clear she wasn't going to speak, I did. "Right. How've you been?"

Raising one eyebrow, Beth took another sip and said nothing.

"Fine. I guess I'll get to the point. What do you know about the Morettis?"

Her gaze fell to the table, and she shrugged.

Leaning closer, I dropped my voice to barely a whisper. "What do you know about your mom wiring money monthly to an offshore account in their name?"

That got her attention.

"What do you mean? That was supposed to—" Beth shook her head and took a big gulp of coffee, burning her mouth. She fanned her tongue, and I nudged my water over to her.

As she gulped down the entire glass, I continued. "Supposed to what?"

Shaking her head, she checked her watch. "Nothing Sasha. Look, I gotta go."

As she stood to leave, I caught her hand. "Please, Beth, I need to know."

She glanced at the door but slowly lowered back down to her seat. We sat in silence for a few minutes before Beth finally spoke. "My mom's a senator."

"Right?"

"She has a secret that could ruin her career." She pursed her lips.

"Okay?"

"She pays for silence."

A little irritated, I snapped, "Well, I could've guessed all of that." I ran a hand through my hair, blowing out a breath. "I don't know what I expected. I guess your confirmation is enough."

Grabbing my hand, she laced our fingers. "I don't know what you're looking for, but I can tell you I didn't know that the Morettis were the ones blackmailing my mom. If I did, I would've said something while you were with that piece of shit."

Heat rose to my cheeks. I was trying to figure out how all this worked, and who knew—not be treated like a fool.

"Baby." her other hand closed around mine, "I'm so sorry. At least you're done with him, right?" She tried to lure me into a false sense of comfort with a pretty smile. Drawing my hand to her lips, she placed a small kiss on my knuckles.

Uncomfortable and disappointed, I gently pulled my hand away. "Thanks. I need to get going. I appreciate your help."

Gathering my bag, I tried to walk around Beth, only for her to stand in my way.

"Sasha, are you okay?" She skimmed her hands down the outsides of my arms. "Has he threatened you? I can get my mom—"

"What? No! I'm trying to figure out what the hell he's been hiding from me all this time. He would never hurt me, at least not like that."

A deep frown pulled her dark eyebrows together. "You're defending him?"

"No—I don't know. This is just so different from the guy I knew."

Her fingers dug into my skin, and she took a step closer, pressing herself against me. "Don't be that girl, Sasha. He's a dangerous criminal. You need to stay away from him. You're too smart to let this monster pull the wool over your eyes."

"No one's fooling me anymore. My eyes are wide open." I peeled her hands from my arms and stepped around her. Leaving

Rise, I wiped my clammy hands on my sleeves and hugged myself. Even after confirmation that Senator Cooper pays quiet money and that Luca and his family are most likely responsible for it, I still couldn't stomach the word criminal and Luca being used in the same breath.

I was pathetic.

—————

A few days later, I was walking up to my apartment after a late night at the office when I spotted a familiar figure walking down the block.

I stumbled on a crack in the sidewalk but managed to right my steps. My heartbeat thumped in my ears seeing Pete on the other side of the street. Taking a deep breath to steady my shaking hands, I unlocked the door and stepped inside. As soon as the door shut, I ran to the window and cracked the blinds. Pete stood in the shadows of the alley until he turned and walked down the street, passing under a few street lights. He was on the phone as he slipped into a nondescript sedan.

On impulse, I snagged my keys and raced to the car. Huffing and puffing, I contemplated whether I should actually follow Pete. It was unbelievable, but as his taillights lit up, I turned the key in the ignition.

I was doing this. I was this self-destructive.

Like any good tail, I let him get to the stop sign before I pulled onto the street. My pulse raced as I followed him for twenty minutes through the center of South City.

I left the radio off, so the only sounds in the car were my continuous mumbling of "Where are you going?" and my stomach growling. The hunger for food I'd felt earlier had been replaced by my stomach gnawing on itself in fear. Flapping my arms, I tried to get rid of the panic sweat breaking out all over my body.

We passed abandoned buildings and strips of closed stores

before reaching a more affluent area. In St. Louis, you can have million-dollar mini-mansions across the street from condemned multi-family units. The disparity was something Luca wanted to address. I had worked with him on many Section 8 approved projects to help revitalize the area without destroying the existing neighborhoods with gaudy high rises.

Thirty minutes and countless turns later, Pete parked in front of The Diamond Lounge. I drove past him and circled the block facing the other direction.

Sliding down in my seat, I peered above the steering wheel, watching dapper men and scantily clad women come and go. Five-star restaurants and upscale clubs line the block, so looking down at my outfit, I knew there was no way I would fit in at this particular bar.

Peeking around the backseat, I smiled. I'd left my show bag in the car after the last performance. With a pinch of discomfort, I squeezed into my corset top and pinned on a sleek black wig without incident.

The overall effect was excellent. I looked like a completely different woman. The corset paired with my trousers in a very "1990s Madonna" way that I planned to recreate when I wasn't doing something positively batty. The black wig made my pale skin and green eyes glow but didn't stand out as much as my flaming red hair. It was a very flattering undercover look.

After a few deep breaths, I stepped into the muggy night and sauntered across the street to the club. Any worry I had about getting in flew out the window when the meathead bouncer couldn't take his eyes off my chest and ushered me through the door.

As dark as the night was, my eyes still had to adjust to the darkness of the club. I had no idea what I would find there if anything. A tremor went through my hands as I quickly got my bearings. The decor and costumed cocktail waitresses gave a distinctively 20s speakeasy vibe. Women drank champagne cocktails while sitting draped around sharp-dressed men smoking fat cigars. I wondered how I'd never been there before—the place was made for me.

I walked around the edge of the bar, careful not to make eye contact with any of the patrons for too long. Toward the back of the large room was a hallway where the bathrooms were located and where I guessed Pete was. Grabbing a stool at the bar, I ordered a gin and tonic and picked out a cigar. With a drink in hand and a thick cigar between my fingers, I sat with my back to the bar and watched the back hallway.

About half an hour passed, and I still hadn't seen Pete or anyone familiar. Bouncing my leg, I tapped my nails on the bar top. What was I expecting? To follow Pete and jump out from behind a bush and yell gotcha? Did I want to see my friend being a violent thug? This whole thing was fucking with my mind.

I checked my phone, shaking my head. This little stakeout was over.

As I set cash on the bar to cover my tab, a short, stout man stalked my way. His piercing blue eyes never left me as he made his way closer.

Standing in front of me, ole baldy blocked the room from my view. "Alessandro Ambrosia. And what's your name, beautiful?"

"Betty." I craned my neck to look around him and caught a glimpse of Pete pulling an unwilling young man behind him.

"Ah, a classic."

Standing up, I slammed my drink back before smiling at the older gent. "Look, you seem like a nice guy, but I gotta roll. Have a good night."

Clammy fingers gripped my elbow as I tried to move past the bar gnat. One tug, and I was free. "Don't touch me."

"Bitch."

With a wave of my hand, I walked away. "You have no idea."

Pete's car was still parked on the street, and I tried to walk to my car quickly without drawing any attention to my super stealth operation.

"Hey! Miss!"

The words hit my back, causing me to stop in the middle of the street. Fixing a smile on my face, I turned, and the doorman jogged up to me, holding a purse. Sweat beaded on the back of my neck as I tried to swallow back my rising panic.

"You dropped this inside." He handed me a red satin clutch.

"This isn't mine."

The beefed-up dude took the small handbag back with a smile. "My mistake, Ms. Mitchell."

My stomach fell to my ass. Why did Jersey Shore know my name?

"A small piece of advice? Maybe you should keep your distance from the Morettis' clubs." A quick wink and my walking warning sign turned, leaving me stunned and stuck in place.

I scanned the street for any sign of Luca, Marco, or, heaven forbid, Mr. Moretti. Someone had eyes on me, or my pic was on some "do not serve" poster circulating in the mafia underground. I wondered who recognized me.

Strange men shouldn't know me.

I glanced at Pete's car, my desire for information trying to overcome my debilitating fear.

A horn blared.

"Ms. Mitchell!"

A car skidded to a stop inches from me. Eyes wide, I stared at the driver as they yelled something, but I couldn't make out the words. The thump of my pulse drowned out everything but the static in my head and my frantic heartbeat. The driver laid on the horn again, and I jumped out of my stupor.

It took a bit of fumbling, but I made it into my car without additional peril.

Once in the safety of my tiny car, I blew out a shaky breath and glanced at where Pete's car had been parked. I deflated. It was gone. My eyes scanned the street frantically. Despite my fear, there was an urgency to follow through on tonight's misadventure.

Toward the end of the block, his taillights flashed as he rolled through the stop.

I shoved the keys in the ignition with trembling hands and crept into the street. Checking the mirrors, I pulled a U-ey. Rubbing the back of my neck, I gripped the steering wheel with my other hand until my knuckles turned white. A giggle spilled from my lips as I checked my rearview mirror, followed by another that turned into full-blown hysterics. Eyes watering and chest burning, I drove through the city with blurred vision, trying to gulp down air. I was tailing a confirmed made man through downtown after he dragged a man from a bar.

"It's official. I've lost my damn mind."

Speeding down a dark city street, I caught up with Pete's car. "And apparently, I have a death wish."

Pete was driving like a bat out of hell. This was not the mild-mannered sweetheart that drove slower than my nana. I couldn't keep up and had to stop near a few warehouses. Looking around, I bit my lip. Lights glowed in a few windows, but the night was quiet and dark.

"Well, shit."

I didn't know where I was. Pulling up Google Maps, I put in my address and waited for the spotty coverage to load the directions. Tapping my fingers on the steering wheel, I scanned the abandoned area.

My shoulders slumped with disappointment. I'm not sure what I was hoping for. To see some violence? To have Pete prove himself a monster?

Shaking out my arms, I tried to get rid of the tightness in my shoulders. This was a reckless thing to do, and I needed to get my ass home.

The stiff, robotic voice told me to continue straight, so I did. At the next stop sign, a string of pops came from a warehouse behind me.

Every muscle tensed, and I ducked down in my seat. I tried convincing myself it was a car backfiring but couldn't. The blinders were off, and even the mind tricks people used to stay brave weren't going to work.

Flooring it, I raced down the streets until I reached the highway on-ramp.

The entire night had been a cluster fuck. I was no Nancy Drew. Hell, I was just acting recklessly with no plan. This was no way to continue. The intelligent part of my brain told me to stop and cut my losses, but the desire to see who Luca was sat in the back of my mind, poking and prodding me to keep going. I told myself that if I saw Luca being a bastard, it would be easier to walk away, but nothing I found out that day kept my heart in check.

As I pulled in front of my building, I had to ask myself, what did I have to see to let Luca go?

What scared me was that I didn't know if Luca could do anything to kill my love for him.

Maybe I was the fucking monster.

NINETEEN

I never considered myself obsessive. In fact, I was told more than once that I should try to care more—be more invested. I don't think my exes or mom envisioned my current state of shifty-eyed compulsion when they hit me with their criticism.

Ryan hopped on my stomach, scaring me awake. I picked up my phone and saw it was only 5 a.m., but it wasn't like I would've slept much later. It had been two months since the shooting, but Luca's blood and our last minutes together still haunted my dreams. I found myself waking up earlier and earlier on less and less sleep.

Dragging myself from my blanket cocoon, I jumped into a hot shower. My morning routine had become more perfunctory than joyful. I used to enjoy the preening and primping, but now I was just maintaining expectations.

The worst part of the morning was when there were no more products to apply, and I was left to sit and stew before work. I'd made the mistake of getting to work early the first few weeks, which left me getting worried looks from Ashley and Miranda and Scott's ridiculous suggestion of sunrise yoga. The boy had lost his damn mind.

Sitting at the kitchen counter sipping hot coffee, I scrolled through the news. My eyes scoured for any mention of Moretti or Chronis, but I always came up empty-handed. A sense of peace would settle over me before reality sank in. Just because the local news didn't say anything didn't mean there was nothing to know. The itch for more information was there, but the memory of my failed sleuthing experiment kept me in check, so I headed to work, determined to stay out of a world that would surely kill me.

Miranda was on the phone as I walked in. With her hushed tones, it was obviously a personal call. I would need to have Ashley talk to her. It had been decided that I was too temperamental to address our receptionist professionally. Apparently, something about my sarcasm was cruel.

Whatever.

To my surprise, the lights in my office were on, and a dark-haired woman sat in front of my desk.

"Uh, hello?"

The tiny figure twisted in the chair. When her dark brown eyes landed on me, I tripped over nothing.

"Mrs. Moretti."

Standing up, she quickly closed the distance between us. Her warm hands grabbed mine, and she squeezed. "Oh honey, call me Rosa."

"Oh-okay." Pulling from her grasp, I circled the desk and set my purse down. "No offense, but what are you doing here?"

The frown on her face made my heart thump wildly. Would they send this tiny, beautiful woman to take me out? Rosa moved back to her seat and reached into her purse.

I put my hands out in front of me. "There's no need to—"

She pulled out a velvet box, cutting me off from groveling for my life. "I was helping Luca pack and found this. You must have forgotten it when you moved out."

With shaky fingers, I took the box from her. Popping it open, I gasped when Luca's grandmother's necklace sparkled back at me. Staring down at the diamonds and emeralds, I swallowed the lump in my throat. "I didn't forget it. It's not mine to keep." Snapping the box shut, I pushed it across the desk.

"Well, I'm just going to leave it here." Patting the black box, she slid it between us, then folded her hands in her lap. Her set jaw and steady eye contact kept me from arguing. The Morettis had a gift. They knew exactly how to drive me absolutely bonkers.

"Fine. Is that everything?"

Warm brown eyes peered at me as her forehead scrunched up. "I needed to see if you were okay."

"I'm fine." Clenching my fists in my lap, I tried to pull back the tears that threatened to spill.

"No, honey, I don't think you are." Rosa crossed her legs, settling further back in the chair.

"I—"

Mrs. Moretti held her hand up to stop me. "Neither is my Luca. Stomping around like a dictator, barking orders at family like he's forgotten who he is. No, I don't think either of you is fine."

"Well, what the fuck am I supposed to do about it?" I deflated, shaking my head.

She leaned forward, and her tiny fist hit the top of the desk, startling me. "Try! You try! Clearly, my son is determined to be unhappy, but you can put an end to this . . . this nonsense."

I pushed myself back into the cool leather of my chair. "I tried. I fucking did. Now . . . now I don't know if I should."

"Ah. I see. You know." Uncrossing her legs, she stood.

Nodding, I couldn't look her in the eye.

"And that's it?" I didn't speak, didn't move. I didn't have an answer for her. "Can't say I blame you."

My chin jerked toward her. "What?"

She shrugged and gathered her purse. "It's insanity to love these men, Sasha. I know that. But I also know what I saw between you and my son and hoped you'd be able to see past the life."

"I love him. I just . . . I don't . . . I'm sorry." I tried to stand, but my legs wobbled.

Rounding the desk, Mrs. Moretti pulled me into a hug. When she leaned away, she gave me a soft smile. "Nothing to be sorry for, honey. I'm sorry for sticking my nose in where it doesn't belong. You'll find your happiness, your match, and so will Luca. I just thought—" Her hand cupped my cheek, her thumb brushing away a tear. "Ah, it doesn't matter. Just be happy, Sasha."

With that, she left me speechless in my office with a necklace that was never meant to be mine.

———

At seven, Ashley bounced into my office. "You ready to go?"

Glancing up from the monitor, I frowned. "I'm in the middle of something."

The joy left Ashley, and in its place was the exasperated harpy I'd become accustomed to battling every Friday night. "Jesus Christ, Sasha! It's Evie's birthday, and you promised to come out with us."

"Oh fuck, I forgot. Ug, is there any way that—"

"Nope! Get your ass up. We gotta get you home and into something less officey." Ashley shut my laptop and grabbed my purse.

She walked out the door without a backward glance. "Ashley! Damn it!"

One wardrobe change, two hours, and three margaritas later, I was in a much better mood.

"So, where are we heading?" Ash slurred over the last sips of her strawberry marg.

"I was thinking Red. What'd ya think?" Evie looked down the long table.

"Let's do it! I haven't been there since it reopened." Jazz hollered as she swung her arm around her latest squeeze. A sweet thing from Alabama that gazed up at Jazz like she was the end all be all of life.

So, eleven scantily clad women and one modest librarian hit the streets, hoofing it the four blocks to the aptly lit Red night-club. A line wrapped around the side of the building—a strange sight in St. Louis.

Evie runway stomped toward the doorman, the rest of us following in her wake. Groans erupted from the line as the bouncer ushered our group inside. The sound only made us strut harder. If they're going to hate, we might as well drown them in it.

It had been months since I'd been to a proper club, let alone been this tipsy in public. The telltale smell of booze and sweat wrapped around me, and my skin got clammy from the humidity radiating off the dancing bodies.

Ashley bumped into me, smiling. "This is gonna be great!"

Shouldering our way to the bar, we lined up twelve tequila shots.

"To our fearless leader, Evie!" I shouted down to our group. Ever the ham, Evie stood up on her stool and led us in the salt, shot, lime ritual.

"To the dance floor!" Evie flew off the stool and into the chaos of bodies. Everyone followed but Jazz's sweet Imani.

"You coming, Imani?"

Her brown eyes widened, and her light brown skin flushed. Pushing back her springy black curls, she bit her lip. "Yeah, I just . . ." Imani's shoulders bunched, and the flashing lights highlighted the creases between her eyebrows. "What am I doing here, Sasha?"

"What do you mean?" I sat on the stool next to her.

"Look at me! I'm wearing a freaking cardigan and flats? It's like I can't help but look like I spend my days in the library." Her hand gestured toward Jazz, who was bumping and grinding with Ashley, howling with laughter. "And look at her. She's everything sexy and wonderful. What am I doing here?"

I wasn't sure if Jazz would appreciate what I was about to say or do, but her girlfriend needed a pick me up and damn it, I was going to be there for her.

Standing up, I pushed her legs apart and stood between them. Her mouth fell open. "Imani, you're a beautiful woman." I let my fingers gently trace from her knee to hip. "These legs are to die for." Continuing to where her generous curves nipped at the waist, I wrapped my hands around and squeezed. Her thick thighs tighten around my legs. "You have these amazing curves and perfect . . ." I grazed the outside of her chest with the side of my palm. Her breath hitched, and I smiled. One hand danced up her neck, cupping her cheek. The heat of her blush warmed my palm. I lightly brushed the pad of my thumb against her full bottom lip, picking up little pieces of salt from our shots. "And these lips." Pulling her waist closer, I leaned in. Counting to three, I waited for our interruption.

Sure enough, I was yanked back long before our lips met.

"What the fuck, Sasha!" Jazz's eyes flared with anger while Imani jumped up to pull Jazz away from me.

"No, baby, it's not. Sasha was—"

"I know what the fuck Sasha was doing." She tore her heated gaze from a shaken Imani to me. "Stay the fuck away from Imani. She's not one of your little distractions. She's . . . she's—"

"Important to you." I smiled at Imani and winked.

Jazz looked between us, a new rage setting in. "You're fucking right, so stop with the winking shit." Giving me her back, Jazz grabbed Imani's hand and pulled her to the dance floor.

"You're welcome!" I yelled behind them. Jazz flipped me off, but Imani laughed and waved.

After another shot, I danced my way to my friends. Jazz smiled at me, letting me know we were okay. Song after song, we danced and sweated up a storm.

As my eyes scanned the dance floor for a distraction for the night, the lights flashed on a face I thought I'd never see again. My breath stopped, but my feet moved toward where I'd just seen

Luca. A big-headed dude blocked my view momentarily, and when I shouldered past him, Luca was gone.

Shaking my head, I returned to the group. I wondered if I was seeing things. It wouldn't have been the first time I thought I saw Luca and was wrong.

Leaning into Ashley, I yelled, "I'm going to the bathroom."

"Want me to go too?" The guy behind her tightened his hold on her waist, and she shoved him back.

"Nah, I'm good."

She nodded and danced away from Mr. Handsy and into the protection of our pack of dancing beauties.

Groaning at the line to the women's bathroom, I scoped out the men's bathroom. Casually, I pushed the door open. No one. Thanking my lucky stars, I booked it into the stall.

Bladder fully relieved, I went to flush when the door flew open with a bang. A few pairs of feet shuffled in, one man grunting.

"I can't believe you had the guts to come here, Alec."

There was no mistaking Luca's voice, even if it was colder and harder than I remembered. I pulled my feet up to sit on the toilet and tried not to move a muscle.

"I . . . I didn't—"

There was the sound of glass breaking, followed by a thud. I leaned to the side to peek through the crack between the stall wall and door. Luca stood over a man with blood gushing from his head. Glass littered the floor and counter, reflecting the dingy yellow light up at my raging ex. A tremor of fear went through my body, and I leaned back against the tank of the toilet.

"Don't bullshit me. You were one of the fuckers that shot me! Your cousin told us everything right before I ripped him apart." The man on the floor moved to stand, but Luca stomped down on his hand. "Don't move one fucking muscle." Lowering himself into a squat, Luca rocked on his feet, causing the man to scream out. "Now tell me, where the fuck is Cy?"

"I don't know. I don't—AHHHHH!" Luca's fingers dug

into Alec's scalp, where the glass had ripped him open. My stomach turned as the blood poured from his wound.

Luca smiled and stood up, pulling a gun from his waistband. I gasped, and my hand flew to cover my mouth. Luckily, Alec's scream covered any noise coming from me.

"Here's the deal. You know I can't let you leave alive."

Alec cried louder. "Please! Please! I—"

"Shh, stop. You tried to kill me in my own fucking restaurant. I'm going to kill you. Your choice is whether I make it quick or drag it out." Cocking his gun, Luca smiled. "I'm hoping you'll let me drag it out."

A hand landed on Luca's shoulder, and I flinched. I'd completely forgotten there was anyone else in the bathroom. "Pete's cleared the hallway. You want me to step out?"

Marco, definitely Marco.

Luca nodded, his eyes never leaving Alec. "Yeah, you and Pete watch the hall. I got this."

Once the door closed, Luca loosened up. "Now, where's Cy?"

Alec shook his head. "I don't know. They don't tell me anything."

Luca pointed his long-barreled gun and shot Alec's knee. The pop was muffled, but Alec's scream was far from it. My racing heart drowned out the thumping of the club's music. It felt like we were in another world entirely, miles away from the drunken scene outside the door. My hands tightened over my lips, silent tears running down my fingers.

"See—" When Alec continued to wail, Luca loosened his tie, taking it off and shoving it into Alec's sobbing mouth.

Luca sighed, his bloody hands leaving a smear on his forehead as he pushed his hair from his eyes. "See, you didn't just shoot me, Alec. No, you and your fucking cousin almost hit someone precious to me. Had that happened . . ." Luca shook his arms out and stepped right where blood gushed from the fresh bullet wound. The tie barely muffled Alec's screams.

With closed eyes, Luca took a deep breath. "Had you killed her, you would've seen my bad side."

A laugh sat at the back of my throat.

This isn't his bad side? Fuck.

Luca opened his eyes, his face grim. "Now, I'm going to remove the tie, and you're going to tell me where Cy is. Okay?"

Alec's eyes shut tight, and tears spilled down his cheeks. Blood and sweat left a shiny mess on his forehead. He nodded, a groan escaping his mouth when Luca leaned down to rip the tie away.

"Cy is in Chicago." Alec moaned as he tried to adjust his body.

Luca nodded as he stood back up. "And does he plan on coming back here any time soon?"

Alec nodded. "Next month for Dimitri's engagement party."

Luca smiled. "You Greeks have no loyalty."

"No, I—"

"Shh. It's fine. Thank you for being honest." Luca pointed the gun at Alec's face. Fear locked my body in place, and my eyes refused to look away or even close.

"I'm a man of my word."

Luca pulled the trigger, and a soft pop filled the room.

The bullet entered Alec's forehead, and his body jerked before it went limp. The pool of blood beneath him grew faster by the second. Luca's expensive leather shoes squished in it as he took a step toward the door.

Vomit pushed up my throat and spewed around my hands. The violence of the heaving forced chunks of burrito onto the floor. My eyes widened in horror as the stall door slammed open. Dropping my hands from my mouth, I braced myself against the stall walls and spewed every bit of food and drink I'd had that day on the floor at Luca's feet.

"Sasha?"

I kept my eyes down and clumsily grabbed toilet paper, trying in vain to wipe myself clean.

Bloody hands reached into my line of vision, and I slapped

them away as I tried to stand. My legs gave out, and Luca hoisted me up against him. His lips brushed against my forehead as he whispered, "What the hell are you doing here?"

Shaking my head, I mumbled, "Had to pee."

A shocked laugh fell from his lips. The whoosh of air blew back loose hairs, and I caught a hint of scotch on his breath. Leaning me against the stall wall, he scanned me for injury, which felt ridiculous as a corpse bled out next to our feet. "I gotta get you out of here."

A sharp knock on the door drew Luca's attention. "Give me a second!"

After he made sure I could stand on my own, he stepped out of the stall. The squelch of blood and vomit under his foot threatened to send me back into a puking fit. Not a second later, he grabbed my hand and pulled me to a small closet in the corner. Gently, he pushed me in next to rolls of toilet paper and paper towels. "Stay here until I come to get you. Don't come out for anyone else. I don't know who I can trust right now."

Kissing my forehead, he closed the door and called Marco in.

"Get Mickey and Tootsie in here ASAP."

The bathroom door closed, and then Marco mumbled, "Is that puke? God, this place is a fucking hole." Then the door closed again.

I stood in the closet for ten minutes as people filed in and out.

"Boss had fun with this one, huh?"

"Hey, you didn't see the other guy. It took me two hours to clean him off the floor."

"You think we should get the vomit?"

"Nah, that's from some drunk asshole. Let the fucking bar handle it. We got our hands full here."

"Wish he'd stop doing this in public spots. I mean, what's the point of having the warehouse?"

"I know, man, but Moretti's not right in the head since that redhead left his ass. Makes me miss Dante."

"Yeah, but look where his sanity got him."

"You're right. You know—"

The bathroom door squeaked open. "Guys, shut the fuck up. The boss is out here, and you're in here gossiping like a couple of teen girls. You got five minutes.

"Yeah, yeah, Paulie. We're almost done."

Sure enough, the two men left the bathroom about five minutes later.

When the door opened again, my whole body tensed. The closet door opened, and Luca stood there holding a towel. "Let's clean you up."

Taking a step out, I looked around. The body and blood were gone. They'd even cleaned up the glass from the broken mirror. Only my vomit sat as a reminder of what happened.

Luca ran water over one corner of the towel. I stood frozen in shock as he gently wiped my face. "Sasha, are you okay?"

I shook my head. Of course, I wasn't fucking okay.

Luca sighed and pulled my hands under the faucet. He took hand cleaner from his pocket and scrubbed my hands free of vomit and the specs of blood he'd left there. When I was visibly clean, with only a couple of spots drying on my dress, he asked me for my shoes.

"No. I need those."

"They're evidence. I need to destroy them."

I stared down at the dark ooze crusted on the edges of my green pumps. A gag rocked my body, but Luca held me and rubbed my back. Calming myself, I stepped out of the heels, and Luca handed me a pair of black flip-flops.

"Really?"

He shrugged. "It's 2 a.m. I doubt anyone will notice."

"Are my friends still here?"

"Ashley is."

Nodding, I turned from him to leave.

"Sasha, wait."

My hand rested on the handle as I glanced back at Luca. "What?"

He pushed his hands in his pockets, staring at me. "I'm sorry."

"I'm not the one you killed." Not wanting his response, I left the bathroom. Looking both ways, I rushed out to the bar. The overhead lights flipped on, and the patrons moved like zombies toward the door.

Standing in the middle of the dance floor was my very own tiny escort. Ashley rushed over to me, stumbling. I caught her, and she held my arms for balance. "There you are! I saw Luca and Marco and wondered if you relapsed on that tall drink of water."

"No, I just got a little sick in the bathroom. No biggie." I patted her hand and headed toward the exit. Near the door, I locked eyes with a pissed-off Marco. He stood across the room next, talking to Pete. I turned my back on them and walked even faster, pulling a giggling Ash behind me.

"Hey, where are your shoes?"

TWENTY

LUCA MORETTI

> You don't have to stay with your parents.
> You'll be safe in your apartment.

> You've missed three days of work. Please tell
> me you're okay.

> Sasha, I'm so sorry. Please tell me what I can
> do to help you.

"Turn back time and leave me alone?"

As soon as the words left my mouth, I knew it was bullshit. I would watch him shoot a hundred guys before I erased him from my life.

I was a fucking monster.

The blue glow from the TV washed over my parents' den as the rest of the house sat dark for the night. After the live execution in a public bathroom, I fused with those couch cushions and had no plans of leaving them. I was safe under those hideous afghans, even if that safety was only an illusion.

My mom fussed and coddled me as only Maggie Mitchell could. And while I usually would've been appalled, at that very moment, I soaked up the maternal loving like a sponge. I promised myself I would get up and go into the office the next day, but that didn't seem likely as it was already 3 a.m. and reruns of Golden Girls aired until 5 a.m.

Cable. A perk of suburban life.

I was polishing off a second bowl of cookie dough ice cream with chocolate syrup when my dad quietly came through the door.

"What are you still doing up, kiddo?"

Rinsing out the bowl, I shrugged. "Can't sleep."

Dad rustled out of his jacket and kicked off his boots. A chair creaked behind me as I put the dishes in the dishwasher.

"Your mom said you've been up all night and most of the day. What's going on?"

I took a deep breath to keep from spilling my guts. My dad had always been the interrogator. He could get me to sing like a fucking canary.

When I finally looked at him, my guts twisted, and my eyes stung with tears. *So much for a brave front.*

"Nothing, just some personal shit I can't seem to shake."

Nodding, Dad got up and took a plate of wrapped leftovers from the fridge. "Boyfriend troubles?" He took off the saran wrap and popped the plate in the microwave. "Girlfriend issues?"

His eyes stayed on his plate rotating as he asked the second question. I didn't doubt that my dad loved me, but I knew that my sexuality would always be a weird spot to avoid at all costs and that fucking hurt.

It took me a couple of minutes to figure out how to respond. "No, nothing like that. It's just. I don't know. I don't feel safe in my apartment anymore."

The microwave dinged, and Dad took out the sizzling lasagna. He snagged two beers from the fridge and a paper towel. Without asking, he slid a beer to me before settling back in his chair. "You shouldn't be living in the city, kid. I've been trying to tell you that."

"Mm-hmm." Anger flushed my cheeks with heat. We had this fight pretty regularly.

"I still have that handgun I got you for Christmas if you want it."

My fingers peeled the label from the bottle as I diverted eye contact. That gun was his "thoughtful" gift after I moved into a studio apartment a few blocks from Tower Grove Park. I refused to take it, and it stayed in his gun safe ever since.

"I know."

"Sasha, look at me."

I begrudgingly pulled my eyes from the torn-up label in my hands.

"I have the next two days off. Why don't we go to the shooting range? Blow off some steam."

Normal "I didn't just watch a man get shot in the head" Sasha would've immediately said no, but I was beyond that now.

"Okay. Yeah, let's do it."

My dad's face broke into a wide smile. "Great! I can't wait to see if you still got it."

"It's been over a decade since I shot a gun, Dad."

"Yeah, but boy, were you a great shot as a kid." He gestured behind him to the den where my NRA trophies sat proudly. Being raised by a gun nut, Dad took me hunting and eventually entered me in a few competitions. I ended up winning a scholarship for my marksmanship. It was one of the stumpers I used when I played two truths and a lie.

"We'll see."

We sat silently as I sipped my beer, and Dad wolfed down his food. "Damn, your mom's lasagna gets better every time I eat it." He pushed his chair back and patted his stomach. By nature of his job, he was in better shape than most fifty-five-year-olds I knew.

Taking the last gulp of beer, I picked up his plate and took it to the sink. The familiarity of this late-night ritual relaxed me. My dad and I had always been night owls, having some of our best conversations when the rest of the world was fast asleep.

By the time I got his plate in the dishwasher, Dad was already grabbing another couple of beers from the fridge. Wrapping his arm around my shoulder, I caught a whiff of smoke on him. "Busy day?"

With a squeeze, he let me go and moved toward the den. "Yeah, there was a big fire in one of those new McMansions in Creve Coeur. We got lucky, and everyone got out safe, but we had a second story collapse on Jerry and Dave." Dad plopped down in his recliner and pulled up the footrest, letting out a heavy sigh. "It was pretty fucking scary for a minute."

"I bet." I crawled back under the afghan and settled in.

We watched reruns of M.A.S.H. until Dad's soft snores filled the room. I grabbed an extra throw and covered him up before settling back into the cushions and finally drifting off to sleep.

After another couple of days of pampering from Mom and dusting off my gun knowledge with Dad, I finally packed up to leave.

As soon as I got behind the wheel, I noticed a black sedan tailing me. Quick breaths escaped my lips, and my heart rate picked up as my fingers fumbled to scroll through the hundreds of numbers in my contacts list.

"Sasha?"

"Someone's following me." I floored it, trying to shake my tail. Unfortunately, the car had no issue keeping up. My heart thrashed against my chest, and my throat was tight, making swallowing impossible.

"Calm down, baby. It's—"

My eyes flashed up to the rearview mirror, bile churning in my stomach. "How the fuck am I supposed to calm down? There's someone following me!"

"Baby, it's just Pete. He's going to keep an eye on you. I should've—"

"Yeah, you should've told me you were going to have me followed. I was about to have a fucking heart attack, Luca! Goddamn it." Ending the call, I signaled and pulled onto my street.

Rage and fear fought for domination as I tried to breathe some peace into my body. When my hands stopped shaking, I grabbed my bags from the trunk and rushed to the door, never looking Pete's way. Who the fuck knew if he could be trusted.

Hadn't Luca said he didn't know who he could trust?

With every lock in place, I finally took a deep breath. I was home. I was safe.

The apartment smelled stale, so I opened the kitchen window. Ryan leapt up on the ledge, rubbing his face against my hand.

"Hey, baby. Did Ashley visit you?" A glance at his water bowl confirmed he was well cared for during my little breakdown. "Don't worry, sweetie. Mommy's home for good."

Carrying a purring, content Ryan to the couch, I plopped down. He kneaded my lap until he fell asleep, leaving me to my thoughts. I glanced over to my suitcase, where my handgun was packed away, not believing things had gotten this bad. I had a fucking gun in my home.

After showering and settling in bed that night, I tried to relax. I wished Luca had never told me he doubted his own men.

Slipping out of the sheets, I dug through the open suitcase before my hands landed on the gun case. I sat on the floor and toyed with the lock. Fear pulsed through me as I contemplated whether I should keep the gun on the side table.

Shaking my head, I slid the case under my bed and went downstairs to find some kind of sleep aid.

My salvation came in the form of a bottle of red wine. Posted up in my bed, I couldn't rid myself of the stomach-twisting nerves that finally pushed me to pull out the small gun and place it next to my charging phone.

Tears blurred my vision as I stared at the Beretta sitting next to the empty wine bottle and my favorite vibrator—a perfect fucking picture of my current life. A small laugh grew until I was shaking from head to toe.

I'm not sure when I finally fell asleep, but when my alarm went off the following day, I felt around to shut it off, and my fingers grazed cold steel. Snatching my hand back, I jolted out of bed.

"Fuck. Fuck."

I stared the gun down, pacing the room. Tugging at my hair and rubbing my eyes, I would walk close to the table, only to stride away as quickly as possible. A pointless dance that I couldn't stop.

Ryan tangled with my feet, as anxious as I was but unsure what was wrong with his human.

At a stalemate with my inanimate foe, I headed to the bathroom to get ready for work. When I came back into the room, my eyes couldn't leave the side table.

Was I really going to keep a gun in the house? Was I really going to sleep with it next to me?

Shaking my head, I shoved the gun into the drawer and grabbed the empty bottle to take down to the recycling. I itched to get the hell out of the house and to work. At least at work, I was surrounded by people and distracted by clients.

Locking up, I scanned the street, quickly spotting Pete down the block.

Did he sleep in his fucking car?

I couldn't get in my car fast enough, and before I knew it, I was walking into the office. Miranda's eyes widened, and she swallowed her coffee with a wince. "Sasha! You're here!"

"That I am." I smiled and hurried past her.

Ashley's office was still dark, which wasn't surprising, as it was only 8:00 a.m. Settling in, I answered emails and set up back-to-back meetings to make up for my week-long absence.

"Sasha!" Ashley shouted from the hallway.

"Yeah?" I kept my eyes on the screen as I crafted an email delicately telling a vendor to fuck off.

Ashley rounded my desk, throwing her arms around my neck. Her petite body pressed hard into my shoulder, her fluffy hair flattening under my chin. "You're back!"

I patted her arm, pulling away. The smile on her face made me nervous. "Yep. I'm feeling much better."

"Mm-hmm." Ashley frowned, then walked over to my office door. She gently shut it and turned the lock.

"What are you doing?" I pushed my laptop to the side to get a better view of her face as she sat across from me.

"We're talking, and I'd rather not have Miranda interrupt us."

Dread sunk my stomach to my ass. I was going to throw up. "About what?"

"You were out for a week, Sash. Do you want to tell me about it?"

Don't get her involved.

My lips parted, but Ashley held her hand up. "And don't bullshit me. I talked to Malcolm."

Fuck. Fuck. Fuck.

"You're talking again? That's great, Ash." I tried to relax my face into a smile, but the tension in my cheeks was too tight.

"Yeah, fucking fantastic." She stared at me as if she was waiting for something. When it was apparent I wasn't going to talk, she sighed. "Fine. Then I'll talk. Did Luca threaten you?"

Her words were a slap to the face. "What?" I shook my head. "No. Never. What the hell?"

Ashley blew out a breath. "Okay. Good. So, has anyone else from his family come for you? Or maybe Dimitri?"

"Damn." I fell back in my chair. "Malcolm told you everything, huh?"

"Yeah, apparently, my best friend didn't think I needed to know what shit she had gotten herself into. Wild, huh?" She pursed her lips.

I closed my eyes. I couldn't take the censure in her stare. "Look, I—"

"No, you had your chance to talk. It's my turn."

My eyes flew open at her near shout. She jumped up from the chair, her eyes wild and raw anger radiating off her. Never in all the years I'd known her had I considered her intimidating, but right then? The bitch was terrifying.

"You were so fucking weird after Evie's birthday, but I figured it was just more of whatever the past couple of months have been. But then you go MIA for a week. So yeah, I made Malcolm tell me everything." She stopped pacing and glared at me, her voice dropping to a harsh whisper. "A fucking mafia boss Sasha? Really? Fuck!"

Glancing away, I forced out, "I know." I didn't even recognize the small, quiet voice that came from me.

I must've looked like a pathetic piece of shit because Ashley's face and voice softened. "What the hell happened?" She sat back down, waiting for me to respond.

Internally, I battled on how much to tell her. "I saw him, Ash. I saw him kill someone." Her mouth fell open, but I continued before losing my nerve. "And he told me he didn't know who he could trust. Like, I watched him kill a guy, and then he tells me there are people like him who aren't on his side? He's so unsure he has a guy following me. That's fucking scary."

Ashley nodded. "But you knew he was, well, you know."

"Right, but knowing it and seeing it are two different things. But you want to know the most fucked up part?"

She nodded, her bottom lip between her teeth.

"I still trust his ass. I noticed I was being followed, and I called him first."

Tilting her head, Ashley narrowed her eyes as she studied me. We sat in silence for a minute before she spoke. "Okay, so he's not what you're afraid of?"

I shook my head. I had a lot of time to think about that night. While watching someone die made me physically ill, Luca still didn't inspire fear in me. The gentle way he cleaned me up and how he protected me from his own family told me more about him than a dead body could.

"You're afraid of the other guys?"

I nodded.

She sunk into her chair. "And Luca has a guy watching you?"

Another nod.

"But you're still scared?"

"Yes." My fingers twisted together.

"What do you think will make you feel safer?"

Shrugging, I thought back to him wrapping his arms around me in that fucking club bathroom. I knew what made me feel safe, the same thing putting me in danger.

"Fuck."

"Yeah, fuck." A chime on my laptop let me know my next appointment was due in fifteen minutes. "Shit, I need to get down to the bank. I have that meeting to go over the loan for the new space."

Ashley worried her lip with her front teeth. "You want me to go with?"

"Nah. I'm just popping in to make sure all our paperwork is in. I'll be back by lunch."

Nodding, Ash got up and unlocked the door. "Okay, but we're figuring this shit out at lunch. If I need to move Scott, Malcolm, Axel, and me in until we can get a handle on what's really going on, I will."

I laughed at the idea of Malcolm and Axel in the same space. Those two would destroy my apartment. "Okay, we'll talk about it."

After a brief meeting with the loan officer, I wandered around the blocks surrounding the bank, sweating my ass off while trying to clear my head before I went back to the office and faced Ashley.

Without realizing it, I ended up in front of Moretti Properties. I stood in the scorching July sun, staring at my reflection in the streak-free windows. Something in my gut told me to go inside. Before I thought through what I was doing, I pushed through the big glass doors and headed to the elevators.

TWENTY-ONE

Entering reception on Luca's floor, I looked for his EA Lauren, but at her desk was a young brunette. Her big blue eyes jumped up to greet me. "Oh, hello! Can I help you?"

Her perfect, natural smile did little to calm the storm raging in my stomach.

"Ah, I need to see Mr. Moretti."

Nodding, she glanced at her computer screen. "Name?"

I adjusted the strap of my bag. "Sasha Mitchell."

When she didn't say anything, I added, "I'm sorry, but what happened to Lauren?"

Not-Lauren's face lit up, and she looked back over at me. "Oh! Her daughter just gave birth, so she's out for a few weeks. They pulled me from downstairs to cover during her leave. I'm Tasha."

Sasha, meet Tasha.

"Oh, wow, that's great! She'll be a great grandma."

"Right? Lauren's the best." Her eyes fell back to her monitor. "Okay, let me see. Hmm. I don't see you on his calendar. Is this possibly a personal visit?"

"Yes."

Tasha twisted her lips and glanced behind her at Luca's office door. "He's wrapping up with legal." Her baby blues swung back to me, and she leaned forward with a conspiratorial smile. "But he has fifteen minutes before his next meeting. Let me poke my head in there and see what we can do."

A little wink, and she was off.

Tapping my foot, I smoothed the front of my skirt. Another second, and I would dash back to the elevator.

Tasha came back, her face a little less cheery. Nicki, Gabe, and a young man I didn't recognize followed her from Luca's office. Nicki looked at me with a bit of confusion, but at least she didn't scowl at me like her father.

Fucking Gabe.

"Okay, Ms. Mitchell. It looks like you can go right in." Under her breath, she muttered, "And I get to move the Perkins meeting. Again." Her eyes scanned the screen, and a tiny frown marred her smooth face.

"Thank you, Tasha. I appreciate all your help."

She gave me a slight nod and smiled, gesturing for me to go ahead.

I made a mental note to send Tasha flowers or something. I knew precisely how annoying Luca's scheduling could be. Meetings were sometimes moved four or more times.

Pausing at the door, I took a deep breath. I wasn't sure what I wanted to get out of his little meeting, but something told me I needed to see him.

I reached for the knob, and the door opened. There stood Luca in all his businessman glory. Even on the hottest day of the year, the man could wear the shit out of a suit. Despite his perfectly pressed clothes and styled hair, he looked worn out. Dark circles and bloodshot eyes marred his usual perfection. His skin didn't have the otherworldly glow I had become accustomed to.

Was he not getting enough sleep? What about water? Was he getting his recommended eight glasses a day?

Worry needled into my chest, but I pushed it away. I wasn't here to check on him.

We stood staring at each other awkwardly, neither one of us moving. The chirp of Tasha answering the phone shook Luca from our standoff, and he gestured for me to enter.

As I walked to the middle of the room, I heard the door lock and the blinds close. Panic seeped into my gut, and I started to get a little nauseous. I wasn't sure I could do this. Whatever this was.

"You can sit. If you want." His voice moved closer to me, the warmth in it prickling the hairs on my neck.

Keeping my eyes ahead, I moved to the small couch and sat on the edge of a cushion. The frame cut into my thighs as I folded my hands. I may not have been sure why I was there or what I expected to get out of this little impromptu meeting, but I knew it felt good just being in the same room as Luca. Fuck, it felt good.

Luca sat in a chair across from me, leaving a sturdy, dark-stained coffee table between us. Leaning forward, he rested his elbows on his knees and steepled his fingers under his chin. His whole body leaned in my direction, like at any minute he would lunge at me. I found my own shoulders leaning forward, trying to close the distance over the table.

We sat there staring at one another, the clock on the wall ticking away. The same fire that was always there licked at us. We were on the verge of fighting or fucking. At this point, I was ready for either.

His full lips parted a couple of times before he finally spoke. "How have you doing since . . ." He trailed off, not able to or not wanting to finish his thought.

Nodding, I fought to keep my eyes on his face. I wanted to look away. I felt guilty. Seeing him shouldn't make me feel happy, but it did. "I'm fine."

Luca lifted one eyebrow but said nothing.

I blew out a breath and shook my hands out. I'd been so sure about talking to him, but now I didn't know what to say. "Fine. I'm not fine. Happy? I'm fucking scared, Luca."

He shifted his feet, his hands dropping between his knees, and he folded in on himself. "I'm so sorry. I—" And then he stopped talking. The fucker just sat there, staring at a spot on the carpet.

After waiting for him to say anything, I snorted. This was fucking ridiculous. "Sorry doesn't make me feel any safer. Sorry doesn't erase the sleepless nights or the fear that someone is going to kill me." Blood pumped viciously through my veins. My legs bounced until I had no choice but to jump off the couch. I vibrated as I circled the coffee table toward him. I wanted to yell in his goddamn face. "Sorry doesn't tell me who the fuck I can trust or if I can trust you to keep me safe."

Luca's head shot up, followed by his body. His whole face shifted into a scowl as he crowded me back against the arm of the couch. My ass perched on the edge, I leaned away from the heat of his body. We were too close.

He gripped my chin tightly, his fingers digging into my skin. "Don't fucking say that, Sasha. If you trust nothing else, trust that I will always keep you safe."

His hold tightened, and his other hand pushed my leg aside so he could move closer. Our chests heaved against one another as I trembled with anticipation of our bodies pressing closer together. His wool pants scratched against my thighs, tempting me to squeeze and trap him against me—lust twisted with anger, turning me into a shaking, panting mess.

"How can you do that when you told me yourself you don't trust your own men?" Pushing on his chest, I tried to make space, only to have him press closer and trap my hands between us.

"I would never put anyone near you I didn't trust. You have to believe me, baby. Either Pete or I have eyes on you twenty-four seven. No one else, Sasha."

My breath caught in my throat as Luca's eyes only increased in intensity. He'd been watching me. He and Pete had been there the whole time.

Why hadn't he just told me that in the first place?

Luca's face moved closer, and he exhaled against my lips. "Pete would die for you. I would die for you."

Leaning in a few inches, I laid my forehead on his shoulder. One deep inhale of his fresh scent, and my body softened against his hold. "That's the thing, Luca. I don't want anyone to die." Pulling back a little, our cheeks brushed. The tiny bristle of his beard raking against my soft skin made me shiver. My lips grazed his ear as I murmured, "I just don't want to be scared anymore."

Luca sighed and pulled his head back, putting us eye to eye. "I handled it. There's no more Moretti threat."

"What do you mean?" I knew what he meant, what he had done, but I wanted to hear him say the words.

Never looking away from me, he answered. "We took care of it."

His eyes held a sadness that made me ache for him. Luca valued family above everything else and had yet again put me before them. My heart swelled for the man I loved, the man that loved me, the man that would kill for me.

I should've been horrified, should've feared the man holding me so tightly. Instead, I felt safe. I felt so fucking safe. And I felt loved.

I don't know who moved first, but before I knew it, our lips locked together. My lungs screamed for air, but I refused to pull away.

I was home.

Luca's fingers twisted in my hair, holding me to him, while his other hand squeezed my ass. I wiggled my fingers, my hands wedged between us. Fingering a button on his shirt, I started the pointless task of undoing that one button and touching the skin beneath. I'd never been so hungry for anyone.

With a gasp, Luca pulled away, his chest heaving. The dark brown eyes I loved so much scanned my face. I could see the questions and doubts swirling in their inky depths. I had no doubts about what I wanted and hoped Luca would get on the same page.

Our mouths only inches apart, I tilted my chin up, asking for more. When he still didn't kiss me, I said, "Fucking kiss me, Luca."

His lips twitched at the corners, but he didn't smile. "We can't be together, Sasha."

"I know." And I did. As much as my heart fucking bled for this man, I understood. If anything happened to me because of him, he wouldn't survive. If he were hurt protecting me, I would burn this fucking world down. Our love was extreme, too volatile to survive.

An oppressive sadness deflated the sexual charge between us, turning our lust into a bittersweet sting.

This is it.

Leaning forward, I nudged his nose with my own before kissing him softly. I put every ounce of love into the press of my lips, into the brush of my tongue. His hands caressed me, memorizing and savoring every inch. We parted, and he slowly shrugged his jacket off and undid his tie, tossing it aside. Never taking his eyes from mine, he undressed, tossing his clothes aside without another look.

A sob-like laugh shook my body at my little perfectionist cutting loose. The round, red scars on his shoulder and torso were a harsh reminder of all his body had been through since I'd known him.

Luca finally gifted me with a small smile as he stood naked in the middle of his office, clothes all over the place. "Your turn."

Shaking my head, I laughed. For the first time in my life, I was nervous about taking off my clothes. My skin felt hot, and my stomach tightened in both excitement and dread.

Luca's eyes followed the path of clothes leaving my body until I stood in front of him, completely bare. "You are perfection, Sasha." He trailed his fingertips down my jaw to my collarbone. "Nothing, and no one will ever compare to you."

Tears blurred my vision. Frozen in my spot, I was scared to

touch him and start something that had an immediate expiration date.

Luca caressed me, slowly walking us over to his desk, where he sat me on the edge. Standing between my legs, he tilted my chin up. "I love you."

Fat, hot tears started to roll down my cheeks, and my heart leapt into my throat. I was just able to croak out, "I love you."

"Whether or not we're together, you own every part of me. Never doubt that." He peppered my face with sweet, small kisses, his big hands cradling my jaw.

I took deep breaths, trying to calm down, but I couldn't catch my breath. It wasn't fair. This wasn't fair. We belonged together.

Luca wrapped his arms around me, crushing our chests together as his hands rubbed up and down my back. "I know." His voice cracked.

Pulling back from him, I wiped my eyes. His hands rested on my waist, his thumbs gently tracing the curve.

"Luca, I've never loved anyone the way I love you. I just . . . I just . . ."

He leaned his forehead against mine. "I know."

Nothing more could be said or done. If this was goodbye, then I was going to make it count.

Tugging at Luca's soft waves, I slanted my mouth over his, and the fire between us flared. Our teeth nipped lips, our tongues tangled, and our hands roamed, creating a manic mess. With every roll of our bodies, his hardness pressed against me. Writhing against him, I became slick with desire.

Luca tried to drop to his knees, but I didn't want his mouth. I wanted him inside of me, completing me.

My hand wrapped around him, pumping a few times before I lined him up with my core. Without missing a beat, Luca slid into me, my body enveloping him.

Our eyes connected as he stilled inside of me. We were drowning in our love, our loss.

Keeping my eyes open, I pecked his lips and grabbed his ass, trying to push him deeper. Luca groaned and started to rotate his hips, his blunt head moving deeper than I could've ever imagined. My head rolled back. It was all too much.

When I looked back at him, his face was flushed, and his jaw was tense. I could see how hard he was working to maintain control. But I didn't want him in control. I loosened my hold on his magical ass, and Luca slowly thrust as if he was savoring the feel of us together. Every meeting of our hips, a wordless 'I love you.'

A strangled moan tore from my throat, and his hips moved faster until each thrust punched the air from my chest. Our eyes stayed locked on one another, afraid to miss a moment.

Luca's hands gripped my hips, his fingers digging into the softness there. My nails scratched down his shoulders, his skin prickling with goosebumps under their attention. My lips followed until I reached the base of his neck at his shoulder and bit down. Pulling back, the impression of my teeth sat red and angry against his skin. It didn't feel like enough. I wanted to mark him all over as if there weren't enough scars already.

In no time, we were both moving against each other at a frenzied pace, the tight ball in my stomach threatening to explode any second. He moved his hand between us, his thumb circling my clit, and I came completely undone.

Crying out his name, I watched as his climax ripped through him. His jaw went slack, his lips parting in a groan. Collapsing, he burrowed his face into my neck.

I wrapped my arms and legs around him, holding him in place. Luca started to shake gently, and I felt a warm wetness on my neck. I dropped my arms to grab hold of his face, and sure enough, tears ran down his cheeks.

Wiping away his tears with my thumbs, I gently kissed his lips. "I love you, Luca."

"I love you, Sasha. I really do."

Blowing out a breath, I tried to shake off the deep sadness sneaking in. "Okay. Okay."

Luca took a step back and gathered my clothes. Once he had them all stacked nicely, he motioned for me to step into my panties. In a move that made my heart clench, he started to dress me. No person had ever dressed me.

With the last zipper zipped, I stood frozen as he quickly slipped on his clothes, smoothing down his shirt despite there being no wrinkles. He swallowed like he was trying to compose himself.

After a little more fussing with his cufflinks, ones I got him for his birthday, he looked at me. "I'm sorry I can't be who you need me to be, who I want to be."

I nodded. "Me too. But I understand." I grabbed his hands in mine. "Please be careful. Don't do anything too reckless."

A genuine laugh spilled from his lips, the skin around his eyes creasing as he grinned. "I'll try. And you stay away from anyone named Moretti or Chronis. Got it?" His smile was all but gone as he mentioned his enemy.

"You got it." I squeezed his hands and pulled away. "Well, I gotta go. I have a lunch date with Ashley to discuss how best to stay away from you. Man, is she going to be pissed."

We both smiled, and Luca put his hand on my lower back and showed me out of his office. At the door, I turned. "Goodbye, Luca." The words gutted me.

"Goodbye, Sasha." Luca's skin turned green. Like any second, he would puke up his breakfast.

With a small smile, I turned and walked away from the person I loved most in the world.

TWENTY-TWO

Closure is a weird thing.

It's supposed to make moving forward without looking back easier.

There's supposed to be a sense of peace or some kind of contentment with how things have shaken out.

For me, closure felt like I would be forever settling.

"Okay. It's been weeks since, well, you know, and I need the old Sasha back."

Glancing up from the book in my hand, I shook my head. "I see you're abusing your key privileges."

Looking back at my book, I tried to find where I left off and ignored Ashley's huffing. As I got sucked back into the raunchy Austen re-imagination, Ash ripped the book from my hands and tossed it across the room, knocking into Ryan's cat tree. My poor, furry son raced from the room, yowling.

"Hey! You owe him an apology."

Ash rolled her eyes but cupped her hands around her mouth all the same. "Sorry, Ryan!" Dropping her hands, she looked back at me. "Now you need to get the hell up and get dressed. We're going out!"

She grabbed me and, with surprising strength, yanked me up off the couch.

"Damn, Supergirl, watch the goods." I rubbed my arms, staring at the red handprints there.

"Go, go, go!"

"But I don't want to. I want to read about Darcy banging Lizzie in the bath."

Ashley landed a sound slap to my ass, and I yelped. She meant business, so I hurried to my room and slammed the door.

I made quick work of my hair and makeup and threw on a jumpsuit.

Strutting into the living room, I found Ashley was no longer alone. Scott, Malcolm, and Axel all sat chatting. The usual tension between Axel and Malcolm was gone. They were actually smiling at each other—freaky shit.

"Well, isn't this cozy? I'm glad you all could make it." Everyone looked up and smiled.

Ashley flipped me off. "Shut it. I needed reinforcements."

Scott smiled as he got off the couch. "Red, baby, you look phenomenal." He scooped me up and spun me around.

"Scott, baby?" My body dragged against his as he set me down. "Don't call me Red." I nipped his nose.

Laughing, he threw an arm over my shoulder, giving me an unobstructed view of everyone looking all spiffy. Ashley smiled at me and got a little misty-eyed—that tiny softy.

"So, what's the plan?"

"First dinner, then drinks and dancing. Maybe, if you're lucky, a little action." Ashley wiggled her eyebrows and shoulders.

The idea of sleeping with someone else turned my stomach. It had been weeks, but I was holding on to the remnants of Luca and I's last time. "Let's not get ahead of ourselves." Her smile fell, and I felt like an asshole. "Unless you're dolling out more spankings."

That did it. Ashley laughed and motioned for us to leave.

Mostly empty plates littered our table. Only wasabi and ginger remained from the epic sushi pig out.

"I'm just saying you shouldn't have banged our tile guy. No dick is worth the headache of taking all those vendor meetings." Ashley tossed her used napkin at Axel.

Catching it out of the air, Axel shrugged. "How was I supposed to know that he was, and I quote, 'in love with me'? We can find a new source. Tile is tile. Right?"

Ash rolled her eyes. "Yeah, Axel, beautiful, designer, hand-crafted tile is super easy to find." She took a sip of sake. "Jackass."

Axel laughed, the potent drink clearly knocking the lumberjack on his ass.

"All right, I'm sorry. Dick move, I get it." Axel took a deep breath, trying to calm down. "No more vendors. I've learned my lesson." He threw his arm over Ashley's shoulder, and she pushed him away, snuggling into Malcolm's side.

Malcolm's smile was blinding. That dude had it bad. If only Ashley would realize how she felt about him.

"Don't hate a man for being attracted to talent. I've landed my fair share of companions because of what these hands can do." Scott wiggled his fingers in my direction.

"Thank you! He gets me." Axel sipped his warm sake while eyeing our waitress. The sway of her hips entranced our whole side of the table. My money was on Scott getting her number. Every time she came to the table, she made a point of bumping his shoulder.

"As fun as all this is, is it time to go home?" I wanted to get into some pajamas and sleep until Monday morning.

"No!" My friends glared at me.

"Per our tiny dictator—" Scott winked at Ashley, and she stuck her tongue out at him. Maybe we all had drank too much sake. "We're going dancing and scouting for your next warm body."

After downing the rest of my drink, I stood up. "If we must," I sighed and gestured to the door. "Please lead the way."

The five of us stumbled into our ride and headed to the club.

A thin sheen of sweat covered us as we danced to top forty hits I'd never heard. Malcolm and Ashley were damn near fucking, while two handsy cuties sandwiched Axel, and Scott was MIA.

I stood the lone dancer, and that was fine. Moving without restriction, I twirled, rolled, and wiggled in the goofiest ways. I dared someone to try and match that energy.

"I need a drink," I yelled to no one in particular since my entire crew was busy.

The bar was packed, so it was a real bitch to flag down the bartender.

"Gin and tonic?" A deep voice shouted in my ear.

Startled, I turned around and found Dimitri grinning down at me. Unease turned my stomach.

"Uh, yeah." I wasn't sure if he heard me over the pounding bass, but I wasn't too worried about that drink anymore. I was too busy thinking about that unanswered invitation sitting on my kitchen counter.

Somehow, Dimitri got the bartender's attention and ordered our drinks, plus an extra. I tried to look anywhere but at him while we waited.

Bad news. Dangerous. Must avoid. Do not speak to him. He will get the message.

"How have you been?"

Damn it.

"Good. I've been good. And you?" My smile must have been weird because Dimitri frowned at me, shaking his head.

"I'm great. You know, just wrapping up last-minute details for the engagement party next weekend. Daphne said you hadn't RSVPed yet."

Damn it.

"Oh, yeah. Um, I have another thing that night. Sorry."

Shaking his head, Dimitri grabbed his two drinks from the bar. "You don't have to lie to me, Sasha. Have the guts to tell me you don't want to come."

His anger surprised me, but he cut me off when I tried to apologize. "It's pretty shitty that one of my oldest friends isn't coming to my engagement party. Are you jealous or something? I mean, you picked Luca over me, remember?"

Gobsmacked. Completely and utterly gobsmacked. In all the years of us fucking around, I never got the impression that he wanted anything more. I'm not sure if it was the liquor or my confusion, but I blurted out, "No! It's because of your family!"

The color drained from his face, and his eyes darted around us. "Moretti told you?"

"Yes."

"You're back with him?"

The ache in my chest intensified. "No."

His frown relaxed as he took a deep breath. "Then there's no problem. It's not like you'd be rolling up with Moretti. You'll be just like all the other guests."

"I don't know Dimitri. Kind of goes against me trying to stay away from the criminal element." I tried to soften my words with a smile and shoulder bump, but Dimitri frowned, looking a little offended, which was fucking ridiculous. The dude was a part of a crime family.

"Look, I need to get these drinks to Daphne. If you get a minute, stop by our booth so we can talk about this. It would mean a lot to both of us if you came." He gave me a quick kiss on the cheek and walked away.

I stayed at the bar, nursing my gin and tonic. Friend guilt ate away at me. Dimitri had done nothing terribly wrong, Luca and Malcolm had confirmed as much, but his family was bad news bears.

Before I could dwell too much on the bullshit that kept

getting thrown at me, Scott appeared at my side, hair mussed, lips swollen, eyes glassy. "Red. Have I told you how fucking hot you are? Like top ten hottest woman I've ever had the privilege of meeting."

I laughed and patted his arm. "Thanks, Scott."

Shaking his head, he pulled me closer to him. "No, Red, you don't get it." He gestured to the writhing dance floor. "We are all but mere mortals next to a goddess like you."

"Okay, someone's met their limit tonight."

A dopey smile spread across his face. "Maybe, but I just wanted you to know I admire you."

I patted his cheek. "I admire you too. Now, let's get you some water."

The bartender delivered a round of waters as the rest of our group assembled.

"Sasha! Look, it's our friends!" Scott was officially tripping.

"Scott, are you on something?"

Giggling, the blond beanpole nodded. "I'm having fun with my friend Molly tonight."

"Scott!" Ashley grabbed his shoulders.

Scott grabbed her right back. "Ashley! Do you know how magnificent you are?" He looked over her shoulder at Malcolm. "It's easy to see why you love her, man. She's everything."

Letting out a dramatic sigh, Scott released Ashley and plopped down on the barstool next to me. We needed to get his high ass home.

"Well, shit." Everything was hazy from the booze, and guilt weighed heavy on my heart as I glanced around the room, my eyes quickly locking with Dimitri's. I thought I'd have a little more time to think this over or at least get drunk enough to make some kind of decision.

Turning to Ashley, I asked, "Can you keep an eye on him? I need to say hey to Dimitri and Daphne before we head out."

Malcolm touched my elbow as I passed by. "Do you think that's a good idea?" His eyes bore into me, trying to communicate the dangers of all things Chronis like I didn't fucking know.

"Not really, but I'll be ok."

Malcolm's forehead wrinkled, but then Ash turned and grabbed the collar of his shirt, whispering something in his ear that had him smiling big time.

I took the opportunity to slide by, bracing for whatever the hell was about to happen.

Beautiful people surrounded Dimitri and Daphne, some of whom I recognized from the fifteen years of friendship Dimitri and I shared, and others from different events around town.

"Sasha!" Daphne jumped up and wrapped her body around me. Rarely did another woman make me feel small, but Daphne was stacked. She dwarfed my five-ten height and had ass for days. Dimitri certainly had a type.

"Daph. How are you?"

Pulling back from the hug, she held onto my arms. "I'd be better if a certain lady was coming to our party. Come on, Sash, why aren't you coming?"

My eyes automatically went to Dimitri, and he nodded. "I'd love to, but I don't think it's a good idea." I pursed my lips, unsure whether Daphne knew Dimitri's little secret.

She glanced over her shoulder and frowned. Pulling me to where she'd been sitting, she pushed me down next to Dimitri. "Ok. We need to sort this out. I refuse to celebrate our engagement without the bitch responsible for us even meeting. Do something, D."

Daphne then sat on my other side and ran interference on some of Dimitri's friends.

"What's it going to take to get you there, Sasha?" Dimitri sounded tired and resigned. I hated that our once happy relationship was being dragged down by bullshit. I hated that it felt like my whole life was being dragged down by bullshit.

"I don't know. I just." The bloody scene from the club bathroom played out in my mind. Luca knew Cy would be at this party. Something could happen at this party. An internal battle raged in me, and I felt the urge to warn Dimitri. I mean, fuck, this dude isn't trying to kill anyone. But then, was that betraying Luca? "I'm just worried something bad will happen. You know?"

There, vague as hell.

"Moretti?"

I shrugged, refusing to say anymore. Loyalty is a hell of a thing. I guess I was on Team Moretti.

Yay.

Dimitri nodded. "Listen, I can't tell you what they'll do, but I can tell you that there will be security and some of the most powerful people in St. Louis there. I seriously doubt Moretti would pull some shit."

That didn't assure me I was safe with the Chronis clan, but Dimitri made sense. Or maybe the alcohol made him make sense.

My eyes darted back to my friends. Scott hung from Axel's shoulders while two girls chatted to the giant man. Ashley had her face buried in Malcolm's neck, but his eyes stayed locked on me.

"I'll come, but—"

"Awesome!"

Dimitri leaned in to hug me, but I leaned back. "But I'm bringing a friend."

He laughed and hugged me. "Bring a million friends. I don't fucking care."

As soon as he released me, Daphne crushed me in against her ample bosom.

Leaving the bar was a blur of kisses and hugs. Axel left with someone, and Ashley and Scott passed out on my couch as soon as we got home. That left Malcolm and me alone to chat.

Great.

After changing into my pajamas, I went to get a glass of water, only to be startled by Malcolm sitting in the dark at my dining table.

"What the fuck, Malcolm!"

He cracked a smile. "I've always wanted to do that." His smile fell. "Now sit your ass down and tell me what you're up to."

I got two glasses down and filled them at the tap. Setting one down in front of Malcolm, I sat down. "I'm going to Dimitri's engagement party. Would you—"

Malcolm sprung up from his chair. "Absolutely not! Are you fucking suicidal? Do you think I'll let you just waltz into the crime world's biggest party of the year? Fuck that!" He paced around the small room.

"I'm going, but—" He stopped moving and glared at me like that would stop me. "*But* I was going to ask you to come with me."

That stopped him in his tracks. Rubbing his bloodshot eyes, he nodded. "Well, that's a start, I guess." His fingertips scraped against the stubble on his jaw. "It's just not smart. You know?"

"Oh yeah, I know. But I figure nobody will pull something in a hotel ballroom, and it's not like I'm with Luca anymore."

"Sure, but why take the risk?" Malcolm dropped back in his seat.

I fell into the chair across from him. "Because right now, I don't have any reason not to. It might sound weird, but going to this party is something that old me would do. I need that right now. And the fact it's for Dimitri makes it a no-brainer."

Blowing out a big breath, Malcolm nodded. "Ok. Looks like I'm getting my wedding suit dry cleaned."

"Tux. It's black tie." I bit back a laugh as Malcolm smiled.

"Fuck yeah."

TWENTY-THREE

The week passed like so many had over the previous years. Sleep, work, drink, repeat. Although I had become awfully popular.

Malcolm texted, called, and dropped by the office daily, trying to change my mind. Every visit chipped away at my resolve that everything would be fine.

On the other side of the fight, Daphne and Dimitri kept me in fresh flowers and treats. Miranda thought I had a new admirer instead of a former hookup trying to trap me into an obligation. Those damn flowers made me a sneezing mess.

Smoothing the green silk on my thighs, I finished getting ready. Any minute, Malcolm would be here, as well as the car service Dimitri arranged to ensure my arrival.

My fingers brushed against the emeralds and diamonds around my neck. In a "fuck Luca" move, I decided to wear the necklace his mom wouldn't take back. There was something satisfying about wearing his necklace to an event he told me not to go to. It didn't hurt that it completed my Irish goddess ensemble.

A knock at the front door pulled me from my reflection. Malcolm stood on my stoop, looking as handsome as ever. Well, handsome and pissed off. I leaned against the door and took my time, giving him an exaggerated perusal.

"Wowie. Looking hot, Mr. Bello."

Malcolm glared at me but gave me a once-over. "You look very nice, Sasha." He glanced over his shoulder at the sleek town car parked in front of my building. "Let's get this over with." He pulled my arm through his and led me down the stairs. A suited driver opened the door, and we slid inside. "Well, this is posh." Malcolm tried and failed to look unimpressed.

Laughing, I settled in for the short ride to The Four Seasons. Malcolm didn't seem up to making conversation, which was perfect. I wasn't feeling particularly chatty.

It wasn't long before we made our way into the elegant ballroom. Candlelight created a warm, romantic glow while large draperies softened the walls. The tables sat eight people, keeping the guests close and cozy. Daphne had somehow made a party for four hundred feel intimate. All hail the Houdini of party planning.

"Is that the mayor? Is that the governor?" Malcolm casually tried to look at the powerful men gathered near one of the bars.

A glance confirmed the Midwest's leaders were throwing back drinks and laughing together. I tripped on nothing as one face stopped me dead in my tracks.

Mr. Moretti.

"What's he doing here?"

Malcolm walked back to me, scanning the group for a threat. I knew the minute he saw him because his body went rigid. "What the fuck is he doing here?"

We both stood, just staring at the region's movers and shakers, unable to be discrete. I suddenly felt lightheaded and too hot.

He shouldn't be here.

I shouldn't be here.

When Mr. Moretti's eyes looked past me, I let out a breath, only to suck it back in when his gaze zeroed in on me. It took everything in me not to run away. Phantom fingers dug into my arms as my body shuddered with the memory of being close to the angry Mafioso. How ignorant I had been back then to think he was just the run-of-the-mill toxic man.

I expected a snarl, a frown. Instead, the motherfucker smiled. He smiled. I shook my head because I had to be seeing things. Then, Mr. Moretti raised his hand and waved. Confused, I slowly raised my hand to wave back, not because I wanted to, but out of a Midwest reflex to be polite, and my brain was too broken to stop it.

"Oh, there's dad. Let's say hello."

At the sound of Luca's voice, my hand froze at my shoulder, and a whole new anxiety put my body on lockdown. My shoulders curled as if I could somehow shrivel up and hide.

I stood perfectly still as Luca escorted a tall, willowy blond past me and towards a far too smiley Mr. Moretti. My eyes immediately zeroed in on Luca's hand resting on her bare lower back, just above the swell of her small but perky ass. I couldn't look away.

"Sasha? We should head to our table."

Even Malcolm's voice didn't pull me from my stare down with Luca's hand and her ass. I wanted to look anywhere else but couldn't. I knew what it felt like to have him maneuver you through a crowd, to smell his rich cologne, feel his warmth on your skin, his breath on your neck as he makes some silly comment.

My chest ached with loss. I felt bereft seeing him be someone else's sunshine.

An ample chest covered in white silk stepped in between me and my new obsession. "Sasha! You're here!"

My stubborn gaze moved up to Daphne's beautiful face, which was made even more perfect by her breathtaking smile. "Well, duh." She crushed me against her. "Wouldn't miss it, Daph."

She let me go and turned toward Malcolm. "And you must be the plus one."

Malcolm tried to smile but couldn't shake his frown. Sticking out his hand, he introduced himself. Against my will, my gaze shifted back to the tux mafia by the bar. This time, Luca was staring at me, his blond companion whispering in his ear.

I pulled in a shaky breath and smiled. The air burned my lungs, but I kept breathing. This was my life: wanting someone so badly it physically hurt but knowing he could never be mine—not in secret, not in public.

My eyes burned, but I kept staring into his stupidly perfect face. His date looked my way, but I didn't give a fuck. Let her see. I hope she asks who I am. Explain that one, Luca.

"I'm sorry I didn't warn you. D's dad invited the Morettis at the last minute. Something about a new building deal. I don't know." After a pause, she muttered, "And I don't know what he's doing with Zoe."

I looked back at Daphne, who was frowning and staring at Luca.

Zoe? Like Zoe Chronis? He's dating a Chronis? What the hell is going on?

Brushing off the icky feelings crawling all over me, I pulled my shoulders back and smiled at the worried bride-to-be. "No worries! I was just surprised."

Daphne pursed her lips.

I patted her hand. "You go, mingle! We'll catch up later." I quickly glanced around the room. "Or maybe not." I laughed, squeezing her hand, and let go. "Good luck chatting with all these people."

That made Daphne smile. "Right? Dimitri's dad turned this into a networking event. I hope you have business cards."

"Guilty." I patted my clutch.

"Fucking hustler." She wasn't wrong. Shaking her head, Daphne laughed as she turned to greet another guest.

Malcolm snatched two champagne flutes from a passing tray and handed me one. We both wordlessly downed them and placed them on a table, grabbing two more from a passing waiter. "Welp. This might not be so bad if they're making peace or whatever."

Malcolm looked around the room, his eyes purposely staying away from Luca, although Luca had never stopped staring our way.

Taking the last gulp, I tried to enjoy the bubbles tickling down my throat, but the heat of Luca's stare made my skin break out in a fine sheen of sweat. A shiver ran down my spine as the air conditioning hit my clammy skin. I was suddenly glad to have an empty stomach because it felt like I was going to throw up my feelings. "I need to go to the ladies."

"Ok. I'll hang out in the hallway."

We left the ballroom and headed to the bathrooms. My hands shook as I sped down the corridor, trying to maintain my composure.

I paused briefly at the door, looking over my shoulder. "I'll just be a minute."

"Take your time." Malcolm leaned against the wall, his eyes scanning the hallway.

The sweet smell of cleaner greeted me as I moved toward the sinks. The lighting was dim, setting the gold fixtures aglow. Marble surrounded me on the floors, walls, and countertops. The sheer opulence of the bathroom was ridiculous. Rich people were a trip.

Setting my clutch down on a dry spot on the counter, I stared in the mirror, taking deep breaths. What a mind fuck. Apparently, the crime lords were going to be besties.

I was safe. I was fucking safe. Probably. There was no way that either side would have time for a small fish like me now that they were at peace. But now I got to have a front-row seat to further heartbreak. Luca was with a mafia princess.

What a fucking joke.

Shaking out my limbs, I growled out my frustrations. I was being a big baby. It was time to suck it up, get drunk, and, well, I didn't have an and, but I sure as hell was going to find one.

When I went to open the door, in waltzed the tall, blond Chronis.

"Ope. Sorry!" She laughed and gave me a perfect smile. It took everything in me not to gag at her beautiful face.

"No worries." I hurried past her and out to the hallway, where Luca and Malcolm were in a tense standoff.

"Am I interrupting?"

Luca immediately moved toward me, his hands reaching for me.

I took an exaggerated step around him to stand next to Malcolm. "I think we should head back in there. Those shrimps won't eat themselves." I trembled while trying to stay calm, cool, and collected. Malcolm noticed my distress, looped his arm through mine, and started to walk away from Luca, but of course, it wasn't going to be that easy.

"Sasha, wait."

I dropped my chin to my chest, blowing out a breath. Without turning around, I asked, "What, Luca?"

"We need to talk."

I shook my head and glanced over my shoulder.

Damn, he's sexy.

"About?" My voice was sharp, but my ankles wobbled. Malcolm pressed into me, giving me his strength.

Leveling me with a look of disbelief, Luca gestured toward the ballroom. "Why are you here?"

"You know Dimitri's my friend. Better question—why are you here?"

Luca's eyes rolled over me, his jaw tensing when they landed on my neck. I lifted my hand to my throat, my fingers pressing into the largest stone.

I shouldn't have worn the damn thing.

With a heavy swallow, his focus rested on my bodyguard for the night. "Business. Can we just—" The bathroom door opening cut him off.

"You waited! What a gentleman." Zoe Chronis floated toward Luca, claiming her spot next to him. They made a striking couple. Her lightness complemented his darkness in every feature.

When Luca didn't respond to her, she followed his line of vision to me. I hadn't turned completely to face him. Instead, I leaned my front into Malcolm's as we stood ready to leave the hallway.

No one spoke. We all just stood there, staring. Awkward doesn't even begin to explain it.

Finally, Zoe regained the function of her mouth. A charming smile replaced her confused frown. "Well, we should probably get back in there before the toasts start."

She tugged Luca along as he begged me with his eyes to talk to him. A tether pulled at me to follow, but I held onto Malcolm tighter. His hands gripped me as if he could feel the tug of war.

We watched them disappear behind the doors and relaxed a fraction.

"Jesus. That was intense." Malcolm snorted and let go of his grip on my arm. "I thought he was about to throw you over his shoulder and run away."

I laughed and nodded, still staring at the heavy doors.

Malcolm cupped my cheek and turned my face toward him. "We can go. We can just walk right out that door and go home."

Shaking my head, I blew out a heavy breath. "No. I can do this. The worst is over. Right?"

"I guess, but that doesn't mean we have to test that theory."

"No. No, I got this." I walked towards the ballroom, and Malcolm followed.

After checking the giant seating chart, he let out a low whistle. "You must be one hell of a good time."

That pulled my attention from the stare off Luca was having with his father. "What do you mean?"

He pointed to the board. "We're sitting next to the family tables and with the mayor. Oh, and the governor." Mischief sparkled in his eyes as he smirked at me. "Just how big of a freak are you?"

His smirk grew into a grin as I laughed—an honest-to-good-ness laugh. While anyone listening would've thought he was a prick, I knew better.

"Now, baby, if you have to ask, you're clearly not mayor-table material." I leaned into him, smoothing his lapels. "And who says it has to be in the bedroom?"

Another round of laughter shook us as we moved out of the way of the other guests. Leave it to Malcolm's dickish sense of humor to ease the tension from the night. Once we both settled down, he wrapped his arm around my waist and led me to our table.

Dinner was a flurry of networking, speeches, and one unfortunate nip slip from the mayor's wife. Occasionally, I would glance over at Luca and find him already looking at me. Well, that or glaring at his father.

Seeing him made me want to be near him, to hold him. I wanted to smooth his forehead and tell him to lighten up. Instead, I watched a blond bombshell hang on his arm, occasionally running blood-red nails up his back. Zoe's touch didn't seem to register as the anger never left his face.

After dessert was served, the dancing started, and I noticed Luca was missing from the ballroom. An uncomfortable dread settled in the pit of my stomach. I had no idea when I would see him again, which was a ridiculous thing to worry about, but hey, I was the queen of ridiculous.

Malcolm's arm brushed against me as he swayed in his seat to the big band music. The man loved to dance, and usually, I would be more than happy to cut a rug, but not tonight. "Why don't you ask someone to dance?" I glanced at the closest bar and the tall woman who couldn't stop looking our way. "There's a tall drink of water by the bar that looks up for a little hustle."

He looked over and quickly, then back at the band. "Nah. I'm good."

"Hm."

Malcolm turned toward me, his eyebrows raised toward his hairline. "What?"

"It's just weird."

He put his hand on the back of my chair, canting his body completely toward me. "What's weird?"

"That you aren't going to dance. That you don't want to mambo with that beauty."

Malcolm shook his head and looked down at his lap.

"You and Ash? Finally?"

He shook his head.

"I'm sorry. She'll get there." I patted his knee.

Malcolm only shrugged. "You ready to go?"

My phone buzzed in my clutch on my lap. Pulling it out, I absently nodded.

Malcolm stood and put on his jacket as I found a text from Luca.

LUCA MORETTI

We need to talk. Meet me in room 551.
Please.

Relief I shouldn't have felt surged through me. Watching him all night made me want to be near him. I wanted to kiss him until he smiled—just once.

One more time. I just needed one more time.

"Um, I actually need to use the bathroom. Let me do that real quick. Then we can track down Dimitri and Daph to say goodbye."

"Sounds good. I need to use the loo anyway."

I walked with Malcolm toward the bathrooms, trying to appear calm. Every step brought me closer to Luca. I waited just inside the bathroom until I heard the men's door close, and then I made a break for the bank of elevators.

My finger mashed the button, and I watched the floor numbers light up.

"Come on. Come on." I peeked over my shoulder, looking for any sign of Malcolm.

Finally, the doors opened with a ding. I scrambled in and hit the five button. A couple stumbled toward the elevator and yelled for me to hold it as the doors closed, so I pretended to try and stop it. There was no way I was waiting on their drunk asses.

The doors closed, and I stared at my reflection in the gold walls of the elevator. It was only five floors, but it felt like the ride up took forever. My fingers dug into the hard case of my clutch. Breathing was a chore. Every muscle in my body was tight, ready to snap.

When the doors opened, I sprinted out and down the hall. Approaching room 551, I noticed the door was propped open. I lightly knocked as I pushed the door open. Shutting it behind me, I called out, "Luca?". There was no answer.

Something felt off as I timidly moved deeper into the room. A bedside lamp was on, but there was no Luca. The sink in the bathroom turned on, and I tried to shake off the bad feeling in my gut, but it wouldn't go away.

Two glasses of champagne sat on the desk near the window, so I took one and downed it. Picking up the second, I looked out at the St. Louis skyline.

When the bathroom door opened, I didn't turn around. Luca's tall silhouette was backlit in the glass's reflection, blacking out the Arch. "This view is pretty spectacular."

He didn't say anything, so I took another sip before setting the glass back on the desk. "So what do we need to—" As my eyes lifted, my mouth went dry.

"We need to make sure you aren't going to be a problem for my family." Mr. Moretti smiled at me, a gun in his hand.

TWENTY-FOUR

My mouth fell open, but no sound came out. I'd been so worried about faceless, unknown dangers that I hadn't even considered Luca's dad.

"Have a seat." Mr. Moretti gestured with his gun toward the bed.

I tried to force myself to move, but my body was frozen in fear. Internally, I screamed for help, but I couldn't even bring myself to run.

This is how I die.

Mr. Moretti sneered. It was amazing how such a handsome man could be so ugly. A humorless laugh left his lips as he moved toward me. Before I could step back, his free hand wrapped around my arm, jerking me from the window. With one hard shove, I fell across the bed.

It was as if that push woke me up, and I scrambled across the comforter to the other side, desperate to put some distance between us. My foot got stuck on the blanket, but I shook it free and cleared the other side of the bed. Jumping to my feet, I walked backward towards the door.

Mr. Moretti tilted his head, a slight smile pulling at his full lips. "You think you're just walking out of here?"

I never took my eyes off him. Lesson one of every action movie—never take your eyes off the threat. I kept inching back. As I reached the bathroom door, my heel caught on the carpet, and I stumbled into the wall. In two long strides, Mr. Moretti was on me.

He gripped my hair, slamming my head into the wall. The sudden attack rattled my brain, and pain splintered through my skull. The room became blurry as I reached out for something to hold to stay upright because it felt like the world had gone upside down.

Another push into the wall, and I cried out only to be pushed face-first into the bedding. Fabric filled my mouth as I screamed. My breath dampened the cover, and I started to suffocate on my own hot sobs.

The weight of him on top of me kicked my panic into overdrive. My hands pushed frantically against the bed, but he wouldn't budge. Kicking out, I hit something, so I kept flailing. I couldn't give up.

Fingers twisted in my hair, and he yanked me up. Pain shot through my scalp, and I yelped, my hands flying up to his, trying to remove his iron grip as I twisted in his hold.

"Quiet!" The back of his hand cracked against my cheek. With his hand buried in my hair, he shoved me onto the bed, climbing over me. His massive body kept me pinned down.

Lifting my head, I could just make out his tousled hair and red face through the tears. The dim lights cast a shadow on half his face, making him a goddamn demon in the flesh.

"Stay fucking still!"

I, of course, did the opposite, wiggling and struggling under him, trying to free my hands. This time, his meaty fist crashed into my face, and I tasted blood as pain spread through my jaw. I cried, but I stopped moving.

"Thank you! Now just fucking lay there."

I sobbed harder, gasping for air. His weight on my chest and my crying kept me from getting a full breath, making me lightheaded. Dots lined my hazy sight, and I tried to tell him I couldn't breathe, but no words came out through the panicked sobs.

As darkness closed in on me, Mr. Moretti got up. The bed shifted next to me, but I stayed still, focusing on taking deep breaths. Every inch of me felt beaten, and I wasn't sure how I was going to get out of the room.

Out of the corner of my eye, I saw his face lit by a phone's screen. Shaking his head, he slid the phone back into his pocket and stood.

"You know, I knew you'd be a problem before I ever met you."

I turned my head slightly, watching as he walked up to the gilded mirror on the wall.

"Rosa told me not to worry." He shook his head as he ran his fingers through his messed hair. "But even before Luca told us he was seeing someone, he'd started to change."

Mr. Moretti's eyes darted to me before returning to his reflection and dabbing his forehead with a handkerchief. "Luca was never like his brother. Never had the spine to carry this family like Dante did. No matter how hard I pushed him, he was soft. But magically, after they murdered Dante, Luca shaped up."

He leaned closer to the mirror, his finger dabbing a spot on his shirt. "You got blood on me." With a sigh, he removed his cummerbund.

"But we're not together," I whispered before I could stop myself.

"It doesn't matter. You're poison to him. With you, he's vulnerable and soft. Without you, he's 'The Butcher.' He's a loose cannon. Do you know he killed his own cousin?"

I shook my head and immediately regretted it as the pain shot down my neck. I cradled my head, trying to stop the room from spinning, and felt warm, sticky dampness. Hands shaking, I brought them in front of my face. Dark red blood coated my fingers. Bile sat at the back of my throat, and I swallowed hard, trying to keep from adding vomit to my blood scattered across the room.

Mr. Moretti shrugged off his shirt and inspected his undershirt for splatter. "For you. He killed family because he found out there were some of us that wanted you gone."

I scooted up to rest against the headboard. "Killing me won't make him any less of a loose cannon."

Tugging off his white undershirt, Mr. Moretti chuckled. "No, but it eliminates the possibility of a reconciliation."

I stared at him. I didn't know if it was the head injury or if I was just missing something obvious, but I didn't understand how killing me helped anything other than satisfy his dickish hate for me.

"And I can use his anger at your death to stop this ridiculous peace he is attempting by marrying that Chronis bitch. It'll be a snap to frame Cy for your death. He's already tried and failed a couple of times."

My breathing became more labored. Luca told me people were coming for me, but Mr. Moretti didn't have to be so nonchalant about it.

"It'll be killing two birds with one bullet. I get my bloodthirsty son back, starting the war back up, and you'll be gone, keeping him focused on what's really important."

He looked down at his hands and shook his head. He surprised me when he went into the bathroom, and I heard the water running. It was my chance to get the fuck out.

I kicked off my heels and jumped off the bed. It took only seven steps, and my fingers wrapped around the handle. I pushed down, and the latch clicked. Before I could open the door, I was snatched back by my hair.

I flew back, landing flat on the floor, knocking the wind out of me. Before I could take a breath, Mr. Moretti was on me. His massive fists rained down on me as I tried to guard my face with my forearms, but he was too fast.

I flailed until my hand landed on smooth leather—my stiletto.

Gripping the middle of the shoe, I jammed the heel at his face. In a stroke of luck, the tip dug into the corner of his eye.

"Fuck!"

He scrambled to get off me, but I followed, shoving the four-inch red bottom into his eye socket.

His scream was deafening as he fell backward, his hands tugging the heel from his face. I didn't give him a chance to get his bearings. I was on him in a second.

My hits may not have had finesse, but they did have the full force of my rage.

"You." Hit. "Mother." Hit. "Fucker." Hit.

He tried to grab my hands, but he couldn't catch me.

Using the heel of my hand, I pushed down on the shoe still stuck in his eye. His fists flew, smacking into my face, but it didn't matter. I only saw red. This time, the blood wasn't making me sick. It was fueling me.

As he pulled at the heel, I wrapped my hands around his neck.

"I don't have some big villain speech, you fucking maniac, but I will say this." My words stilted between heavy pants, I forced out, "You can't beat me, motherfucker."

His face turned purple, and his hands pulled at mine, but he didn't have the strength. He bucked under me, trying to knock me off, but I only tightened my thighs around him.

I leaned into my grip, putting all my weight against his throat. Slowly, Mr. Moretti's body stopped bucking under me. His mouth fell open as he tried to talk, tried to scream.

I squeezed harder, my arms shaking with the effort. The blood vessels in his good eye burst, and I watched as the light started to go out.

But I didn't stop. I couldn't. If I didn't do this, I would be dead. Hell, I was probably already dead. Why not take the fucker with me?

My whole body tensed as Mr. Moretti went limp beneath me. I shook his neck once, and his head lolled back.

I killed someone.

SASHA AND THE BUTCHER

I killed Mr. Moretti.

I killed Luca's dad.

Fuck.

Reality set in now that I was safe, and my body sagged with relief. I pulled myself from him and leaned against the wall, sitting in a splatter of my own blood.

I looked around the expensive hotel room and marveled at the utter destruction our struggle had caused. The carpet was dark, but it was darker where blood puddled.

My dress was torn and stained, and I knew my face was a busted mess. Gently, I probed my cheek and winced.

I was fucked.

For a few minutes, I just sat there. I didn't know what the hell to do.

I killed a mafia boss. A laugh bubbled up in my throat.

I choked out a giant motherfucker. A chuckle fell from my mouth.

I killed Luca's dad. My whole body shook with laughter until it turned into sobs. I wasn't worried about having literal blood on my hands. I was worried about Luca.

Snot ran down my lips, mingling with the blood there. I slowly slid down to the floor until I was facing Mr. Moretti's lifeless body.

I lay there staring for who knows how long. There wasn't really a "what to do when you've killed your ex's dad, the mafia boss" checklist.

Suddenly, a phone ringing broke the silence. I pushed up on my elbow and saw Mr. Moretti's pocket light up.

My hand shook as I reached into his pocket and pulled out the vibrating phone. "Dad" flashed across the screen. I frowned down at Mr. Moretti's mangled face. I knew his dad was dead. How was he calling?

Just as the phone stopped ringing, there was a knock at the door. "Dad, I think you grabbed my phone by mistake. I have yours."

I held my breath and sat as still as I could.

"Come on. I know you're in there. The front desk gave me your room number."

Looking down at Mr. Moretti, I didn't know what to do.

"If you and mom are in the middle of something, just stick your hand out in the hall with the phone. I need to get Zoe home."

Tears pooled in my eyes. I needed to do something.

Luca knocked again and cursed under his breath. His shadow under the door rocked back and forth. Then the door beeped and cracked open. My breathing sped up, and I dragged myself toward the bed.

"Final warning. Cover any bits you don't want me to see!"

The light from the hallway poured over Mr. Moretti's body, Luca's figure casting a large dark shadow. I couldn't see his face as he gasped. The door closed behind him with a click.

My eyes adjusted back to the darkness of the room, and I watched as Luca approached his father. He stood next to his body, just a few feet from me, and fell to his knees. Trembling hands ghosted over the wounds on Mr. Moretti's face, and his shoulders began to shake. Without thinking, I moved to hug him.

When my hand grazed his shoulder, Luca turned quickly, shoving me against the wall. My head slammed against it, and I whimpered. It only took a second for him to recognize me and slacken his grip on my shoulders.

"Sasha?" His eyes widened, and he cupped my cheek. Pain shot through my face, and I jerked back, only to smack my head against the wall again. "Fuck, baby, stay still."

I nodded. "Luca, I—" The distance between us was becoming too much. I threw myself into his arms. "He was going to kill me." His jacket muffled my words.

"Shh." His hands gently rubbed my back. "It's going to be okay."

I shook my head and tried to pull away, only to have Luca

hold me closer, placing kisses on top of my head as he took deep breaths. We sat wrapped together on the floor.

After a deep sigh, Luca moved back and inspected my face. "What happened?"

I rested my hands on his chest. "I got a text from you telling me to meet you, but when I got here, it was your dad. I don't know what his plan was because when I got the chance, I made a run for it."

Luca nodded, his gaze falling on the heel planted deeply in his dad's eye. "I'd say you got the upper hand." He shook his head and looked back at me. "We need to get you out of here. Do you trust me?"

It wasn't a question. "Always."

"Good." He gently lifted me and guided me to the bed. "I need to get Marco up here. He'll get you out of the hotel and to safety."

I nodded, my hand holding his so tightly that his fingers turned red.

"This isn't our hotel, but we shouldn't have any problem cleaning this up. But we need to get you to the hospital without anyone knowing what happened."

"Probably an obvious answer, but no cops?"

Luca frowned and shook his head. "No cops. No one can know you did this. There are too many balls in the air."

"Okay. So what do I tell the hospital? Or Malcolm?"

Luca stood in front of me, smoothing my hair. "You're going to be in a car accident."

"Come again?"

"I'm going to put you in a car, and Pete's going to crash it. We'll make sure one of ours comes to the scene. I'll tell Malcolm we got into an argument, and you left. I'm guessing he won't buy it, but he's the least of my worries right now."

My head was spinning at the thought of being in a car accident. "And what about him?"

Luca's gaze fell on his dad. "I'll take care of it."

I stood up and pulled his face toward me. "No, I did this. I should—I should—"

"You should what?" His hands traced my waist. "This isn't your fault, Sasha. If I had been more observant, I could've stopped him before you had to. I'm so sorry." His lips gently pressed against my forehead. It hurt like a motherfucker. "I'll take care of this."

He stepped away for a second and shot off some texts. Sliding his phone in his pocket, he knelt between my legs. "I need you to listen to me, okay?"

I nodded. Honestly, I didn't even know what to say.

"You need to forget about tonight. You need to forget about me. This right here is proof I can't keep you safe, and I would die if anything happened to you."

"But—" Luca shook his head, and I swallowed my words.

"I'm going to marry Zoe Chronis." He shook his head as my lips parted. "Our marriage will unite the families and stop the day-to-day bloodshed. It will keep you safe. I should've never brought you into this world." He looked away for a moment before nailing me with his dark stare. "I will never forgive myself for this."

Tears welled in his eyes. My hands framed his face as I placed a kiss on his lips, my split lip stinging. When I pulled back, I thumbed the blood that stained his perfect pout.

"I love you, Sasha Mitchell. Never doubt that."

As I battled the pounding in my head to make sense of every-thing, there was a knock at the door. Marco rushed in. He looked surprised but weirdly unbothered by his uncle lying dead on the floor.

Luca stood, and the two had a quick, hushed conversation before Marco whisked me from the room. Luca watched us walk down the hall before reentering the room and moving out of sight.

Marco cradled my elbow, his voice soft as he reassured me, but I didn't hear anything he said because I was too busy spiraling.

I was a murderer.

We moved at a snail's pace. A trip that should've taken five minutes took twenty, with me limping on one high heel while Marco shortened his long strides to match.

Pete met us at the garage level with a town car. When he opened the door, I screamed. Mr. Moretti's body sat on the other side of the backseat, strapped into a seat belt. My stiletto sat in his lap, leaving his eye a gaping wound. I bent over and finally threw up the expensive dinner Daphne had so meticulously chosen.

Wiping my mouth with the back of my hand, I pleaded, "I can't get in there!" I dry heaved as I gripped Marco's lapels. He had to understand just how fucked up this was. Faking the cause of my injuries is one thing, but we were faking his death?

He patted my back but pushed me back to the car. "You have to."

"Please! No!" I clawed at his arms as both men moved me into the backseat.

Pete held me in the seat and fought to buckle the seatbelt. He backed away, murmuring apologies.

Marco peeked his head back inside. "Hang in there, Red. Luca is stubborn and thinks he's doing the right thing. He'll figure it out." He closed the door and hit the roof twice.

Pete pulled away from the elevator doors and out of the parking garage. "Are you okay, Ms. Sasha?" He glanced in the rearview mirror, his face drawing into a tight-lipped frown.

I glared at him and his ridiculous question, never looking at the body next to me. My side pressed tightly against the door to avoid brushing against his arm.

Pete left it at that and drove down the dark city streets. Ten minutes later, he broke the silence. "All right, time to brace yourself."

Before I had time to grab onto anything, the car was spinning, and bright headlights smashed into the passenger side door. My head smacked into the window, and everything went black.

TWENTY-FIVE

"Sasha! Oh, thank God! Greg, get the doctor!" Mom's voice pierced my eardrums as she shouted at my dad while still facing me. Everything north of my shoulders throbbed in intense pain, but the woman kept bellowing for the doctors despite sending my dad running into the hallway.

Lifting my hand, I went to cradle my forehead, only to have a stinging sensation stop me. I slowly open my eyes to find my hand stuck with all manner of IVs and tubes.

"Mom, can you stop yelling and turn down the lights? My head's fucking killing me." The fluorescents were blinding, which didn't help my blurry vision from what I suspected was a concussion. I shut my eyes tightly, trying to keep the spots at bay.

She mumbled apologies as she fidgeted with the lights. Once the room was dim, I opened one eye to a slit before fully opening both.

"What the hell happened?"

Mom pulled her chair closer and grabbed my needle-free hand. "You were in a car accident, sweetie." She stared at our hands as she caressed my fingers. "You and Mr. Moretti. Do you remember anything?"

Like a movie montage, the night's events came back to me.

The party, the fight, me killing someone, and the car accident all hit me one by one until I folded over and threw up into a perfectly placed bin.

My mom's hands smoothed over my back as she whispered soothing nonsense.

"Ah, I see we're awake." A cheery voice came from beside me.

Wiping the corner of my mouth with a paper towel, I dragged my head up to greet the doctor. The tiny man looked all of twenty and was positively beaming down at me. I managed a grunt in response.

The doctor gestured toward the pale, and a nurse came and switched it out for a puke-free bucket. "How are we feeling, Ms. Mitchell?"

Another grunt as I tried to sip down some water. I wasn't sure how to tell this doctor that I wasn't throwing up because of head trauma but because I was a goddamn murderer. I glanced down at my hands and noticed they were clean, not a speck of blood in sight.

"That's to be expected. Migraines and vomiting are common symptoms of a concussion. We'll be keeping you overnight for observation, and we'll assess you tomorrow to make sure you're safe to go home."

I nodded, still sipping down the ice-cold water. It didn't matter where I spent the night. I knew I wouldn't be able to sleep. The sight of Mr. Moretti's lifeless body sat at the back of my mind.

The pocket-sized doc looked down at his clipboard and nodded. "It looks like, besides your head and face taking a bit of a beating and that wicked bruise on your chest from the seatbelt—you came out of the accident relatively unscathed. You're a lucky one, Ms. Mitchell." Looking at his watch, he grimaced. "All right, I'll be back to check on you. If you need anything, just buzz the nurses." He bounced out of the room.

Dad came and sat down next to Mom, his eyes still on the door. "I don't know that I believe he's old enough to be a doctor."

My mom slapped his arm. "Stop it. He's been very profession-al." Shaking her head, she looked back at me. "Oh honey, we're glad you're okay."

I squeezed her hand. "Me too." I finally took a good look at my parents and realized they were all dressed up. "What were you guys up to tonight?"

Mom blushed. "The Fire Department banquet was tonight."

"I interrupted date night? Damn it! I'm sorry, guys."

Dad smiled at mom. "No worries, kid. I got to dance with my girl before we got the call."

My mom's blush deepened outrageously. These two drove me crazy, but damn if I didn't want what they had with each other.

"As long as you got to dance." I laughed and rested back on the pillows behind me. "Now that I'm awake and you know I'm fine, why don't you two head home and finish date night?"

All humor drained from my parent's faces, and Dad added his hands to Mom's and mine. "We have to tell you something, Sasha."

I chuckled to ease some of the tension out of my body. "You guys aren't getting a divorce, are you?"

They both shook their heads, but neither cracked a smile.

"Unfortunately." Dad paused, shifting on his feet. "Luca's dad didn't make it."

A bark of laughter left my mouth before I could measure my response. Thank God my parents misunderstood, thinking I was in disbelief. Mom moved closer and rubbed my arm. "Sweetie, I'm so sorry. I know this must be a shock to you."

Nodding, I forced my face into a frown. "I can't believe he's gone." I tried to cry, but it wasn't happening. Mourning for the evil dead wasn't in the cards.

Tears glistened in my mom's eyes. "I know. We saw Luca in the waiting room. The poor boy looked devastated."

A shiver went down my spine, and I felt the tug of that invis-ible tether. "Is he still here?" Hope wiggled in my chest. What if he came for me? What if he realized he was wrong?

"He's right out there. He wanted to check on you before he went home." Frowning, my dad shifted in his seat. "I told him we'd have to see what you said because, well, you know." He pursed his lips.

There was no question, of course, I was going to see him. I would just have to deal with the emotional fallout after—something I'd gotten pretty good at doing. "Right. Yeah, you can bring him in."

Sighing, Dad stood up and left the room. Mom ran her fingers through my hair for a last-minute primp. If it wouldn't have hurt too much, I would've smiled, but my cheeks were throbbing. "Let's prop you up." She shoved another pillow behind me, aggravating my sore muscles.

Batting her hands away, I pursed my lips to hold back the groan. "That's good. Thanks, Mom."

Just then, Luca and my dad walked into the room. Dad rejoined us while Luca stood at the door. He was no longer wearing a tux. Instead, he was dressed in joggers and a hoodie. Memories of Sunday mornings spent lazing about while Luca cooked me breakfast in bed ran through my head.

God, I love him.

Coughing, Luca pulled a colorful bouquet from behind his back. "Uh, I brought you these." He set them on the table below the TV and then came to stand at the bottom of the bed. "How are you feeling, Sash?"

Luca's dark eyes traced over me, taking inventory of every scratch and bruise. They stopped on my cheek, which was being held together by stitches. His brow furrowed, and he raised a hand toward me, even though there was no way he could reach me.

"We're going to grab a coffee from the cafeteria. Be back in a minute." My parents shuffled out of the room as Luca and I stared at one another.

Finally, Luca looked toward the door. "I see Maggie Mitchell is as subtle as ever." Shaking his head, he drifted toward the chair and sat. I watched as he raised and lowered his hands a few times until he ultimately clasped them around my free hand.

After a deep breath, his gaze met mine. "I'm so sorry."

I shook my head. "There's nothing to be sorry about it. You didn't do anything."

Luca scowled and parted his lips, only to press them back together and shake his head. "We don't have a lot of time. Officer Russo will be here soon to take your statement. We need to be on the same page."

My chest deflated. He hadn't come for me, at least not like that. Summoning all my strength, I sat up as tall as I could and nodded.

Blowing out a breath, Luca squeezed my hand. "You and I argued about Zoe, and my father was there. He offered to take you home as a way to apologize. You can decide on the details of that conversation. Pete lost control of the wheel, and the truck crashed into you."

Tears burned at the back of my eyes. "Got it." I tried to pull my hand back.

"Please, just let me hold your hand a little longer. Let me be here with you, knowing you're okay."

"Fine." My words came out like a whisper.

We stared into each other's eyes, the only sound coming from the machines monitoring my body. There was nothing more to say. I'd said the same thing over and over, and it always ended in him telling me no and me running off to lick my wounds.

A knock at the door drew my attention from Luca. Officer Russo stood with his notebook in hand and a grimace on his face. "Can I come in?"

"Sure."

He walked to the end of the bed and tipped his chin at Luca. "Mr. Moretti."

"Officer Russo." Luca didn't let go of my hand. If anything, his grip tightened.

"I just need to ask you a few questions, Ms. Mitchell. Then I'll be out of your hair."

"Shoot."

"Can you describe what happened?"

"Well, Pete was driving me home from the engagement party."

"That's the engagement party of Dimitri Chronis?"

"Correct."

"Go on." Officer Russo pulled a chair to the end of the bed and sat down.

"I was sitting behind the driver's seat, Mr. Moretti—" His name caught in my throat. Fear wedged itself between the words, and I needed to press on to get this cop out of my face. I cleared it and continued. "Mr. Moretti was on the passenger side. Pete lost control of the wheel, and the car spun. The last thing I remember is headlights coming at the passenger side."

Russo nodded and flipped his notebook closed. "That's all I needed. The driver who hit you was over the legal limit, and with Mr. Moretti's passing, we need to have all eyewitness statements accounted for."

"Wait. What's the other driver being charged with?"

"That's what we're figuring out." He stood up and reached a hand out to Luca. "My condolences for your loss. Mr. Moretti was a good man."

Annoyance radiated off Luca as he stood and took Russo's hand. "Thank you. Do you need anything else?"

Officer Russo looked between the two of us, his eyes darting back and forth as if he was trying to figure something out. "Not right now." He finally settled his gaze on me. "I'll be in touch."

One head nod and he was out the door.

I sucked in a breath to calm my nerves. Luca dragged a hand through his already mussed hair. Someone was going to be charged for Mr. Moretti's death. Guilt churned in my gut. Even if we didn't make the driver drink, we did throw an accident in their path.

Chalk it up to another life I've ended.

"I guess we're in the clear then."

Luca turned and raised an eyebrow.

"I mean, your plan worked. We can go back to normal."

"Right."

Then he just stood, his face giving away nothing.

Irritated, I snapped, "What?"

"I'm trying to figure out what the hell I'm supposed to do now."

"Okay?"

Luca shoved his hands in his hoodie pocket and went over to the window that had a fantastic view of the parking lot. "I mean, now he's gone. He won't be there to push his agenda. He won't be there to handle the shit I don't want to. It's all me now." The fabric pulled taught around his fists. "I'm in deeper than I ever thought was possible."

I stayed silent. Luca was right. I had nothing to offer him. Over the course of an evening, he went from being the transitional leader of the most powerful crime family in the Midwest to the leader. All because we couldn't let go.

"I hoped that dating Zoe and eventually marrying her would calm things down enough to take the heat off me, but now even that's fucked."

My forehead scrunched, and as I tried to ask what he meant, there was a knock at the door. Ashley flew into the room, not even glancing Luca's way. "Sasha! What the hell!"

A tall, tuxedoed, angry man followed in her concerned wake. "Yeah, what happened to not leaving my side?" Malcolm's eyes did clock Luca by the window, and the two men stared each other down.

"I'm sorry, you guys. I just—" I looked at Luca for help, but he was too busy glaring at Malcolm.

"We'll talk about it later," Ash mumbled, finally noticing my brooding ex.

"I think you should go." Malcolm's voice was cold and menacing.

"Wait a second," I tried to shout.

Malcolm raised a hand in my direction, cutting me off. "You've caused enough trouble for Sasha. Go back to your girlfriend."

Luca's jaw ticked, but he didn't respond to Malcolm. Instead, he walked over to the bed and bent down to my level. "I'm sorry, Sasha." He gently kissed my busted lips, mindful not to put too much pressure. Too bad I wanted more. I would take every miserable moment of pain if he would really kiss me. "I love you. Feel better."

Standing to his full height, he nodded at Ashley and stalked out of the room, knocking into Malcolm's shoulder on the way out. Malcolm huffed out a laugh and came to sit by Ashley. "What happened, Sasha? One minute, you're in the bathroom. The next, I can't find you, and I'm getting a call from Ashley that you'd been in an accident with Mr. Moretti." He arched an eyebrow, his lips flattening into a severe line.

I grabbed Ashley's hand for support. "I got a text from Luca asking me to meet him in his room. After watching him all night, I wanted to see him, even if it was a bad fucking idea." I looked around Malcolm to make sure the door was closed. "When I got to the room, it wasn't Luca."

"What do you mean it wasn't Luca?" Ashley practically growled out.

"It was his dad, and things got ugly." I blew out a breath to keep from crying. "Long story short, Luca helped me, and we had to come up with a plausible story for the cops. Case closed."

"Not case closed. Case mother fucking open, Sash." Ashley shot out of her seat like she was about to run after Luca. "That man's got you lying to the cops? Hell no!"

Malcolm grabbed the pint-sized warrior and sat her on his lap. His arms acted as a cage. "Calm down. Sasha's safe now."

"For now. What happens when he tries to get her back?"

The two of them were wrapped up in each other and talking about me like I wasn't there.

"That shouldn't be a problem." My voice startled Ashley out of the trance Malcolm put her in. "He's with Zoe Chronis now. He's going to marry her."

Ashley frowned, shaking her head. "Well, now I'm really confused."

"You and me both."

I spent the night chatting with my mom and Ashley, who got to stay after saying she was my sister and my mom vouching for her. Weirdest fucking sleepover I'd had in a while.

As the sun rose outside the window, I flipped on the news.

It surprised me when the anchor launched into a story about our accident and Mr. Moretti's passing. She didn't mention my name—thank all things holy. I made a note of the tentative memorial service information, knowing I shouldn't go but also knowing my ass would be there. If there is any opportunity to see Luca, I'd be there. Pathetic didn't even come close to describing me.

I wondered if I had any dignity left when the anchors said a name that caught my attention.

"A missing person's report has been filed for socialite Zoe Chronis after family members found her home ransacked. She was last seen leaving the engagement party of Dimitri Chronis and Daphne Dukas. If you know anything regarding Zoe Chronis' disappearance, please contact the number at the bottom of the screen. A fifty-thousand-dollar reward is being offered to anyone who comes forward with information that leads to her discovery."

Surprise! The hits just kept on coming.

TWENTY-SIX

Cars lined the street leading up to the Moretti estate. It took half an hour, but I valeted my car and found my way into the foyer. Walking behind a tall couple, I tried to stay out of sight until I found Luca.

Too bad luck was never on my side.

"Sasha!" Arms wrapped around my hips, and I looked down at Dante. His eyes were red and puffy. It was clear the little boy had been crying. Of course, he had. He'd been Mr. Moretti's shadow. My heart ached for Dante and the loss I'd caused.

"Hey, bud!" I ruffled his hair, and he frowned. "Where's your mom at?"

Dante glanced behind him and shrugged. "In the kitchen with grandma. I got kicked out for eating all the cookies." His little brow furrowed. "But that's why they're there, right? To eat?"

"You're not wrong. Why don't we go see if I can sneak a couple of cookies for us."

Nodding, he grabbed my hand and pulled me through the dense crowd of mourners. The closer we got to the kitchen, the fewer guests we encountered.

Caterers bustled around the ample space, getting out tray

after tray of treats. Pulling Dante back a little, I stopped when I spotted Mrs. Moretti by the stove.

How do you face the widow of the man you killed?

The sight of her face twisted my insides with guilt. The normally glammed-up goddess was plain-faced, her skin blotchy and her eyes red. Every line of her face had deepened with sorrow, but she fought to give me a small smile.

She spread her arms wide, gesturing with her hands. "Sasha, dear. Come here."

As wrong as it was, I ran to her. Rosa wrapped her arms around me tightly, her entire presence calm and collected as if I was the one who needed to be comforted. And as selfish and shitty as it was, I needed that hug.

"I'm so sorry for your loss." I teared up as I took a step back. I didn't deserve her warmth and love.

"Thank you. I'm sorry you were there and had to see that." Her sad smile was like a vise on my chest, and I couldn't take a full breath. The image of my hands wrapped around Mr. Moretti's neck as he jerked for the last time put me right back in that hotel room, fighting for my life.

Black dots filled my vision, and I sagged against the counter.

"Adriana! Get a chair for Sasha!"

Rosa helped me sit down, her hands rubbing my back in gentle circles. "I'm so sorry, dear. I shouldn't have mentioned the accident. You must be having a hard time."

If I wasn't breathing heavily into the brown paper bag Adriana had handed me, I would've laughed. I guess our cover story was a convenient one. No one would question why I wouldn't talk about that night or why mentioning it would send me into a tizzy.

Survivor's guilt.

"What's going on in here?"

Hearing Luca's voice, I tried to sit up, but Rosa and Adriana kept me hunched over with my head between my knees.

"It's my fault. I mentioned the accident. I wasn't thinking."

Rosa sounded distraught, and all I wanted to do was tell her she had absolutely nothing to be sorry about because I was the problem. Thinking about why I was the guilty party only made breathing more difficult.

"It's okay, Mom. She'll be fine." Large hands replaced Rosa's small ones on my back. I could just pick up the smell of Luca's cologne through the paper bag. "Why don't you guys go out and sit with the family? I can handle this."

"Are you sure?" Rosa's voice was thick with worry. Luca squeezed my shoulders, and I guess he must have nodded because Rosa continued. "Let me know if she needs anything. Once she's a little better, take her to your room for a lie-down."

Adriana's and Rosa's heels clicked away. "Put that cookie down, Dante. So help me!"

"Come on, mom! Just one more!"

"No!"

Then Luca and I were left surrounded by the clinking and clanking of the wait staff. His hand never stopped rubbing my back, and slowly, I was able to take a normal breath.

He helped me sit up, but I couldn't bring myself to look at him.

"Better?" Luca brushed his thumbs under my eyes.

"I guess."

He cupped my cheek and turned my face toward him. When our eyes met, all the hurt and anger I expected to see wasn't there. Instead, his gaze was full of worry. "You think you can make it up the backstairs with me?"

I nodded, and he helped me up the stairs to his room. Easing down onto the bed, I took in the familiar surroundings.

Luca shut the door and locked it. After a beat, he joined me on the bed, his movements slow and unsure.

"I can't imagine how hard all this must be for you." His voice shook with emotion.

"Me? Are you fucking kidding me?" I pushed his shoulder to catch his gaze.

Luca's eyes widened, and his cheeks puffed out. "What do you mean?"

"Oh, I don't know, Luca! Maybe the fact I killed your father? Or maybe that you had to help me stage his death? Take your pick!"

He cringed as I got louder and louder until he covered my mouth with his hand. "For fuck's sake. Keep your voice down."

I relaxed my shoulders and nodded.

Inching his hand away, Luca shook his head. "You did what you had to do. If you hadn't killed him, I would've." Honesty laced his words, and I felt a little relief.

Grabbing his retreating hand, I kissed his palm. "It doesn't change the fact you lost your dad. Shitty or not, that's still your dad, and it's okay to be sad."

Luca looked at me, his eyebrows pulling together. "I don't think I'm sad he's gone." He shifted closer to me. His knees bumped into mine. "I'm sad that I'm not sad. We never had a great relationship, not like him and Dante." He stood up and went over to a picture hanging on the wall. Tracing his fingers over the glass, he shook his head. "When Dante was alive, I was just the disappointing extra son, but when he died, I was the disappointing son fucking up the family legacy." He stopped moving and looked at me. "I feel free, which makes me feel so fucking guilty."

"I can see that." I rose to my feet but didn't step toward him. "I'm not going to tell you how to feel because fuck if I know what is "normal" in this situation, but I will tell you I'm here for you, whatever you need."

Luca took a tentative step toward me, stopping just out of reach. "How can you say that? If it weren't for me, your life would've never been in danger. You would've never had to kill someone." He pounded his fist on his chest. "That's on me, Sasha. This should have finally scared you away, but instead, you're here consoling me. Why?"

I shrugged and closed the gap between us. "It's like I told you the first time you brought me to this room. You could never scare me away, Luca. I'm the crazy bitch that loves you." His lips twitched, but he didn't smile. I could tell he would need more convincing.

Wrapping my arms around his waist, I stared up at him. "I love you unconditionally. I tried leaving you, and you've tried to keep me away, but nothing has worked. We belong together."

Luca's arms loosely wrapped around me. "That doesn't change how much danger you're in just being with me. I'm not as arrogant as I was when we first got together."

Arching a perfectly sculpted eyebrow, I smirked. "Are you actually worried that I can't handle myself? I hate to point it out today of all days, but I'm kind of a badass."

His plump lips pulled into a smile. "That you are, baby."

Encouraged by his relaxing posture, I continued. "I'm not oblivious to what I'm walking into. I know who you are." Luca winced, so I rushed out, "But you're not just the guy I saw in that bathroom or the man who protected me in that hotel room. You're the softie that makes me breakfast in bed, the uncle that has sing-a-longs and does voices while reading at bedtime, and you're the only person I can imagine making a life with, danger and all."

Luca blew out a breath, opening his mouth, but I cut him off before he could say anything to ruin my momentum. "So that's the danger thing." I held up a finger, then another. "Next is your ridiculous arranged marriage idea. This might be in poor taste, but Zoe is missing, and I assume the Chronis family is already blaming you?"

"Yeah. Fucked timing."

I pressed into his body. "No. Perfect timing."

Tilting his head, Luca waited for me to continue.

"You were planning on using the wedding to squash any beef —" Luca laughed, making me smile. "Shut up. I don't know the mob lingo yet." He chuckled and squeezed me closer to him. A lightness filled my chest as I felt Luca's defenses crumble. "Like I was saying, you were using Zoe to bring peace between the families, a peace your dad wasn't keen on. I assume he was working against you?"

"He was."

"Well, he's gone now—time to get your house in order, Mr. Bossman. Once everyone is in line, you can work out a real peace with Chronis, not some weird feudal shit. I'm sure you have business interests that would form a tighter bond than a sham marriage."

"Who are you?" Luca's eyes sparkled with admiration.

"The future Mrs. Bosslady."

We both laughed, his chest shaking against mine, making my heart beat faster.

"Are you sure you want to be a part of this world? Once you're in, that's it."

I fought against the smile playing on my lips.

I had him.

"I'll be honest with you. I don't like the violence and will probably hate a lot of other things, but that pales in comparison to how much I love you. I'm here for good. Can you trust me enough to be honest with me? This doesn't work without honesty."

"I've never trusted anyone more." He leaned down, placing a sweet kiss on my lips. "Okay. We're doing this. Shit." He vibrated with excited energy. "So, you'll be my mafia queen?"

That did it. We fell into a fit of laughter.

"I just heard what I said. Jesus, that was corny." Luca hugged me even tighter as we shook with laughter.

"You're going to have to work on not being such a cornball if you're going to run this shit."

Luca pushed me back by the shoulders, his grip tight and his face set in a determined scowl. Too bad the corner of his mouth twitched. "I'm Luca Moretti. They don't call me "The Butcher" for nothing."

"The Butcher, huh?" I slinked closer, skimming my hand down the front of him.

A hum rumbled from his throat as his perfect white teeth sunk into his bottom lip. He ran his hands down my back, grabbing my ass roughly.

"I seem to remember there being talk of fantasies involving that desk over there."

Luca's lips tilted up. "The desk, the bed, that exercise ball over."

I cupped his growing length and gave it a squeeze. A moan fell from both our mouths. "Where should we start?" I stood on my tiptoes, nibbling his neck.

"The—"

"Uncle Luca! Why's the door locked? Is Sasha okay?" Dante's sweet voice was an instant boner-killer.

"Shit." Luca cursed into my hair. "Give us a second, kiddo."

I gave Luca one more squeeze, earning myself a glare and shove away. Laughing, I went over and opened the door.

Dante looked up at me, relieved. He pulled his hands from behind his back, shoving various treats in my face. "I brought you some cookies and a brownie. I figured it might help you feel better."

"Thank you, bud." I glanced over at Luca, who had his back to us and was muttering. Why don't we head downstairs and give your uncle a minute to collect himself?"

Dante nodded solemnly. "Mom said today is a hard day, and we have to make sure everyone has space." He leaned around my body. "Uncle Luca, it's okay to cry, and if you want to cry up here, that's okay."

It took everything in me to even respond to mini Dr. Phil.

"Let's go find your mom." Dante took my hand, and we started down the hallway.

I gave one more look back at Luca, and he was watching the two of us over his shoulder with a smile on his face.

Any lingering doubts melted away, and I knew I was exactly where I belonged.

EPILOGUE

"Did you see them?" I looked at Luca in the bathroom mirror as I pulled the bobby pins out of my hair. "I swear I just watched Malcolm impregnate Ash."

Luca dabbed at a spot on his shirt that I couldn't see, but he had assured me it was there and that it was a serious problem. "Pretty sure the whole club saw them. You know, I've never been at a conception before. I feel honored."

I laughed, leaning over to dig through the cabinet for my makeup remover wipes. Our new ensuite bathroom was double the space of the old one, but I still struggled to find a place for all my beauty junk.

"It'll be a great story to tell my godchild when they're older." Closing my eyes, I rubbed away the expertly drawn, winged liner. "Do you think they made it home, okay? One minute they were there fucking through their clothes, the next . . . Poof! They were gone!"

"I'm sure they're fine." Luca sighed heavily, yanking off his shirt and tossing it on the floor. "Damn it! Another shirt bites the dust thanks to Evie's colorful cocktails!"

He stood there pouting, but all I could focus on was his drool-inducing body—his chiseled muscles covered in scarred tan skin, the hint of dark hair above his waistband, and a single tattoo over his heart, marking him as mine.

"You're not even listening."

With a herculean effort, I tore my eyes away from their bodacious feast. "I'm sorry, what?"

Huffing, Luca left the bathroom, and I heard clothes rustling. He came back in only his boxer briefs. "Adriana and Marco. They were all kinds of cozy." He went to his sink and pulled out his water pick. "It was weird to see."

I watched his muscles jump a little as he lifted the device. I hummed in agreement as my gaze traced from his hand up his arm to his broad, glorious shoulders. Dude was fucking stacked. He interrupted my ogling when he casually added, "You know they dated before she met Dante." He started shooting water between his teeth, somehow not making a mess.

"Come again?" I dropped my cotton rounds, and they fell all over the floor.

"Damn it, Sash!" Luca put down his water pick and got down on his hands and knees.

I sat on the edge of the tub, watching him scoop up the mess, completely taken aback. He shook his head and leaned back on his heels. "Yeah, Marco and Adriana went on a few dates before Dante met her, and, well, you know what happened then."

"That's wild. How did I not know this?"

Luca's back flexed as he reached for a rogue piece.

He was too fucking beautiful.

My eyes never strayed from his form as I mumbled out, "I'm all for my girl getting it, even if it is with asshole Marco. Maybe she can pull the stick out of his ass while she's at it."

When Luca laughed, his stomach tensed, and I pressed my legs together. With enough pressure, I could've come by watching him clean up my mess.

He could make money just recording himself cleaning up naked—so much money.

The room fell silent for a minute, and when he looked up, he caught my lust-filled gaze. A smile pulled at his plump lips, and he glanced down at his full hands. Pulling out a random drawer, Luca cringed as he shoved the cotton rounds next to whatever the hell I'd crammed in there.

He shook his head and knee-walked over to me. Every inch of me felt his stare. He licked his bottom lip, and I couldn't help but mimic him. There was no mistaking what was about to go down.

My heart sped up the closer he got, and my knees fell open, making room for him.

Luca shuffled between my legs, pressing into me. The heat from his body clouded my already frazzled thoughts. Running his hands down my side, he kissed the corner of my mouth. "As great as you looked tonight, I have to say I'm a big fan of this look."

"Noted. I'll start going out in my underwear." I placed a hand on his chest as my other lightly gripped the back of his neck.

"Perfect." He traced the edge of my bra. His touch was so gentle goosebumps followed in its wake. His fingers traced down my spine, sending a shiver up my back before he reached my ass. Cradled between my legs, his growing length pressed hot against my core, creating a hunger in my body that only he could satisfy. Luca quietly groaned before tugging my face to his. When our lips met, all restraint disappeared.

Our teeth clashed as we kissed with little finesse. Our frantic movements jarred me from the edge of the tub and on top of Luca. He landed on the bathmat with a soft grunt but never stopped his conquest.

Before I knew it, my bra was in the sink, my panties were on the toilet seat, and Luca's boxers were lost to the shower curtain.

Rocking my hips, I slid Luca's length between my lips, making him slick. My muscles tightened with each pass as I clawed his chest to steady my movements. The feel of him under me pushed me closer to my climax, even though I promised myself I would hold out.

A hard slap to my ass pulled me from my sexual trance. "Up," he grunted, squeezing my hips.

I raised enough for him to slide his head between my legs. His fingers dug into my fleshy thighs, bringing my pussy to his mouth, where he started to torture me with long, slow strokes of his tongue. I held on to my knees as I moved my hips against his mouth. When he flattened his tongue against my clit, I ground down, not caring one bit about how he would breathe. From my clit, he slid back and speared my slit.

My pussy fluttered around his thick tongue, and I huffed as my nails scored my palms. It was too much and not enough at the same time.

Luca turned his head and bit the inside of my thigh. I yelped, moving back on his chest, my wetness leaving a trail. Not wasting a moment, he lifted me up and over his cock. The tip grazed my opening, and my thighs quivered. My eyes stayed locked to where I ached for him most. The anticipation made my legs wobble and my heart beat wildly. I wanted him more than I wanted my next breath.

Trying to move down, Luca held me in place. Lifting my eyes from where our bodies should've already joined, I frowned. "Um, I'm trying to do something here."

Luca chuckled, causing his head to bump my clit, and I nearly jumped out of my skin. "I love you, Sasha."

"Okay. I love you too. Now can we . . ." I gestured to where his hands held me still and blew my hair out of my face.

Luca looked at me with so much love that it made my chest hurt. "I never want to take this for granted, baby."

His words melted me to the core, and I leaned down to place a sweet kiss on his mouth. I nibbled his lip as I smiled into the kiss. I loved this man with all my heart.

Without warning, Luca surged up and slid into me. I gasped against his lips, and his tongue began to fuck my mouth as his hips raised to meet mine.

I pulled away, pressing my hands against his chest and holding him to the floor. That didn't stop his hips from thrusting up and taking my breath away—every move harder than the last.

When it all became too much, I sat all the way down, pinning his hips to the floor, and kissed him deeply. The taste of scotch and my pussy on his tongue gave me a perfect moment of calm in the storm.

Twisting my hips, my clit ground against him, and the beginnings of a fantastic release grew. He matched every swivel. Our bodies locked together, creating the most incredible pleasure with the slightest movements.

Pulling away from Luca's lips, I sat up and cupped my breasts, squeezing them roughly. Luca's impossibly dark eyes simmered with a heat that threatened to burn me alive.

I teased my nipples, the sensation overwhelming my body. Too much was happening. Luca bucked up under me, sending me into a bounce. My thighs burned with the constant up and down, and my breath came out in heavy pants, but I knew I couldn't stop.

"Fuck." I inched closer to oblivion with every thrust. When Luca licked his thumb, then massaged small circles against my clit, I exploded.

My walls tightened as I stilled above him. His hips continued their punishing rhythm as I rode wave after wave of bliss. Spent, I fell forward, my mouth landing on his neck. I kissed and sucked up to his ear before he mumbled and finally collapsed against the cold tile floor.

"Damn." His chuckle rumbled through my chest, sending aftershocks, as he was still very much inside me.

I eased up on my elbows and smiled down at his perfect face. "Yeah, damn."

We slowly made our way off the bathroom floor and finished getting ready for bed. Occasionally we'd give one another a swat on the ass or a kiss on the neck, but we moved in silence.

"I need a glass of water. You want one?" Luca asked as he walked toward the door.

"That'd be great. Thanks."

He nodded and left me to get settled in bed. I reached for my phone charger cord, but it wasn't on my bedside table. Looking through my drawers and then Luca's, I came up empty-handed.

"Well, this is just ridiculous," I muttered as I dug through the suitcase we'd taken to Chicago.

The pink cord was wedged in the front pocket. "Bingo!"

When I reached in, my fingers brushed against a felt box. I pulled the cords out and then a small ring box. My heart raced.

Was this a . . . ? No. It can't be.

Taking a deep breath, I opened the box. Sparkling back at me was the biggest rock I'd ever seen. The setting was antique, which made me wonder if this was another family heirloom.

"I'm going to make a grilled cheese. You want one, babe?"

Luca's voice startled me, and I dropped the box on the floor. I scrambled to grab it and shove it back in the suitcase.

"Babe?"

"Uh . . . yeah. Yeah. Do you even have to ask?" I shouted as I walked out of the closet, only to find Luca standing all naked chef in the doorway. He'd already put on an apron. Post-sex cooking always called for an apron to avoid possible grease injuries.

"Why do you look like you've seen a ghost?" Luca eyed me suspiciously.

"I saw a spider."

"No, you didn't." He looked behind me as if a giant monster was about to jump out.

"Yeah, but don't worry, I got 'em."

Luca nodded, blowing out a breath. "I hope you used one of your shoes."

"Of course! Now chop-chop!" I grabbed his shoulders and turned him around, slapping his delicious rear. "Mama needs a sammie."

Luca tried to look stern but ended up smiling over his shoulder.

I crawled into bed and tried to calm my racing heart.

He has a ring.

Luca has a ring.

He's going to propose.

I waited for commitment panic to set in.

A minute went by, then another.

I sat in our bed, waiting for ultimate dread to wash over me, but it never came.

Eventually, Luca came in carrying a tray with a couple of glasses of water and some sandwiches.

"I cut up an extra apple and warmed up some of that dipping sauce you like so much and—Why are you smiling like that?"

I traced my fingers over my lips. Sure enough, a smile wide enough to split my face was front and center. "Because I love sandwiches, and I love you."

At that moment, I knew I wasn't scared. In fact, it wasn't only that I wasn't scared, but that I was fucking excited. I couldn't wait to marry Luca Moretti.

Giddy and ready for more of my soon-to-be husband, I crawled to the edge of the bed and took the tray from his hands, setting it on the floor. "Before I eat that, there's something else I want to taste."

The front of his apron failed to hide his growing interest in my hunger.

"The chef in me wants to point out the food will get cold, but the man in me wants to wrap your hair around my hand and give you exactly what you're hungry for."

"Let's go with option two."

Thank you for reading Sasha and the Butcher. If you want more Sasha and Luca, read book 2—Sasha and the Stalker—available now!

Want to get sneak peeks, free short stories, and stay up to date on new releases? Join Stephanie's mailing list!

Acknowledgments

I want to thank all the writer and reader friends I made on Wattpad—Karma, OP, Natalia, Tay, Rose, Stephanie, Maggie, Julie, Rachelle, Cole, and so many more. You all read the roughest draft of this book and gave me the confidence not only to write the damn thing but to finish the first draft.

I want to thank my beta readers—Brittany, Karma, OP. Your feedback was huge!

I can't thank my ARC readers enough. From help with my blurb to finding those lingering typos, you all have made this whole process possible. Thank you for taking a chance on a new author.

A huge thanks goes to my best friend Bonnie for designing my covers. When I started this process knowing I had no money, she stepped up and offered her keen eye and skills. I feel like the production of this book is as close to the DIY zine vibes as I could get, and I love that my friends and community supported me and made it happen.

And last but certainly not least, I want to thank Jordan. He was my proofreader, and together we tackled commas. He's put up with my late nights and gave me the time to write free of the kids on weekends. He's basically everything you could ever want in a partner as a creative.

I am surrounded by love and support, and there aren't enough words to describe just how thankful I am. I love you all.

On to the next!

ABOUT THE AUTHOR

After becoming something of a romance fiend, Stephanie Kazowz decided to try her hand at writing some good old-fashioned love stories. Never one to narrow her focus, she plans to write the banging multiverse, weaving as many tropes and subgenres together as her smut-loving heart can handle—and it can handle a lot.

Stephanie lives in St. Louis, Missouri, with her husband, two bonkers babies, two codependent dogs, and two cats who are perpetually staring at her like she betrayed them by bringing the motley group home.

Made in the USA
Columbia, SC
22 November 2024

47334534R00186